SECRETS AND LIES
SPUN INTO A
WEB OF DECEIT

AMANDA—Beautiful and defiant, the fashion world called her special "look" The Granger Woman . . . but her life had become a dangerous lie.

PAUL—Rich, sensual, and devious, his society friends knew he was a playboy—only Amanda believed his promises.

MATTHEW—As passionate as he was handsome, his "perfect" marriage ha~~~~ ~~~~come a perfect hell—and only Amand~~~~ ~~~~ ~~~~ him free.

SYDNEY—C~~~~ ~~~~ ~~~~ ~~~~ ~~~~r money gave her~~~~ ~~~~ ~~~~ ~~~~ ~~~~anted— and ~~~~ ~~~~ ~~~~ ~~~~d.

Other Avon Books by
Catherine Lanigan

ADMIT DESIRE
BOUND BY LOVE
SINS OF OMISSION

and writing as Joan Wilder

THE JEWEL OF THE NILE
ROMANCING THE STONE

WEB OF DECEIT

CATHERINE LANIGAN

AVON
PUBLISHERS OF BARD, CAMELOT, DISCUS AND FLARE BOOKS

For J.R. who has all my love

For Ryan who is a most special son

For Zoni for giving me inspiration
and being a friend.

With love and thanks to my mother,
Dorothy, for all her help with the
tremendous amount of research that
went into this book.

And for Susanne Jaffe, my editor,
whose keen eye made this book better,
and who shared in the good time.

AVON BOOKS
A division of
The Hearst Corporation
105 Madison Avenue
New York, New York 10016

Copyright © 1987 by Catherine Lanigan
Published by arrangement with the author
Library of Congress Catalog Card Number: 87-91586
ISBN: 0-380-75311-1

First Avon Printing: November 1987

AVON TRADEMARK REG. U.S. PAT. OFF. AND IN OTHER COUNTRIES, MARCA
REGISTRADA, HECHO EN U.S.A.

Printed in the U.S.A.

K–R 10 9 8 7 6 5 4 3 2 1

Book I

THE LIE

CHAPTER ONE

London, 1894

Shelton Street was just wide enough for the rolling fog to pass. Forty houses, two and three stories high, teetered against each other, like rusty links of an old chain. More than two hundred families occupied their tiny, filthy rooms. The little yards in back were crammed with dustbins, water closets and cisterns meant to serve six or seven families.

Few people were up this early since most of them had no jobs, no place to go, no appointments to keep. Less than a dozen windows looked out onto the street and all of them remained shuttered against the dawn. There were no window boxes filled with colorful petunias or geraniums as were found on most London houses. The people of Shelton Street kept to themselves, which in its way was an act of charity, for none wanted to inflict their burdens on others. Lives lived here were meager both financially and spiritually. For the old, Shelton Street was an end to a wasted life; for the young it was a tormentor to be overcome and subdued.

Gambling, drunkenness, foul language, and even murder grew on Shelton Street. It was no place for pride.

Amanda Granger buttoned her cotton skirt and tucked in her blouse as she raced along the perilously narrow sidewalk, being careful not to tear her clothes on the projecting nails that studded the housefronts.

She was late. She hated being late.

Lady Kent would be furious; recently, a perpetual state of being for her employer, Amanda thought.

Amanda had no time for remorse or guilt for her tardirness.

3

She'd worked long past quitting time too often with no pay and no kind words from Lady Kent to worry over a few minutes' extra sleep this morning.

Amanda's excuse was a good one, to her mind. She'd been writing again, late into the night. She was struggling . . . battling, actually, with her poetry. No matter how many times she'd tried to copy Keats and Shelley, she'd failed. The translation of her thoughts into words resulted in hodgepodge. She was better at prose, much better. However, Lord Kent had clearly instructed her that once she mastered poetry, she could write anything. Almost as much as she wanted to write, she wanted to please him.

She crossed Mercer Street where the morning sun peaked through the passageways between the buildings and burned away the fog like a hot poker. At Cutter's Row, she stopped at the haberdasher's shop kept by Mrs. Bird. Amanda opened the sparkling glass door. Mrs. Bird was especially proud of her glass door when her fellow merchants could offer only wood doors.

"Good day, Mrs. Bird."

"Amanda. How sweet you look today. That a new blouse?" plump Mrs. Bird asked, inspecting the fine white linen cloth.

"To me it is," Amanda replied proudly. Mrs. Bird knew, as everyone did, that Amanda's clothes were secondhand, though not the rags sold at Sunday auctions by toothless old women on Chapel Street. Amanda's clothes were unsoiled, unripped, and often, worn but once. Eloise Kent, the sixteen-year-old daughter of Lord and Lady Kent, always gave her unwanted clothing to Amanda. It was one of many privileges Amanda had enjoyed all her life.

"I've come for Eloise's hair ribbons."

"I have them here," Mrs. Bird said, withdrawing six palest pink satin ribbons from a wooden box.

Amanda inspected them and wrinkled her nose. "Much too pale for Eloise. She needs more color near her face. Let me see the ice blue ones."

"Amanda, I don't think it wise to make decisions without your employer's permission."

"Tonight is the Queen's birthday ball. There will be two hundred and fifty debutantes coming out this year. Eloise *must* look her best. This blue will make her eyes more lively."

Mrs. Bird burst into laughter. "Nothing could put spark into that girl's eyes!" Then, suddenly remembering the Kents' position and their very good patronage of her store when they could easily choose to go elsewhere, Mrs. Bird said protectively: "I think you should get the pink. That's what she ordered."

"No, the blue is better. And let me see those matching lace gloves."

"Amanda! Lady Kent did not authorize you to buy gloves."

"They will complete the outfit. Eloise will look wonderful. Wrap them up."

"I don't like this."

Amanda signed the bill and then took the receipt and box that Mrs. Bird had tied with string. "It'll be all right. You'll see." Amanda smiled with assurance, but it wasn't until she was out on the sidewalk again that she felt her heart resume beating.

She was taking a great risk at further upsetting Lady Kent. But Amanda was counting on the customary weekend bustle in Kent Manor to deflect any confrontations.

By the time Amanda reached Regent Street, the sun was completely up. She whisked through the lacy wrought-iron gate, ran through the precisely manicured gardens to the back of the imposing four-story brick house to the back door that led four steps down to the kitchens, butler's pantry and servants quarters.

"You're fifteen minutes late!" Georgia, the red-haired, obese cook snarled as she hastily slammed a ladleful of porridge into a china bowl and put it on a wicker tray.

Amanda watched as Georgia fried sausages, scrambled eggs, buttered muffins and dished up fruit with a skill that could only be evolved from forty years as cook and the well-kept secret that she was ambidextrous and had grown eyes in the back of her head.

Amanda quickly donned a stiff white apron and cap. She plucked an early May rose from the basket resting on the drainboard, placed it in a silver bud vase, and picked up the tray.

"You won't tattle on me, will you, Georgia?"

Georgia whirled around, hands on hips, lips pursed tightly. One look at Amanda's smiling face and her anger melted.

"Go on with you. Miss Eloise didn't sleep at all last night. She's been ringing since dawn."

Amanda pecked Georgia on the cheek and dashed up the steps before the older woman could growl at her for showing her affection, something Georgia never wanted the other servants to see.

"Morning, Elrod," Amanda purred to the dour-faced butler as she passed him on the back staircase. He harrumphed as usual, paying her no mind. Elrod had been in a bad mood since the day Lord Kent had announced he was "automating" the household.

Every day for the past five months, carpenters, plumbers, and electricians had been scurrying in and out of Kent Manor, gearing up the two-hundred-year-old house to enter the new century.

The last of Lady Barbara's Waterford chandeliers had been electrified. An automatic dumbwaiter and an elevator had been installed. The new bathrooms were finished: lavish ceramic baths replaced the old copper tubs; porcelain commodes, bidets, and gold-edged oval sinks occupied every floor. Lord Kent had scoured Germany for the fixtures, Portugal for the hand-painted tiles for four new shower stalls, and gone to Vienna and Paris for the Art Nouveau mirrors and electric wall sconces. There was an intercom system built into the walls and a telephone on each floor, plus the study and the library.

However, for the past three days, amid debut preparations, gown fittings, deliveries from the florist, and an avalanche of invitations, when Lady Barbara could have put every invention and innovation to good use, everything . . . had broken down.

Amanda gently rapped on the mahogany door to Eloise's room and entered.

Eloise was sitting ramrod straight in bed, not allowing herself the comfort of three rows of lace-edged, down-filled pillows. She was gazing into a hand mirror. There was no sign of delight or girlish giddiness about her as Amanda had expected. Instead, Amanda saw a tightness to her mouth, a strain around her eyes. Amanda remained silent while she placed the tray in front of Eloise. Eloise didn't move a muscle, nor did she acknowledge Amanda's presence. Amanda placed the box from Mrs. Bird next to the tray. Eloise still said nothing.

Calmly, Eloise placed the mirror on the bed and looked at her food. Normally ravenous in the mornings, Eloise moved the tray aside.

"I've had a dreadful night. Now I'm to have a dreadful day."

"What *are* you talking about?" Amanda asked as she opened the thick lace draperies and let the morning sun wash the room in a pink-gold glow. "You should be happy. It's your debut, all your friends will be there, you'll get to wear your beautiful new gown. What could be better?"

Eloise picked up the mirror and again did not comment on the box Amanda had brought.

"I'm supposed to be in my prime. How will I find a husband, a proper husband, if *it* hasn't happened yet?"

"*It?*" Amanda asked coming over to look into the mirror with Eloise.

"Beauty, womanhood, whatever *it* is. I don't understand. I've waited all this time. I have my father's blond hair and blue eyes, my mother's alabaster skin, and my grandmother's aristocratic nose. Somehow, it's not put together correctly."

"What a terrible thing to say of yourself . . . why, you're everything a real English lady should be!"

"You think so?"

Amanda nodded firmly. "You just need more confidence." She handed her the box. Eloise pulled out the ribbons.

"They're supposed to be pink! Pink, Amanda!" Eloise tossed the covers aside, nearly knocking the teapot over. Where once she'd been friendly and intimate with Amanda, now she turned on her. It was a scene that had been occurring more and more frequently over the past year.

Amanda quickly grabbed the hairbrush from the vanity table, took Eloise's arm, and pushed her—gently—to the stool. Amanda brushed Eloise's long, thick, wavy hair to one side. She laced a piece of ribbon around a hank of hair, wove and twisted it until she'd created a masterpiece.

"Blue, Eloise. Never pink," was all she said.

Eloise stared at her reflection. The two tiny blue plates that looked back at her, out of a face seemingly devoid of bone structure, brightened and gleamed.

Amanda took the gloves and pushed them onto Eloise's hands.

"Every time you lift your hand to your face—the color of your eyes intensifies."

Eloise tried it. It was true. Her colorless skin blushed pink as the blue shadow of the glove passed over her cheek, played with a tendril of hair, patted her lip.

Just then there was a solid, purposeful knock at the door. Amanda knew instantly it was Lady Kent. She glanced disapprovingly at the untouched breakfast tray, walked over to Eloise, fingered the blue ribbon, and turned to Amanda. "I ordered palest pink, Amanda. Have you gone against my orders again?"

"I thought that . . ."

"This is a debutante ball, Amanda. I know you have no knowledge of these things, being from the . . . with your background. But all the girls must wear white. Only pale pink bordering on white is acceptable. And these gloves. They are vulgar and crass."

"They're effective," Amanda mumbled to herself, knowing Lady Kent would hear her.

"Amanda, your impertinence lately has been intolerable, but I have been patient. Don't press me again."

Amanda curtsied. "Yes, ma'am."

"Take the gloves back and bring the pink."

"Yes, ma'am," Amanda replied, looking to Eloise for salvation.

Eloise dropped her head and removed the gloves. Lady Kent picked up her skirt and left the room.

"Why didn't you tell her you wanted the blue, Eloise? She would give in to you."

"She was right. The rules are very specific about these things. I can't breach etiquette," Eloise said, firmly reciting the credo that had always been her life.

"What good are rules if they don't help you?" Amanda asked as Eloise went into the adjoining bathroom and quietly shut the door on Amanda and her probing words.

Amanda ironed Eloise's white silk and lace ball gown, taking great care not to crease the four rows of wide ruffles at the bodice. She could hear the carpenters banging upstairs on the main floor and Sally, the head housekeeper, yelling at them about the sawdust, their grimy shoes, and their overall lack of concern for her and her "schedule."

Schedules—Amanda remembered when everything at Kent Manor had run like a precisely tuned Swiss clock. That was when her mother, Harriet Granger, had been head housekeeper. From nearly the day she was born, Amanda had accompanied her mother to Kent Manor. She had learned to walk in the back gardens and spoke her first words in this very kitchen. Amanda had grown up with Eloise, Emily, and Jonathon Kent. She'd felt like they were her brother and sisters. Though she lived on Shelton Street in two cubicles with her own brother, Andrew, Kent Manor was more a home to her.

Many times Harriet would carry a sleeping Amanda home in her arms, except for those nights when Eloise would demand that "little Amanda" sleep in her room with her. At Lord Kent's instruction, Amanda was allowed to study with the tutor along with his three children. Amanda learned to read, write, and cipher. She had almost a photographic memory and could remember the names of nearly every guest who'd ever called at Kent Manor. She could ride as well as Eloise but not as well as Jonathon, which bothered her tremendously, for Amanda had always believed she could do anything as well as anyone else if she only tried long enough and hard enough. This belief was a cornerstone of Lord Kent's preaching to his children. Amanda seemed the only one to have heard him.

Life had been nearly idyllic for Amanda until she was ten. With no warning, Lady Kent fired Harriet, stating that the "efficiency in the household had dropped." To this day, Amanda never understood how her mother could have failed, since Lady Barbara had never been able to find anyone to replace Harriet. However, nearly daily, the walls of Kent Manor echoed with Lady Barbara's voice as she demanded "efficiency" from the staff.

Shortly after Harriet's dismissal, Burt Granger died. At the time, Amanda was too young to realize that Burt's alcoholism had destroyed his liver and pancreas. She also felt no remorse as she stared down at his lifeless body lying in the plain, cheap wooden box.

To Amanda, her father had been a cold, self-centered, mean man. Fortunately for Amanda, she wasn't exposed to him all that much during the week. But on the weekends, their apartment at Number 8 Shelton Street was a living hell. Often he would come home late on Saturday night after being to the pubs and start an argument with his wife. To this day, Amanda could hear her mother's screams of pain as he beat her. Amanda, powerless to defend her, prayed to God or the Devil, whichever would take him first, to kill Burt on the spot. Finally, when Amanda reached the age of ten, one of them had listened to her.

Life on Shelton Street improved—for awhile. With no income for Harriet other than what she earned shelling peas near the cathedral, and the absence of Burt's income, Harriet went back to Lady Kent to plead for her job. She was turned down, but she did manage to get Amanda a job as lady's maid to Emily and Eloise for five shillings a week.

Five years later, Amanda was making over ten shillings a

week, two shillings more than the neighborhood girls, who worked at the garment factories or as telephone operators. Hers was not a difficult job. She was responsible for both the care and the acquisition of wardrobes for both girls, their personal care, their social schedules, and their studies. Eloise was just as disciplined as Amanda. Emily, however, was lazy and always looked for the easiest courses. But Emily was fun and full of pranks, and when her mischief wasn't getting her into trouble, it was difficult for Amanda not to like Emily.

Amanda finished ironing the dress, stuffed it with tissue, and repadded the bustle. Quickly, she carried the dress upstairs.

Eloise was bathing when Amanda entered the room. She knocked on the door.

"We're running late, Eloise. Hurry!"

While Amanda gathered white silk stockings, a lace teddy, the new white kid ball slippers, and the pink gloves, Eloise finished drying and came into the room.

Hastily, Eloise dressed. "Do you realize this could be the most important night of my life?"

"Of your whole, entire life?"

"Yes."

"Why?"

"Sometimes I think you are so smart, Amanda, and then sometimes you are just so . . . obtuse."

"A lifetime is a long time, Eloise."

Eloise waved off Amanda's help and stepped into the Parisian gown. "I could be meeting the man who will change my life. Just think of it. Somewhere in that room tonight . . ."

"Here, put these on," Amanda said, handing Eloise the gloves while Amanda buttoned the spine-hugging covered buttons on her dress.

"You're not impressed."

"I am. It's an important night, as you said. Just not *the* most important."

Disgusted with Amanda's lack of awe, Eloise checked herself in the mirror. As she had earlier that day, she raised her hand and played with the tendril of hair that hung from her temple. The pink gloves did not have the impact of the blue ones. Eloise could almost hate the rules. Almost.

Amanda continued speaking. "I would hate to think that a night when I was sixteen—only sixteen—"

"A year older than you." Eloise interrupted.

"—that tonight could be the apex of your life. What happens to all the rest of the years?"

"You live them."

"How?"

"The way you're supposed to. Oh, I don't know why we have these conversations, Amanda. You're so hardheaded."

"So are you." Amanda laughed.

Eloise laughed too, her tension broken. So she would have to wear pink gloves and pink hair ribbons; she would be as polite and charming as she knew how to be. What did Amanda know anyway?

"You've never looked so wonderful."

In a rush of fondness for a lifetime of shared moments, Eloise embraced Amanda in the way she had last year—before things, and she, began to change.

Eloise ceremoniously walked down the stairs with Amanda trailing her. At the foot of the stairs waited, a bit nervously, breathlessly, the entire Kent family.

Lady Barbara, her imperious nose set high, scrutinized her oldest daughter. Finally, she gave her a snort of approval. Though she had spent a minor fortune on Eloise's gown, there was no mistaking that the bell of this ball was Barbara. She wore an emerald green silk Balmain gown, cut perilously low to reveal an abundance of cleavage. By focusing attention on the bosom, the designer was able to draw attention away from Lady Barbara's thick waist. Four rows of perfectly matched diamonds sparkled in a waterfall effect against her skin. She looked every inch the direct descendent of royalty that she was.

Emily Kent, thirteen years old, was obviously dreaming of the day she would wear her first Paris ball gown, thinking she would look ten, no, a hundred times better than either her mother or her sister. Emily had blonde hair, like her sister's, and Lord Kent's slim build and his huge blue eyes. Like Eloise, she had the right ingredients for beauty, and she eagerly awaited the day she would cross the border into womanhood and make her dream a reality.

Jonathon Kent, home this first week of May from Cambridge, watched Eloise descend the stairs. He was as anxious about the ball as was his sister. He was one of the top ten most eligible bachelors going to the ball. At eighteen, he was a choice target for one-tenth of the debutantes. To his calculations, that meant twenty-five marriage-thirsty girls and their parched mothers would be gunning for him.

Amanda looked over at Lord Alvin Kent. Of the entire group, he was the only one whose love for Eloise shone in his eyes. Amanda could almost hear the mental images of Eloise growing up click off in his brain. He walked over to Eloise and took her arm and gently placed it through his. He kissed her cheek.

"You'll be the prettiest girl at the ball."

"Father, I . . . thank you."

Amanda could feel the tears welling in her eyes as she came down the stairs. Of all the things he could have said, he chose the perfect lie. Eloise's smile had never been so lovely. Amanda loved Lord Kent. He always knew the right thing to say. He had always made her feel as if she belonged. He'd given her privileges he hadn't accorded other servants. When Lady Barbara's tongue became too sharp, he planed the edges. He was truly lord of the manor and he ruled with a quiet, gentle, and effective hand. Amanda wanted to rush over and hug him; instead, she placed her hand on his arm.

He turned and smiled down at her. The affection in his penetrating blue eyes could not be hidden.

Emily, always jealous of her father's obvious feelings for Amanda, bristled.

"Amanda!" Lady Barbara's voice snapped. "Go downstairs so the *family* can have a private moment."

Still caught in that split second of unspoken feeling with Lord Kent, Amanda said nothing as she slowly backed away and Lady Barbara continued.

"Your manners lately have deteriorated. I take full responsibility for it, however. I've allowed you too much freedom with Eloise and Emily. You're going to have to learn your place."

Amanda crept along the wall to the kitchen. She could hear Lord Kent's voice.

"Don't be so hard on her. She's just a child."

"She's nearly as old as Eloise."

"As I said, just a child."

CHAPTER TWO

Harriet chopped two potatoes, a carrot, and a rutabaga and tossed them into the pot. The steam rose, engulfed her face, and wilted her hair. She pulled out a pin from the chignon and replaced the errant lock. She straightened and heard, more than felt, her back crack. She was exhausted from being over her sewing machine at the garment factory. She was thirty-five years old and felt a hundred and thirty-five. It was a good job, she supposed, bringing in thirteen shillings a week. They certainly lived better than anyone else on Shelton Street.

The three Grangers lived on the ground floor. The main room held her tiny kitchen with a small round table and three chairs near the window that looked out on the backyard. Amanda had planted two rosebushes—to hide the view of the cistern, Harriet guessed—but they had never bloomed. There was a battered old sofa with new pillows she'd made herself with scraps of fabric she'd stolen from the factory, and a lamp and table where Amanda kept her books. Andrew slept on the sofa; she and Amanda slept in the bedroom in back. Still, there was little privacy, but they lived better now than they had all the years when Burt was alive.

Unlike the other apartments, theirs was clean and tidy. Amanda had asked Lady Barbara for all the old sheets and linen towels and in a magnanimous gesture, she'd consented. There was a swirl-patterned cranberry glass pitcher and plate on a shelf in the bedroom which Amanda was constantly filling with fresh flowers from the Kent gardens. There was an odd-shaped Chinese urn on the floor next to the sofa that Lord Kent had brought back from

13

Hong Kong three years ago for Jonathon. Disappointed in his gift, he'd given it to Amanda—just to "get it out of his sight."

Their household was an odd mix of rags and fine linen, porcelain and chipped stoneware, poverty and riches.

Many times Harriet thought there was just enough of the "dream" in their lives to keep them all hungry—and hopefully striving.

The pendulum clock, also a Kent discard, struck eight just as Amanda came in the door. She placed a small package wrapped in brown paper on the table. Harriet looked at it and smiled.

"Georgia said to double dip the meat in flour, then brown it."

"She's a good friend. I miss her."

"Why don't we go to St. Silas's noon service and see her?"

Harriet, long wise to Amanda's ways, watched her daughter as she unwrapped the meat. "You've already arranged it, haven't you?"

"Well . . . she did send this beef."

"And so now we both must confess pilfering from Lord Kent."

"Mother," Amanda began sweetly, "you know very well that if I'd asked Lord Kent for the meat, he would have given it to me."

"I know, I know," she said, going to the stove and following Georgia's instructions.

"Andrew isn't home yet?"

"He's come and gone. He should be back soon. Said he had some errands."

"Hmm." Amanda frowned as she set the table. God only knew what "errands" he was on, she thought. She did know that he was courting a new girl. She was the daughter of one of Mr. Sloan's clients. Andrew had been very fortunate to get the job as assistant bookkeeper. But then, Andrew was very good with numbers.

Just then, the door flew open and Andrew rushed in, boxes tumbling from his arms. She should have known, Amanda thought. It was Saturday and as usual, Andrew had spent all of his pay on clothes. Once he went to the pubs tonight with his friends, which she was certain he would, there wouldn't be any money left over for the household. He hadn't contributed anything to the grocery money or rent for months. She wished her mother would be more firm with him. But as she looked at his smiling, excruciatingly handsome face, she knew she would give in to him too, just as Harriet had.

"My lovelies," he said, sweeping Amanda into his arms and whirling her around the little room. "Don't you look especially pretty tonight, my lady. Would you care to sup with me?"

Amanda laughed as he spun her again. She was dizzy when he stopped and went over to Harriet and kissed her cheek. He was in a good mood, and he hadn't been drinking—yet.

"Three shillings," Harriet demanded.

"What?"

"You owe me three shillings for the month. I'll forget the past months."

"Aw, Mum. Can't it wait till tomorrow?"

"No." She stuck out her hand.

Amanda started going through his purchases. There was a fine linen shirt that must have cost a whole week's wages. A new black tie, socks . . .

"Hey, hey!" Andrew instantly came to the rescue of his purchases. "Poke around where you're not wanted and you'll regret it."

Amanda lifted the collar on the shirt. "That's from Harrod's! What are you doing at Harrod's?" Amanda had been to Harrod's on shopping trips with Eloise and Emily. She knew that even with a raise at double his salary, Andrew still couldn't afford these clothes. Amanda guessed he'd "borrowed" from one of his friends. She wondered how long it would take him to pay it back.

Harriet instantly came over and looked at the clothes. "No wonder you can't pay the rent."

"Damn it, I can pay!" He took out three shillings and handed them to a startled Harriet.

Harriet examined him. "You stole this."

Andrew's smile shattered. His eyes glazed red in anger. "Must you always suspect the worst from me? I got a raise today, that's all. So I spent a little money to celebrate. So I went overboard. Who cares? The two of you always acting like pack rats—penny pinchers. A man needs a little trust. But do I get any?"

Feeling all the guilt Andrew had intentionally thrust on her, Amanda said: "You're right."

"Of course I am." He dropped his defensive tone. "Mum, you know I'm seeing Lucy Attington. She's a wonderful girl, from a fine family. How will it look to her parents if she goes out with a ne'er-do-well?"

"You are *not* a ne'er-do-well. Your father was, but not you. No child of mine will ever be anything less than what they want to be."

As she spoke, Amanda went to the stove, stirred the stew, and mouthed the words along with her mother. Amanda was certain she must have said those words the day she gave birth to Andrew. And she'd been saying them ever since.

"I have dreams of my own, Mum. And I'm gonna make it. I got this raise; Mr. Sloan says I show more promise than any other apprentice. I wanted to celebrate. I'm taking Lucy to church tomorrow."

Amanda laughed. "You? In church? I've got to meet this girl."

"I'm meeting her family."

Amanda dropped her banter, for she realized just how nervous Andrew was about all this.

"Is she special to you, Andrew? I mean, do you like her?"

"She's the prettiest girl I've ever seen. *And* she's from the best family I could ever hope to marry into."

"That isn't what I asked," Amanda said.

"When do we get to meet her?" Harriet wanted to know.

Suddenly, Andrew started picking up his parcels and fidgeting with the tissue paper. "Soon," he said. "Very soon."

A cool breeze gently ruffled the leaves of the oak trees on the common. Amanda wore a green-and-white cotton lawn day dress—a two-year-old castoff from Eloise—and green ribbons in her long blonde hair. The dress didn't fit her as well as it had last year. It was much too tight across the bodice, it pulled at the shoulders and was curiously baggy in the waist. She liked the dress and so she forgave its deficiencies.

"I just knew Andrew wouldn't be at church," Harriet said.

"This is the first Sunday in years I've seen him up before noon. He looked very nice when he left. What if Lucy's parents don't like him . . . ?"

"Andrew can be very charming and persuasive, but once they start questioning his background . . . well, he must be very careful."

"But if Lucy loves him . . ."

"It will take more than that. I don't know how high he's set his sights this time. Dr. Pierson's daughter was a disappointment for him. But Andrew has a way with girls."

"You sound as if his 'way' was not something good. How could anyone resist him? He's charming, handsome, and fun. He has a job with promise. . . ."

Harriet peered at her daughter. Her eyes travelled the length of her as if she had never seen her before. "Amanda, I think it's time you stopped thinking about what's best for Andrew and me and started thinking of yourself. Before long, you'll be a woman. As we've walked around today, I've noticed that at least four boys stopped to stare at you."

"They have?" Amanda quickly looked around to find them.

Harriet threw up her hands. "You didn't see! When are you going to pay attention?"

"I didn't know I was supposed to."

"How many times have I told you, Amanda, that the only way out of the slums is a good marriage. You meet the right man— not one on the commons, not one who is also from the slums— you meet a *good* man, with family and a future, then make your move. You're a pretty girl and soon you'll be a beautiful woman. Don't sell yourself too cheap. Andrew is right to shoot for the stars; so should you."

"I know, I know. You've told me a hundred times."

"Then when are you going to listen? Amanda"—Harriet used her most cajoling tone—"I want to tell you about my friend Sylvia. Sylvia Hendrickson was a governess for some friends of the Kents when you were still a baby. For five years she saved her money and then sailed to America. Many times Sylvia had told me that in America there aren't the class restrictions there are in England. She always told me she was going to New York to get a better job, but I always suspected it was to marry up. And I was right. While Sylvia was on board ship she met Charles Hendrickson, a New York banker. Sylvia said he wasn't wealthy, but I know otherwise. It took her less than a month to get him to the altar. She lives in a fine house in New York, goes to parties, and wears beautiful clothes."

"Like Lady Kent?"

"Exactly. I'm sure Sylvia lives even more lavishly. She has always understated herself. Sometimes I think it's so that I won't

go to New York and find the same good life she has. Women can
be petty like that, Amanda. Be careful.''

Amanda nodded, deferring to her mother's superior knowledge
about these matters.

"The time is right for you to groom yourself for the future,
Amanda. I worked in Kent Manor for fifteen years. I watched
and listened, just as I've told you to do. Those books of yours
and your writing, well, that's all fine and good, but it doesn't get
you a husband, now does it?

"Well, I don't . . .''

"Looks and good manners. That's what counts. I want you to
listen to everything Lady Kent tells Eloise. Watch how she
walks, talks, and handles herself. The summer social season has
just begun. You can learn a great deal by staying close to Eloise.
Pay attention. You can be just as much a lady as she is. After all,
blood isn't *always* everything. . . .''

They stopped under a clump of apple trees, waited for two
bicyclists to pass, and then continued on. The park was getting
crowded as the sun climbed in the sky. Picnic cloths were spread
under trees as young men and women dug into baskets with
nearly as much relish as they gazed into each other's eyes.
Children played ball, skipped rope, and played hopscotch.

Rounding a trimmed hedge of holly, Amanda spied Andrew
and a beautiful red-haired girl, whom she assumed was Lucy.
Amanda raised her arm, waved her handkerchief, and called to
her brother.

Upon hearing his name, Andrew stopped and looked around.
Then, suddenly, he took Lucy's arm, turned around, and walked
very quickly in the opposite direction.

"What on earth?''

"Where's he going? I'm sure he knew it was me.''

"Yes,'' Harriet replied bitterly. "I'm sure he knew.''

CHAPTER THREE

Monday morning saw the normal bustle of early week. The three laundresses came in to do the linens. The grocer delivered four boxes of fresh vegetables, fruits, and canned goods. Jonathon had gone back to school to study for final exams, and Lord Kent went to Threadneedle Street to check on his bonds. Lady Barbara had a luncheon engagement, and Emily was sequestered with the tutor until she learned her geometry.

Amanda sorted through the calling cards and invitations that had arrived by post and by messenger. "The ball must have been a big success," Amanda said to Eloise, who was about to leave for a fitting at the dressmaker's.

"Why do you say that?"

"You'll have to be two people in order to attend all these parties!"

Eloise shrugged her shoulders apathetically. "I wouldn't be caught dead in over half those homes."

"What about the Charles's? You were always good friends with Nancy."

Eloise chuckled, then lifted her nose in much the same way Amanda had seen Lady Barbara elevate hers. "That was when we were children."

"And now it's different?"

"Of course. Nancy Charles is a commoner, royal blood notwithstanding. I must go to the very best parties, where I have something to gain by being there, not where my hostess has everything to gain from my presence." Then, with a hint of doubt in her voice, she added: "At least, that's what Mother said."

"I see," Amanda said, hoping she could remember all this. She *had* to pay attention. That's what *her* mother had said.

"An invitation from the Palace would be a real coup for me. Once that happens, the caliber of my suitors will escalate."

Amanda knew this, too, was Lady Barbara talking.

"After my fitting, I'm meeting Mother at the theater for the matinee. I'll have the dresses sent here. Now remember, the blue is for next Saturday; put the lavender in plenty of tissue. I won't be needing it until Derby Day at Epsom Downs in June."

Eloise fastened her tight brown vest and hurried out the door.

Amanda went to the kitchen, got a cold glass of milk, and sampled some of Georgia's ginger cookies. Methodically, she broke the cookie into pieces and slowly savored them as she'd seen Eloise do. Georgia was rolling dough for kidney pies. She kept eyeing Amanda as she ate.

"What're you doin'?" Georgia asked.

"Eating cookies."

"An' since when do you not gobble down a half dozen of my finest in minutes?"

"I'll get fat."

"You should worry. You're too scrawny as it is."

"I am not. My waist is up to eighteen inches!"

Georgia laughed. "I was talkin' about the rest of you."

"That'll come—in time."

A persistent rapping at the kitchen door stole Amanda away. A young girl about Amanda's age, dressed in a skirt and blouse with a soiled apron, placed a bucket and brush on the step.

"I'm here to do the steps."

"We didn't call for a step-girl. We have someone for that."

"Are you sure? They don't look all that good to me."

"I don't make those decisions."

"Then I want to see the woman in charge."

"One moment," Amanda said and went to the drawing room where she found Sally.

"Couldn't you get rid of her, Amanda? Honestly, *must* I do everything?" Sally stomped off to the kitchen door, angry that her duties were not running on time again.

"No one in all of London does steps as good as me," the step-girl said. "It'd be worth yer while to sign me up. Just look at these here"—she kicked at a brick step caked with mud—"a disgrace."

Amanda and Sally looked down at the grimy steps. Considering all the workers who had tromped in and out, Amanda was surprised the steps looked this good. But the young girl's persuasive tactics were working on Sally.

"I can guarantee I'll do twice the job any o' yer people could do—and in half the time."

"Half the time?"

"Yes, ma'am."

Sally was hooked.

"Go ahead," Sally said. "Amanda, give her a shilling wnen she finishes—and make certain it's a good job. I'll hold you responsible."

Sally went back to the drawing room to finish dusting the precious Venetian glass chandelier. Sally had never entrusted the job to anyone else.

The step-girl got right to work. She filled her bucket with water, soaped her brush, and started scrubbing the bricks. "So, you work here?" she asked Amanda.

"Yes. I'm lady's maid to the two misses. And I have some household duties—not too many though."

"I wouldn't have your job for all the tea in China."

"Why not? I have a very, very good job."

"You got nothin'. Me, now. I got it all."

"How do you figure that?"

"I come and go as I want. I don't have to be nowhere at no particular time. When I feel like workin', I work. When I don't, I don't. I wouldn't be tied down to some old pinch-face like that one there. And I bet the lady . . . bet she's a real pistol. You gotta answer to everybody. How many you figure that is?"

"Well, I never thought about it that way. There's Sally; Georgia; Elrod; Miss Eloise, of course; Miss Emily; Lady Barbara; and Lord Kent."

"Awful . . . a crime it is to do that to someone as young as you. Me, I'm having fun while I'm young. Me and Alice, my friend, she works at a bank—she makes lots of money . . . I make good money, but not that good—we're getting us a place of our own."

"You are?"

"My sister did when she was sixteen. 'Course, she went amuck."

"What happened?"

"She got married."

"But I thought that was what is supposed to happen."

"Who told you that? Some ignorant person? I'm never gettin' married. No one is gonna tie me down to brats and an ole man who drinks all day Sunday and who's gone whorin' the rest of the week."

As the step-girl spoke Amanda remembered when Burt was alive. He'd been that kind of man. Amanda had never considered, even once, that she would have a marriage like her mother's. It simply wasn't in her plans. She would marry for love, but her criteria for a man were stringent. He must be at least as intelligent as she, kind and thoughtful, and he must love her back. She'd never actually *seen* a marriage like she envisioned, but she'd read about them in the novels Lord Kent kept in his library. She knew, somehow, that what she dreamed of was possible. Still, what the step-girl was talking about made sense. Amanda had never considered that she might have *options*.

"Things are changin' for women," the step-girl rattled on as she vigorously scrubbed the fifth and last step. "It won't be long before we get the vote . . . I went to a rally last night."

"You saw Emmeline Pankhurst?"

"I did. It got a bit rowdy, somebody threw a rock at the window of the *Lloyd's Weekly Newspaper* building, and Mrs. Pankhurst was tossed in jail again. But it won't stop her . . . or us."

Spellbound, Amanda was about to follow the step-girl to the front steps when Georgia opened the back door.

"Are you still out here? Miss Eloise's dresses were just delivered. You'd better see to them before Sally has a fit." She wagged a finger at Amanda and then went back inside.

Amanda looked at the step-girl. An impudent smile creased the girl's lips.

"Like I said, all the tea in China wouldn't tempt me to have your job."

Amanda wanted desperately to explore this girl who would risk deprivation, even jail, for her beliefs. And for a moment, she considered it. But her sense of responsibility prevailed and she went inside.

* * *

Amanda unboxed the dresses and shook them out. She chuckled to herself when she saw the ice blue silk taffeta gown Eloise had chosen. It was *exactly* the same ice blue as the hair ribbons Amanda had purchased from Mrs. Bird.

Amanda heated the warming plate for her iron, then tested it to make sure it wasn't too hot. This gown was cut low, with satin leaves ringing the neckline and continuing over the shoulders. It fit tightly in the waist and had an overlay of white organza on which vines and flowers had been hand painted. It was a beautiful gown, probably the loveliest Eloise had ever owned, but Amanda could tell from its inferior construction that it was a copy of a Paris original. The lavender gown was an odd shade of pink lavender that Amanda knew was wrong for Eloise. As she pressed it and then stuffed it with tissue and carried it upstairs she wondered what had possessed Eloise to buy it.

Amanda opened the cherry wardrobe, hung the gowns, and checked the shoe drawer to make certain the dancing slippers matched. As she went about the room gathering lingerie to be laundered and replenishing towels, Amanda found her eyes going back to the ice blue gown. There was something about it that beckoned to her. Perhaps it was because the color was so very near her eye color. She walked toward it, mesmerized. She wondered what it would be like to wear a dress brand-new, for the first time, for its silk never to have touched someone else's skin but hers.

What would it be like to wear soft kid shoes before the holes appeared on the bottoms or the stitching had come apart? For the first time in her life, Amanda wondered what it would be like to *be* Eloise.

She took the gown off the hanger. With trembling hands she unfastened the buttons, slipped off her faded black bombazine skirt and white blouse. Dressed in a yellowed and mended cotton chemise, she boldly stepped into the exquisite gown. Quickly she fastened it, as if it would vanish if she didn't hurry.

Standing in front of the cheval mirror, she held her breath. She blinked twice. This vision in the mirror couldn't be real! She spun around, then leaned forward and inspected herself. The ice blue had done for her eyes what it could never do for Eloise. She took off her cap and pulled her blonde hair over her shoulder, then pushed it up on her head. She looked older, elegant, even . . . regal.

"My lady." She curtsied low to the mirror. She picked up Eloise's fan, spread it open, and fluttered her eyes as she had seen Eloise practice. The effect was incredible.

Amanda did not see the bedroom door creep open, nor did she see Emily on the other side as she watched through the crack.

Amanda was in a dreamworld. "Are those flowers for me?" Amanda chimed. And then in a deeper voice, emulating a man's: "For my darling Lady Amanda. The most beautiful girl . . . wearing a most beautiful gown."

Emily had started to burst into the room and join in Amanda's fun until she realized what was happening. Her delight in a bit of mischief evolved into indignation, then anger. How dare Amanda call herself royalty? How dare she assume a standing equal to her own? Even in a daydream Amanda was being impertinent.

Though Emily didn't harbor an abundance of sisterly love for Eloise, she felt every wave of jealousy Eloise would have felt seeing Amanda in that gown. Emily's eyes became wrathful slits. Amanda had always lived better than anyone of her station, thanks to the bounty of the Kents. As children, the class lines dividing them had been blurred, many times even obliterated, but now they were all nearly adults. Wasn't that what Father had said to her just the other day? That soon her responsibilities as a Kent would present themselves and Emily must be prepared for the challenge?

Emily watched Amanda pretending to be a lady, a Kent, while inside her jealousy raged unchecked. This was her chance to show her father that she was meeting her responsibilities. When she informed him and her mother about Amanda, he would be proud of her. More important, once and for all, Lord Kent would see that Amanda was *not* special.

Emily closed the door and quietly slipped down the stairs, knowing that today she would obliterate the nightmares she'd had for years. When she was three years old, Lord Kent had promised Emily a new pony for her birthday. She was frightened of the pony and wouldn't ride it. With Lord Kent's help, Amanda had mounted the pony and ridden him about the yard to show Emily she had nothing to fear. When Emily finally had the courage to ride, she instantly slipped off and fell into the mud. Lady Barbara had taken Emily inside to change. When they emerged, Emily had seen Amanda successfully "jump" over a clump of rosebushes and then pull to a halt. Thrilled with her ride, she had flown into Lord Kent's arms. They had laughed and hugged, and Emily had watched in shock as her father kissed Amanda, the servant's girl, in a way he'd never done with her. Rubbing salt in the wound, throughout that evening he had extolled Amanda's riding skills to their guests.

Emily had never forgotten that day. In her mind, she'd been striving to win her father's love ever since. Eloise had often told Emily she had conjured all this in her mind. But Emily *knew* that her father did not love her.

Emily went to the library and found it empty. She passed Elrod but didn't speak; her mind was on the revenge she was about to exact. Finally, she found her mother in the main drawing room with Eloise, who had just arrived.

Emily flung back the door. "Mother! Where's Father?" she asked breathlessly.

"He went to the Reform Club."

"I need him!"

"Emily, control yourself. What could possibly—"

"It's Amanda. . . . Someone must stop her."

"What?"

Knowing she would lose the impact of the moment, Emily motioned to them to follow her. She nearly raced up the stairs.

Standing at the closed mahogany door, Emily could still hear Amanda talking to herself. She smiled triumphantly as she flung open the door.

Amanda spun around and gasped. Her smile vanished as her eyes took in one furious face after the other.

"My gown! What have you done to it?" Eloise demanded.

"Nothing . . . I . . ."

Devastated, Amanda watched as Jane, the upstairs maid, and Molly, the first-floor maid, clustered just outside the door. They wore the same smile of triumph that Amanda saw on Emily's face. They had waited a long time for Amanda to be dressed down. She knew the time had come.

"Take it off!" Eloise nearly screamed and Amanda quickly did as she was commanded.

Eloise took the dress and carefully hung it up. She gazed at it, knowing that now it would never be the same, that it had been defiled somehow.

Amanda stood before Lady Barbara dressed in the ragged chemise. She might as well have been naked, she thought. She wished she could run away, but instead she held her chin high, bit her tongue, and fought back her tears.

Emily sidled up to her mother. "I heard her talking to herself. She called herself Lady Amanda."

Amanda looked at Lady Barbara, who was fighting her fury with Olympian control. She looked like a volcano ready to explode.

"Is this true, Amanda?"

"I was just pretending. I didn't mean any harm. . . ."

"For months you have been trying my patience. But this escapade of yours today goes much deeper than your playing dress-up. I haven't decided if it is your stubbornness or your naivety that leads you to trouble, Amanda. In either case it must stop."

"Yes, ma'am."

"I'm afraid it isn't as simple as that. Perhaps I'm at fault just as much as you."

"I don't understand."

"I know you don't. You see, Amanda, for the past year I have been preparing my girls for life. They know precisely what is expected of them. They know what their duties will be, their responsibilities. I've involved both of them in charity work for the poor, church work; drilled them in etiquette and taught them about fashion, deportment . . . all the things that are part of being a lady.

"If you learned all these things, Amanda, even if you learned them better than Eloise or Emily, you could never be a lady. A lady is born, Amanda. It takes *bloodlines*, proper bloodlines, to be a lady. You can never be something you weren't born to be. You are a servant girl, Amanda. You have a particular place and life you must assume."

Amanda looked into Eloise's stern face, Emily's triumphant one. "But we were friends. Eloise and I still talk as if we were . . ."

"Sisters? No, Amanda. Never mistake youthful friendliness for anything more than exactly that. And that will stop too. Eloise will now have her own friends who have the same advantages and bloodlines that she does. You are no longer friends with Eloise, Amanda. You are here to serve Eloise and Emily. Nothing more. It was a grave mistake you made today. You hurt

Eloise's feelings tremendously. For that you must be punished. I'm docking your pay by one half.''

"A half?" Amanda knew instantly what hardship that would bring to her family. This couldn't be happening! And all because she'd tried on that dress.

Lady Barbara continued. "If you conduct yourself as a lady's maid should, I will *consider*, but *only* consider, raising your pay a shilling a week. You must learn that there is a limit to my good graces."

She turned to Eloise and Emily. "I think Georgia has tea ready for us in the salon."

They started for the stair. Lady Barbara turned back to Amanda.

"I want this room picked up. It's time to air the rugs and drapes. Have Jane help you."

Amanda watched her leave. Never in her life had she been talked to like that. It was demeaning and she hated it. Amanda knew—oh! how she knew—that Lady Barbara was right. The reality of her future had been creeping in on her for months. And each day, Amanda had willed it away, as if she could alter the social balance of England by herself. She didn't think Lady Barbara was being cruel, any more than life itself was.

Amanda felt a shroud of doom cloak her shoulders. Was that all there was for her? She could choose the option the step-girl had presented. She could find freedom that way. She could leave Kent Manor and be a step-girl. She could marry as her mother advised her and live in a better section of London and pray every day that her husband would be good to her. But as she looked at her future from both angles she didn't like either alternative.

Amanda wanted more for herself. She wanted a life even better than Eloise's or the step-girl's. Her childish dreams of a beautiful house appointed with Persian rugs, fine furniture, and fabulous art, the beautiful clothes and parties, faded in the light of Lady Barbara's words.

For years she'd been reading philosophy and literature that touted man's inherent dignity. Amanda believed she was no better and no worse than the next man. What she did with her life was *her* choice, however. She couldn't believe she would not find independence and acceptance. She knew Lord Kent cherished the same values she did. He'd taught them to her. Yes, she thought, Lord Kent would tell her the truth.

* * *

"What is it, Amanda?" Lord Kent's soothing voice asked as he closed the library doors behind him.

Amanda tried to wipe her tears unnoticed. The sun had set, and normally she should be home by now. But after the ruinous day she'd had, she wanted to hide. It was easier to hide here than anywhere on Shelton Street. No one but Lord Kent ever came to the library, much to his chagrin.

"I didn't know you were back. I'll be leaving."

"Nonsense."

"I know how special this place is to you. I can't intrude."

"And why not?"

"It isn't . . . my place."

"And what is your place?"

She raised her head. Did he know of the incident that afternoon? She couldn't be sure. She wondered if this was one of his "tests."

"I'm a servant."

"You're a human being, Amanda. As we all are." He walked over, turned on the new electric Tiffany lamp, and sank into the forest green leather sofa. He rubbed his eyes. He looked tired, though a faint smile parted his lips.

Amanda stood rigidly in the corner. She knew if he scolded her, this time she would surely cry. There was only so much pride a person had.

"Tell me what you've been learning."

"Sir?"

"From the books I gave you."

He didn't know. "I'm learning about society and its structure. I know that we all have a certain destiny at birth and it is our duty to see it out."

"That's one theory. Not everyone believes it, however."

"They don't?" Amanda felt hope renewing itself.

"It's interesting you should bring this up. We were discussing this very subject today at the club. I have always believed that it is education that will bring the lower classes up. When men are better able to read and write they will find better jobs. We're moving into a new century, Amanda. I believe that soon most of the jobs done by men will be done almost entirely by machine. We've seen much of that in the last thirty years, but it is nothing compared to what is about to come. That's why I've stressed your studies so much with you. The rest of the girls working here, they don't care about anything past their weekly wages and having a good time on Saturday night. You aren't like that.''

"I try to be more responsible."

"And you are. The others will never rise above their station."

"You think if they studied, they could become better than what they are?"

"Absolutely. Why, if you kept to your writing, Amanda, you could become a teacher at a university."

"But could I ever become like, well, like Eloise?"

"How like Eloise?" he asked, looking at her intently.

"Could I ever live like a lady?"

He considered this a moment, and when he spoke he chose his words carefully. "Yes. You could live like a lady. You could do charity work as Eloise does, which is one of her most important responsibilities. It is our task in life as nobility to leave the world in a better position than it was when we were brought into it. I suppose if you married a rich man, you could have the advantages she does." He saw from her face that his answer was not the one she was looking for. He continued. "I trust that you will be a good and kind wife to the man you marry. Raise your children as Christians, of course. Yes, it is possible for you to live like a lady."

"But . . . I could never actually *be* a lady, could I?"

Suddenly, he realized the direction of the conversation. He had always prided himself on speaking the truth. In fact, Barbara had often said that she knew he'd never lied because on the one occasion when he'd even considered it, he had trembled so much his knees had rattled. He wished he'd learned to lie so that he could spare Amanda this overwhelming slice of reality.

"No."

Amanda gripped the edge of the sofa. She steadied herself. Lady Barbara was right. No matter how much he tried to sugarcoat it, she was from the slums. Bloodline was everything.

He hated himself for being the cause of her heartache. All those years when he'd put her on an equal level as his own children, he had blinded himself to the fact that this day would come. It was stupidity on his part, for he'd never planned for any of them to grow up. He'd adored those years when the children were small . . . egalitarian days when in their innocence, they knew nothing of the world, of its restrictions. Being only four years apart from the oldest to the youngest, they'd banded together to extort favors out of him and only fought when they felt one or the other had been slighted. It was a simple world he'd tried to keep just that way. He knew now that the idyll he'd so carefully created was over.

Amanda said nothing as she closed the doors quietly behind her.

CHAPTER FOUR

"How will we make it on only five shillings a week?" Harriet asked as she donned her apron.

"Maybe it's time Andrew—"

"Please . . ." Harriet sat next to Amanda. "It took me three months to get five shillings out of him."

"Why do you favor him so much?" Amanda asked angrily. Tonight she was angry with her mother, Eloise, herself—the world.

"You know the old saying . . . that your son will take care of you for the rest of your life? I keep thinking that he will sprout some responsibility and take care of me when I'm in my twilight years."

Amanda softened and put her arm around her mother's shoulders. "You don't have to rely on him. I'll take care of you."

"And how can you do that?" She looked at her daughter incredulously.

"I don't know, but I'm not giving up like this!"

"Give up?"

"How can you talk about having Andrew take care of you? Only you can take care of yourself. Why must you rely on him? There's got to be another way," Amanda said, looking at her mother's stunned face. She lost the head of steam that propelled her. "There's got to be."

Harriet shook her head. "That's the way the world is, luv. Men rule over women, the rich over the poor. But that's not to say you can't get what you want. I think there is another way for you."

"What? How?" Amanda asked as her eyes brightened.

"I'm going to write to Sylvia in New York. I've known for a long time that you belong in America. You've got dreams that will never happen here. There's too much against you here. Nobody can fight these odds. But in New York, with a new name . . ."

"No. I like my name."

"Then a new background . . . we'll make one up. We'll get you the best clothes we can. And you'll sail for America. *Then*, after you marry a rich, nice man, then you can take care of me."

"Oh, Mother! Do you think it's possible?"

"Of course." She hugged a jubilant Amanda. Amanda looked at her mother for a moment. Then, as she thought more about it, her face fell.

"I can't go to America. It must cost a fortune to book passage."

"You let me worry about that. If it's just money we have to worry about, then it's not that impossible."

"But you just said we couldn't make it because my pay was cut by a few shillings. I don't understand."

"Never let it be said I didn't like a challenge myself once in awhile. Now, you go to Lord Kent and tell him about the row with Lady Barbara. My bet is he'll raise your pay back up. I have some friends who can get me a job at night. In the meantime, you start preparing yourself for the future. It'll take some time, but I know we can do it."

May moved into June. Amanda had gone to Lord Kent about her dilemma and he promised to pay her the full ten shillings a week provided she didn't tell Lady Barbara. Amanda asked if there was anything else she could do to earn extra money. Sally consulted with Lady Barbara and they agreed to give her three shillings more a week for polishing the silver. A gargantuan task, it consumed a full three extra hours four nights a week. Lady Barbara was pleased with Amanda's new attitude. She believed that though the "incident of Eloise's dress" had been an unpleasant one, it had taught Amanda her place.

Harriet told Amanda she'd procured a second job herself as a seamstress for one of the better dress shops. She was not able to bring the work home, however, but was instructed to work only in the workrooms. The owner was cautious about sending piecework out until she knew she could trust her employees.

With the bulk of the summer "season" upon them, Amanda had more than her share of work load at Kent Manor. The Royal Horticultural Society flower show had been outstanding that year. Eloise had met Ashton Parks, son of Lord Parks. She said she liked him when they first met, but by the time of the Royal Ascot races in mid-June, Eloise had altered her opinion.

Rather than accompany her on Thursday, Ladies' Day and the most fashionable day of the races, the day when the crème de la crème of society wanted to see and be seen, Ashton chose to go on Friday. Friday, as everyone knew, was strictly for the horsey set. They were the most enthusiastic of race fans.

Owning three horses, Ashton was more than passingly interested in the races. He was an excellent polo player, had won several national cups, owned no less than fourteen trophies for dressage, and he was only interested in a woman who loved horses as much as he. By June 19, the "romance" had ended.

Queen Victoria's choice of Lord Rosebery as her prime minister had kept most of the political and financial circles bubbling and battering at each other. Lord Kent was forever being called upon to speak to Parliament, to offer his advice to coalitions of Whigs and Liberals. He believed that Victoria's Salisbury administration would find a very important rise of imperialism that her reign had not enjoyed since the days of Disraeli. It was clear to him in his audiences with the queen that she was far more comfortable with her present cabinet than she'd been in years. To him, it was a sign that England would enter the new century as a strong and powerful country.

Amanda arrived home most summer nights around ten. Fortunately, the sun had been down long enough for the stale little rooms on Shelton Street to air out and become habitable once again. Harriet worked past midnight almost every night now, but when Amanda begged her to rest, Harriet assured her that the money was too good to pass up.

Andrew's life-style had not altered in the least. He worked until six each day and then went to the public houses and pubs all night. Somehow, however, Harriet had coerced him into paying her two shillings a week for his room and board. Harriet squirreled the money away in a false-bottom drawer in the bedroom she shared with Amanda. On the night she'd shown her hiding place to Amanda, she made her daughter swear on the Bible she would never reveal her secret to Andrew. Knowing what a spendthrift her son was, Harriet's concern was well founded.

Amanda unlocked the front door and lit the gas lights, wishing Shelton Street would get electricity like Kent Manor. She opened the window next to the table and took a deep breath. The air was rancid. She turned and noticed that the bedroom door was closed. The door was never closed unless Harriet was home.

"Mother?" she called and went to the door. It was locked. Harriet had never locked a door in her life.

"Mother? Are you in there?" There was no light coming from under the door. Then she heard feet shuffling. And what sounded like a drawer closing. Or the window?

Suddenly, the door unlocked and opened.

"Andrew! What are you doing in there?" She tried to peak over his shoulder, but it was dark and she couldn't see.

"I couldn't sleep, so I came in here," he said going past her to the ice box. He opened it and withdrew a jug of cold water, put it to his lips, and drank deeply.

"I thought you'd be out with Lucy."

Amanda noticed that whenever she spoke of Lucy, a sly grin creased his face. There was no happiness in his eyes as she would have expected from a man in love. He still had not introduced her to Lucy. Amanda suspected that Andrew had lied to Lucy and her family about himself and his background. Amanda wondered if he'd even told her he *had* a sister.

"Lucy couldn't see me tonight . . ." he said, his eyes momentarily revealing his pain. Amanda instantly regretted her misgivings about her brother. Perhaps he did love Lucy. Perhaps there were problems Andrew could not surmount. "She went to some party . . . her mother insisted . . ."

"I'm sorry," was all Amanda could say.

He turned his back on her and rather than probe him for information he wouldn't give, she went into the bedroom. She lit the lamp and began undressing. She carefully folded her blouse and went to the chest to put it away. When she did, she noticed that the bottom drawer was crookedly inset.

It was the false-bottom drawer. Had Andrew discovered their mother's hiding place? Could it be possible Andrew was stealing? Amanda pulled it out and checked the inside. There seemed to be a great deal of money there, more than she knew her mother could have made in the past month from her extra job.

Where had it all come from? Had Andrew been giving Harriet money without Amanda's knowledge? Philanthropy was not in her brother's character, so she strongly doubted it.

Something was very wrong. All three of their wages for nearly half a year wouldn't add up to this much. However the money had gotten there, Amanda knew it had been dishonestly gained.

Amanda stuffed the money back in the drawer and replaced it. It fit smoothly into its resting place. She didn't want to see the money or even think about it, for if she did, then she would have to admit that her mother—or her brother—was leading a life she knew nothing about—and didn't *want* to know about.

How could they keep such secrets from her? They lived out of each other's pockets as it was. She sat on the bed. Or did they?

Andrew had always been closemouthed about his life. The only things she knew about him were the obvious. He believed he could marry his way out of the slums, just as she did, and she was certain he was a hard worker, as she was. She had always assumed they were of the same mind. They *were* brother and sister, after all.

No, she couldn't believe Andrew was guilty of anything more than spending too much money.

As Amanda thought of her mother, she knew that Harriet had found a way, though she couldn't think what, of amassing the boat passage. After so many years of poverty, Amanda found it incomprehensible to think that her mother suddenly had the means at her disposal to alter her life, all their lives.

Harriet lifted her arms above her head to fasten her hairpins and when she did, her naked breasts rose voluptuously. She smiled at the reflection of the man in the mirror. He was sitting up in bed, his head against the walnut headboard, admiring her. She turned around on the vanity stool and slowly bent down to pick up her stockings. She raised her leg into the air and pulled the new silk hose up over one knee and then slipped on a lace-edged garter. She knew her languid, sensual movements were driving him mad.

"You like those stockings I gave you? Chinese silk. Nothing but the best for you, Harriet," he said and patted the bed next to him.

She ignored the gesture. "Next time, I'd like a new chemise and perhaps a peignoir. Green, I think. To match my eyes."

"Aren't you afraid you're asking for too much?"

She smiled, rose, and went to the bed. She eased herself onto the bed, letting his eyes feast on her breasts. She pulled the sheet away from him. Slowly, she traced a path with her hands from his chest down to his stomach, bulging from too many years of sitting at a desk pouring over stocks and bonds, down . . . down to his penis. She grasped him and held him tightly.

"But your rate of return, Arnold, is very"—she squeezed—"very, high."

"Anything . . ." he gasped.

"Just think of all those years you've wanted me. Thought about what I would look like . . . naked . . . like I am now."

He closed his eyes.

"Every time you came to Kent Manor, you wanted me. Every time you sat at dinner with your fat old wife, you watched me. And I saw you watching me."

"You were always so cold toward me."

"Because I knew this day would come, Arnold. And it would be all the more grand for the waiting. I know," she said, pulling on him, then releasing the pressure until he grew hard, "you've never had anyone like me, have you, Arnold?"

"No."

"I'm worth half a gold crown . . ." She pulled. "A whole gold crown."

"Yes," he said, beads of sweat springing onto his forehead and upper lip. "Even more than that."

"Two gold crowns, Arnold, plus the new lingerie, and the world will be yours."

"Yes! Yes! All of it! It's all yours . . . just . . . please."

She lingered, waiting for the right moment. "I just didn't want you to think I was cheap."

"Never! I know better." He was gasping and it sounded as if he were dying.

Harriet smiled triumphantly at the bargain she'd made, then lowered her open mouth onto him.

CHAPTER FIVE

Amanda didn't say anything to her mother about the money. Nor did she talk to their neighbor, Mrs. Jenkins, about her mother's comings or goings during the day while Amanda was gone. All the next day, Amanda pretended that she'd just been dreaming about the money and that she didn't have to fear the bobbies coming after them. But that night when she arrived home, finding no one there as usual, she checked the drawer again. She could swear the two gold crowns had not been there the day before. This time she counted the money. There was nearly a hundred pounds. Again, she replaced the drawer and waited for Harriet to come home.

Amanda worked on her studies, wrote two poems, which were coming a bit easier now, and finished reading her Jane Austen novel. She fell asleep before midnight and did not hear Harriet come in, place a new chemise and green peignoir beneath two moth-eaten sweaters on the shelf in the closet, and then climb into bed.

For over a week Amanda saw Andrew as he dressed to go out with Lucy or go to the pubs, and she only saw her mother in the morning when she left for work. But each night, Amanda counted the money and found that the tally was growing at an alarming rate of speed.

Still, Harriet said nothing to Amanda. Amanda could not broach the subject because she didn't want her mother to know she'd been spying on her. All Amanda could do was worry.

Amanda replaced her book on the library shelf and started for the doors. She heard voices. The past few days had taught her that sometimes it was necessary to pry, to eavesdrop. Rather than show herself, she leaned closer and listened.

"Pack a steamer for each of the girls, two for myself, and just Lord Kent's summer suits. He'll be coming into town during the week," Lady Barbara instructed Sally. "I don't think we'll ever get that man away from the bond market."

"Lord Kent works too hard, if you don't mind my sayin' so, ma'am," Sally said.

"I know. But he's hired a new manager, and I'm hoping he will make a difference. There's more to life than stocks."

Lord Kent walked into the vestibule where Lady Barbara and Sally were talking about him. "But my investments pay for this house you're so fond of, my dear," he said tersely. "And if you want to take the children to the seaside for the summer, that's fine. I just can't join you, is all."

Lady Barbara's voice rose an octave as it always did when she wasn't getting her way. Sally slipped away, leaving them alone.

"Our friends are spending the summer in the Cotswolds. Why can't we go there?"

"Because we own a house at Tresco. What's the matter with the seashore? I thought you loved the seashore."

"I'll need more servants at the seashore, and you told me to cut back this summer."

"Good God, Barbara! You never stop, do you? All right, then. You can take Amanda."

"She's no help!"

"Since when? I've seen how you've been working her. She's here till almost ten every night. It looks to me like she does more than the rest of the staff."

"I want Jane."

"You can take Amanda. It's time she saw the seashore anyway." Lady Barbara grabbed his arm. "I should have known you'd do this."

"What are you talking about?"

"Your favoritism toward her must have its limits. The children are growing, and Amanda must know there is no place for her in their world."

His eyes narrowed. "I wondered why Amanda was suddenly so concerned about the social order of things recently. You've never liked her. You've gone out of your way all her life to push her back, when I've tried to educate her, pull her above her roots."

"Why, Alvin? Why have you given Amanda so much?" Lady Barbara asked with a rush of breath.

"Why does her very existence bother you so much?" he retaliated.

Lady Barbara backed down. "Amanda is only a servant. I deny that I'm overly concerned with her." She started to walk away, then turned back to him. "Thank you, Alvin, for letting me take her to the Scillys."

Lord Kent smiled, knowing he'd worked his way around his wife again. He'd gotten what he wanted. Curiously, though, he realized *she'd* gotten precisely what she'd wanted too.

"I don't believe you!"

"It's true," Amanda said as she continued to pack.

"The Kents have never taken you to the seashore. Why now, all of a sudden?" Andrew barked.

"Amanda has been with the Kents since she was born. Why does that upset you?" Harriet asked.

"You don't see my employer taking me away for six weeks of holiday!"

Harriet continued cutting up apples. "Your jealousy is showing."

"I'm not jealous. It just isn't fair. I have to work twice as hard as she does."

"That's ridiculous. Amanda works harder and longer hours than either of us. If anyone here has an easy road of it, it's you, Andrew."

Andrew was instantly on his feet. "I knew you'd take her side. You always did—and you still do. Well, I don't have to stay around and listen to it."

He walked over to the bedroom and watched Amanda as she dug around in the closet for nicer clothes, things that weren't there.

"Have a *good* time, Amanda," he said sarcastically. "I'll see you when you get back."

In three strides he was across the room and out the door before Amanda could stop him. She looked blankly at her mother.

"Did I do something?"

" 'Do'? No, I don't think so."

CHAPTER SIX

Two boys, one seven, one nine, waited impatiently on the street corner. It was three hours past race time. A beer wagon, piled with wooden kegs, rounded Mercer Street. The wooden wheel of the wagon slipped over the curb and nearly ran over the younger boy's foot. He jumped back out of the way. An ice wagon passed, then two carriages and three new motorcars. They made a horrid noise, sputtering and spurting the way they did, but the boys were fascinated with their claxon horns. The streets were noisy this time of midday.

The boys looked up and down Mercer Street, straining their eyes. Finally, their faces lit up and they began waving frantically.

From the left, a boy on a bicycle with reams of pink paper in a cloth bag he'd slung over his back was pedaling toward them at record speed. He tossed a bundle of papers at the boys, gave them the familiar wave, and was off to the next street corner where another pair of boys waited for him.

The elder boy took out his pocket knife and cut the piece of jute that held the papers together. Shouting at the top of their voices, the boys were back in business.

"Speshul! Speshul! Read all about it!"

"Mark your winner!" the other boy said, racing into the factory yards where clerks and supervisors grabbed up his penny paper.

Rapping on retail and office doors, the boys poked their heads in and sold every one of their papers. In England in the summer, the biggest business was betting.

Andrew paid the boy and quickly scanned the pink sheet. Yes, it was another good day for him. Quickly, he went back inside, finished auditing the last two columns of numbers for the day, and was off.

As workers from the lumber mills, the wood yards, garment factories, and ice houses streamed out of the company yards for the day, the majority of the men sought out their bookmakers.

On any given afternoon, bookmakers could be seen on the street corners marking bets in plain view of the police. Everyone knew who the bookmakers were, for they were very public about their vocation. All except Andrew Granger.

Andrew hated making book. It was time consuming and demeaning to associate and work with men who couldn't even sign their names. He couldn't afford to run his "business" as the others did, for he wanted someday to marry Lucy Attington. If Lucy's father ever discovered this sideline, he would not be allowed to walk the same city as Lucy.

Andrew, then, kept his clientele exclusive. His roster was taken from the list of Mr. Sloan's clients. Most of these men didn't want their wives to know about their gambling, and so they placed most of their bets by phone or did so late at night at one of the pubs where Andrew made certain to be.

For years he'd kept his secret from his mother and sister. Not to protect them but to protect himself. He didn't want either of them getting any of his money. He needed every penny he could earn or steal to get out of the slum. His courtship of Lucy had cost him dearly, over four hundred pounds, to dress himself and take her to the ballet, opera, and the finest restaurants in London. Lucy's father had chosen another man as Lucy's suitor. Gerald Attington wanted Lucy to marry a professional man, not an accountant clerk with no college education. Andrew should have felt fortunate he'd made it this far with Lucy.

Andrew had one major advantage with Lucy: she was in love with him.

However, Andrew also knew that love wasn't enough. He had to show Lucy's parents that he could care for her as well as Collin Bratton could.

Collin was an attorney whose future would include a partnership in a two-hundred-year-old firm run by his uncle and father. Someday, too, Collin could have a political career.

Andrew always took Lucy to those places where she would be certain to see her friends. They went to the cathedral on Sundays, never to St. Silas's where his mother and sister attended services. They went to Albert Hall, where several times he'd seen the Kents at the concerts and operas. They went to Alexandra Place, Boswell's Coffee House, tea at the Dorchester, and dinner at Boulestin's.

All this cost money. As did the flowers he sent, the candy from Fortnum and Mason's, the gold bracelet and earrings he'd purchased at Royal Jewelers.

In the past month, Andrew's bookmaking business had doubled. With next month's exodus of nearly his entire roster of clients as they headed for the country, Andrew was faced with a decision. He could pull back from Lucy and hope that for a month she would not fall prey to Collin's overtures, or he could take to the streets and make book along with the Cutter's Row and Mercer Street bookers.

Andrew prided himself on being a risk taker. And he was also intelligent enough to know that by September, when his regular business was good again, Lucy might be engaged to Collin.

CHAPTER SEVEN

Amanda looked out the train window at buttercup-sprigged meadows, speckled here and there with magpies who nose-dived near grazing herds of Holstein cows. The Cornwall coastline, brick red in color, fascinated her as the train chugged along to Penzance. After several hours, the train pulled to a stop at a tiny, dilapidated station.

It took three porters and all the Kent accompanying staff to unload the luggage. The house had not been opened for two summers, and most of the supplies had been moved back to London. Now everything had to be moved back to Tresco. Rather than having the staff coordinate on their own, Lady Barbara insisted that she be present. She had brought both her daughters along, thinking it would be a good time to teach them about the rigors of preparing the summer cottage for the holidays.

"Never leave all the details to the staff," Amanda had heard Lady Barbara say. "Supervision is everything." Amanda had thought "efficiency" was everything.

Jonathon was to remain in London during the summer to learn the brokerage business with his father, and both father and son would come to the seashore on weekends.

From Penzance, the family was ferried by boat to one of the one hundred small islands known as the Scillys. Amanda, never having been to the Kent summer home, had read everything she could on the area. But nothing had prepared her for such splendor.

The "summer cottage" was twice the size of Kent Manor. Sprawling on top of a hill overlooking the sea on the south and acres of hilly forest on the north, the three-story white-and-blue-shuttered structure boasted turrets, catwalks, gingerbread, wrap-around porches, and at least a hundred windows, Amanda guessed. The Kents had ridden in the carriage in front of them, Amanda, Jane, Sally, and Georgia stayed in the open wagon with the luggage.

Amanda had never seen hedgerows blossom in quite this shade of pink and lavender. Brilliant, fiery red azaleas studded the ground beneath shady oaks. The yards had been clipped, and to the left a whitewashed fence enclosed an area where horses grazed. And everywhere was a brilliant blue sky that almost made her eyes hurt to look at it. Used to the diffused light of a smoggy London, Amanda had never seen air this clean. Awed by both nature and architecture, Amanda stood dumbstruck while everyone began unloading trunks, china barrels, silver boxes, and suitcases.

"Amanda!" Lady Kent boomed. "I did not bring you to the seashore to stand and gape. Lend a hand. There is much to do."

"Yes, ma'am!" Amanda replied willingly. This was such a beautiful place that even though she was a servant, she couldn't imagine *anyone* not being happy here.

After two long weeks of ironing fine Egyptian cotton bed linens, washing windows—there were seventy-one—painting the wicker porch furniture, polishing dark oak floors, and refilling the barren pantry and four iceboxes, everyone at the summer house was exhausted and ready for a rest.

Because the neighboring houses were still empty, since Lady Barbara had a rush on the season, there was no one to give a party for—except themselves. In an uncustomary gesture, Lady Barbara suggested that staff and family join together for a day of swimming, picnicking, and frolic. Since none of her friends were around for her to worry over propriety, Lady Barbara felt safe in being magnanimous.

Amanda jammed a bright yellow canvas umbrella into the sand and tilted it against the sun. She spread a huge blanket beneath it and then walked down the beach a few paces and jammed another umbrella into the sand. The sky was cloudless, a sparkling sheet of blue; it hovered over Amanda, making happy promises. Everything at Tresco seemed clean and new, though it wasn't. Amanda liked the way the wet sand squished between her toes. Every morning she got up an hour early just to sit at her window and look out to sea. She wondered what was out there—if her destiny did indeed lie on the other side of the Atlantic. She didn't know what America was like, but right now, Tresco was the most beautiful place in the world and she thought she could live here forever. But as she heard Lady Barbara's voice reeling off instructions to the servants as they marched over the sand dune, she realized this was only an interlude, a time that didn't count.

Emily raced over the sand and plopped down under the first umbrella.

"This is mine! No one else can have it," she said pointedly to Eloise, who arrived with a bit more poise. Eloise kicked sand at her sister and went to the next umbrella that Amanda had prepared.

Amanda chuckled to herself. Since they'd arrived Emily had weaseled her way out of most of her chores. Eloise, being the dutiful daughter she was, had taken up the slack. Her sense of responsibility obviously did not squelch Eloise's anger.

Amanda prepared the third umbrella, taken by Lady Barbara, then two more, all in yellow. They looked like inverted spring tulips, Amanda thought as Emily and Eloise, clad in new bathing costumes, raced for the waves.

"Remember the current, girls. The undertow here can be very strong!" Lady Barbara said.

Sally erected two canvas and wood folding loungers. She took out her embroidery and sat in the shade of another umbrella near Lady Barbara's. "Aren't you going for a swim?" she asked Amanda.

"Yes. Maybe later. What are you making?"

"A summer dress. I thought some decoration around the neckline would be pretty."

Georgia started laughing as she took out a lemon meringue pie from a picnic basket.

"She's hoping she'll see Gregory this year," Georgia said to Amanda with a wink.

"Who's Gregory? I never heard you speak of him."

Sally tossed Georgia a blistering look and then went back to her needlework. "He works at Lord Edgerton's house a mile down the coast. We see each other from time to time."

Amanda was fascinated with this side of Sally. She'd always thought of Sally as a rigid, rather unfriendly spinster. But ever since they'd arrived at the seashore everyone was acting differently.

Though they worked long hours, there was much whistling and song singing, joke telling and a mutual respect Amanda hadn't seen before. For the first time in her life, she worked side by side with Eloise and Lady Barbara. She'd actually seen Lady Barbara baking in the kitchens with Georgia. They'd talked about Georgia's family, her sons and grandchildren. Lady Barbara knew all their names and ages. Amanda had been more than surprised by the revelation.

Something happened to them all at the seashore. There was a relaxation of mood, of character, of order. Amanda didn't understand it, but as she sat on the blanket next to Sally, who was telling her about her beau, and looked at Lady Barbara's happy face out of the corner of her eye, Amanda wished with all her heart that it could always be like this.

"You should ask him to supper, Sally," Lady Barbara offered as if she were one of Sally's oldest confidantes."

"Isn't that a bit forward? I mean, what would he think of me?"

Georgia laughed heartily. "He won't think of you at all if you don't give him a bit of a push now and then."

"I agree with Georgia," Lady Barbara said. "Men need some prodding. After all, you've been coming here to Tresco with us for ten years."

Amanda's mouth flew open. "Ten years? And you aren't married yet?"

As soon as she'd said it, Amanda flung her hand over her mouth. She was so embarrassed, she wanted to die.

Everyone, including Sally, burst into uproarious laughter.

"I didn't mean . . . Sally . . . I'm so sorry. . . ."

Sally stopped long enough to say: "You're so right, Amanda. Never be sorry for that." She looked down at her dress. "I think I should cut the bodice just a bit lower." And with that, she ripped the embroidered panel off. "That ought to get him started!"

Amanda laughed so hard she thought her sides would split. Their laughter was very loud—so loud that it filled the air and was carried out to the water. Their voices beckoned to Emily who, tired of swimming, started back to shore to investigate.

Emily was so intent on finding the source of the laughter that she didn't pay any attention to Eloise.

Eloise was farther out than Emily, swimming toward Flat Rock—she'd named it when she was only six. It was a big water-smoothed rock that they used as a diving platform. It was gray with pink and silver colorations like marble. She'd always pretended that underneath was buried pirate treasure and that long ago buccaneers had placed this unique-looking rock in precisely this position for her to find. Hundreds of times she'd plunged into the sea around the rock, searching its base for a hint of a treasure chest.

Not since she was eight had she told anyone about her fantasy. She knew her mother would think it was foolishness. Jonathon would side with her mother. Emily would use the information to make her life miserable, bringing it up every chance she had. And her father . . . he would approve.

It had been two years since she'd been in Tresco. Two years of growing taller and stronger would certainly aid her in her quest. She knew she shouldn't think about such fairy tales anymore. But—what if there really *was* something down there?

Eloise reached the rock, climbed on top, and rested for a moment. Had the rock moved farther out to sea in the past two years? or had she just never noticed before? She stood up and gazed into the turquoise waters. It fascinated her how the water's colors seemed to be layered one on top of another like a parfait.

Amanda took a long drink of her lemonade and picked up a piece of chicken. Absentmindedly, she looked out to sea just long enough to see Eloise dive off a big rock.

After a few moments, Eloise's head popped out of the water. She climbed the rock and dove in again. Amanda stood, shaded her eyes with her hand, and smiled as Eloise executed a perfect dive. There was very little wake as she gracefully entered the water.

Amanda wished she could dive like that, but her only experience with swimming had been when she and Andrew had sneaked down to the Thames to cool off during hot summer nights when they were children. It had been years since she'd been in water. And she'd certainly never had the leisure to learn to dive properly.

Amanda watched as Eloise dove in again. The reflection of the sun off the white sand was blinding. Amanda walked down to the edge of the beach where the breaking waves slammed against her knees. She could see better from here. Again, Eloise emerged from the water, climbed onto the rock, and readied herself for another dive. This time, Eloise took off her bathing cap, her stockings, and the sash around her waist.

Amanda thought this quite odd behavior. Had Eloise found something? This time her dive was not as precise as before. It was a sign Eloise was tiring. Amanda strained her eyes trying to get a glimpse of Eloise. It seemed like an awfully long time for Eloise to be underwater. What was she doing down there? Suddenly, Amanda felt the hair on the back of her neck stand on end.

Eloise was in trouble. Amanda didn't wait a second longer. She plunged into the oncoming waves and swam as fast as she could. Kicking with as much thrust as she could, she remembered to keep a steady rhythm to her arm movements. She tried to be patient with herself. If she panicked she would use twice the effort and cover half the ground.

Unused to athletics, her arms burned and she thought her legs would fall off, but she kept going. She looked for Eloise, but there was no sign. She was almost there.

By now she could hear the voices of the others, from shore, Lady Barbara's screams, someone else swimming behind her, but she didn't know who.

When she reached the rock, she only paused for a split second to take a deep breath and then hurled herself underwater. Kicking like a frog, down, down she went. She was astonished at how clear the water was. She could see almost everything. Everything except Eloise.

She went deeper. Her lungs felt as if they would burst. Still nothing. There were no bubbles, no sign of underwater movement.

Amanda could hold her breath no longer. Quickly, she darted up to the surface. She took another deep breath and went back again. Only this time, she went to the back of the rock. There, only fifteen feet below the surface, was Eloise, her long blonde hair entwined around a jutting piece of rock.

Eloise looked lifeless, but Amanda wouldn't give up hope. In one swift movement, she ripped Eloise's hair from the rock, most of it remaining around the rock. She put her arm under Eloise's chest and shot for the surface.

When she emerged, Sally was on top of the rock ready to dive in. She grabbed Eloise's arms and pulled her onto the rock.

She held Eloise's nose and breathed into her mouth. Three times she did this, then turned her over on her stomach and pressed on her back.

Amanda climbed onto the rock and watched in fear and horror as Eloise remained lifeless. She should have swum faster; she should have been with Eloise when Emily came to shore. She should have watched out for Eloise. Eloise was *her* charge, *her* responsibility.

"Breathe, Eloise!" Amanda commanded.

Sally pressed again with all her weight and force.

As if she'd heard her, Eloise choked, coughed, and vomited water.

"Yes! Eloise! Get it all out!"

Eloise continued spitting up water. Finally, exhausted, she sat up. She looked at Amanda, then Sally, as the realization of what had happened sank in. She smiled at Amanda.

"You saved me, didn't you?"

"Sally helped. . . ."

"But you risked your life for me. Down there . . . somehow . . . I knew it was you, Amanda."

Eloise reached out to Amanda and hugged her closely. It was an embrace Amanda remembered from their childhood. Eloise hadn't hugged Amanda in a very long time. It wasn't proper for her to feel affection for a servant, her mother had told her. It felt wonderful being with her friend again. She was indebted to Amanda . . . and she liked the feeling.

"How can I repay you, Amanda? You should receive a reward."

Amanda smiled back at her, tears mixing with the seawater. She squeezed Eloise's hand, touched her cheek. "I just did."

CHAPTER EIGHT

During the following two weeks, the beaches at Tresco became studded with London families on holiday. Every morning, Amanda went to the beach and erected the yellow umbrellas, which now mingled with blue ones from the Saliston household, green ones from the Harringtons, and white ones from the Dukes. Lady Barbara held informal tea each day at four, which many of the neighbors attended. Amanda liked this world where everyone wore informal linen clothes, slept late in the morning, and dined at ten in the evening.

Sally's schedules were tossed into the sea. But at Tresco, even she didn't seem to care.

Most of all, Amanda liked the rediscovered closeness between herself and Eloise. There were no other children near Amanda's age. In fact, the Dukes had no children, and those of the Harringtons and Salistons were all under the age of seven. Eloise, Emily, and Amanda spent cool evenings on the porch playing cards, swinging in the glider, and talking about the next day's activities. For Amanda there was no future, no past at Tresco.

Even Emily seemed unduly calmed by the rhythmic lapping of the waves. There were no classrooms to bind her, no parties she couldn't attend because she wasn't old enough, and, since her father was in London, she didn't feel the pressure to compete with Amanda for his affection. For the first time, she had the opportunity to get to know Amanda, not as they had known each other as children, but now as almost adults. Emily sensed that, given a good background, Amanda might have been a person to reckon with someday. Amanda possessed the kind of confidence

50

and intelligence that Emily had only seen in people like her father.

She, too, was grateful to Amanda for saving Eloise. She knew she didn't love her sister the way she should, but she would never wish any harm to come to her. Eloise was, after all, her foil. Eloise was the tension in her life. Emily needed Eloise to keep her senses keen. Emily liked competition, and more than anything, she wanted always to best Eloise.

"The Americans are coming!" Eloise exploded as she raced up the five wooden steps to the front porch where Lady Barbara was rocking and fanning herself. She handed her mother the opened letter.

Amanda had just finished slicing golden summer pears. "Who is coming?"

Eloise's face was flushed as she plopped down next to Amanda on the swing and stole a pear slice. "The Dooleys. From San Francisco."

"California? Why, that's a very long distance. What are they doing here?"

"Mrs. Dooley is a very dear friend of mine, Amanda," Lady Barbara piped in. "She and I went to school together in Switzerland. I haven't seen her for five years. She says her youngest is two years old now. How ghastly!" Lady Barbara let her hand fall to her lap. "To be having children at her age! It's not dignified at all!" She took the letter, rose, and went indoors.

Amanda looked at Eloise and they both covered their mouths to stifle their laughter.

"Do they have other children?" Amanda asked.

"Yes. Two girls and a boy. They used to come to England every summer when they lived in New York. But Mr. Dooley was transferred to San Francisco five years ago. The girls are a bit rowdy, but that's expected . . . they're Americans."

Amanda was fascinated as Eloise rambled on. "And the boy?"

"Billy. Last time he was here, all he did was dunk me under the water and hold my head down. I don't really like him all that well. He was sort of fat and spent most of his time with Georgia . . . near her cobblers," Eloise said, stealing another pear slice.

"I'd better take this to Georgia while there's still some pears left."

"Yes, you'd better. And tell her that it'll take more than one cobbler to keep Billy Dooley happy."

Andrew lifted his champagne flute, clinked the edge of Lucy's glass, and let his eyes roll over her face. He'd never wanted a woman so badly in all his life. He'd lusted before, he'd wanted before, but he'd never felt like this. Lucy was a paragon to him. She was the rainbow's end, the goddess of his dream. And his was a big dream. The last meeting had gone well with her parents. He'd told them his sister was spending the summer at Tresco with friends. He could tell they were impressed.

The waiter came to the table.

"Would you care for dessert, sir?"

He looked at Lucy. She smiled sheepishly.

"No, thank you."

"Andrew . . ." She took his hand and caressed it sensuously.

He grabbed her hand and kissed it. Christ! If she kept this up, he'd never be able to walk out of here. He knew he couldn't take this much longer. No man should have to endure such torture.

Her luminous green eyes told him she wanted him too. But he knew he couldn't have her until their wedding night. He didn't want to tarnish his golden egg.

"Let's get out of here," he said, tossing a very large tip on the table and then nearly dashing for the door.

He hailed a hansom cab and they climbed in and shut the door. He took Lucy into his arms and kissed her. She clung to him, pulling him closer. She willingly opened her mouth and accepted his probing, sweet tongue. He caressed her breast and pulled her closer. It was torture, it was rapture.

"Andrew . . ." Lucy finally pulled away. "We can't go on like this."

"I know, Lucy. But I can't ask your father for your hand until I know the timing is right. He's just now beginning to come around."

"I know. I know. Sometimes I think it would be better if we didn't see each other so often. There's something about you . . . I just . . . lose control. I'm not like that."

"I know. But don't you think it is the same for me? I love you, Lucy. And I want us to be married as soon as possible. It won't be long. Trust me."

"I do, Andrew." She crushed her mouth to his, devouring him.

Andrew thought his entire body would explode from wanting her. He was trembling as he held her. He kissed her cheeks, throat, and bosom. He pulled her under him until he was almost on top of her. And all along he knew he would have her if he wanted. Lucy was his . . . all his. She would do anything for him. It was *he* who kept them under control. It was *he* who was going to make certain this wedding became reality.

Suddenly, the horses pulled to a stop.

"Oh, we can't be home already," Lucy complained.

"I'll see you Sunday, as usual," he said and jumped out of the cab. He held out his hand to assist her. He walked her to the door. He could see the maid waiting on the other side of the lace curtain.

He kissed Lucy's hand.

"It was a wonderful evening, Andrew."

He whispered: "I love you, Lucy. Dream about me tonight. Dream about my lips on yours, my body next to yours . . . dream, Lucy."

Before she could answer, he was back in the cab and had driven off.

"Driver, this is fine. Let me out here." Andrew jumped out, paid the man, and looked around the street.

Midnight in central London was like being in another world. Gas street lamps cast a muted golden glow on the dewy brick streets. Huddled in corners were whores casting about for a nibble. Millworkers, bankers, politicians, and meat cutters vied for their favors. As the night wore on the price went up. Some of the pubs had closed, a few remained opened.

Ordinarily, Andrew would have gone to Barley's pub for a cold beer. But the hot summer night combined with the lingering scent of Lucy in his nostrils kept him in the street. He walked slowly down the sidewalk.

"Come see me, honey," a brunette prostitute called. She wore cheap glass beads wrapped around her neck, too much lip rouge, and not enough rice powder to cover the pox scars on her cheeks.

Andrew continued on. As he listened to their catcalls and sexual innuendoes, he became impatient. He wanted a redhead with green eyes like Lucy's so that he could pretend.

It would probably be best for him to go to a brothel or a "house of accommodation." He'd never used a street whore before. Everyone knew they were the lowest grade of prostitutes. He wanted one who dressed well, one who was probably a secretary by day.

He stopped. Just ahead, walking hurriedly toward one of the ladies' public lavatories, was the woman he wanted. As she passed under the lamplight he could see that she wore a beautiful china blue silk shirt and a crisp white linen skirt. Her hair was carefully combed into a tight chignon. It was only the fringed shawl, a bit too flashy, worn seductively slung over her shoulder, that let him know what kind of woman she was. She continued on, then stopped under a gaslight to check the time. As she leaned down to read the numbers off a pendant watch she wore around her neck, Andrew gasped in shock.

"Mother?"

He strained his eyes as he backed into an alley so she couldn't see him. It *was* her, he could tell. She wore lip and cheek rouge, though no kohl around her eyes as some of the prostitutes did. The dark auburn wig she wore looked real. But it was Harriet.

She went into the lavatory to wash off her "paint" and change her clothes, as did most of the prostitutes who were not bound to a brothel.

Andrew's sexual need flagged.

"So, this is where the money came from. I should have known."

Andrew remained in the shadows while Harriet emerged and started on her journey back to Shelton Street. She was now dressed in the old black cotton skirt and faded shirt he'd seen so often. She carried her "working clothes" in a bulging satchel.

Andrew forgot about the whore he'd wanted. It had been a long time since he'd felt this kind of power. He wouldn't use his new-found information—yet. The timing wasn't right.

CHAPTER NINE

Amanda dove off Flat Rock precisely as Eloise had instructed.

"That's perfect!" Eloise clapped her hands when Amanda emerged from the water.

She was exhausted. She'd spent the last half hour diving. Finally, she'd mastered it. "I can't believe it! I never thought I'd get it right."

"But you did. It just took some time."

"And a good teacher."

"Eloise! Eloise!" Emily shouted as she swam toward them.

"What is it?"

"They came a day early. . . . The Dooleys are here!"

With a broad smile, Eloise dove into the water and headed for shore. Amanda was right behind her. The three girls, blonde hair streaming down their wet backs, raced over the dunes and up the wooden stairs that led to the front lawn. Barefoot, they jockeyed with each other for position as they rushed to the house.

From the lawn Amanda could see the familiar open wagon that had brought them all here. She saw a handsome, dark-haired woman, dressed in a powder-blue-and-white-striped summer dress, two girls about nine or ten, and a tall, broad-shouldered boy of about sixteen standing on the porch.

Amanda, Eloise, and Emily were laughing and completely out of breath as they reached the steps.

"Don't come another step!" Lady Barbara commanded. "You'll get sand all over the porch. Where are your towels? And your shoes?"

"Down at the beach," Emily said, winking at the two Dooley girls.

"Did you leave your brains down there too?" Lady Barbara scolded.

The beautiful Mrs. Dooley turned to Lady Barbara, and in the most melodious voice Amanda had ever heard she said: "Don't be so hard on them. Can't you see they were excited to see us? I don't know when I've been paid a more dear compliment."

Mrs. Dooley came down two steps, looked them over, went to Amanda, and took her chin in her hand. "I think I would know you anywhere, Eloise. You look so much like your father."

Eloise frowned, Emily chuckled under her breath, and Lady Barbara gasped.

"We may all have the same coloring, but I'm not Eloise. I'm Amanda. I work for the Kents."

Mrs. Dooley stepped back. "I'm sorry." She turned back to Lady Barbara. "It's been so long, Barbara. They all look a bit alike—wet and all."

"It was an honest mistake," Lady Barbara said coldly. "Girls, get dressed. Amanda, you help with the luggage. Then help Mrs. Dooley unpack. There'll be no more swimming today."

"Yes, ma'am," Amanda said going over to the wagon.

As the Dooleys and Kents filed inside, Amanda was unaware that Billy Dooley was the last one into the house. Nor did she see the appreciative smile on his face as he watched her juggle hatboxes and suitcases.

Amanda balanced three teacups on her tray as she set it before Lady Barbara, Mrs. Dooley, and Mr. Dooley. Intent on their mutual exchanges of news, they paid no attention as Amanda slipped in and out of the drawing room, bringing biscuits, scones, and more hot tea.

Nancy and Sharon, the two Dooley girls, were napping while Emily played croquet with Billy. Eloise, still upstairs, rang for Amanda.

When Amanda walked into the room, it looked like a cyclone had hit it. There were clothes, shoes, lingerie, and stockings everywhere.

"Thank God you're here, Amanda!"

"What is it? What's happened?" Amanda asked, shocked at the mess.

"What am I going to wear?" Eloise asked, hastily flipping camisoles and blouses over her head. Eloise was not acting like Eloise at all.

"Did you see him?" Eloise asked breathlessly.

"No—who?"

"Billy, of course! He's the most handsome boy I've ever seen. And when he looked at me . . . I felt my stomach flip over. I actually did. Do you think this is love, Amanda?"

"I . . . I don't know. Is love supposed to feel like something?"

"That's what love is, dummy. Feelings. This has to be it. I've never felt like this."

"I thought you didn't like him. You said he was fat."

"He *was*. Five years ago. But now . . ."

Eloise continued rifling through clothes, not stopping to see what she was discarding. It would take Amanda hours to press out the wrinkles she'd put into all these cotton and linen skirts and blouses.

"Wear blue, Eloise. How many times do I have to tell you?" She handed Eloise a sheer voile dress with blue flowers painted on the skirt border and around the collar and cuffs.

Amanda hung up the rest of the clothes while Eloise dressed.

"What's he doing now?"

"Playing croquet with Emily."

"What?" Eloise quickly sat at the vanity. "Hurry! Do my hair! There's not a moment to waste."

"Emily isn't doing anything."

"Emily always has a motive, Amanda. Surely you know that by now."

Harriet rang for room service. She ordered a pot of tea and fresh raspberries and cream. She kissed her sleeping lover on the head, went into the bathroom, and started a steaming bath.

As she sank down into thick, scented bubbles, she wondered why it had taken her thirty-five years to get smart.

She'd spent the majority of her adult life working for the Kents. She'd waited on them, run their household, nursed them through their illnesses, and comforted them through death, and what thanks had she ever gotten for it?

She'd wasted her youth on dreams. She'd pretended that some-day she would live like they did. She'd told herself that working there was the next best thing to actually owning Kent Manor, being Lady Kent.

Instead, the real Lady Kent had tossed her out on her ear. Now, her daughter worked for them. If it was the last thing she did, she was going to make certain that Amanda had more. But Amanda was smarter than she was. Something told Harriet that Amanda would never wind up as she had.

Although, as she looked around her lavish suite at the Dorchester, what she had now wasn't all that bad. Harriet had finally used her beauty to its fullest advantage. When she'd been younger, morals had been paramount to her. Now, as her years were fading—a bit too quickly—morals did not have the value they once had.

Harriet had once believed in love. The kind of love that could surmount all barriers, the kind that would burn and last a lifetime. She was wiser now. She would take what she could get and would relish it for what it was. She knew that very few people married for love. Why had she ever believed she would be so fortunate? No, she was much, much wiser now.

Harriet dried off, dressed in her new clothes, and started to wake her lover, but didn't. He'd been tired. And she knew there would be a next time. He was a special man and she'd made him feel very, very good. Yes, there would be a next time.

Quietly she drank her tea and finished the berries. She wrote him a short note and left it on the pillow. Tomorrow was a working day for her and she'd have to be up early. Carefully, she shut the door behind her.

Coming out of the public lavatories, now wearing her familiar worn clothes, Harriet crossed Mercer Street. She saw two of her supervisors from the garment factory standing under a street lamp talking to a third man.

"I made that bet on time and now you owe me!" one of the men boomed so loud Harriet could hear.

"You got a reputation among all the bookers that you chisel, Grady. I'm not payin' for something you aren't due!" Andrew yelled back.

Instantly, Harriet stopped dead in her tracks. What was Andrew doing, talking to thugs like that about betting?

They continued their argument. The one called Grady picked Andrew up by the collar and threatened him. With a swift kick,

Andrew felled the larger man. He crumbled on the sidewalk, his companion backing away, letting the large man work out his own negotiations.

Harriet was frozen to the spot as she watched Andrew kick the man repeatedly in the ribs.

"Never, never, threaten me, Grady. I despise scum like you. You, all of you, make me sick!" Andrew then stalked off.

Harriet stayed back for a few moments until Andrew was gone. She watched as the large man's friend came back to help him up. With much cursing and swearing they went into a pub.

Harriet continued home, wondering why she was shocked. She'd known somehow that Andrew hadn't been getting all those raises like he'd said. Why hadn't she just asked Mr. Sloan herself? Why had she trusted Andrew when she knew she shouldn't have? Andrew never thought of anyone but himself.

She had believed what she wanted to believe. It was simpler that way. She had pretended that Andrew was truly in love with Lucy, but in light of what she'd seen tonight, she realized Andrew had many secrets, many motives. Andrew wanted Lucy only to better himself.

But above all, Harriet had to face the fact that *she* was responsible for Andrew's behavior. She had given him the dream and the way to get out of the slums. She had loved once and so, in her own naivety, she believed that her children could find what had eluded her.

She had to talk to Andrew. She had to stop him before it was too late.

Lamplight shone beneath the door to Harriet's bedroom. As she walked across the room, she knew what she'd find. She no longer held any illusions.

Quietly, she turned the knob and let the door creak open.

"Get what you wanted?"

He stood and faced her. The drawer had been replaced. He clutched a wad of bills in his hand. There was no shock at being discovered. He was as cold and dispassionate as she knew he would be.

"Not all, no."

"I saw you tonight, Andrew. I saw you making book for those men."

A perverse grin cracked his face. "It's how I make my living."

"You make an honest living at Sloan's. Why isn't that enough?"

His anger churned in his gut. "You know why. Because I hate living like a worm, a lowlife. I hate this flat . . . this life. . . . I hate you!"

"Andrew!"

"Who are you to accuse me of anything? Just where did you get all this money, Mother? You didn't make it honestly, sewing dresses for rich women, did you? No, you didn't. Well, I saw you too, Mother. I saw you changing from fancy clothes to work clothes. I know how you got this money.

"That money is none of your business!" She tried to grab it away from him.

"Oh, no!" He jerked his hand away. His smile disappeared, and there was a flash of maliciousness in his eyes that almost made her shudder. "It's for your precious little Amanda, isn't it? She was always your favorite. You didn't give a damn about me . . . never!"

"That's not true. I've been lenient with you about many things over the years. Obviously, that's where I went wrong. You think the world should revolve around you. You're lazy, Andrew, and you'll never be any good."

"I could be a lot of things if I had the chance. You're giving Amanda a chance to get out of here. Why won't you do that for me?" He came closer until they were face to face. She could feel his hot, angry breath on her cheek.

"You're a man, Andrew. It's a man's world. You'd almost have to be deaf, blind, and dumb not to make it if you wanted to. But you don't want to work for it. Amanda isn't afraid of hard work. She will never have the opportunities handed to her that you will, simply because she's a woman. You're just as clever as she is, maybe even more so. If you'd just apply yourself to one thing, Andrew, you could take all three of us out of here."

Harriet backed away, straightened her spine. She was as angry as he was. She could feel her fists balling, but she wouldn't hit him. She had to show him she had power over him. Her facial muscles constricted; she ground her jaws.

"I wonder what Lucy's parents would think if I paid them a call, me bein' almost family." Her smile was tight.

"What are you saying?"

"I can ruin your chances with Lucy. And she *is* what this is all about, isn't she? The money, the bookmaking. You need it to get her. I could expose you for the cheat, the liar—the *thief*—that you are.''

Andrew felt his nerves tingle. The old bitch. He wasn't going to let her get away with this. He could play just as hard as she.

''You do that and I'll make sure Amanda knows about your nighttime activities.''

Harriet didn't falter. ''That would be unfortunate—but not devastating. Amanda will probably hear about it anyway. The streets have eyes and mouths. However, it's possible that I could get her off to America without her knowing. I would rather she think better of me. You have a point.''

Andrew couldn't believe how cool she was being about all this. Could it be true he had more to lose than Harriet did in this bargain? He'd never seen this side of her before, but he should have guessed. He'd gotten his brains from one of his parents, and he knew it wasn't from his father. Harriet's relationship with Amanda was a strong one. It would take a lot to break it. Clearly, he wasn't winning this battle. But there would be other times, when his position was stronger. . . .

''You keep your mouth shut and I do the same. Is that it?'' he asked.

''Yes.'' She held out her hand. ''My money please.''

Reluctantly, he handed it over.

''Do I have your word?'' she asked.

''Is it worth anything to you?''

''No, it's just a formality.''

They studied each other, probed into each other's eyes, trying to find the soul. They stood for a long moment gazing, this mother and son, each wondering how one could be part of the other.

CHAPTER TEN

Barefoot, Amanda crossed the lawn. The grass felt cool with night dew. Though there was a slight breeze to fend off the remains of the hot summer day, Amanda couldn't sleep. The maid's room she shared with Jane seemed to grow smaller every day, probably due to the increase in the volume of Jane's snoring. Amanda pulled a light wool shawl around her shoulders as she reached the edge of the hill. She sat at the top of the wooden steps that led down to the beach.

The moon was full and cast a silver beacon across the sea. It started at the horizon and led straight up to shore. Amanda had the eerie feeling it was beckoning to her. She fantasized that if she walked into the light, she would find the happiness she sought.

In the last ten days that the Dooley's had been at Tresco, Amanda had never felt so alone. And yet there wasn't anyplace she could go where there weren't people. Neighbors were constantly in and out. There were swimming and fishing, and croquet games every day. It was a perpetual party. But the closeness, the warmth she'd felt those first days at Tresco, was gone.

It wasn't that Eloise didn't show her gratitude to Amanda for saving her life. In fact, Amanda thought she went a bit overboard with her praises sometimes. Lady Barbara had again donned her usual haughty manner. In fact, Amanda noticed that Lady Barbara had several times been quite arrogant with her guests. Though Mrs. Dooley was her friend, Lady Barbara let it be known that because she was married to an American, Mrs. Dooley was beneath Lady Barbara's station. Amanda was still learning about rules of etiquette as her mother had instructed, but something told her that in this situation, Lady Barbara was in the wrong.

Emily was stirring up mischief again, and this time she'd involved both Nancy and Sharon Dooley in her schemes. The three girls had gone into the forest and, at a tiny brook, gathered a dozen frogs, brought them home, and put them in the laundry chutes. When Jane began gathering sheets and towels, green frogs hopped everywhere. Amanda had been in the kitchen when a frog leapt off a laundry basket and into Lady Barbara's favorite teapot.

Four hours later, the frogs had been rousted and the girls reprimanded.

Two days later, the trio of girls went fishing, filled the fish gullets with live worms, and brought them to Georgia, who planned to prepare them for the evening meal. When she slit open the bellies, long, slimy worms greeted her. Georgia had not been amused, and to punish the girls, she had locked up every cookie, pie, and cake in the house.

Nancy and Sharon, unused to the foibles of prankstering, turned their backs on Emily and found more acceptable forms of amusement.

"I'm being treated like an outcast!" Emily complained to Amanda. "Not even Jonathon will speak to me."

"He doesn't like frogs in his socks or dead fish under his comforter. You don't have to play tricks on people to get their attention, Emily," Amanda said.

"Who do you think you are to lecture me? You're just a servant!" Emily spat and stomped off.

For the next three days, Emily kept to herself, harboring her anger and vowing vengeance.

Emily's seclusion was self-imposed. Amanda's was not.

Amanda wanted to be close to Eloise, but Eloise was preoccupied with Billy Dooley. She only saw Amanda when she was changing clothes for one activity or another. Always conscious of her looks, Eloise became obsessed. She experimented with several hair styles, none of which she liked. She buffed her nails, creamed her arms, and went through two bottles of her mother's cologne.

None of her tactics worked. William Dooley was not impressed with Eloise Kent. And the more uninterested he seemed, the more infatuated Eloise became.

As the days passed, Amanda noticed that Billy seemed to appear wherever she was. If she was dusting in the salon, he wandered in. He wouldn't say much, just chat, pick up a book, and leave. When she cut roses for the house, he'd be sitting in the gazebo. He didn't follow her around but rather seemed to anticipate her destination and beat her to it.

Often she would be helping Georgia make lemonade and she would feel his eyes on her back. But when she turned around to look out the screen door, there was no one around.

When she helped serve dinner to the family, she could feel Billy watching her out of the corner of his eye. She didn't understand her suspicions, for he'd never been forward and besides, Eloise liked him and she would never do anything to hurt Eloise.

Silver moonbeams danced on the rippling waves. Thinking about Billy, she wondered what it would be like to follow those moonbeams all the way to America. She was just about to go back to the house when she thought her name was being called.

"Amanda! Down here!"

She looked down at the bottom of the stairs. It was Billy.

"Come down and walk with me!"

"I'd better not. . . ."

He raced up the steps and pulled on her arm. "Come on. It's a beautiful night. The sand is cool, the air is wonderfully invigorating. It's the kind of night that poets write about."

"Poets?" She could feel her resolve weakening.

"Yes." He tugged on her arm and she followed.

It was an almost magical night, she thought as they walked in silence.

"You're afraid of me," he said bluntly.

"I am not. What a ridiculous thing to say."

"Then you're this cold with all men."

"What?" She stopped walking and looked at him indignantly.

"Aloof, then."

"I don't know what you're talking about."

He took her elbow; she could see the gleam in his eyes. Or was it moonlight reflections?

"I think you're very, very lovely, Amanda," he said, his voice lowering an octave. "I know I've never seen anyone in San Francisco as pretty as you."

"No one's ever told me that before—no boy, I mean."

"I'm glad I'm the first," he said, moving his face closer to hers.

Amanda knew he wanted to kiss her, but she couldn't let it happen. She had to think of Eloise. She would never forgive Amanda if she knew that Billy had kissed her.

"What's it like, San Francisco?" she asked, pulling away from him. She turned and motioned for them to continue walking.

He smiled and gave in. "It's the most beautiful city in the world. More romantic than Paris, more exciting than New York, hillier than Rome. I'd like you to see it someday."

"I'll do that," she said firmly.

He laughed. "Ho! I was just teasing."

"Why? Don't you think I will ever come to America?"

"Well, I suppose you could . . . if the Kents decided to visit. . . . Yes, they would probably bring you."

"If the Kents . . . ? No! I mean I'm going by myself!" She faced him squarely, but she could tell he didn't believe her.

"It costs a lot of money to sail to New York."

"I know that."

He looked at her intently. Then his smile vanished. He nodded his head. "I believe you'd find a way, Amanda. I think that's why I like you. You seem to know where you're going."

"Everyone has to have a plan for the future. Lord Kent told me that."

"I know what I want right now." He moved very close to her, looked into her eyes, and before she knew what was happening, Billy kissed her.

It was an odd sensation, the pressure of his lips on hers. She kept her eyes opened until he stopped.

"You shouldn't have done that!" she scolded. "Eloise . . ."

"Eloise be damned," he growled and put his arms around her. Only this time Amanda broke away from him and started for the steps.

Billy was laughing. "I knew you were afraid of me."

Amanda whirled around and faced him. "I'm not afraid of you or anybody. I don't want you to kiss me, that's all. I didn't ask you to, did I? Eloise likes you a lot and she's my friend. I wouldn't do anything to hurt her feelings."

"She's your employer."

"She's my friend too."

Amanda started up the steps and nearly tripped on her gown.

She yanked her shawl around her shoulders and held her skirt with the other hand. She was so angry she could hit him. As she raced up the steps with Billy only a few paces behind, she didn't realize they were being watched from the third window on the left.

CHAPTER ELEVEN

Amanda ran Eloise's bath, clearing away the morning tray, and took out a new white linen ensemble for Eloise to wear.

Amanda's mind reverberated with the conversation she'd had with Billy. She was not flattered by the encounter at all, despite his pretty words. Billy was brash and needed to learn some manners. She wondered if Eloise had any idea what kind of boy she'd fallen in love with.

Eloise hummed to herself as she bathed. Every morning she awoke in a good mood. Amanda knew that Eloise made more of Billy's feelings for her than what existed. She was living in a dream world. Amanda wanted Eloise to be happy, but she knew it wouldn't be with Billy.

Eloise towel-dried her hair as she walked out of the bathroom. "Jonathon and Father arrive today. Mother says they'll be staying for five days. I'm glad. I've missed them."

"I didn't think you'd had time to even think about anyone but Billy."

"Oh, you!" Eloise said and threw her wet towel at Amanda.

"Lady Barbara told Georgia they were bringing a guest. The earl of Donnet."

"No, his son. He's some college friend of Jonathon's."

"Any more guests and Lord Kent will have to commission a new wing."

Eloise's eyes widened. "Wouldn't it be terrible if we had to double up? Billy could stay with me. . . ."

"Oh, you!" Amanda said and pitched the towel back at her.

* * *

"This is our daughter, Eloise. She debuted this spring," Lady Barbara introduced Eloise to Henry, destined to be the sixth earl of Donnet.

Eloise curtsied, lowering her head, and then coyly lifted her eyes to him. She was practicing again, and she wondered if her maneuver would have any effect on him.

Henry Donnet took Eloise's hand and kissed it. "Charmed," he purred.

Lady Barbara watched as Henry kept his eyes glued on Eloise. She had high hopes for a match between Eloise and Henry. They were from similar backgrounds, they were evenly matched in intelligence, and, from what Jonathon had told her about Henry, he was ready for marriage.

It was clear to Lady Barbara after this visit that Billy Dooley was not the choice she'd thought when she had initially invited the Dooleys to Tresco. Mr. Dooley's fortunes had been hard hit in the depressed stock market last year. It was evident to her that Billy would insist on living in America. He was out of his element in England. Eloise's bad showing at the balls in the spring had caused Lady Barbara to feel unnecessary pressure where Eloise was concerned. Most of the pretty debutantes were spoken for by now. The man who wanted Eloise would have to be special, she thought. He would have to want Eloise for her finer qualities. Henry Donnet was the right man.

Henry instantly extended his arm to escort Eloise into dinner. She looked over at Billy, who had already linked arms with his sister Sharon. Jonathon took Nancy Dooley's arm, and they all followed Lord and Lady Kent and Mr. and Mrs. Dooley. Sulking, Emily was last into the room.

Amanda helped Jane serve. Throughout the dinner, Amanda noticed that Eloise kept her eyes glued on Billy, who sat across from her, while deftly carrying on a conversation with Henry, who was seated to her right.

Lady Barbara expounded on Henry's virtues so much that it became painful to listen. However, everyone, including Billy, was impressed.

"I've always thought the law was a noble profession," Billy said, watching Amanda bring slices of ice-cream cake.

"I enjoy it tremendously," Henry said, following Billy's eye.

"I'm thinking about medicine myself. Possibly research."

"*That* is noble."

"I believe we were all put here for a purpose. I intend to do something with my life," Billy said almost pointedly to Amanda, who was standing behind Lord Kent's chair.

Amanda wondered if this was his way of apologizing for last night.

This time, Eloise couldn't miss the wink he gave Amanda.

Her fork clattered against the china plate when she dropped it.

Amanda continued serving the cake, her eyes pleading with Eloise to understand, but Eloise turned away from her.

Lord Kent spoke to Billy. "I couldn't have said it better myself, young man. You have no idea how refreshing it is to hear that. Why, I've been saying the same thing to my children for years."

Amanda bent down to Eloise's ear as she served the cake.

"It's nothing, Eloise. Truly."

"I don't want to hear it!" Eloise whispered back.

No one at the table heard the exchange, but Emily saw it. She could almost read their lips. She listened with the ears of a bat and watched with the eyes of a hawk. Of all the times in her life, Emily knew that this moment had been created expressly for her. There were minidramas taking place all around this table. Eloise, Henry, and Billy were the pawns, though none of them realized they were being manipulated by their parents. But Emily knew it. She watched the eager faces of her parents as Henry whispered to Eloise. She watched the disappointed faces of the Dooleys as they realized that the obvious title-bearing marriage for their son was vanishing quickly.

Always feeling she was the outsider, Emily had honed her skills as onlooker, observer. When the moment was right she would pitch them all into a tailspin.

Billy continued: "There is so much going on in America right now. Two years ago Charles Duryea invented the horseless carriage. He's perfected the engine now . . . why, already they're shipping them to England. Look at Edison's moving pictures. Look how far he's come in just five years. And everyone has electricity now. . . ." He looked up at the candles in the chandelier overhead.

Lord Kent laughed. "Not at the seashore—yet. Next year."

They all laughed except Eloise, for she realized that Billy was speaking directly to Amanda. It was as if he was trying to sell her something.

"Anyone can do anything in America. There are no limits," Billy said emphatically.

Emily carefully placed her silver dessert fork on the white damask cloth, making certain the strawberry ice cream would leave a stain—one that Amanda would have to wash out.

"No limits at all, Billy?" Emily asked.

"Not if you want it badly enough and are willing to work for it."

"You mean that in America, a rich boy like you, from a fine family, could marry a servant . . . like . . . Amanda?"

Mrs. Dooley's spine cracked when she straightened. "No!" Her eyes darted from Billy to Eloise to Lady Barbara.

"Yes!" Billy replied, looking pointedly at Amanda, who was clearing away the dishes.

Amanda looked at Emily and saw that evil, cold glint she'd seen before. She trembled but tried to hide it. Emily was a born conniver. Amanda should have known that Emily would graduate from frogs and worms someday. But she had trusted Emily. She had wrongly assumed Emily was her friend. Amanda had been wrong about many things. And many people.

"Did you propose to Amanda last night while you were walking on the beach?" Emily's voice was like syrup studded with malicious spikes.

Eloise's hand flew to her throat. She thought she would choke. Her eyes welled with tears. "Amanda?"

Forgetting her "place," Amanda rushed to her own defense. "No, Eloise."

"Billy?" His mother's voice cracked.

"It's not true." Billy realized the danger of the situation, both for Amanda and for himself.

A vanquisher's sneer contorted Emily's face. "I saw you both. It was after midnight. Amanda was only wearing her nightdress."

"Good God!" Henry whispered snootily to Eloise. "With a servant?"

Lord Kent was instantly on his feet. "Amanda. Go to the salon. Immediately!"

"Sir, I didn't . . ."

"Now!" he commanded.

"I didn't do anything!"

"I'm sure you didn't. But that doesn't alter the fact that you were there, he was there." Lord Kent took Amanda's hand gently and led her to the sofa. "We've never had this talk because, well, I'm not your father. But in this instance . . . well . . . I think you need some guidance.

"It's very important for a young girl to guard her reputation. Eloise and Emily must be even more careful than you."

Amanda hated him for stating it like that, as if she were vermin.

"Whether you and Billy did anything or not, it is your name and purity that will be sullied. Because you are an employee here, it is a reflection on this house and my name. Do you understand?"

"You want to get rid of me."

"I don't want to, but I have to. There's a tension here that's never existed before. Being away from the family these few weeks has helped me to see things. Emily is jealous of you—for whatever reason. It is growing and will continue to grow as long as you're here to spur her on. I don't want that. Emily is a good girl, though rambunctious. I think it's because she isn't challenged enough. But that's not your concern."

Amanda agreed with him. She didn't understand Emily at all. Maybe someday she would.

"Eloise is smitten with Billy. I can't stop that either. But because of him, Eloise will not be able to tolerate your presence. Lady Kent is convinced that Henry Donnet will be a suitable husband for Eloise. I think that with a proper courtship period, Eloise will get to know Henry and eventually come to the same conclusion as we have."

Caught in the whirlwind of all he was saying, and thinking of her own problems, Amanda suddenly realized the impact of his words.

"Eloise and Henry? But she just met him. She likes Billy. She can't *think* of anything *but* Billy. How could she be happy with someone else?"

"Eloise knows the duties of her station."

"Duties?" Amanda hoped her shock didn't show. Was it possible Eloise was just as much a prisoner of her society, her class, as Amanda was of hers? What Eloise wanted she couldn't have, any more than Amanda could. They were both trapped.

"We'll be leaving for London in two weeks. You'll stay here, close the house with the other servants, and then return. I'll give you a month's severance pay and references. I'm sure I can find you a job in another good home.''

"But I don't want to work for someone else."

"I'm sorry, Amanda. But it has to be." He smiled down at her fondly.

She could see pain in his eyes as he bent over her, but she knew he couldn't be hurting as much as she. He had money, position. He wasn't being booted out into the world. She had never thought it would end like this. She'd always thought her termination would have been at Lady Kent's hands. For that reason, it was twice as painful for her. This was the man who had guided her nearly all her life. He had pushed her to study, to better herself. He'd been confessor, teacher, god.

She wanted to touch him, to tell him how much he'd meant to her. She was grateful for everything he'd given her. But as she watched him walk out of the room, she said nothing. He was above her station.

CHAPTER TWELVE

Sky blue shutters were clamped down tightly against the wind and rain the day Amanda and the rest of the staff left Tresco. They sat beneath a tarp in the rickety open wagon that had brought them there. Amanda looked out at the angry gray ocean, wondering how soon, if ever, she would see it again.

The past two weeks had been a nightmare for Amanda. Lord Kent, Jonathon, and Henry had left shortly after *that* night. No one in the household would talk to Amanda except for Billy, which only seemed to anger everyone the more.

He apologized to her and told her that when she did come to America, he would like to see her someday. He gave her his address and promised he would never be brash with a girl again. He told her he loved her.

Amanda didn't believe him, not really. She thought they were all too young to know about love. She knew she didn't ''feel'' anything for Billy. What she did feel was sad, lonely, and very, very guilty.

Eloise had not spoken a single, solitary word to her in two weeks. She didn't say good-bye when they left, nor did she ever say she was sad that Amanda would not be working for them anymore.

To Amanda, it was as if her entire childhood had never existed. Amanda didn't understand it at all.

She picked the situation apart, trying to uncover the bones of justice. But she found none. She had been accused of something she hadn't done, and she was being punished for it.

The wagon jostled over muddy ruts in the road. Amanda

swayed back and forth as they journeyed to the coast to the boat
that would take them to Penzance. The driver was saying they
might have to stay at an inn that night, for the storm showed no
sign of passing.

Amanda didn't care. She was in no rush to get back to
London. There was nothing to go back to. She had no job. There
had never been any life for her on Shelton Street. She was at a
crossroads in her life. It was up to her to do something about her
future.

"All talk and no do. That's what you are, Amanda Granger,"
she mumbled to herself.

For the past six weeks, she'd spent every spare minute she had
looking out over the ocean. She'd conjured every thought about
America that existed. She was tired of dreaming and planning. It
was time for her to get on with her future. When she got back to
London, she was going to take that job Lord Kent would find for
her. She was going to ask her mother to help her find a second
job. She'd do anything and everything it took to buy her passage
to New York.

"Don't go."

"I have to. You know that," he said, brushing his blonde hair
back and setting his bowler hat at a slight angle on his head. He
looked incredibly handsome.

Harriet pulled the sheet up over her breasts. She looked at the
wad of bills sitting on the nightstand. There were tears in her
eyes as she thought about what that money would mean to
Amanda.

He came over to the bed and leaned down. "Next Tuesday?"

"Yes," she said breathlessly, waiting for his kiss.

"I'm counting on it." He opened the door and was gone.

"Thank you," she whispered, but he couldn't hear her. It
didn't matter. She knew he knew.

She would put the money in the bank where it would be safe
from Andrew. Ever since their "bargain" she'd been extra cautious about her comings and goings. She made certain Andrew
never followed her. She didn't want Andrew to know about her
lovers. They were prominent men, with families and positions to
protect. That's why she had chosen them. They didn't mean
anything to her—except as a means to help Amanda—all of
them, that was, except the man who had just left. He was

different. He was the one she would write about in her diary tonight. He was the one who'd known she needed a lot of money and he'd rightly guessed the money wasn't for herself.

She should have guessed he would have given her anything she asked for. But her pride wouldn't let her beg. No, this way was best. At least—the very least—she wasn't taking charity.

She picked up the bills and counted them. Amanda would be home tomorrow. Harriet smiled to herself as she thought about her daughter. She'd missed her, more than she ever thought she could. She wondered how she'd tolerate Amanda's voyage to America.

"Not well, milady. Not well," she mumbled to herself as she rose and dressed to go home.

Amanda stood rain soaked in the middle of the tiny kitchen on Shelton Street hugging her mother.

"I'm so glad to be back."

"I thought you would have loved the seashore, it bein' so cool and all."

"It was wonderful—up till the end." Amanda took off her wet clothes and hung them near the stove to dry while relating the story about the Dooleys, Emily, and then finally her dismissal.

Harriet seemed unusually calm through all this, as if she already knew the story.

"I thought you would be upset," Amanda said.

"It was a matter of time, Amanda. You wanted your life to continue as it had when you and Eloise were children. Though we talked about it and about your going to New York, I knew it still hadn't registered in your head yet. You had to *live* what I, and Lady Barbara, were trying to tell you. It isn't anybody's fault, Amanda. It's just the way things are."

"I know that now. That's why I'm going to work two jobs just like you've been doing."

"No, you aren't. You don't have to."

"Why?"

"I've already booked your passage. You leave from South-hampton at the end of next month."

"Is it really true?"

"We have just enough time to get a suitable wardrobe together."

"That will take just as much—even more—money. How can we do it?"

"I've been working very hard while you were gone."

Amanda looked at her quizzically. "How could we possibly have that much money that fast?"

Harriet didn't miss a beat. "I've been keeping a secret from you for many years, Amanda. Every week for years, even before Burt died, I've put away a little bit of money. In a bank . . . and the interest has mounted over the years. So it didn't take as much as I'd thought."

Amanda considered this. It was possible. Her mother did keep secrets, she thought, remembering the false-bottom drawer.

"And," Harriet continued, "I had some very good jobs while you were gone. Even a wedding dress."

"Ah!" Amanda replied, knowing such fees could be very high.

"So tomorrow after work we'll get started. You go to Mrs. Engle's shop and ask her for the finest woolens she has. Top stuff. No remnants either. You want the newest patterns for fall too."

Amanda couldn't believe her ears. It was happening too fast. In little more than a month, she would be leaving England . . . home.

She looked at her battered suitcase. She'd just gotten home. She had the oddest sensation of being suspended above herself. As if she didn't have any control. What a ridiculous thought! she chided herself under her breath. This was her dream, wasn't it? Hadn't she vowed only yesterday to do everything she could to get to America? She should be grateful . . . and she was . . . it was only that . . . She looked at her mother, her face full of anticipation. She wished she could have everything she wanted and not have to leave. She wished for the impossible.

Mrs. Engle rolled out a fabulous Black Watch plaid and held it to Amanda's face.

"These are your colors, Amanda. Your blonde hair with the black and dark green is very dramatic." She held up another blue-and-green plaid. "This too, and this taupe Irish tweed." She showed Amanda many patterns, but Amanda chose the most classic designs for her basic pieces. For blouses and a dressy ensemble, she chose the newest designs.

"I heard yer mather talkin' 'bout you goin' to New York. 'Course I didn't believe her at the time."

"Oh, I knew I'd be going. Just not this soon." Amanda smiled.

Mrs. Engle's eyes flashed as she leaned forward and whispered conspiratorially, "I shouldn'a doubted that one. She's always been a looker. Nearly as pretty as you when she was young. I knew she wouldn'a had no trouble."

Amanda was confused about the conversation. "Trouble?"

"Gettin' the men to come around. Been keepin' late nights while you were gone. Ha!" Mrs. Engle jabbed her elbow into Amanda's side and then picked up the fabrics.

Amanda was dumbstruck as she watched Mrs. Engle's retreating back. "Men coming around . . ." How could she have been so stupid not to see it? Of course—it made sense now. Even if Harriet had saved since the day she was born she could not have come up with the nearly thousand pounds it was taking to underwrite this trip, the wardrobe, even the new luggage she'd bought. Harriet kept telling Amanda about "appearances." That it was necessary for Amanda to look the part of a lady. Props; she'd needed many props.

Just the past week since Amanda had been home, Harriet had been out very late on Tuesday and again on Thursday. She'd told Amanda she was working for Lady Sedgwick—"a very special gown," Harriet had said.

Amanda paid Mrs. Engle for the fabrics and patterns with the money her mother had given her. As she stuffed the remaining bills back in her skirt pocket, she wondered how many men her mother had slept with to get it.

It must have been demeaning for her mother to do such a thing. Harriet had always taught Amanda that her virginity was something to save, even revere, until her wedding night. But then, Harriet wasn't a virgin anyway. Was it different after you were married?"

Amanda knew that if it weren't for her, Harriet would never have become a prostitute. Harriet had pride too. Right or wrong, Amanda was humbled by her mother's self-sacrifice. Amanda instantly wished she didn't know. Not that she thought any less of her mother: she didn't. It was just that Amanda didn't know what she could ever do to make it up to her.

Harriet wanted this new life for Amanda more than Amanda had realized. There were times when Amanda felt she was just going through the motions, that none of it was really happening.

But it was for Harriet. Harriet was making it all happen. Perhaps it was good that Amanda knew. Now she would know never to waste a single minute or forego a single opportunity when she found it in New York. She would do everything she *had* to do to bring Harriet across the Atlantic. Amanda admired her mother's courage and tried not to think about her morals.

"She's no worse than anyone else I know," Amanda mumbled to herself.

Many of the women on Shelton Street weren't even married to the men they lived with. Harriet had insisted she and Burt be legal—even though she'd told Amanda many times she hadn't loved Burt, not really.

Amanda wanted to confront her mother with all her questions, but she knew instinctively she couldn't. Harriet had gone to great lengths to lie to Amanda in order to preserve a semblance of morality; Amanda would let her preserve the illusion.

Amanda sat at the kitchen table stitching the last of the decorative braid to a black wool coat. It was beautiful, the pattern copied from one worn by Kaiser Wilhelm's wife. Amanda was certain Eloise would have one just like it, only trimmed in white mink or blackest sable.

Thinking of Eloise brought Lord Kent to mind. She was glad she hadn't needed his help in finding a job. It would have been too embarrassing, too degrading.

The autumn days were growing short she thought as she lit the gas lamp above her. It had been a wet October and cooler than most. A perfect time for her to be indoors working on her travel clothes.

Just then the door opened. Andrew breezed in, a satisfied grin on his face.

"What are you so happy about?" Amanda asked.

"You are looking at a full-fledged auditor. No more apprenticeships for me."

"Andrew! That's wonderful!"

His chest was puffed up a full three inches. "I thought you'd be impressed."

"I am." She smiled at him but didn't say anything more. She went back to her sewing.

His spirits deflated. He had expected more accolades. It had been damn difficult to get this job, especially since Sloan had threatened to fire him a month ago. He'd given up booking for two whole weeks to put extra hours in. But it had paid off. He would keep his respectability.

He pulled a letter out of his pocket and tossed it on the table. "This came for you."

Andrew went to the stove, dipped a wooden spoon into the vegetable soup Amanda had simmering, and tasted it.

Amanda looked at the letter. "It's from Sylvia!" She ripped the envelope open. "I wrote to her asking her to find me a job."

"And did she?"

"Yes! I'm to be governess to a seven-year-old girl who lives near her in Washington Square."

"Washington Square? Where's that?"

"I don't know. I'm certain it's a very prominent area, Sylvia being as rich as she is and all."

Andrew suddenly became very interested in his sister's future. "Do you suppose it's as elite as Belgrave Square here?"

"Well, at least as good as Grosvenor Square, anyway."

"Hmm." He sat across the table from Amanda. "You and Mum have been pretty closemouthed about this trip of yours."

Amanda smiled. "Not at all. You're just never around. I didn't know you were interested."

"Amanda! How could you say that about your brother? I love you. You're my baby sister. Of course I would care about you and want only the best for you." He made certain his words rang with great sincerity. "I know how hard Mum has worked to get the money for this trip."

Amanda's eyes darted up to see if there was any inkling that he *knew*. There wasn't. She continued sewing.

"I had no idea this friend of Mum's was so . . ."

"Rich?"

"Fortunate," he continued. "You should do very well in America. I'll tell you what! After Lucy and I are married, perhaps I'll ask her father to send us to America for a honeymoon."

"Oh, Andrew! Do you think he would? Wouldn't that be lovely? We could all be together again. Because after I get some money together, I'm going to send for Mother."

Instantly, Andrew's eyes clouded. "You would send for her and not for me?"

"I didn't mean it that way, Andrew."

He rose and put his back to her. Theatrics had always worked on Amanda.

"Andrew." She rose and went to him. "It's just that you are so resourceful. I know you could get the passage money together in no time, Lucy or no Lucy."

"I wouldn't be too sure about that."

"Why do you always underrate yourself? Look at what you did at Sloan's! This new promotion. Why, I'll bet that in two years' time you could be manager."

"Two years?" To Andrew it seemed like a lifetime. He wanted everything and he wanted it now. He could never be as patient as Amanda. Just look at her stitching some goddamned coat together. She'd been working on these clothes for nearly three weeks. He could barely stand the wait while the clerks at Harrod's wrote up his tickets. No, he could never be like Amanda. And he didn't want to be either.

"And by the time you are thirty, you will be invaluable to Mr. Sloan. Maybe he'll even make you a partner."

"Partner?" Andrew couldn't think of a worse fate. To live his entire life going to that little hole, bending over ledgers with not enough light to see. It was a life designed for moles, not men.

"You know I'm right, don't you?"

He turned to face her. "Yes. You are. I have to use my life better than I have been."

"That's right! You can do anything."

"Yes, Amanda. I guess I *had* forgotten that for awhile. Thank you for reminding me."

CHAPTER THIRTEEN

Amanda walked in and out of billowy clouds of steam as she searched for Track 8. Three locomotives stood side by side, exhaling steam and smoke like huge dragons. Bells clanged, conductors yelled. Passengers scuffled and raced past Amanda as she waited for Andrew and her mother to catch up to her.

Amanda had been more anxious about this trip than she'd let on. For the past two nights she'd had nightmares that the train had left without her. Then the boat had sailed, leaving her behind.

Harriet walked up, all smiles, and handed her a sack of warm chestnuts. "You might get hungry." She choked back a tear.

Amanda knew this was hard for them all. She already felt a wrenching inside and she hadn't even left yet.

"You have your trunk tickets?" Andrew asked.

She nodded. "They're in my purse."

"Remember what I told you. Don't be overtipping the dockhand when he loads your trunk and suitcase for you. You hang onto what you've got."

"Spoken like an accountant." She hugged him and kissed his cheek.

Harriet turned to Andrew. "I want a minute with Amanda."

"I'll get a newspaper." He left.

"Do you remember everything I told you?" Harriet delved into Amanda's eyes. Amanda looked so young—so in need of protection. But she would do all right. She was her daughter, after all. "Sylvia got this job for you, but she has also promised

81

to introduce you to some nice young men. These are good men, Amanda. Men with real futures. You remember that."

"I will. And don't you forget that I'll send for you as soon as I save some money."

"Don't worry about me. You find yourself a good husband. You're getting more beautiful every day. You'll do just fine." Harriet hugged her tightly. "Oh. I almost forgot," She pulled a little package out of her pocket. "You'll be celebrating your birthday on the Atlantic Ocean. Open it then."

"You didn't need to do this. You've already paid for the trip."

"It might be a while before I can celebrate your birthday with you."

Amanda tried to smile. "Just till next year . . ." It might as well be a century, Amanda thought.

Amanda waved from the little iron steps one last time and then boarded the train. She went straight to her compartment and then rolled down the window. She looked for her mother and brother, but they were nowhere to be seen. It was just as well, she thought. She didn't want to know there could be a face any sadder than hers.

From the time she'd boarded the ship at Southampton, Amanda had wallowed in self-pity, fear, and sadness. The cold first days out underscored her bleak mood. But on the third morning, the sun rose gloriously in the sky, teasing Amanda with hope that her life hadn't ended after all.

She took her book, one she had purposely *not* returned to Lord Kent, and went to the top deck. Could it really be this beautiful? she thought gazing out into the endless horizon. Blues, from the deepest indigo to an almost lavender pink, drifted above and below her. For long moments she lost herself in the silver foam of the ship's wake.

"It's lovely, isn't it?" a masculine voice coming from behind her said.

Amanda sighed. She didn't feel like talking to anyone. Not today, maybe never for the rest of her life. Slowly she turned. Her rejection would be polite but to the point. She opened her mouth to speak.

"I'm sorry . . ." She stopped immediately, for she was looking into one of the most handsome faces she'd ever seen in her life. He was almost as good-looking as Andrew.

"Paul." He smiled. "Paul Van Volkein."

Before she knew it, he was kissing her hand. She gazed into deep green eyes that twinkled merrily in an aristocratically boned face.

"You're American."

"Yes. And you're British."

"And we haven't been introduced," she said and walked away. She rounded the corner and slipped down the steel steps that led to the lower deck and her cabin.

She shut the cabin door and leaned against it. She felt flutters in her stomach, just like the ones Eloise had described when she first met Billy. And her legs felt tingly too. If this was love, it was a lot like a cold, she decided.

Amanda sat in a gold-damask upholstered chair. She had to think.

She and her mother had carefully worked out every possible situation that could arise. Amanda was masquerading as a "lady," but not in title. She was a commoner, but of royal blood. A descendant of King Charles II and his mistress, Lucy Walters. She had already stated this point-blank to her dinner companions, and she'd made certain the porter knew her "station." She had watched Lady Barbara all her life. Amanda was making certain propriety was in order. She wasn't hiding in this cabin, she was only acting the way a lady would act. She couldn't afford any blunders. She had let Paul Van Volkein know that she was special. If he had any background, he would see to it that they were properly introduced.

Reassured that she'd done the right thing, she opened the door. It was a beautiful day and she planned to spend it on deck.

Amanda was disappointed that the afternoon had passed and she hadn't seen Paul again. Perhaps she'd made too much of the situation. She knew she shouldn't have reacted so strongly to him. If she saw him again, she would will herself to be calm.

The day was not a total loss. She read, played shuffleboard with a middle-aged couple from Chicago, Illinois, and met a young girl from Boston and her governess at tea. Dinner, she knew, would be the same as it had been the two previous nights. She would sit with the Van Allens from Baltimore; the Goldbergs from New York; the Weintraubs, also from New York; and young James Sealy from Denver, who was only eleven years old but who had crossed the Atlantic six times in his young life. His father had been stationed at different embassies all over the world. For the bulk of the year, he lived with his grandparents in Denver. And until this morning, James Sealy was the most exciting person Amanda had met on board.

Amanda was surprised to learn, as she spread her teal green silk skirt over her chair, that James Sealy would not be dining with them that night.

"He's caught a cold," Mrs. Goldberg said. "I sent for some hot soup. That will cure it."

"I'm sure it will help," Amanda said.

Amanda smiled at her dinner companions. Everyone was in formal dress, de rigueur for such an evening, but she noticed that with each passing night, the women wore more and more jewelry. Mrs. Weintraub had six strings of black jet beads wrapped around her thick throat. Mrs. Van Allen, in keeping with her reticent nature, wore fabulous pearls. Mrs. Goldberg was already wearing a double strand of diamonds and two diamond bracelets. The dress ball wasn't until Saturday night. Amanda wondered how far these women would go to impress each other.

She looked around the opulently appointed room for Paul. The room easily held five hundred passengers, all seated at linen-covered tables, each centered with fresh roses, ruberum lilies, and ivy. She couldn't see into the burgundy-draped alcoves to the left. She assumed he must have been placed at the seven o'clock serving time.

She sipped her wine and looked at the menu. Just then, out of the corner of her eye, she saw a hand clamp down on the back of the chair next to her.

From the gold braid on the cuff she instantly knew it was the captain.

"Good evening," his gruff voice said politely.

She looked up. Standing next to the captain was Paul. He was smiling.

"Miss Granger, I would like to introduce Paul Van Volkien. Mr. Van Volkien, this is Miss Amanda Granger from London."

Amanda nearly burst into laughter. "How do you do?" she said with forced restraint.

"Very well. I'm pleased to make your acquaintance."

The captain clapped his hands. The maitre d' rushed over. "A bottle of champagne for this table," the captain said, then winked at Paul and left.

Paul seated himself next to Amanda.

"Was that *proper* enough for you?"

"Very," she answered, noticing that everyone at the table was snickering at them. And Paul's smile was a bit *too* wide. "Did I miss something?"

Mrs. Van Allen was first to speak. "Paul! You didn't need to involve the captain in your games. I told you I would introduce you to Amanda when I arranged your seat here this evening."

"You arranged? Then James wasn't ill?" Amanda asked.

"No, but he has a new train."

"You bribed a child?"

"It's always worked before. . . ."

Amanda was flattered, and as the waiter took their orders, she again felt that tingling.

The orchestra on the main-deck ballroom played a Strauss waltz. Amanda had never waltzed with a man before. She and Eloise had practiced together to the scratchy sounds of a Victrola, but she'd never been held like this, gently but firmly. Paul guided her with his arms and her feet naturally followed. When the dance ended, her head was spinning, though she wasn't sure if it was from the music or the man.

"Could we go out on deck for a minute?" she asked.

"Absolutely."

They stood next to the railing looking out at the moon. It was even more luminous than at Tresco. But tonight, as she looked up at Paul, his dark hair woven with moonbeams, she knew no other moon would ever be like this one.

"So how is it a beautiful girl like you has escaped my attention? I've been to London many times. Do you know the Penningtons?"

"No. Do you know the Kents?"

"No. I've heard of Lord Kent, though."

Suddenly uneasy, Amanda moved a bit farther down the deck. She hadn't bargained for an inquisition on her third night into her lie.

"Where did you go to school?"

"I had private tutors."

"Of course."

"Actually, I spent most of my life in Cornwall. My father died when I was young. My mother and I retired to the seashore. We preferred it there. So that's why you wouldn't associate me with any particular London group.''

"Cornwall, eh? Where? I've been to the Scillys myself.''

"Tresco.'' She held her breath.

"Don't know it.''

Thank God, Amanda thought. This was more difficult than she'd thought. Perhaps an offense would be a better play for her.

"Now that you've grilled me, perhaps you'll tell me about the man I've spent most of the evening with.''

"Oh, I'm a nasty sort. I know most of the people on this ship. I suppose if you went back far enough we'd all be related. My mother died when I was young, and my father passed away last year. He left me stinkingly rich, and I've spent the last year in Europe trying to forget the old bastard.'' He paused, took a cigarette from a gold case, and lit it. He seemed to be talking to himself and not to her. Amanda said nothing and let him continue.

He leaned over the railing and fixed his eyes on the wake. "I suppose he wasn't a bad sort, as fathers go. It's just that he plotted out my entire future for me. Now I'm not so sure I can go through with it.''

"Do you have to?''

As if he'd just remembered she was there, he turned to her. "Why, yes . . . I think so. . . .''

"I've always heard that in America a person could do anything they wanted.''

"Land of golden opportunity and all that, huh?''

"Yes.''

He pondered this for a moment and touched her cheek. "How old are you, Amanda?''

"Tomorrow's my birthday. I'll be . . . eighteen,'' she lied. Sixteen sounded so childish suddenly.

"That's old enough.''

He moved closer, his green eyes intent on hers. When he kissed her, she felt as if time had stood still. This was different— very, very different—from Billy's kiss. Suddenly, she understood everything Eloise had tried to tell her. She knew she must be in love.

"Happy birthday, Amanda,'' he whispered.

They heard the orchestra leader announce the midnight dance. They walked inside, and Paul took her in his arms and guided her across the floor. She smiled up at him, thinking that no other birthday had ever been or ever would be this wonderful.

CHAPTER FOURTEEN

Wildfire in a parched forest has more control than gossip on board a ship.

However, for those who were accustomed to being the topic of gossip, news of Paul's budding romance with the Granger woman was not malicious.

Paul Van Volkien had been raised by the elite of New York society. They had consoled him when his mother died, forgiven him his imperfections as he matured, and understood his reasons for spending this past year in Europe after his father's death. They were his conscience when he spent his fortune too freely or played too recklessly.

Paul's background and life-style had taught him how to charm the staunchest of his father's friends, how to wrangle a larger allowance from his accountant, and how to precisely woo beautiful young women.

Paul was a playboy. And he was New York's favorite. He'd never intentionally hurt anyone or caused a single heart to break—for everyone who was anyone *knew* about Paul.

Paul was on his way back from Europe to announce his engagement to Christine Whitley. It was his father's dying wish that she and Paul marry. The alliance of his son with his oldest and dearest friend's daughter was paramount to the old man. Without the marriage, Paul would not receive his entire inheritance—a fact Christine was not aware of.

They, then, were unconcerned when talk spread. And since Amanda was from the proper circles in London, she certainly would have known about Paul. His infatuation with Amanda was a lark, then, for them both.

And so it was that no one on board sought to warn Amanda about Paul.

Because there was a five-hour difference between London and New York, every day that Amanda rose it was an hour earlier. By the fourth day out to sea, Amanda calculated that she was rising at three o'clock London time.

She didn't care. Asleep or awake, all she could think about was Paul.

When the seven o'clock breakfast bell rang, Amanda was already dressed in her new tweed skirt and matching waist-cinched jacket. She opened her cabin door and was met face-to-face with a porter carrying an enormous wicker basket of fresh flowers.

"Miss Granger? These are for you."

She took the flowers, placed them on the bureau, and read the card:

Happy birthday to the most beautiful girl on board. Meet me on the main deck. Paul.

She placed the card in her pocket and hurried out the door. There wasn't a minute to waste. Paul was waiting.

He stood next to the railing holding a rifle, another resting on the deck. A porter stood next to him.

He smiled widely as she approached.

"The flowers were beautiful. Thank you."

"You're welcome." He paused for a long moment and gazed into her eyes. He seemed to be somewhere else.

The porter coughed, then cleared his throat.

"You shoot skeet?" Paul asked.

"Pardon?"

"You do shoot, don't you?"

"Uh, well, no. My mother was opposed to firearms."

"It's not that I don't respect your mother, but you need to learn. Here." He handed her a loaded rifle. "Now, watch."

He aimed his gun over the deck out to sea. "Pull!" he shouted to the porter, who pulled a cord. A round clay disk went whizzing over the ocean. Paul fired and it shattered into a thousand pieces.

"Your turn."

He helped her aim, again shouted, "Pull!" and Amanda fired the gun.

The rifle slammed into her shoulder so hard, Amanda's arm shot up, missing the target.

"You said nothing about pain!"

He smiled. "You'll get used to it. Now, again."

Angry that he took her injury so lightly, she aimed again. If he could do this, so could she.

"Pull!" she yelled and the disk went slinging overhead. She fired and missed again. This time she was ready for the "kick" and compensated for it. She felt more confident.

"Again," she said to the porter, who nodded.

For the next hour, Amanda shot at the whirling clay pigeons. By the third box of shells and the second box of skeet, her hit-to-miss ratio had increased to fifty percent.

"Aren't you getting tired, Amanda?"

"No," she said, readying for another shot. She hit it dead center. "I like this, Paul." She fired again. A direct hit.

"Remind me never to introduce you to new sports."

"I hate dress balls at sea." he said pulling her closer as they danced.

"Why?"

"Because it means the trip is almost over."

"It *is* lovely, being at sea. It's very . . . romantic," she said, looking into his eyes.

He kissed her cheek. "True. But I have a feeling you'd be romantic on a tugboat." He whirled her around again. "We were just getting to know each other."

"You . . . say that as if you were never going to see me again. We'll be living in the same city, you know."

He looked away. "Oh, I know."

"Is something wrong?"

"No." He looked back at her.

There was an intensity to him she hadn't seen before. He'd always kept the conversation light, his remarks flippant. He was fun and charming and wonderful. He was the kind of man she'd known had existed out there for her. He was everything her mother had said he would be. She wondered if Sylvia Hendrickson had felt like this when she'd first met her husband.

Because Amanda was expecting romance to come to her, she

never questioned its existence. This was the way it was all *supposed* to happen. Amanda knew that once they were in New York, he would court her, then propose and, being in love as she knew they both were, they would live happily ever after.

"I've never met anyone quite like you, Amanda. You're trusting, for one thing. And there isn't much that frightens you."

"Is there anything wrong with that?"

"Not at all."

As the music ended, he waltzed her out on deck, where beneath the steel steps leading to the upper deck, he kissed her. It was a lingering kiss that built to urgent passion.

She held him closely, her arms around his neck. She met his intensity, refusing to let him go. She made him believe in things he'd never imagined . . . like love.

"Amanda," he said kissing her throat and ears. "You make me want to protect you."

"From what?"

"From me."

"What a silly thing to say."

"Yes. It was. I've never felt like this before. It's as if I'm alive for the first time in my life. I don't know what it is. . . ."

"I do." She smiled at him. But something stopped her from saying it. He was supposed to do the proposing.

"But we've known each other such a short time."

"I didn't know we were on a time schedule. We have all the time in the world, Paul. Once I'm at Sylvia's . . ."

"Sylvia?"

"I'll be living with Sylvia Hendrickson. She lives near Washington Square."

"I know," he said despondently. Of all the people! Sylvia Hendrickson was one of Thalia Whitley's closest friends. And he knew that Thalia Whitley's life mission was to see her daughter Christine married to him.

He would never get out of this. And as he looked at Amanda, God help him, he didn't *want* out, either.

"Is that far from where you live?"

"Across town. But not far. Not really." He kissed her again, savoring her mouth for as long as she would let him. "Even if you still lived in London, I would track you down, Amanda."

Her eyes gleamed with love. She trusted him—completely. Paul knew his responsibility to his dead father. He knew that everyone on this ship and in New York expected him to marry Christine. But sometimes he had been known *not* to do what was expected. He'd certainly never thought he would find romance on this voyage—he'd never thought he was worthy of love. His father had never loved him. He couldn't remember enough about his mother to know for certain. Paul knew he'd never find a girl like Amanda again. He also knew second chances were rare.

"We're going to have a *wonderful* life!" he said suddenly, picking her up and whirling her around.

CHAPTER FIFTEEN
New York City, 1894

Amanda saw her, standing tall, proud features facing the sun. She was beautiful, regal, and strong.

"She's my first love," Paul said as they passed the Statue of Liberty.

Amanda knew instantly what he meant. Even though she wasn't American, the statue gave her a sense of belonging, of caring. She looked to the statue knowing that she would find the freedom, the equality, in America she could never have in London.

The ship churned past the statue as little tugboats came out to meet the ocean liner. They ferried it to a small island that contained a fortresslike wooden structure.

"What are we doing here?" Amanda asked.

"This is Ellis Island. The immigrants must get off here."

Sylvia had taken care of Amanda's necessary papers and passports. Amanda hadn't given Immigration a second thought. But as she watched hundreds of ragged-looking families board the tugboats, suddenly she was reminded of her roots. She pulled her shawl around her shoulders to ward off the internal chill she felt.

She watched a young girl, about her own age, being hustled into one of the crowded boats by a gruff-looking deckhand. She wore a scarf on her head. She carried a tied-up bundle in her hand. She turned and motioned to a small boy. Amanda assumed it was her brother. They seemed to be alone, for she saw no adults concerned with their whereabouts or welfare.

Just as the boat pulled away from the ocean liner, the girl looked up to the upper decks. Her eyes met Amanda's. Had they

92

been face-to-face, Amanda couldn't have been hit with any more
intensity. They were eyes of the wanting, the determined. Amanda
wondered what kind of hardship the girl had undergone just to
get this far.

Bloodlines separated that young girl from Amanda. But, Amanda
thought, my bloodlines are a lie. If not for Harriet, Amanda, too,
would be coming to America in precisely the same manner.
Instead, she'd feasted on fine cuisine, danced her nights away,
and met the man of her dreams. It was a thin, thin line she
walked. She must be careful.

"What's going to happen to her . . . them?"

"They have to go through Immigration. They'll be checked for
diseases. The really bad cases will be sent back to their mother
country. The rest will come to New York where they will live
like sardines—four and five families to an apartment. Can you
imagine? Whole families trying to live in a single room—or two,
at the most."

Amanda thought of Shelton Street. It seemed very, very close
and frighteningly real. "I can't imagine," she said coldly.

"Every year their numbers rise. I keep thinking that there can't
be that many unhappy people in the world, but I guess there
are."

Yes, Amanda thought, more than you know. "I . . . I didn't
even know they were on board," she said, looking at another
boat filling up. They were like lemmings, racing to the sea.

"It's another world below decks. Not a pretty sight. Especially
not for your eyes." He turned her toward him.

"Hold me, Paul," she whispered as she closed her eyes to the
people headed for Ellis Island.

"It won't be long. We'll sail up the Hudson and dock. Is there
someone meeting you?"

"Yes. Sylvia will be there. And you?"

He thought of Christine. Yes, he thought, she would be there.
Even though she hadn't cabled that she would. This would be
Christine's idea of a surprise. Christine wasn't very imaginative.

"I haven't even packed, Amanda. And I have some cables to
send. I'm afraid this will have to be our good-bye."

"Good-bye?"

"Don't look so frightened. I meant for today. I'll call you once
you're settled in." He kissed her. "I'm not going to let some

other guy find you and steal you away." He traced the length of her nose with his forefinger. "Until then . . ."

"Until then . . ."

Sylvia waved a red scarf over her head. Since Amanda didn't know her on sight, this was their signal to each other. Amanda waved a similar scarf. The ship pulled into the dock, and as the passengers leaned over the railing waving to families and friends, the dockhands secured the ship to the moorings.

Sylvia was close to her mother's age Amanda knew, but she was not as pretty as Harriet, though she actually looked younger. Her face was bright with anticipation, and she seemed happy to see Amanda. Amanda was relieved, for she'd worried that she might be a burden to Sylvia. There was a woman servant with her, but no one else.

It seemed like ages before the passengers were allowed to disembark. Amanda searched the crowds for Paul, but he was nowhere to be seen. The cargo crew was already unloading hundreds of trunks and suitcases. Beautiful carriages and hansom cabs waited at the far end of the dock. It was cold for the last day of October, and she noticed that most of the women wore fur coats or fur-trimmed coats. Their bonnets were the latest fashion. The vision of the well-dressed crowd sat juxtaposed with the one of the immigrants in Amanda's mind.

She wondered if someday the immigrant girl would stand on this dock, dressed in fine clothes, waiting to receive her family. She hoped so. She wanted a lot of things for the immigrants—and for herself.

Amanda walked down the plank and was met with open arms by Sylvia.

"I can't believe how much you look like your mother when she was young!" Sylvia inspected her more closely. "Incredible. You're quite tall for your age, aren't you? You're tall for any age. That's wonderful! You can wear all the fashions, then. New York men are fascinated with tall women. Irene Langhorn started it all, you know, She's a legend already. The Gibson Girl, they call her. We'll have to put your hair up like hers. Yes, you'll look wonderful."

Amanda was amazed that anyone could talk that fast. She wondered if it was because she was lonely. She didn't have any children, and her husband was dead.

"Thank you for everything you've done, Mrs. Hendrickson. I realize now how important my papers and passports were."

"It was nothing. I have friends who *do* that kind of thing. Think nothing of it. This is Julia, my housekeeper. She is my right arm. . . ." She smiled at Julia, a pinch-faced woman who said nothing, only turned and walked toward the end of the dock. Sylvia shrugged her shoulders and whispered at Amanda: "She just has to get used to you, is all. Give her time."

They went to the waiting hansom cab and rode south on Eleventh Avenue. Sylvia explained that the docks were located in midtown and that they were now passing through Chelsea. This was where the Hudson River Railroad had opened in 1851. In the past forty years the area had become filled with slaughterhouses, breweries, and the shanties and tenements of the workers. Sylvia said she lived in Greenwich Village.

"Tomorrow I'll take you around the city. Brooklyn Bridge is something to see. It's wonderful to view both Manhattan and Brooklyn through a filigree of cables."

The streets were wider here than in London. Most of the buildings were five or six stories high. So far, she hadn't seen ancient towers, forts, or houses like London had. There was a flavor here that did not exist in London. Everything here seemed so *new* to her. Not new in that there was an abundance of new construction, but new in that the whole city was only two hundred and fifty years old.

And it was fast. People moved fast, carriages moved faster. She wondered where they were all going. Perhaps they were just anxious, like she was, to find their futures.

Above all she noticed the people, all kinds of people talking, arguing, and cursing in their native tongues, as the carriage rolled on from street corner to street corner. And there were so many of them.

Paul had been right. In Manhattan people did live like sardines. They would have to. All these people who filled the streets and bought their food on the street corners would have to live somewhere.

Coming to a pleasant park where the autumn trees looked as if they'd been gilded with gold, the carriage stopped. Amanda saw a huge stone memorial arch at the entrance. There were men playing checkers, nannies strolling with bundled babies in wicker prams, and children running in and out of the trees.

"Here we are," Sylvia said, getting out and paying the driver.

As they walked inside, Amanda realized that Julia still had not spoken a word.

Sylvia's brownstone was very much like those in London but nothing like what she'd imagined, Amanda thought. Number 6 on Washington Square North had once housed a socially prominent New York family, Sylvia said, as had the neighboring houses. Henry James and Williams Dean Howells had lived at Number 1.

Two stories high, and with large windows that looked out onto the park, it was pleasant but not lavish. Sylvia's furniture was light pickled oak and upholstered in French brocade in pastels. Amanda was glad Sylvia hadn't chosen the oppressive dark reds and olives that were currently in vogue.

"Your room is upstairs," Julia finally said, standing on the stairs.

"Go ahead. I'll start some tea and then we'll have a wonderful chat. You must tell me all about your mother. And Andrew. How they're doing."

Amanda followed Julia upstairs to a high-ceilinged room that was surprisingly large. A four-poster bed was canopied in white openwork crochet. There was a bureau, two fauteuil chairs, and a rose-pointed carpet underfoot. Julia pointed to the two doors to the right.

"The bath is in there. There's your closet."

"Thank you, Julia." Amanda paused. There was no reply. "My trunk . . ."

"Will arrive late this evening."

Amanda smiled and Julia left.

"What an odd person!" Amanda mumbled to herself. She sat on the edge of the bed and leaned all the way back. "My own room . . . my own chairs . . ." She went to the window and pulled back the French lace curtain. "My own view." This was even better than Tresco, she thought. She was *here*. This was America. Soon, but not soon enough, she would see Paul again.

The golden leaves of the trees waved at her. How right she had been to come to this land. What had Paul said? "The land of opportunity." Yes, she thought, she had found it all.

CHAPTER SIXTEEN

Luxury, Amanda found, is a personal experience. To a czarina, luxury must come from jeweled Fabergé eggs. But the morning Amanda woke to breakfast in bed and heard Julia run her bath, Amanda knew luxury had entered her life.

As she sank a sterling spoon into an out-of-season melon, flashes of her mother, dressed in work clothes, raced across her mind. She wondered what her mother was doing today. She wished she was here so she could tell her about Paul. Amanda remembered the little gift her mother had given her. She'd stuffed it into her valise and forgotten about it. She'd forgotten nearly everything once she'd met Paul.

Pushing the tray aside, Amanda went to the closet and found that Julia had already pressed her dresses and skirts and unpacked her trunk and bags—a job Amanda knew too well. The little wrapped package rested atop a shelf where Julia had laid out her hairbrush, comb, and pins.

Amanda quickly opened it. "A diary," she mumbled. Inside the cover she read: "I started a diary when I was your age. *Your* dreams, I know, will come true."

Amanda held it to her breast. She didn't feel nearly as homesick as she thought she might. She would tell her diary about Paul, about Sylvia, and about Julia. She wondered what Julia might think if she knew that Amanda was really nothing more than a maid, just like her.

Just then there was a knock at the door, and before Amanda could answer it Sylvia breezed into the room. She drew the drapes, checked the closet to see if Julia had done her job, and looked askance at the tray, all the while keeping up her magpie chatter.

"Good morning. Good morning. Although it isn't really anymore. Nearly noon. Not hungry, I see. Well, I have a glorious day planned for us. Your steamer trunk arrived early. I had Julia put your things away. I noticed that you don't have anything suitable to wear."

"I don't?" Amanda's eyes darted to the closet. She thought they'd done so well choosing the right patterns. All that work . . .

"There's only one party dress in the bunch. What were you going to dance in? A skirt and blouse?"

"Party dresses? I thought these things would be quite suitable for a governess. . . ."

"Governess? What are you talking about? Oh, yes. That teensy lie I told your mother."

"Lie?"

"I've known your mother a long time. Sometimes her pride gets stuck in the wrong part of her brain. And you're probably just like her too, aren't you? Well, the truth is, there is no job waiting for you here. At least, none other than being my companion. How would it look," she asked sitting on the bed, taking a bite of the melon, "if you, a royal descendant, which by the way is our little secret, were to have to *work* for a living? Why, I'd never be able to introduce you to the 'right' people. No, my way is much better. After all, you're here now and that's what counts, isn't it?"

"If I'm not going to work, how can I afford to pay you back?"

"You can't. That's the point, don't you see? I've never had a daughter. And now I can pretend I do. I can dress you up and show you off. Plus I have the added bonus that you know nothing about New York or the whole country, for that matter. I've been so looking forward to this. I have so much to show you. Selfishly; I'm doing this mostly for myself. And I want to help you too, Amanda."

Sylvia bounced off the bed, gave Amanda a quick hug, and went to the door. "I'll send Julia up to help with your hair. The carriage will be here in forty-five minutes, so don't dawdle. Hurry, hurry."

Amanda felt as if she'd been visited by a whirlwind. The bedskirt actually rustled when Sylvia flitted out the door.

"And I thought I was controlling my own destiny," she muttered.

If royalty existed in New York, it was fashion. Amanda had never seen Paris, but she couldn't imagine Parisians dressing any more richly than New Yorkers.

Dashing over wide, smooth, white asphalted streets, Amanda and Sylvia stopped at the crossing of Broadway, Fifth Avenue, and Twenty-third Street. The sidewalks were teeming with begowned matrons and young girls. The children were exquisitely dressed, as were the rich liveried coachmen and footmen.

Carriages with crested panels and snorting steeds rolled up in front of the city's finest hotels, restaurants, and department stores. Amanda saw millinery that combined colors and hues she'd never seen before. They were monstrosities bedecked with feather and plumes from rare South American birds that defied gravity and imagination.

There was an air of flamboyance and excitement here that was poles apart from Washington Square.

Sylvia pointed out the newly finished Madison Square Garden. "Do you like horses?"

"Yes. I ride quite well."

"Oh, no, dear. That's not what I meant. On the fifteenth is the National Horse Show at the Garden. I have a friend who bought a box when they were auctioned off. They have to take their own easy chairs and Persian rugs, of course. But I think they'll have room for two more."

"Do you think we should impose?"

"Me? Impose? Never. Remember, I have friends who *do* this sort of thing. It's nothing. Really."

Amanda didn't understand about Sylvia's "friends," but she guessed she soon would.

They went to Lord & Taylor where Amanda was fitted for tea gowns, which were loose fitting with cascades of lace down the front. These she would wear only at home. For parties, she chose a rich emerald velvet with a voluminous skirt, square neckline and exaggerated puffed sleeves. Amanda was content with this and the lemon silk with the ruffled neckline and bustle in back. Sylvia, however, insisted they also purchase the apricot taffeta, the champagne crepe de chine, and two theater cloaks, one in black velvet lined with white satin, the other in off-white velvet with brown satin lining.

There were also three carriage dresses in light wools and heavy linens, all in autumn colors of mustard, burgundy, and rust. A day coat in sable brown wool tweed with leather buttons was more fashionable than the one Amanda had sewn, Sylvia told her. To accessorize these, there were calfskin shoes in four colors for day wear, kid dancing slippers to match each gown, and six pairs of gloves, three opera length and three wrist length.

At noon a light lunch was brought to them in the fitting room. Amanda tried to eat a watercress sandwich, but she'd only gotten one bite when yet another saleswoman came in. She carried a trio of wool vests and matching short jackets.

"Ah!" Sylvia said. "These will go with the skirts you already have, Amanda."

Amanda examined the leather-edged vest pockets and braid along the coat lapels. "They *are* beautiful."

"Then you shall have them."

Amanda knew that Sylvia was reveling in this day. And yet, Amanda wished there was some way she could repay her. But there wasn't. Perhaps there never would be. She felt guilty. She always seemed to be on the receiving end. She wondered what she'd ever done to deserve such generosity. The only thing she *could* do was to promise herself that she would make it up to Sylvia.

"You're much too generous, Sylvia. You shouldn't be doing all this."

"And why not? I promised your mother I would introduce you to New York's finest. To do that, you must look the part. This is nothing. And you are to think nothing of it. Agreed?" she asked firmly.

Amanda could tell this would be the last time Sylvia would discuss the matter. "Agreed."

As they climbed into the carriage at the end of the day, Amanda sank back into the seat, wondering if she'd only gotten two blisters on her feet from the day's walking.

"I'm exhausted."

"You've only begun, my dear. Tomorrow is the milliner's. It takes me days to choose a hat."

"Days?"

"The hat is the crowning glory. It requires great skill to choose the *right* hat."

Amanda looked at the beautifully attired women passing them on the street as they drove off. "I believe you."

Sylvia owned a telephone, paid for a full-time housekeeper, and her mail was delivered at precisely ten o'clock every morning. On the third day after her arrival, Amanda noted there were no letters addressed to her, no notes had arrived by messenger, and Julia had not reported any telephone calls.

Paul had forgotten her.

It was the only explanation Amanda could give, along with an easy five hundred other explanations her anxious mind had conjured. He was in the hospital, he'd left town on an emergency, he was being held prisoner. All of these were more acceptable than the truth. She thought about him at least five or six times an hour. Probably more. But as each day passed it became more and more obvious that he had forgotten her.

Despondently, she picked at her dinner.

"What's the matter, Amanda?"

"I guess I'm just tired. I never knew it could be so much work being . . . a . . ."

"Lady?" Sylvia winked.

"Yes. Being a lady."

Perhaps he had discovered the truth about her. That had to be it. She wouldn't let herself believe that he'd fallen out of love with her so quickly. She knew she meant more to him than that. Didn't she?

She refused dessert but savored the dark coffee Sylvia served. She liked it like this, laced with thick cream and sugar.

"Tomorrow I have errands to run and a lunch meeting with my attorney. You can entertain yourself, can't you?" Sylvia asked.

"Yes." Amanda sighed. This was perfect. Maybe now she might have a chance to telephone Paul. She had to know the truth.

She wished she could discuss him with Sylvia, but something told her not to. It was all too soon. If Paul had truly forgotten her, she didn't want to look like a fool to Sylvia. And if he hadn't—well, there really wasn't much to tell. He had proposed, she guessed, although it wasn't on bended knee. Nothing was *formally* set—although *she* knew it was. In her heart she knew she and Paul would be together. This absence of his was just temporary. It meant nothing.

*   *   *

Amanda plunked at the ivory keys trying to elicit a melody from the piano. She was depressed.

After Sylvia left, she'd gone through the telephone book looking for Paul's number. She called a number on Fifth Avenue, but there was no answer. How could she find the truth if she couldn't find him?

The jangling telephone wrested Amanda from her thoughts. She went to the tiny alcove in the hallway and lifted the receiver.

"Hendrickson residence."

"Amanda? Is that you?"

Julia walked into the hall. Amanda smiled and waved her away, and she went back to the kitchen.

"Paul."

"I've been thinking about you."

"You have?"

"I would have called sooner, but I've been tied up with attorneys all week over this estate thing."

"It must be the day for it. Sylvia had to see her attorney today too."

"Really? How long will she be gone?"

"She told Julia not to have dinner ready till eight."

"Perhaps I could break away and see you. If I send a carriage for you, would you have lunch with me?"

"Of course." She hoped her voice wasn't too jubilant.

"Until then . . ." He rang off.

Amanda raced up the stairs. She pulled the burgundy wool dress out of the closet, and when she turned around there stood Julia.

"I thought you didn't know anyone in New York."

"It's a friend of my mother's."

"Do you need me?" Julia asked, gesturing at Amanda's hair. "It could use a repinning."

"Yes. Thank you."

As Amanda sat for Julia she remembered how the world "below stairs" has ears and mouths all its own. A tiny piece of information can become amplified, distorted, and then transmitted. Amanda didn't want Sylvia or anyone to know about Paul. She had to be sure about him, about her feelings. Of course, after today's phone call she had proof that everything was fine between them. She probably didn't have to worry about Julia at all But just the same . . .

* * *

The carriage arrived, but Paul wasn't in it.

"He said he'd meet you at the restaurant." The driver helped her into the carriage.

They rode down Seventh Avenue, then west of Washington Street near Leroy she could see the New York Central Railroad tracks. It looked odd to Amanda to see railcars elevated in the air like that. The new Sixth Precinct police station was just being finished. They passed a few more blocks of brownstone houses, rounded a corner, and the carriage stopped.

Through the windows she could see the coffeehouse was full. And there, coming through the door, was Paul. His face was bright. He opened the door, climbed into the carriage, took her in his arms, and kissed her.

"How I've missed you!" he said moments later as he helped her from the carriage and they walked into the coffeehouse. "All those meetings . . . the nights when I haven't even been able to telephone. You're more beautiful than I remember."

"It's only been four days," she said.

"You didn't miss me?" he teased.

"Yes, I did." She noticed that suddenly his face had grown solemn.

"What did Sylvia say when you told her about us?"

"I haven't told her."

Amanda could swear his eyes gleamed at the news.

"Amanda, I think for the time, until this thing is settled with my father's estate, that we should keep our relationship under wraps."

"I don't understand."

"Oh, don't get me wrong. It has nothing to do with my feelings for you. It's just that probating the will has gone quite sticky. It's all very complicated . . . I still want to see you, every chance we get. Do you mind terribly?"

"I could see you?"

"Yes, Amanda." He kissed her hand. His eyes were anxious, and when she smiled her approval, his face lit up again. She was amazed at the power she could wield.

For the next two weeks Paul met Amanda on the days when Sylvia worked on the charity ball to be held the weekend after Thanksgiving. Sylvia had been a principal fund-raiser for half the charities in New York when her husband was alive. Now she spent her time on her favorite organization, and they worked her to death.

Amanda would call for her own cab, telling Julia and Sylvia she was visiting an art museum, shopping, or going to a matinee on Broadway. None of this was an actual lie, for she *did* do these things. She simply neglected to tell them it was with Paul.

She noticed, however, that they went to obscure restaurants and out-of-the-way spots. She noticed that he never took her to places near his home facing Central Park. He took her to Coney Island where she rode a new invention called the Ferris wheel. When they got to the top, he kissed her, and she was never sure if it was Paul's kiss or the quick descent of the Ferris wheel that caused her stomach to sink. She tasted salt-water taffy, hot dogs, and cotton candy for the first time. She kept the Kewpie doll Paul won for her under a pile of sweaters in her closet.

The days became heady in their wealth of new experiences and new places. But mostly, Amanda was giddy with the new feelings she had for Paul. And she wondered if it was she who had the power over him or vice versa.

Fabulous carriages with magnificent horse teams ringed all four sides of Madison Square Garden. The horses wore exotic and brightly colored plumes and gold tassels on their heads. But as they came to the front of the building for the National Horse Show, Amanda noticed the most magnificent carriage of all. Its dark wood panels gleamed like mirrors in the electric street lamps. Its hardware, lamps, and crest looked as if they were fashioned of gold.

"That," Sylvia said pointing to the carriage, "belongs to Diamond Jim Brady."

Amanda didn't know who Mr. Brady was, but as he emerged from the carriage, she knew she'd never forget him. He was enormous, though expensively dressed in tails and top hat. The top of his cane was encrusted with jewels. And even from her window, Amanda could see that his shirt studs were diamonds.

"They say he never goes out wearing less than fifty thousand dollars worth of jewels."

Amanda was amazed at such flamboyance. It was impossible for her to imagine. As Diamond Jim turned toward the carriage door, her eyes followed him. This was someone Amanda did recognize.

"Lillian Russell!" Amanda said. "She's more beautiful than her pictures."

"She is. And look at that perfect Gibson Girl figure. Oh, Amanda! Now there's someone else you should meet . . . Irene Langhorn . . . the real Gibson Girl. Yes," Sylvia said, getting out of the carriage, "I'll have to arrange that too."

Sylvia was right. Nobody came to the horse show to see the horses, although Amanda had never seen Arabians that magnificent or Belgian and Austrian Pinzgauers as sturdy. Lord Kent had only the lighter breeds. But as fascinated as Amanda was with the horses, nothing could equal New York's fascination with her.

They sat in the Van Rennselaers' box, on French chairs that Sylvia *knew* had came from Versailles and the threadbare Persian rug they had cushioned the feet of the Medicis. Gold-waistcoated waiters passed silver trays of Mumm's champagne—compliments of Diamond Jim Brady. Amanda and everyone in their box lifted their glasses to thank him. As she sipped her wine, she could swear the wink Diamond Jim gave was meant for her.

The Jays spoke to Sylvia about a dinner party for a few—a hundred—friends next week. They wanted to be the first to "launch" Amanda. Caroline Astor was effusive with praise. She would have a luncheon for Amanda.

And so it went. By intermission, Amanda felt as if she were a celebrity. And she was, for with each introduction, Sylvia made certain she recited Amanda's credentials. "My ward, Amanda Granger; you know, dear, *the* Grangers—she's descended from King Charles II and Lucy Walters." They, *all* of them, Amanda noticed, beamed with pleasure and fell into the trap. None of them would check, of course; Sylvia Hendrickson's word was good enough for them.

Amanda grew queasy. Sylvia had never lied to these people. And Amanda's lie was not so innocent anymore. Now she needed it. She needed it to keep Sylvia's honor and to keep Paul.

She knew instinctively these people were Paul's friends too. It would be important not only for her but for Paul, too, to keep her mouth shut.

When the show was over, Amanda's head was reeling. She hoped she could keep all the names and faces straight. If she were to accept the many invitations she received that night, she wouldn't have a spare moment to spend with Paul.

The driver helped Sylvia into the carriage first. Amanda followed her and just as she looked out the window she saw Paul. She started to wave to him when she noticed a beautiful brunette with him. She wore a full-length sable fur with a hood. There were diamonds in her hair, around her neck, and on her ears. She was smiling up at Paul. He leaned over and . . . he kissed her.

Maybe it wasn't Paul after all. She looked again. She could never mistake that handsome face.

"Sylvia." Her voice cracked when she spoke. "Who is that couple there . . . under the lamp? I've met so many. Did I meet them?"

"That's Paul Van Volkien and Christine Whitley, his fiancée."

"His . . . what?"

"Well, actually, dear, they aren't engaged yet. Of course, they will be. Everyone knows about them."

"I don't."

"Before his father died, he made Paul promise to marry Christine. The Whitleys and the Van Volkiens go way back—before the Revolution. Anyway, there's a rumor that Paul is dragging his feet over the whole thing. You never know how much is rumor and how much truth, but I heard that if he doesn't marry Christine, he only gets half his fortune. The way Paul spends money, he'll need it all. I think it's all hearsay. She's too beautiful for him not to want. And besides, Paul or no Paul, her mother, Thalia Whitley, will make certain that's one wedding New York sees. She's been working on it for over a year."

Amanda thought her nerves would explode. This was a joke—an awful, stupid joke. Or a nightmare. Paul loved her. He'd told her so. She couldn't believe he would tell her they would be together when he was promised to someone else. She wouldn't believe it. But Sylvia said he'd been "dragging his feet." She wondered if it was because of her. It had to be. There was no other explanation.

As they rode to the Waldorf and went inside, Amanda promised herself she would find the truth.

CHAPTER SEVENTEEN

The crime of the century required less plotting than Amanda's confrontation with Paul. That night, she'd searched the crowd for a sign of him. He was nowhere to be seen. Discreetly, she asked a few people about him and learned that he lived on Millionaire's Row on Fifth Avenue across from Central Park. North of Fifty-eighth Street was a mansion designed by Richard Morris Hunt, who had designed Mrs. John Jacob Astor's house, and this palace belonged to Paul Van Volkien—his bequest in his father's will.

As the evening drew to a close, Amanda was convinced Paul and Christine must have gone to the party at Delmonico's. Unfortunately, she did not have an invitation, and etiquette could not be breached.

No amount of champagne could have made Amanda sleepy that night. She tossed and turned and reshaped her down pillow a thousand times. Morning would bring her closer to the truth.

As she dressed and ate breakfast, Amanda thought she'd lost the entire mass of her insides. She consciously had to *think* to breathe, she was so nervous.

After Sylvia left, she called for a carriage. She told Julia she was going shopping for an ensemble for the luncheon with the Astors. The ride to Central Park was hideous. It was cold and threatened to rain. Amanda felt as if she'd already lost her heart, so she had nothing to keep her warm.

When the carriage stopped she gasped at the elegance before her. The structure was five stories high, executed in red brick with a Georgian facade. It looked as if it took up half the city block.

With trembling legs she alighted from the carriage. She noticed there were four other carriages waiting across the street. She mounted the steps and rang the bell.

The butler opened the door. "May I have your name? I'll announce you."

He ushered her into a fabulous reception area with marble statues, pillars, and oak flooring. She could hear voices coming from the salon to the left where the butler had gone. Rather than wait for him to come back she followed him. She didn't want to be turned away.

She stood inside the double doors. There were six couples, beautifully dressed, enjoying a brunch buffet. A maid carried a silver coffeepot and refilled English china cups. They were talking about the party last night, the people they'd seen.

Then Amanda saw Paul standing next to the French doors talking to Christine.

At precisely the same moment, he saw her. His face went ashen. He didn't excuse himself but went straight to Amanda.

"Paul?" Christine was frozen to the spot.

Eyes darted from Christine to Amanda.

"Who is she? Mary Hadden asked.

"A friend of Caroline's. I saw her last night," David Simon replied. He moved closer. He wanted to hear *everything*.

"What are you doing here?" Paul asked Amanda.

"Do I need an invitation?" Amanda answered.

"No, of course not." He was nervous and unsure of his moves. She was in control and she knew it.

Amanda could see Christine out of the corner of her eye. Her anger overcame her better judgement. She wanted to fly at him with balled fists, but she forced her emotions to stay hidden.

"Surprised to see me, aren't you, Paul?" she said sweetly but with a cutting edge to her voice. She didn't wait for an answer. "I saw you last night. I was there. Sylvia told me about you— and your engagement to Christine."

"That's not true! It's not official. . . ."

"Paul!" Christine moved closer.

". . . yet." He turned to look at Christine. He couldn't afford to upset her. She was his tie to his inheritance. He glanced back at Amanda. She held his heart. "I didn't mean for it to go this far."

"What's that supposed to mean? I'll bet Christine wouldn't like to know that you've been seeing me nearly every day since we docked." She looked over his shoulder at Christine. "I had to know the truth, Paul. I'm glad I came here today. You needn't worry, Miss Whitley. He's all yours."

Amanda knew her face was blazing when she whirled away and stalked out the door. She raced down the marble steps and dashed into the carriage. Once they were past the Plaza Hotel and headed south, she finally allowed the tears to flow. She never knew it was possible to break one's own heart.

David Simon, artist, leader of the avant-garde in New York, and a sought-after bachelor in his own right, stared openmouthed at the fantastically beautiful tall blonde who had obviously had an affair with Paul Van Volkien. It took him precisely fifteen minutes to discover who she was and where she'd come from.

David didn't believe Paul's protestations and denials to Christine about his "affair" with Amanda. Paul was a randy sort. Of course he would have bedded her. This was bad for the Granger woman.

The more David heard about her, the more fascinated he became. She was a mystery to most of them, and yet *everyone* knew Sylvia. All David knew was that he'd never seen a more beautiful woman in his life. And he wanted to paint her. He knew he, and only he, could bring that face to canvas.

Those eyes, piercing blue, rimmed with thick lashes, and the *bone structure*. God, the bone structure was a painter's dream. She'd be the new Mona Lisa. Better than Mona Lisa. Her portrait would hang in the finest gallery in New York. People would come from all over the country to see her. She would be famous, and he—*he* would be immortal.

Amanda's eyes were swollen, her silk blouse tear-soaked, by the time she reached home. Sylvia was waiting for her.

"Where have you been, Amanda?"

Guilt riddled her like bullets. "Sylvia," she began her confession, "I've made such a fool of myself. I've ruined everything you and Mother have worked for."

Seeing Amanda so distraught, Sylvia's heart went out to her. "Come sit with me and tell me." She put her arm around Amanda.

"I thought he would be like Charles—your husband. I met Paul on the ship, just like you did. I thought that's how it was *supposed* to happen. And then, last night, I found out about Christine. I went to his house and confronted him—in front of her—everyone. It was humiliating.''

''Why didn't you tell me before? I could have spared you this grief.''

Amanda shook her head. ''It was too late. I already loved him.''

''Perhaps you're right. And perhaps it's not over at all. The next step is up to Paul. After all, maybe Christine doesn't have as strong a hold on Paul as you think.''

Paul sipped a glass of sherry after his guests had left. He could hear the staff cleaning up in the kitchen. Even they were talking about the ''incident'' today. He wondered how long it would take to get around town. Had he pushed his good luck too far this time? His ''friends'' had been known to crucify many a young man in similar circumstances—and without as much cause. How stupid he'd been not to see that Amanda could never be tricked. She was too smart and too headstrong for him to contain. He smiled when he thought of her, her eyes flashing, her cheeks burning with anger. She was in love with him, there was no doubt. He'd had numerous affairs, but he'd never seen love before. It humbled him and made him feel guilty.

Paul's weakness was money. He loved Amanda, but not enough to forsake his fortune. However, he also refused to buckle under to the pressure Christine and Thalia Whitley were exerting on him over a wedding date.

This scandal, minor though it was, was enough to keep Christine off his back for a few weeks. He needed the time to think. In a way, he should thank Amanda, for the incident today had crystallized his future for him. He would never be able to follow his heart and marry Amanda. She was already a part of his past, an interlude, where for a moment, he'd had the poor man's luxury of falling in love.

Sylvia had worried that the linkage of Amanda's name and Paul Van Volkien's would besmirch Amanda's good reputation. She needn't have worried. As the weeks passed and more of her friends met Amanda and came to know her goodness, her charming naivety, she was exonerated of any wrongdoing. Paul, on the other hand, by refusing to announce his engagement, was treading a precarious line. He no longer had his father's power and influence to fall back on. New Yorkers had never been known to be overly forgiving.

To forget Paul, Amanda volunteered to help Sylvia with the charity ball. From early morning till dinnertime, they worked side by side with a dedicated group of a half dozen women. The proceeds for the ball were to go to a cultural-arts center. Sylvia had founded the organization fifteen years ago. She wanted a place where all the arts could be viewed and performed. If the ball this year brought the proceeds she expected, her hard work would see fruition. Amanda felt doubly honored to be a part of the work.

Amanda was given the job of making posters. Through Beatrice Kane, a fellow worker, she found a young sketch artist, who drew a cachet of pink roses against a purple background. Amanda composed the copy and laid out the final poster. Everyone agreed it was eye-catching. With three weeks to go before the ball, Amanda and her crew plastered every vacant building and wooden fence. They coerced shopkeepers into displaying the posters in their windows. Amanda suggested they run an ad in the newspaper.

"*Pay* for publicity? Ridiculous!" Sylvia and Beatrice condemned the idea.

The days flew and Amanda found herself thinking of Paul only in the evenings when she came home. There were no messages, no letters, and, Julia reported, no phone calls.

It was clear to Amanda that she was not as important to Paul as she had hoped. She went to bed each night and wrote in the diary her mother had given her. The notes these days were sad, homesick, and tear-stained. They held none of the hope she'd had when she first started her entries.

"America is a land of dreams—shattered dreams," she wrote.

The Society for the New York Cultural Arts Ball was held at the Savoy. Ward McAllister, who had coined the phrase the Four Hundred, handled the invitations and guest list for Sylvia. Though the ball was "open to the public," everyone knew that "the public" could not afford the hundred-dollar tickets. For those hoping to become one of the Four Hundred and for those who only wanted to rub shoulders with the elite, the Cultural Arts ball of 1894 was a must.

Amanda wore the emerald velvet gown, and because she was a committee member and Sylvia Hendrickson's ward, it was acceptable that she had no escort. Truth be known, there were many who advised her to attend unescorted—to put Paul Van Volkien in his place.

The orchestra played beautifully, the dinner was divine, and everyone was full of praises about the decor of pink roses against lavender silk tablecloths.

"The turnout is even greater than we'd hoped. A lot of the credit goes to you, Amanda. Those posters of yours got people excited," Sylvia said.

"This is your night, Sylvia, not mine. You deserve all the credit."

"I agree, but"—she waved her finger— "never underestimate the power of public relations. We've never had such good advertising as this year's."

Sylvia was giddy with her success. She could almost hear the first boards being nailed on her new arts center.

Amanda moved in and out of the crowd, making certain everything went smoothly. She was glad Paul had stayed away, and yet his absence was almost deafening.

The party was nearly an hour old when she tasted her first glass of champagne.

"You look magnificent," said a male voice behind her.

Amanda smiled automatically as she turned to face him. "Thank you, sir."

"David Simon." He smiled. "I've been watching you. And I noticed you haven't been asked to dance."

She kept her smile. "Oh, I've been asked. I haven't accepted."

"Would you now?"

She considered him for a long moment, liking his warm smile. "Yes." She put her glass down on the nearest table and led the way to the dance floor. He took her firmly in his arms.

"You're a good dancer," he said, his sandy hair reflecting the subdued lighting.

"Thank you," she said and began to relax. He was quite tall, with broad shoulders and a slender torso. But more than the deep, smoky eyes and the perfectly trimmed mustache, she noticed his hands. They were large, with long, tapering fingers. They reminded her of Eloise's piano teacher's hands.

"Do you play the piano?"

"No. Should I? Would that interest you more?"

She laughed. "I was wondering about your profession."

"I'm an artist. Ergo, my concern that the center become a reality."

"Ah." She nodded. "You look so familiar to me. Have we met?"

"I'm surprised you remember—you were quite preoccupied at the time, as was our host, and there were no formal introductions. But then, what could you expect under the circumstances?"

Amanda stopped dead still. "Oh, my God . . ."

She turned and tried to flee. He grabbed her arm and pulled her back into his arms.

"Don't be embarrassed. I thought the old boy had it coming to him. We're all on your side, Amanda."

Amanda felt as if her nerves were on fire. How long would it take to live this down?

He continued. "I like Paul. I've known him since we were kids. My family wasn't as wealthy as his, though banking ran in the blood, and after my parents died, his father helped pay my college tuition. We're both only children. I guess this isn't very interesting to you," he said, looking down at the crown of her head.

Amanda finally looked up. "Not at all. Especially the parts about yourself."

"You needn't flirt with me. I already think you're the most beautiful woman God created. I'm sold."

"And you needn't flatter me. It won't do you any good," she said firmly.

"Because you're still in love with Paul?"

"Because it takes more to 'sell' me, Mr. Simon."

He cocked an eyebrow as he studied her. "I'm sure it does, Miss Granger, I'm sure it does."

He waltzed her across the floor, keeping perfect time to the music. He was an excellent dancer, and whenever she would look at him she found him scrutinizing her with those dark eyes. It made her feel self-conscious, as if she were some sort of specimen.

The dance ended. Amanda thanked him, and before he had a chance to ask for another dance she walked away to find Sylvia. She wanted to be back with her committee crew where it was safe.

David Simon watched her through the dinner, the dessert, and the award presentations to the largest donors and sponsors. He didn't press himself on her because he knew she was still mending a broken heart. He'd made his presence known to her, and for now that was enough.

He hadn't been trying to flatter her earlier. He'd spoken the truth. He was an artist, and an artist sees things other mortals don't. Amanda Granger had a face that was an artist's dream. Even up close he found no flaws. Her skin was perfect—not a single mole or blemish to mar it. He'd watched how the light settled in the plateaus of her face, enhancing the bones, shading the valleys.

David would make it a point to be wherever Amanda Granger was invited this season. He would move surely and cautiously. He didn't want to blunder like Paul had. David Simon was no fool.

The St. Nicholas Day Ball held on December 6 raised over fifty thousand dollars to feed the hungry immigrant children of the city. Amanda had found that charity work was the best part of her role as a "lady." It demanded long hours and indefatigable spirits. Simultaneously, she was able to banish Paul from her mind and, hopefully, to better the position of the immigrant girl she'd seen from the boat at Ellis Island.

Throughout the Christmas season that year, Amanda volunteered for one project after another. She interspersed Christmas shopping and decorating with worthy causes. She baked cookies for St. Joseph's bake sale. She helped gather old clothes for a clothes drive for St. Luke's Episcopal Church. She served on the invitation and publicity committees for the New York Hospital Association and assisted Sylvia on three of her charities. Amanda went with her church choir to carol in the homes for the elderly and at New York Cancer Hospital. By Christmas Eve she was exhausted, but never had she ever felt the true meaning of Christmas so deeply before.

Amanda stood atop a ladder placing a porcelain angel on the tip of the Christmas tree. Sylvia walked around the tree and scrutinized its every detail.

"Unequivocally the finest job I've ever seen."

Amanda smiled and came down the ladder. "Thank you." She stood back and admired the eight-foot fir tree. It was filled with over a hundred beeswax candles, and there were twice as many glass ornaments from Germany and Austria. Amanda especially liked the twelve glass pipers that glistened in multicolored costumes. They were quite old and had belonged to Charles's mother.

"Lady Barbara's decorations were beautiful. Every year florists brought in armfuls of holy and ivy, and her tree was magnificent, but this tree is even more lovely. I can't explain it. . . ." Amanda said.

Sylvia smiled indulgently. "Perhaps it's because your heart was never in it before. This is your home now."

Amanda didn't know what it was, but she did feel differently about so many things this year. It was if she were a new person. Her old life seemed as if it had happened to someone else, and yet she'd only left London a few months ago. So much had changed. *She* had changed.

She shot down the image of Paul in her mind as if he were one of those clay pigeons she'd learned to annihilate. "Not on Christmas," she mumbled to herself as she turned to put the ornament boxes away. Amanda walked into the hallway when she heard the knock at the door.

Sylvia came to the doorway. "Who can that be? It's too late for deliveries. I'm not expecting anyone. Are you?"

"No." Amanda opened the door. It was a messenger. He handed her a large, flat package. Amanda tipped the man and closed the door.

"Who is it from?" Sylvia asked.

Amanda tore away the brown paper and found a huge, homemade Christmas card. Inside was a small pen-and-ink sketch of herself. It was from David Simon.

"It's very good," Sylvia said, looking at it. "I've seen some of his work, but this is better than most. But then, this," she said, pointing her finger at Amanda, "is my favorite subject. You told me you saw him at the ball. I had no idea he was this interested in you, my dear."

"Neither did I," Amanda said. "I'm impressed. He did this from memory. And except for two dances at the St. Nicholas Day Ball, I haven't seen or talked to him since. That's very odd behavior, don't you think?"

Sylvia smiled. "He's hoping you'll be as intrigued as he is."

Amanda looked at the little portrait again. It was uncanny how well he'd caught her likeness. She *was* intrigued. And flattered. "I'll have to thank Mr. Simon . . . properly. Perhaps we should have invited him to Christmas dinner. Surely he's made plans. . . ." She looked at Sylvia.

They both looked down at the portrait.

"Surely," Sylvia said.

After dawn services, Amanda telephoned David Simon at home and thanked him for his gift. She invited him to Christmas supper that evening at seven. To her amazement he accepted.

Sylvia Hendrickson's Christmas supper was an annual affair. For seventeen years she'd invited her closest friends, who in the beginning had all lived on or near Washington Square but who now lived on the Upper East Side. Only Sylvia Hendrickson's Christmas supper could steal New York's finest from their children on this night. Though she was not as wealthy as they, her position was not to be taken lightly. And to her credit, not one guest ever attended begrudgingly. They came out of love and admiration, not out of duty. This Christmas, however, had the added inducement that her ward, Amanda, had the town aflutter with gossip. There were no empty places at Sylvia's table that year.

Amanda wore a red-and-green plaid taffeta gown with a green velvet bustle and green velvet leg-o'-mutton sleeves. Julia had piled her hair into a perfect upsweep and decorated it with a tiny spring of holly. She wore Sylvia's emerald drop earrings and an emerald brooch at the neck. As Julia and two hired serving girls carried away the remains of the roast beef, David Simon raised his wineglass.

"I'd like to toast our marvelous hostess Sylvia for a Christmas none of us will soon forget."

"Hear, hear," came the response, and all drank.

Dana Gibson helped his wife Irene with her chair as they all rose and adjourned to the parlor for brandy. David smiled at Amanda as he took her arm. The Joneses, Crosbys, and Chandlers followed. They settled around the crackling fire, admiring the decorations, complimenting the hostess.

It was the first chance David had to speak to Amanda without everyone hearing him.

"I'm glad you like my gift. It was crude, just from memory. I could do so much more if I had the model. . . ."

Just then Irene Langhorn, who had been inspecting the tree, came over. "Amanda," she said, not realizing she had interrupted David, "I know you don't know me well—which I hope isn't always true—but I just wanted to tell you how grateful we all are for what you've done for Sylvia."

Amanda was confused. "What *I've* done?"

"Sylvia has always been one of my dearest friends. But I don't think I've seen her this full of life since Charles died. She's a strong woman, no one would refute that . . . it's just that ever since you've been here, it's as if she's found herself again. She has done so much for us—for New York—that, well, we'd like to thank you." She motioned to her husband to join her.

Dana Gibson, who'd been waiting for his wife's signal, arose.

Irene continued. "Dana and I thought that it would be a wonderful surprise if he painted your portrait and then gave it to Sylvia."

David immediately bristled.

Amanda's mouth dropped. *"You* want to paint *me?"* She'd never been so flattered. This was the man who'd made his wife the Gibson Girl. Dana Gibson painted only the most beautiful women in America. They were all tall, with wasp waists and hair in overstated upsweeps, and normally he depicted them with infatuated men groveling at their feet.

David's eyes flitted from Dana to Amanda to Irene. He couldn't believe this was happening. Dana Gibson was his competition—his only competition. Of all the artists he wanted to best, it was this man. David had known from the first day he'd seen Amanda that he'd finally found a woman to take Irene Langhorn's place. For three weeks he had tried to capture Amanda's essence on paper—and from memory to boot. He'd tossed out a hundred sketches before he'd mastered the one he'd sent her last night. He had tried to follow her around town, but she'd been so busy with her damn charity work that she'd eluded him most days. But it didn't matter. He'd accepted the invitation here tonight solely for the purpose of getting her permission to paint her. And now here was his nemesis, undermining his efforts, stealing his property, attempting to destroy his future.

"I couldn't agree with you more, Irene," David began, using his most charming smile, the one that had always worked. "But I'm a step ahead of you. I've already painted Amanda—a small sketch, to be sure. But I rather fancied doing a large oil of her myself. However, I would never want to usurp some territory that wasn't mine. . . ."

Dana, a bit flustered, answered: "I had no idea, David. Irene and I wanted something special for Sylvia, that's all. I suppose it doesn't much matter who paints her. Only that it be done."

David breathed a bit more easily. "Wonderful. It's decided then. I'll paint your portrait, Amanda."

Amanda knew she should be smiling back, but somehow she'd felt as if she'd just been bartered off, and she didn't like the feeling at all. However, she agreed with Dana. The painting was for Sylvia. She would do anything for Sylvia.

"I would be most pleased to sit for you, David."

"North of the Vanderbilts' and east of the park," was how David had given Amanda directions to his house. It was snowing the morning Amanda arrived. Only a few holiday decorations remained on those houses where there were not enough servants to store them on a timely basis, or where the owners had already left the city for winter resorts in Florida, South Carolina, and Georgia—houses whose taskmasters were lax.

Unlike Paul's house, David's brownstone was unassuming, spare even in its exterior simplicity. When she entered, though, she found all the crimson velvet plush and gilt that was popular in the era. The piano was draped with a deeply fringed shawl, and, in fact, she saw fringe on everything—draperies, club chairs, lamp shades. There was also a profusion of Moroccan-design fabrics on huge pillows adorned with gold tassels at the corners, on tablecloths, and on throws. This was the Bohemian style the artist colony embraced. However, David's ties to his society friends were clearly seen in the antique Chippendale chairs, the French settee, and the Viennese mirrors. It was a balancing act of the two worlds David inhabited, and like the unusual symmetry of the room, somehow he carried if off.

"You're beautiful . . . as always," he said as he helped her off with her coat, muff, and hat. "Come by the fire and warm yourself."

He instructed the housekeeper to bring hot tea. Amanda went to the fire and warmed her hands. David sat in a huge overstuffed chair. With hands knitted together, he rested his chin on them as his eyes studied her face, her form. She was perfection. Nothing less.

"Must you look at me like that?" Amanda asked. "I feel like some—foreign object."

"I'm sorry. I don't want to make you uncomfortable. Quite the contrary."

"Are we working in here?" she asked.

"No. In the studio. Upstairs. It's where I spend nearly all my time. Would you like to see it now?"

"Yes," she replied eagerly.

They mounted the stairs to the third floor, where there was a small landing, a narrow hall, and two doors. He opened the one straight ahead. They walked up four more steps.

Amanda entered a room whose ceiling was nearly all glass. It was covered over with a thin film of snow outside. The room had a soft white haze, and she had the feeling she was buried, yet she did not feel closed in. She felt—safe. She turned to David and smiled.

"It's wonderful here! I'd spend my time here too."

"I'm glad you like it. That's important for our work together."

She looked around at the easels, the stretched canvases waiting to be filled with imagination, with life. The end wall held six shelves with every conceivable color of paint in pots, tubes, buckets, and jars. There were hundreds of brushes and different-sized pallet knives.

"Where do I sit?"

"Here," he said, pointing to a thronelike chair made of alabaster, purple velvet, and gilt. It was near the left wall, where the sunlight filtered in through six windows.

As she sat down, he instantly came to her side, adjusting her skirts, turning her head this way and that. He turned her shoulders, tilted her chin up and then down. He turned her entire body to the other side so that she was facing the opposite wall.

He became increasingly frustrated. "It's not right. None of it!"

"I don't understand."

"Perhaps it's the chair. I thought—something regal—you being of royal blood and all—but it doesn't fit."

Amanda's back stiffened and she squirmed in the chair when he mentioned her bloodlines. It was there, wasn't it? she thought. The Lie was always trying to trip her up, show her hand.

"Drape your arm over the back casually," he said, standing back a pace. "Yes, better. Now tilt your head back and laugh."

She laughed.

"Now, pull one leg up onto the seat of the chair."

"Are you sure about this?" Amanda asked. She'd never seen anyone ever pose like this.

"Keep your skirts over your leg. Don't even let me see the shoe. Perfect! Insolence. Defiance—that's what I saw that afternoon. No, Amanda, don't frown at me. You were wonderful that day. Still are. Even more so," he babbled as he donned his smock and took out pen and paper.

His hand flew over the paper as he sketched. She watched him, thinking it impossible for anyone to work that fast. How odd he should create such a pose for her. And how right it was, and he didn't even know it. Sylvia would appreciate it though. A few moments later he handed her the sketch for her to look at while he started a second. It was amazing. With the regal chair behind her she was sprawled all over it, defying it, just as he'd said. It was as if he knew she didn't give a damn about society—its rules, it prohibitions.

In the respect they were very much alike—she and David Simon. He was born to a station that he defied through his life-style and his chosen vocation. He was fortunate, for bloodlines afforded him supplies, tools, and warm surroundings to work in, whereas many artists nearly starved. His connections with patrons of the arts in New York would always ensure a market for his work. She wondered why, with all the advantages at his disposal, he was not more renowned.

She looked down at the sketches he peeled off his tablet and let flutter at her feet. They were exquisite. They were genius.

Perspiration covered his brow as he sank to his knees next to her chair. His dark eyes were steady and pleading when he spoke.

"I've waited for someone like you to come along, Amanda. I knew you would be the *one*."

"What 'one'?"

"The model I needed to inspire me. You are my dream, I beg you to let me paint more than this one portrait for Sylvia. I'll pay you to sit for me. You have no idea what you can mean to my work. With you, I can become the artist I've always known I should be. Please, please say yes."

She looked at the sketches once again. They were better than anything she'd ever seen. Even better than Dana Gibson's. David was right. She had unleashed something here today. Even she could feel it. There was an energy in the room that hadn't existed when she'd walked in. She still couldn't believe that so much was owed to her. But she could see something, that elusive quality every painter strives for his life long; that something was there on the paper.

"Yes," she replied.

CHAPTER EIGHTEEN

By Easter the finished portrait hung over the mantle in Sylvia's parlor. By May, nearly all of Sylvia's friends—five hundred, if one used the roster from which she'd sent personal valentines in February, had been invited or invited themselves to see the painting. By June, David Simon's portrait of Amanda was famous, just as he'd predicted.

David worked feverishly on three more portraits of Amanda, all of which he placed in galleries, all of which sold at good prices. But it wasn't enough. If he worked twenty-four hours a day, it wouldn't be enough for David. Dana Gibson had an incredible head start; his sketches of the Gibson Girl were now being carried by newspapers and magazines across the Atlantic. David Simon had a long way to go before he could make such a claim. But he intended to do it if it killed him—and Amanda.

"But I can't sit today, David. I told you that last Wednesday Enough is enough."

"I'll double your fee. Just one more week."

"I could buy the Taj Mahal with the money I've made from you. I need a rest."

"You don't understand. The lighting this time of year at twilight is perfect. And I need some sketches of you near the docks. . . ."

"You're obsessed, David. No!"

He relaxed a bit. He was getting nowhere. "All right. What is it that *you* want to do?"

"I want to help Sylvia and her committee."

He slapped his forehead with his hand. "Jesus! Another charity?"

"But I like this work. All I have to do for you is not move. I want to move, David. And think and create. I have those needs too, you know."

He smiled indulgently. He had to be careful with Amanda. Working with her for six months had taught him that. She had a mind of her own and usually when she'd set it—he was in trouble. Difficult was hardly the word to describe her when she got like this.

"Create? What will you create?" he said patronizingly.

"I'm doing the entire promotional campaign for the Fourth of July charity picnic. I know it doesn't sound like much, but I'm pretty good at slogans and copy material for the posters and newspaper ads—now that Sylvia has discovered my idea for paid advertisement works," she said defensively. "I've always liked writing. This kind of writing appeals to me very much. But ever since I started modeling, I've barely been able to write in my journal."

He watched her chew the bottom of her lip as she looked out the window of the ice cream parlor. She jammed her straw into her chocolate soda, then stirred the contents. He noticed that she didn't take the first sip. It had been her idea to come here. She was more angry than he'd thought.

He took her hand and caressed it. "Truce. We'll compromise. Maybe I need a break too. You do your work for Sylvia. But I get one day—Tuesdays—"

"Not Tuesdays. Wednesdays," she said.

"Wednesdays," he conceded. "We'll skip the oils for now and just do some sketches. I've got a few ideas of my own and need to spend some time away from the easel to promote them. Is it a deal?"

She smiled. "Deal."

Amanda put together a fabulous Art Nouveau poster to announce the picnic. She also created the special invitations that were to be sent to the city's most elite homes. Pre-picnic ticket sales had never been as high, nor had there ever been quite as much "talk" about the picnic. Amanda helped Sylvia in every area she could. They were beginning to garner a reputation for spearheading creative, exciting, and *profitable* fund-raising events.

Amanda learned quickly what it had taken Sylvia nearly twenty years to learn as she'd climbed the rungs of New York society.

She knew what florists to use, which orchestras, caterers, bakeries, and distilleries to contact for the best prices without sacrificing quality. For charity, one did not employ "popular" vendors and service people; they were too expensive. She knew which volunteers would actually work and which ones were only glory seekers. She made certain the latter never got what they came for. She organized and reorganized the subcommittees until only three phone calls in the morning would give her an update on everything she needed to know about the picnic. Sylvia commented that things had never run as smoothly.

On Wednesdays Amanda sat for David, who, once he was resigned to their weekly date, seemed quite happy with the arrangement. He was busy with other matters himself, he said.

The Fourth of July, 1895, dawned like a firecracker. By eleven o'clock it was nearly ninety-five degrees. But Amanda was un-ruffled. Wearing a white cotton skirt and blouse trimmed in red and blue ribbons, with sashes and hand embroidery around the hem, she set out for the picnic site with Sylvia.

"The Bronsons were wonderful to donate their Long Island estate this year," Sylvia said. "I didn't much like having the picnic in Central Park like we did last year. It's too difficult to keep a head count."

The Bronson estate stood majestically on a hill overlooking the gently rolling bay waters. English Tudor in style, it reminded Amanda very much of London, but as they alighted from the carriage and were ushered by the butler to the "grounds," she knew she'd never seen anything like this in London.

Over fifteen acres of rolling, lush lawns extended out and down to the water. The area was heavily studded with enormous hundred-year-old sugar maples, oaks, and walnut trees.

There were seven red-and-white-striped tents under which were round tables, each seating ten. Each table was skirted in white cotton and each was centered with huge baskets of red, white, and blue flowers and tiny American flags.

Behind huge smokers stood volunteers, men and women, clad in aprons as they grilled hot dogs and chicken. There was huge pots of Boston baked beans and chilled potato salad—a summer's feast for the price of a quarter.

Around the perimeter of the area were carnival booths, each set up to make money. One sold pies, another sold corn on the cob, another sold watermelon, and still others sold handmade quilts, lacework, aprons, and wooden toys. There was an ice-cream booth, a photographer's booth, and a kissing booth. In one booth a man would cut out a silhouette of the customer in black paper and paste it onto a sheet of white for a nickel. In another booth, for the price of a dime, any well-muscled young man could try to knock over a stack of weighted wooden milk bottles and win a Kewpie doll for his lady.

It all turned out just as Amanda had wanted. Except for the Ferris wheel this was as close to a re-creation of Coney Island as she could get. Already the grounds were filling up with excited children anxious to play ring toss, dart games, and games of chance.

Between the shade from the trees and the breeze off the bay, no one seemed to mind the high temperatures. By two o'clock every table under the tents was occupied and Amanda was scurrying around trying to find blankets to place under the trees for the crowd that continued to pour in.

She had just come from the house, where Mrs. Bronson had her entire household staff stripping beds—they were using sheets now, since all the blankets were taken—when David walked up.

He stood with her on the terrace overlooking the throng. Her face was filled with elation and triumph. She looked magnificent, the wind whipping tiny golden tendrils around her face. Every time he looked at her, he felt as if he was going into shock. Was it possible for a woman to become more beautiful every day? He wondered what she would look like a year from now, five, ten. . . . He also knew he wasn't the only man to see it either.

He took the stack of sheets from her. "Looks as if you could use some help."

"Isn't it wonderful? Sylvia says we've doubled our projected goal already. And there seems no sign of it stopping. I don't know where they're all coming from."

"They came to see you."

Amanda's smile vanished. "Honestly, David. I hardly think these people care a whit about this face you paint."

"Maybe they don't, but I do." They walked down the steps and across the lawn to where Ethel, one of the young volunteers, was waiting for the sheets.

"I hope these help, Ethel," Amanda said as four families waited with loaded plates.

David took Amanda's arm. "Just to show you what a good fellow I am, I came here to help."

"No!" She laughed.

"I'm crushed. You have so little faith in me."

"How's your arm?" She squeezed his muscle. "Just right. I think I have exactly the job for you."

They walked over to the ice-cream booth. "Samuel, this is David. He wanted to help make ice cream." She smiled coyly at David. David rolled his eyes.

Samuel was drenched in sweat, his sleeves rolled up past his elbows. He wiped his face with a wet towel. "I could use some help."

"But Amanda—" David pleaded. Resolutely, he took the crank. He'd never done anything like this for anyone . . . any woman. He couldn't believe he was doing it now. But Amanda wasn't just any woman.

Christine Whitley took Paul's arm as he helped her out of the coach. They followed her mother, Thalia, around the brick walkway to the Bronson mansion to the picnic in back.

Christine knew she would be seeing Amanda today and so she'd taken incredible pains with her outfit, her hair, and her understated but expensive jewels. She had to be perfect, more perfect than Amanda. She had cajoled her mother into buying the two-hundred-dollar silk and organza dress she wore. Christine knew every one of her mother's weaknesses and which ones she could manipulate to her advantage. First and foremost was Paul. Thalia would do anything to make certain this engagement of Christine's resolved itself in a marriage. Paul was taking his sweet time, but Christine wasn't worried. She knew eventually she would be his wife. She was still one of the five truly beautiful women in New York. And three of them were already married. Except for Amanda Granger, a newcomer, Christine had no competition. In the meantime, she would use this time to wheedle more clothes and jewels from her mother and more favors from their friends who thought she was being abused by Paul. The only real threat Christine felt was that from Amanda.

Christine didn't trust Paul's protestations that he was not seeing Amanda. She didn't really care if he did or not, as long as no one found out about it. Christine never, never wanted to look the fool again. The weeks after their first encounter with Amanda had been difficult for Christine. But she'd weathered them, and many of her mother's friends had stated that Christine had acted with propriety and a cool head. Thalia was proud. She bought Christine the Balmain gown she'd seen in Paris that fall.

What Christine didn't like was having a rival. Christine was not considered a "smart" girl. However, she was wise enough to recognize this fault: Christine was insecure about her position in society. She needed this marriage to Paul to catapult her to the top.

Christine Whitley's father had never been good enough for her mother. Thalia Whitley had commented on it nearly every day while he was alive and at least twice weekly since he had died six years ago. Thalia had come from one of the oldest New York families. She had married Garrison Whitley in a moment of passion. They met while on vacation in the Adirondacks, and, while standing next to glistening Mirror Lake, he had proposed and she had accepted. It was the one and only time in her life Thalia had let her emotions rule her judgement. The marriage cost Thalia greatly when measuring her social standing. A marriage to one of the Howards, Roberts, or Cuttings would have been more appropriate. Her father took Garrison into his law firm and gave him a respectable business name. And for the rest of their years together, Thalia spent every moment striving to better her lost social position.

Christine was raised on the credo that her social position was her mind, body, and soul. She felt the same ambitions her mother did. She wanted to be the hostess whose name fell from everyone's lips with reverence. She wanted *her* parties to be the most well attended. She wanted to know that the absence of an invitation from Christine Whitley could send a young matron into depression or cause a young debutante to throw angry tantrums. It was too easy for her to name the times she'd been snubbed and left out. Christine had always been indulged by both her parents—her father especially. He was easier to manipulate than her mother. She'd found that men did not disguise their weaknesses as well as women did. Women, being in competition with each other all their lives, had too many years practicing deceit. Christine's indulgent past had taught her one thing—that she liked it—and she intended that society should cater to her, just as her father had.

Marrying Paul, then, was essential to her plan. As his wife, she would be a dictator of style and trends. Caroline Astor would beg to come to her parties.

She'd heard the rumors about the Van Volkien will, but she didn't trust them. She couldn't be *that* lucky. Christine liked the easy way, but that was too easy. And if she truly had a rival in Amanda she needed to know it now. That was why she'd insisted they attend this charity picnic. Amanda had kept herself so busy with David Simon that she hadn't been seen much of anywhere all winter and spring—at least not anywhere Christine had been. Christine couldn't be sure about Paul.

She watched him out of the corner of her eye as he scanned the crowd. Was he looking for her?

Thalia turned to Christine. "I see Caroline," she said with the breathlessness of one who wants but does not have. "If you'll excuse me," she said to Paul.

Thalia lumbered over the steps and down to the tent where the Astors, the Roosevelts, and the Chandlers were seated.

Amanda instructed the caterer to haul out a dozen more chickens and cut them up. She could see no slowing of the demand. She started toward Sylvia, but before she did, she looked over to see David churning merrily away at the strawberry ice cream. She turned around and came face-to-face with Paul and Christine.

She hadn't seen either of them since *that* day. She was surprised after all this time that her heart could leap to her throat that fast. She felt the blood pulsating in her head.

"Christine," she said pleasantly. "And Paul. I'm glad you could come today."

Paul smiled, and when he did, she remembered the way he'd looked at her that first night. She felt a tear sting her eye, but the breeze dried it.

"You look wonderful," he said wistfully as his eyes delved into hers. Then he remembered himself. "Doesn't Amanda look . . . fit?" he asked Christine.

Charm oozed from her lips as Christine replied: "Yes. Like a little flag, all in red, white, and blue."

Amanda could feel Christine's hate seething beneath the surface. And well it should be, Amanda thought. What she didn't understand was Christine's willingness to stand in the fire. Why wasn't she tugging at Paul's arm, wanting to leave?

"You have a remarkable turnout, Amanda," Christine continued. "I mean, it was quite a drive from the city."

"None of us was prepared, but I'm glad. I think we'll nearly triple our expectations. And that's what we're all here for, isn't it—*Charity?*" Amanda said pointedly.

Paul pulled at his collar. He was getting nervous. He knew what a spitfire Amanda could be, and for some reason Christine was prepared to spar. He didn't like any of this.

"How's David? We haven't seen much of either of you."

"Were you looking?" Amanda quipped, but then noticed the tension in Paul's face. This was difficult for him. She was almost glad. "I only pose for the man. He's a gifted artist and I believe in his work. But he is *not* my escort."

"Really?" Christine pointed to the tent where David was making ice cream. "Don't I see him over there?"

Amanda was becoming incensed. "He believes in the cause as much as I do."

This time Paul had to laugh. "David Simon has never done anything charitable in his life. Amanda, if you've truly managed to alter David's personality, make a human being out of him, every one in New York will pay you homage."

Amanda lifted her chin. "You don't think I could?"

Christine chuckled but frowned when she saw the intensity in Paul's face.

He paused for a moment. "I think you could do anything."

Christine opted for retrenchment. "Come, Paul. Let's talk to David."

Amanda watched as Christine pulled Paul away. She turned around, walked to an empty chair, and slumped into it. She felt as if she had just come out of battle. Sylvia walked up behind her. She placed a hand on Amanda's shoulder.

"Are you all right?"

"You saw?"

"Only I and two hundred others sitting ringside. You handled yourself and the situation beautifully."

"It was strange seeing him after all these months. All I could think about were those days on the ship. . . . How long before I forget?"

"Maybe never. I know you don't want to hear that, but it's true. First loves are difficult to get over. They last until a new love comes along."

"A new love? I'm never going to be that stupid again. No, Sylvia. I'm going to be much smarter about love from now on."

Amanda rose purposefully and placed her social smile back on her lips where it was supposed to be. She looked over at David, who was watching her. She waved and he smiled back. He started churning the ice cream again, and this time he was whistling.

"Yes, I'm going to be much, much smarter," Amanda promised herself.

David had been pacing outside Sylvia's door since dawn, when the first editions had hit the newsstands. He nervously smoked a cigar and choked on the smoke. He didn't normally smoke until evening, but he hadn't slept in two days, and his days and nights had all run together. He glanced at his watch. It was only seven-thirty. He put the watch back in his vest pocket and looked up at the bedroom windows. The draperies were still closed.

"Christ! Doesn't she know what today is?" He sat on the step for only a moment; then, too anxious, he rose and resumed his pacing. He'd never realized how quiet New York could be until this morning. It was as if the whole city had died. Especially Washington Square. He hated the silence. He felt as if he were being ignored—he looked at the window again—as if Amanda were ignoring him. He slammed his fist into his palm. How could she sleep at a time like this?

Just then he saw the draperies part.

He raced up the steps and banged the brass knocker four times, then another four times. He heard the window above him opening.

"David? What are you doing down there?"

"Amanda!" He took a step back and waved the magazines over his head. "They're out! Don't you want to see?"

She broke into a grin. "I'll be right down."

Amanda grabbed a lacy summer robe, jammed her feet into her slippers, and knocked on Sylvia's door. She cracked it open and stuck her head in. Sylvia pushed herself up on her elbows.

"David's here! Hurry!"

"Tell Julia to fix coffee! How can I greet guests when I haven't had my coffee?" Sylvia groaned.

Julia, dressed but still not quite awake, opened the door for David as Amanda came racing down the stairs. "Coffee's finished," Julia said in her usual stoic tones. Amanda wondered when she would get used to Julia's psychic abilities.

"David! What did you think?"

"I haven't even looked."

What? How could you control yourself?"

"You seemed pretty calm—sleeping," he teased as he handed her a copy of the September issue of *Harper's Magazine*.

Amanda tore through the pages as they went into the salon. She sank onto the settee. Suddenly, she stopped.

"A whole page I . . . I can't believe it."

David was about to burst with pride. "And they'd told us only half a page. They must have really liked it. Do you think they really liked it?" He was afraid he was seeing a mirage.

"Let me see *The Delineator,*" she demanded. She opened it and here, too, her face filled a whole page. "You're a miracle worker," she said breathlessly.

He took the magazine and inspected it.

Three months of begging, pleading, and cajoling just to get the editors of *Harper's* and *The Delineator* to look at his work had finally culminated in more than he'd dreamed—at least at this point in his career. He'd known he'd get there sooner or later. But he also knew how tough it was breaking into the magazines— especially when all he'd heard for four years had been: "Sorry, we don't need anyone else but Dana Gibson," and, "The Gibson Girl is all any publisher needs to insure sales."

Finally, David had convinced two publishers that the market was ready for something new, something fresh. And he'd given them Amanda. But it had been Amanda's idea to call herself The Granger Woman.

She was beautiful, sophisticated, and fashion conscious. But above all, she was adventurous. Whereas Gibson sketched his models outdoors, playing croquet or tennis or fishing, David went a step further. He sketched Amanda moving within society but always poking fun at it. The sketch in *Harper's* had Amanda riding in a hot-air balloon above a sedate garden party. *The Delineator* had chosen David's sketch of Amanda wearing a captain's uniform on board a yacht. It was one he hadn't particularly liked, although he agreed with the editor that he'd captured Amanda's independent spirit. It was that same independence that kept Amanda outside his grasp.

David's kind of lampoon could easily backfire on him. New Yorkers might think he wasn't taking them seriously enough. It was a big gamble. And he hadn't won—yet. The final verdict would come from the sales figures.

Amanda shoved the magazines into his hand. "I'll get dressed right away. There's no time to waste."

"What are you talking about?"

"We'll go up to Herald Square and see what people are buying. We'll talk to the newsboys. I have to know."

Within two days every copy of *Harper's* and *The Delineator* had disappeared from the newsstands in the city. Rather than that being a good sign, Amanda soon learned that it could be a bad one too.

"Curiosity?" she asked. "They would buy simply out of curiosity? I hadn't thought of that."

"Max says he won't know until next month if they liked us or just wanted to see what all the ruckus was about," David explained." We may be in big trouble."

"But the good sign is that both magazines want your sketches for another issue."

David's face showed no elation. "What good is that if I never get published again?"

"Maybe we should have kept to a tried-and-true formula."

"And always be second-best? Never! I think the gain is worth the risk. I couldn't stand it if everyone said I could never do any better than to copy Dana Gibson."

Amanda was pleased when he talked like this. His eyes flashed with determination—something she knew a great deal about. She uncoiled herself from the floor where he had her posed in an Indian turban sitting on a cushion playing the flute to a rubber cobra.

"David, you're worrying too much about this. All we've done is work for the past three weeks. If you aren't meeting with publishers, you're painting or divising some costume for me to wear for yet another sketch. Can't we have some fun?"

He put his brush down slowly and looked at her. For nine months he'd kept her at arm's length but always in his sight. She had no idea how closely he watched her itineraries. He made it his business to know exactly which charity she was working on, what parties she was invited to, and if there was any possibility that Paul would be around. Amanda was David's business—his only business; without her, he knew he wouldn't have come this far. He had to protect his investment.

David also knew that until Amanda was completely over Paul,

it would be disaster on his part to make a move for her. When the time came for him to propose he wanted to make certain she wouldn't turn him down. For now, they were both comfortable with their working relationship. She considered them to be friends. And *he* made certain that everyone knew it was strictly business between them. He couldn't afford to have Amanda's name blackened.

However, David also knew he couldn't wait forever. After all, he wasn't made of steel. He didn't know many men who could work with so beautiful a woman day after day and not go insane. He'd never wanted a woman so much, but he had to be sure.

"Fun? What kind of fun?" he asked.

"Sylvia has extra tickets to that new revue you wanted to see."

"I'd like that," he said moving very close to her face and letting his eyes probe hers.

They stood for a long moment, saying nothing, asking a million mental questions of one another. But David didn't kiss her, though he wanted to, and Amanda waited for his kiss as she had for so many weeks. She didn't take the initiative, but she didn't back away.

CHAPTER NINETEEN

Caroline Astor's Halloween masquerade ball was held at Delmonico's, where the best taste prevailed. Three rows of gold, crimson, and rust chrysanthemums lined the sidewalk along the Fifth Avenue side. At the main entrance on Forty-fourth Street, there were four valets dressed in yellow satin pants, black top hats, and tails. When guests arrived they were ushered into the Palm Garden, where tropical palms, banana trees, and plants brushed against the floor-to-ceiling windows. The Elizabethan Oak Cafe was transformed into the bar, where the drinks were served, and the dancing took place in the third-floor ballroom directly above the dining rooms, where its rich, muted tones created a serene backdrop for the wildly colorful costumes and Halloween decorations.

Amanda wore a white, blue, red, and yellow satin harlequin gown she'd had especially made. She had wanted to wear real pantaloons, but Sylvia, and David too, had thought that a bit risqué. Maybe next year.

Now that the October magazine issues had sold out and David's sketches had been purchased for November, Amanda believed that it was a good time for him to pull back and relax. David thought otherwise.

It was becoming increasingly apparent to Amanda that David's obsession with Dana Gibson would not go away. There were many times she wondered if David would paint at all if it weren't for trying to best Dana.

That night as she watched Irene Langhorn and Dana Gibson weave in and out of the crowd, she noticed how serene they were. Perhaps that was the measure of success. Dana didn't need to feel that cutting edge that David seemed to nurture. The Gibsons had proven they were the couple to emulate. Amanda watched how eyes, both male and female, glanced appreciatively at them. If a monarchy were possible in America, Dana and Irene Gibson would reign.

Amanda took a glass of champagne and smiled at David. She did not realize as she did so that the same eyes that admired the Gibsons were now looking to Amanda and David as their new prince and princess.

"Hello, Amanda," Christine's voice purred. "And David. It's a wonderful party, isn't it? But then, Caroline's affairs always are," she said as if she'd never missed one her life long.

"Yes," Amanda replied. Paul looked older . . . or more tired. She'd heard he was having a difficult time running his father's investments. Word was he'd forsaken his days of spending money and lately become fascinated with making it. She hoped it was true. The lines around his eyes were honestly earned then. Christine was dressed as Marie Antoinette. An appropriate choice, Amanda thought, not too kindly.

Just then Dana Gibson walked up. He slapped David on the back.

"Let me shake your hand, David. Those sketches of yours are genius. I know I couldn't have done any better."

"Thank you," David said, wishing Dana wouldn't be so magnanimous. He didn't want to like the man.

Irene interrupted. "Perhaps you should have Amanda sit for you, dear," she said to Gibson.

Christine gasped. This was almost insulting. It was bad enough Amanda was gaining fame. Just this week, Christine had noted that the society columns were giving Amanda more space than they were her.

"I'm afraid there's only one Granger Woman. And I'm it. I sit only for David."

David smiled, Christine sighed with relief, and Dana frowned.

"I understand," Dana said.

Christine's reactions had gone unnoticed by everyone except Irene. "Christine, perhaps you'd like to sit for Dana?"

Dana nodded in agreement. "A good choice. I have something coming up for Christmas for *Collier's Weekly* that you'd be perfect for."

Christine beamed, but only because she didn't want everyone

to see her disappointment. Again she was second choice—a position she couldn't tolerate.

"It would be an honor," Christine replied.

"Wonderful. I'll telephone you and make arrangements," Dana said as he and Irene excused themselves.

Paul ground his jaws. "A triumph for you, Christine. Let's get some champagne and celebrate." He hurried her away, knowing he couldn't stand being this close to Amanda. He was in control only when he didn't see her.

By midnight the party began to wind down, even though over two hundred guests remained. David had found a representative from Scribner's publishing company. He had plans to put together a book of his collected sketches, and he believed this was as good a time as any to approach a publisher.

Amanda went to the roof conservatory above the third-floor ballroom where she could cool off. She stared off into the distance . . . toward London.

It seemed like a lifetime since she'd left home, and it was only a year. But what a year! A year ago she'd never believed—well, not actually believed—that she could impersonate a Lady. But she had. There wasn't a single soul in New York who had ever doubted her. She'd even found a way to work within propriety and yet maintain her own personality. All of this was due a great deal to Sylvia and David. Sylvia had given Amanda the credentials and David had shown her the way to make it all work.

When she went shopping or had lunch she could hear people whispering about her or pointing at her. Only this time it wasn't because she was from the slums. It was because she was The Granger Woman.

Amanda was immersed in her thoughts and didn't hear the door open. Paul stood for just a moment before speaking. He could not resist being with her again, but he wanted to catch her alone, unaware. That was why he'd followed her up here.

"Long way from home, isn't it?"

Amanda whirled around. "How did you know what I was thinking?"

"I read tarot cards too." He laughed and walked over to her. "Maybe I was just thinking of the same thing."

"What?"

"That is was a year ago today that we met. I'll never forget you shooting at those clay pigeons. I think you went through all the shells on board. Or trying to beat me at gin. I should have told you I've been playing since I was six." He moved closer. "I know I could never forget anything about you, Amanda. Ever . . ."

He kissed her and she let him. She had to know if she still felt anything for him or if all that remained were ashes of a few memories. He put his arms around her and crushed her to his chest. For him all the passion remained. He kissed her cheeks and eyes and ears. But Amanda remembered all too easily his lies and deceit. And when he held her, she knew then he was clinging only to a dream.

"Happy birthday, darling," he said.

"You do remember well," she said as she let her arms fall.

Paul didn't notice. "Oh, Amanda. you don't know how hard it's been for me to see you with David. I've tried to fight my feelings for you, but it's no good. I don't love Christine. I never did. I love you. I don't care about anything anymore except you and me. I came up here tonight because I want to ask you to marry me."

"Why has it taken you a whole year to decide this?"

"Just stupidity, I guess."

Amanda's eyes narrowed. "Or greed. I think the only reason you want me now is because you've found a way to have me and your precious money. Isn't that it? A year ago, I wasn't good enough for you—at least, I wouldn't get you what you really wanted. Now you're ready to toss Christine aside and come back to me. It won't work, Paul." Before he could answer, Amanda stalked out of the conservatory.

Dejectedly, Paul followed her out. As he closed the door, he did not notice the rustle of palms on the far right side next to a white wicker chair.

Christine walked out from her hiding place, eyes blazing with angry tears. She was glad no one else was around to see her humiliation. For the rest of her life she would never forget this Halloween, when twice she'd had to take second place to Amanda Granger.

"So help me God, it will be the last."

David's proposal came precisely two weeks after Paul's, but this time Amanda's answer was in the affirmative.

"I've thought about this a great deal," she said to Sylvia the following morning at breakfast. "David and I are perfectly suited.

We both have artistic talents; we're both ambitious and hard-working, and we work very well together.''

"And you think that's a sound basis for a marriage?"

Amanda thought about the rocky emotions she'd experienced with Paul. "Yes, I certainly do. David will provide well for me; he's from a good background. He's never been unkind. . . . He's everything a husband should be." Amanda knew this time she was right. Everything Harriet had taught her, every criterion she knew, told her that David was husband material.

"What about love?"

"I do love David. I care very much about him, about his well-being. And he cares about me."

"Oh, I don't doubt that. David can't let you out of his sight. But as to whether a one-sided love makes a good marriage or not . . ."

"Will you hush about this? My mind is made up. Everyone in this town has expected me to marry David for almost a year. Now they're getting their wish."

"But are you getting yours?"

"Yes," Amanda said flatly. She wished Sylvia would stop these questions. This was one time when she didn't want to think so much.

Amanda's engagement to David Simon was announced two days prior to Christine Whitley's engagement to Paul Van Volkien. Although Christine received more column space than Amanda did, she was still not pleased. In Christine's mind, she had been bested once again.

Both weddings took place in December: Christine's on the twentieth and Amanda's on the twenty-eighth.

Thalia Whitley's planning did not go wasted. Her daughter's wedding, with fifteen bridal attendants all dressed in burgundy velvet gowns and carrying white roses on white ermine muffs—provided by the bride's family, of course—and five hundred guests in attendance at the lavish reception at the Waldorf Hotel, would not see a rival for decades.

When Amanda married David in a quiet ceremony at David's house, with a small wedding breakfast for a hundred guests at the New Netherland Hotel, everyone complimented the bride on her "good taste" and "restraint when others had allowed weddings to become a three-ring circus that rivaled Mr. Barnum's."

Amanda received three inches more column space than Christine in the *New York Herald;* four inches more in the *Times;* and *Harper's Bazaar* ran David's sketch of his bride in full bridal gown and veil for their January issue.

Dana Gibson's sketch of Christine Whitley did not appear in *Collier's* until February, after they'd utilized their entire inventory of Gibson sketches.

Book II

MURDER

CHAPTER TWENTY

London, 1896

Andrew kissed the end of Lucy's taut nipple before helping her back into her corset. She held onto the bedpost as he yanked at the strings that would make her waist a mere handspan of seventeen inches. Was it imagination or was it harder to tie these lacings? he wondered.

"I read about your sister's marriage in the newspaper," Lucy said as she simultaneously held her breath and sucked in her stomach.

"What of it?"

"She's getting to be quite famous and all, isn't she?"

"I suppose," he said, finishing and then stepping into his pants.

"It must have been a lovely party. I think our wedding will be just as lovely, don't you?"

Andrew tried to hide his frown. Now that Amanda's fame was growing in America he'd found the backlash of it had helped him—even in London. Just two weeks ago, Mr. Jackson's daughter had lingered after picking up her father's ledgers. She wanted to talk to Andrew. Samantha Jackson was rich, far richer than Lucy Attington could ever dream of being. It didn't take Andrew long, either, to realize that Samantha found him irresistible. She invited him to a party at her home. And he'd gone. It was in a neighborhood not far from the Kents, and most of the guests knew of Lord Kent, though none of them were of the same social standing. Still, it was a giant step up for Andrew. For the first time, he realized he didn't need Lucy.

"Andrew," she said, putting her bare arms around his waist as he buttoned his shirt. "I'm so glad we didn't wait any longer. I couldn't stand not having you."

"Ummm," he said, wondering how he would break their date for Saturday, when Samantha had asked him to accompany her to the opera. Mr. Jackson had actually encouraged Samantha. Andrew could kick himself for wasting nearly two years with Lucy and her overly strict father.

Lucy pulled on her skirt and fastened it. Andrew turned around just as the button popped off. He looked at her quizzically.

She smiled sheepishly. "Too many chocolates, I guess."

Andrew put on his shoes. "We'd better hurry. I don't want your father raising a ruckus about how late I keep you out."

Lucy slipped into a velvet bolero jacket, and again Andrew noticed how tightly her clothes fit.

"Father won't say anything to you—I promise. Especially not since . . ." she started, but as usual her tongue got all twisted up in her mouth and she lost her words along with her nerve.

"Since when?"

"I told him that you and I were getting married on Valentine's Day with or without his consent."

Andrew shot to his feet. "You did what?"

"I told you I couldn't wait any more. And you do want to marry me, don't you?"

"Well, yes. But I would never go against your father's wishes. What did he say about the dowry?"

"Nothing. Besides, I don't give a fig about that dowry. We love each other, Andrew. What do we care about money?"

"What do we . . . ? Are you out of your mind?" A lunatic, that's what Lucy was. How could she be so stupid? He wanted to shake her by the shoulders; instead he tried to calm himself. He saw the vision of Samantha Jackson begin to fade. "Tell me why you did this, Lucy. Why, after all these years, suddenly you give your father an ultimatum."

Before she opened her mouth, he knew.

"I'm pregnant."

"Jesus." He sank onto the bed and ran his hand through his tousled hair. "This isn't happening."

"Oh, Andrew. You don't hate me, do you? I didn't know how to tell you. I've tried. But I couldn't. I was just so scared. It seemed so . . . common."

"How long?"

"I'm three months gone."

"Three months . . . oh, God."

Lucy was frantic. "Andrew, don't talk like this. It isn't the end of the world. We'll get married just as we'd always planned. It won't be any different."

"Different? How naive can you be, Lucy? Of course everything is different know. Your father will never give us his blessing . . . there won't be any dowry . . . no job in his firm . . . no inheritance when he dies. God, it's over. My dream is over. . . ."

"Andrew, you aren't making any sense. What dream?"

Andrew looked at her; there were tears in her eyes, and she was frightened. He had to control himself. He was still in shock. And he knew he shouldn't make decisions without thinking things through. Perhaps there was still a way for him to get what he wanted. Maybe Lucy's father wasn't all the ogre he pretended to be.

"It's all right, Lucy. We'll get through this thing together. I promise. Come on. I'll take you home and then we'll talk again tomorrow. Don't say anything about this to your family just yet."

"I won't."

"Good." He picked up his coat. "It's going to be fine. Just fine."

Andrew checked the room one last time before they walked out. Just as he was about to close the door, he could almost swear he heard Samantha Jackson laughing at him.

Harriet Granger pulled the threadbare comforter up to her waist as she repositioned herself under the lamp. She wanted to finish this entry in her diary before Andrew got home. She liked using this time of night to reread her letters from Amanda or to write ones to New York. Now that Amanda was married, Harriet had begun thinking about going to America herself. Amanda had said she would send passage money, but something was holding Harriet back.

For years she had imagined how easy it would be for her to go to America and start over in just the way Amanda had, but now that the opportunity was here, she found it wasn't easy at all.

As much as she despised Shelton Street, this was her home. She would miss old Mrs. Jenkins, her friends at work, Mrs. Bird at her haberdashery, and of course Georgia, whom she saw more often now that Amanda was gone than when she was at home. But most of all, she would miss *him*.

When Harriet wrote in her diary these days, there was nothing to tell of the lovers whom she had used for Amanda's passage. She no longer needed their money, and though a couple wanted to continue seeing her, she explained why she'd done what she had and they understood. Harriet's life now was a series of long days at work studded with a rendezvous a few times a month with the only man she could ever care about. He'd made certain there was enough money for Amanda—enough money for her—if she wanted to go to New York. But for now, she didn't.

She didn't hear or see the door open and Andrew come in. She got up and walked across the cold floor to the bureau. She pulled out the false-bottom drawer and slipped the diary among the stacks of Amanda's letters.

"Almost as important as money to you, isn't she?" he asked.

She turned around. "You both are," she said smoothly, shutting the drawer. She must remember to put the diary back in its hiding place under the floorboards. There were things in it she didn't want Andrew to see.

"What have you heard from my dear sister?" he asked with a snide tone in his voice.

Harriet had noticed that since Amanda's departure, Andrew had become increasingly tense. Whenever she mentioned Amanda, Andrew never let the moment pass without a derogatory comment. Harriet felt as if she were forever defending her daughter and trying to restrain her son. He'd always been jealous of Amanda because of the bounties the Kents had bestowed upon her. Harriet thought it curious that precisely when Andrew should have been more relaxed about his position and have a better sense of himself, he was still battling his sister.

Harriet went past him into the kitchen and put a pot of water on to boil. "Amanda writes that she's moved into David's house and says she has been redecorating. There have been lots of parties, but mostly it sounds to me as if all they do is work."

"I don't believe it. Rich people don't work."

"That's not true. I know a lot of wealthy people who work—and very hard too."

"You know so many . . ."

"A few . . ."

"I'll bet you do at that." He sneered at her. He hated the way Harriet's voice lifted when she talked of Amanda. He wanted her to remember that she was still a part of the slums.

Harriet ignored him—again. It seemed to her that Andrew had grown increasingly hostile toward her ever since Amanda left. He was evasive about his activities and always on the defensive. They never conversed anymore, only argued. Everyday pleasantries were a partially sealed Pandora's box of animosity.

"What's the matter, Andrew?" she asked, pouring herself a cup of tea.

He noticed that she didn't offer him a cup. It was just like her . . . to think only of herself. "Nothing is the matter," he said grinding his jaws and reaching for a cup. He poured the tea and downed it like it was whiskey. He wondered what it would have been like to have been Harriet's only child. Would she have given him more attention? Would she have loved him more? In his mind he believed that all that had been Amanda's—the clothes, the tutors, the exposure to the wealthy—by rights should have been his. After all, he was a man, the namesake. But he was a Granger . . . a name he despised.

Andrew realized then and there what was the matter. He hated his mother because she had chosen her husband so badly. Being beautiful in her youth, she could have married better, but she'd been stupid and had not thought of the repercussions—ones that would determine *his* life. He knew the kind of men she attracted—rich men, men with influence. How incredibly selfish she'd been not to plan for the future. She'd saddled him with the Granger name and thus burdened him with the responsibility of carving a future for himself, when he could have just as easily been born to privilege.

Harriet could almost see his mind whirling. Though she didn't understand him, he was still her son. She wanted things to be right between them. "Please talk to me, Andrew. Maybe I can help."

He scoffed at her. "You never have before."

"That's not true!"

"I see no sense in becoming buddies when you'll be leaving soon."

"Leaving?"

"Amanda said she'd send for you when she got married. Christ! I still can't believe how easy she's had it. She sails off and before we know it, she's married some rich fellow who makes her into a public goddess. My sister! It's unbelievable.''

"I'm proud of her too."

"Proud? She didn't do anything for all that. She didn't have to work at it like I've had to. It's always come easy for Amanda. Always . . . hasn't it, Mum?''

She watched him guardedly. His anger seemed to heat the air around them. "I don't understand, Andrew. I thought things were going well for you. I noticed your betting business is on the rise. You'll be a rich man yourself.''

He glared at her. She had the familiar air of disdain when she talked about his bookmaking. How could she, a whore, be so judgmental? He would never earn her respect. He knew that now.

"And how is *your* business, Mum?'' he sneered.

Harriet knew instantly what he meant. "Don't talk to me like that!''

"Like what? Like a whore? That's what you are.'' He moved closer. "What I want to know is, where are you keepin' all that money?''

Suddenly, Harriet felt the first real fear in her life. Andrew's eyes blazed. "There is no money. I gave it all to Amanda,'' she told him.

"I don't believe it. It wouldn't take you two months to raise enough to send us both to New York, would it?''

"No,'' she hissed.

"Then do it!'' He ground his teeth as he talked so that spittle shot angrily through the tiny crevices.

"No! Why do you want to go to New York all of a sudden?''

"I want the same kind of chance Amanda's had. I'll never get anywhere stayin' here.'' The pressure of the situation with Lucy screwed itself into his temples, tightening its hold on him. For months he'd known he didn't really love her anymore. He knew now he never had. As he matured, he began to realize just how far his good looks and charm could take him. Certainly farther than Lucy Attington. He'd been stupid to sleep with her. He should have broken it off with her. Now he was going to have to pay for his dalliance.

Harriet tried to keep cool with Andrew, but she was just as ready for this fight as he was. It was time he moved out on his own. She wanted her life to be her own again. They were both at a breaking point.

"You could be in America by spring if you'd save your bookmaking money instead of spending it on Lucy."

Andrew moved closer to her. "I'm not seeing Lucy anymore."

"What?" Harriet stood calmly as his eyes bored into her. "How could you break that girl's heart? She loves you."

"She's pregnant."

"Oh God."

"So you see, Mum, I need that money of yours—badly."

She didn't like the way his voice had lowered. "Never. You made your bed. More than once, I see."

Andrew didn't know how his rage traveled so quickly from his brain to his hands, but it did. He leapt at her, grabbing her by the shoulders and shaking her furiously. All the years of contempt, of believing she had favored Amanda, washed over him, engulfing his mind like a typhoon. He could hear himself breathing hard, but somehow he knew he was holding his breath. He watched rather than felt his hands travel to her throat.

Her hands shot to his face as she tried to scratch at his eyes, but he held her off. She tried to scream, but he stopped it as he tightened his grip. She squirmed, and it took all his energy to keep his hold on her. She kicked at his legs, his knees, his scrotum, but he jerked away at precisely the right time.

He didn't want to kill her, he just wanted to frighten her. If she knew that he *could* kill her, then she would give him the money. He would go to America and be free of Lucy—free of the worthless existence he'd built for himself.

Suddenly, with superhuman strength, she grabbed his hands and pried them off of her. She started for the door, but he got hold of her and pulled her back. He flung her across the room with a force greater than he'd believed he was capable of exerting. She slammed her back against the stone mantel. Her eyes bulged out of her head, and her jaw dropped open as she sank to the floor.

"Mum?" Andrew raced to her, knowing she was momentarily stunned from the blow. He looked down at her for a long moment. Her eyes stared blankly up at him. "What's wrong?" he asked as he slowly bent down to her. He put his hand on her shoulder and shook her. She felt like a rag doll.

He put his arm under her head, thinking if he lifted her, maybe carried her to the couch, she would be all right. But when he did, he felt something wet and warm against the back of his hand.

"Mum . . ." He quickly wiped the blood on her sweater, not wanting any of it to stain his new shirt.

He felt her pulse to be sure.

"Now what will I do with you?" he mumbled to himself as he sat on the couch. He stared at the corpse, measuring it, taking into account its weight and length. He couldn't leave it here. The neighbors would find out. "My God, the neighbors." Andrew shot to his feet.

He went to the door and listened. There was no sound in the hall. He heard nothing from the flat above him. He turned the lights down and looked out the window. Most of the surrounding apartment windows were black; everyone was asleep. He wondered if anyone had seen them through the window. He checked his watch. It was long past midnight. He remembered that Mr. Jenkins was always out late at the pubs. Andrew would have to wait until he knew Mr. Jenkins was in for the night before he left or made any preparations.

"What a mess you've made of things, Mum!"

None of this was working out the way he'd planned. With Harriet dead, there was no way he could get the passage money out of her. Still, he didn't believe for one minute that she'd given all the money to Amanda. He knew his mother better than that. She liked her new-found life-style. He'd seen the pretty clothes that had worked their way into her closet. He'd found all her little hiding places, including the unnailed floorboards under the rag rug next to her bed. Harriet had always been a woman of secrets. His earliest recollection of her had been woven around a secret she'd told to Burt one night in the middle of one of their battles. It was a nightmare he'd never forget, for it was then he'd learned that Amanda was a bastard—the daughter of Alvin Kent.

For a time, Andrew had felt superior to his baby sister, knowing he was legitimate and she was not. Then came the years of privilege for Amanda, and the stark, heartless reality for Andrew— Amanda's royal blood overcame her bastardy. It was Andrew who was the lesser. Early on, he'd realized The Secret was one that could not be told—at least not until he'd placed all the advantages on *his* side of the board.

Somewhere in that bedroom, Andrew knew he'd find the money.

He opened the bedroom door, went to the bureau, and took out the false-bottom drawer. He found that diary he'd seen before.

He checked it and noted she'd made a new entry. How foolish Harriet had been to think she could hide anything from him. He stuffed the diary into his jacket pocket. There was no money, only stacks of Amanda's letters and a pair of small sapphire earrings. They weren't worth much, but he took them anyway. He found a few scraps of paper with scrawled notes. One was the address of a hotel he knew. The other was a series of numbers and two capital letters: B E.

"Bank of England." He smiled to himself. Andrew carefully memorized the numbers, and to be doubly safe, he put the piece of paper in his pocket with the earrings. He checked under the floorboards, but found the space empty.

As he put the drawer back, he began devising his plan.

He went to the kitchen and withdrew the strongest, sharpest knife they owned. He stood for a moment over the body; then, with a deep breath, he went over to the couch and began to slit the cushion from one end to the other along the seam.

Carefully, he peeled back the fabric along the side seams, for this he would have to repair. He took out the cotton stuffing, the wire coils, and the horsehair and emptied the base of the couch. It took over an hour to create the coffinlike cavity he needed for Harriet.

He carried the cotton into the bedroom and shoved in under the worn coverlet and shaped it into the form of his supposedly reposing mother. He tucked the sheet and blanket around the "head," perfectly re-creating the way she'd snuggled in her bed for thirty-seven years.

When he went back to Harriet, she was still staring up at him and still bleeding. He took an old rag and tied it around the wound on her skull. Then, placing his hands under her armpits, he dragged her to the gutted couch. He placed shoulders and head first, then picked up her legs and stretched her out. This time, he closed her eyelids.

Using vinegar and water he scrubbed the blood off the wood floor, but some of the stones on the hearth wouldn't come clean. He used a brush and ammonia, but as he stood back to inspect his work, he saw that the stones he'd washed were too clean. Now he had to clean the entire mantel and hearth.

Cursing to himself, he worked on each stone, until one by one they all looked the same. Sweat was dripping from his face when he finished. He'd never worked this hard in his life. "Christ! Even in death she's still getting her way."

He took just enough cotton to cover the body and make the bottom of the couch look smooth. It was perfect as long as nobody sat on it.

He took a long, sturdy needle from her sewing basket and chose a thread to match the upholstery. He followed the seam lines as best he could. Having only sewn one button on a shirt in his lifetime, he did not have a deft hand. But it would do. By the time he was finished it was nearly dawn.

He'd listened all night for Mr. Jenkins but had heard nothing. If he could keep calm about his tasks, Andrew knew he could make this work.

Andrew made himself a breakfast of eggs, coffee, and toast. While he ate, he took a pencil and paper and practiced forging his mother's name.

He went out as usual and bought his paper. As he did every morning, he saw Mr. Barrows on the streetcorner.

"Mornin', Mr. Barrows," Andrew said pleasantly.

"Mornin', Andrew. Looks like snow again today," he commented, looking at the gray sky.

"Yes, it does, Mr. Barrow. Yes, it does." Andrew walked back the two blocks to his house, unlocked the door, casting a glance at the Jenkins' apartment, and then went in.

Andrew waited half an hour until he saw Mrs. Jenkins go out the backyard to the cistern. She placed her garbage in the can and quickly returned to the house. Andrew waited fifteen minutes more, then went to the Jenkins's apartment and knocked on the door.

Mr. Jenkins came to the door. His eyes were clear. He had not been drinking the night before.

Damn, Andrew thought to himself.

"What do you need this time, Andrew? A bit of flour for your mum?" Mr. Jenkins asked.

"Nothing like that. I came to ask if you could help me out tonight after work."

"Doin' what?" Mr. Jenkins asked suspiciously. He didn't trust anybody.

"I've sold our couch, and I need to deliver it across town. I've rented a wagon . . . if you could help me carry it down to the street . . ."

"That's all?" Jenkins asked with narrowed eyes.

Andrew smiled that smile that had always worked for him. "That's all. Just a tiny favor. I'd be grateful."

"Well, I don't know."

"Beer's on me at Grady's."

Mr. Jenkins parted his thin lips and revealed his two cracked front teeth. "I'll do it."

"I'll see you tonight, then," Andrew said and started out down the street. He walked several paces before turning around. It was just as he'd thought. Mr Jenkins was still watching him. Andrew waved back using *that* smile, and then continued on. Once he rounded the corner, he stopped. He counted to fifty before doubling back around the rear of the building so that he came in from the opposite side. He wanted Jenkins to think he'd left for work at his regular time.

Quietly, he slipped back into the apartment. He stripped off his clothes and went to his mother's closet. He pulled out her black wool skirt and an old white shirt she often wore to work. He shoved his arms into her coat, but the sleeves were very tight and much too short. He found a pair of long wool gloves and pulled them up over his exposed wrists. He took out her biggest and, he thought, ugliest winter shawl and flung it around his shoulders. He pulled a knitted red wool cap over his head and down around his ears. He tied a wool scarf around his face so that the only part of his anatomy that was exposed were his eyes—the part of him that looked like Harriet.

He bent slightly at the knees to make himself shorter, picked up her purse, took the scrawled note with the numbers on it from his jacket, and set out. He'd gotten just out the the door when Mrs. Jenkins called to him.

"Off to work, Harriet?"

Andrew froze in his tracks. He had to disguise his voice and fool Mrs. Jenkins at the same time. It wouldn't be easy. Mrs. Jenkins did not drink and had not known a dull-witted day in her life.

"Yes," he said hoarsely.

Mrs. Jenkins was instantly on the alert. "Somethin' the matter, Harriet?"

"I've a terrible cold. I think I should have stayed in bed," he creaked.

"I'll bring over some soup tonight. That'll help."

"Don't bother. I'll be fine."

"You've nursed me through many a bad time, Harriet, Don't argue."

"All right," Andrew answered and walked on. He would worry about Mrs. Jenkins's soup later. He glanced back and noticed that she had gone inside, satisfied with the answer. His disguise was working.

It was a miserably cold day and just as Mr. Barrows had predicted, it snowed. By the time Andrew had walked across town to the Bank of England, he thought his fingers and toes had fallen off from frostbite.

He was fourth in line at the teller's window. When his turn came, his hand was still numb. He didn't know if he could successfully forge Harriet's name or not. He wrote the account numbers on the withdrawal paper.

"I want to close out my account, but I can't remember how much I have," Andrew said in his hoarse imitation of his mother.

The young man looked at him strangely. "You sound terrible, Mrs. Granger. Got a bit of a cold, eh?"

Andrew nodded.

The teller straightened his back and moved away so as not to become infected himself. He went to the account ledgers and checked the amount. He returned to his window.

"You have slightly less than two thousand pounds."

"Two thou . . ." Andrew was stunned. Harriet could have lived for a decade on that kind of money, as frugal as she was. He not only had enough for the passage but plenty to start him off in America. "Could you fill this out for me? My hands are so cold . . ." he asked sweetly.

The teller smiled graciously. "Of course, Mrs. Granger."

Andrew signed the slip as instructed and waited patiently as the teller counted out the money. He folded the paper bills and stuffed them into his mother's purse, then left.

Dressed as Harriet, he arranged for a wagon to be at the corner of Mercer and Long Acre at eight o'clock when it would be dark. He booked passage to New York City on a ship leaving Southampton in three days. He cabled Amanda in New York telling her that Harriet was ill with pneumonia.

He arrived home at six, when Harriet normally returned. He waved to two other neighbors, coughed loudly as he unlocked the door, and made certain he sneezed several times just as the door closed.

Quickly, he took off Harriet's clothes, for he knew Mrs. Jenkins would be true to her promise. He'd just donned his jacket when he heard the knock on the door.

"Andrew, I brought this for your mother," she said, trying to push her way in.

He took the soup from her. "She went straight to bed, Mrs. Jenkins. I'll take this to her immediately. Poor thing. She seems bad off."

"Maybe I can help." She tried to push past him again.

Andrew pressed his hand against her shoulder. "I couldn't let you expose yourself, Mrs. Jenkins. You aren't a young woman . . . although you're still as lovely as a girl. You need to be careful."

As always, she fell for his charm. "Yes, you're right . . . and thoughtful too. I've always said that about you, Andrew, despite . . ." she stopped herself short.

"Despite what my mother says about me?"

"I'd best be going. I'll send Mr. Jenkins over to help you with the furniture."

"About eight. I don't want to interrupt your supper."

She smiled widely. "Thank you, Andrew."

Andrew closed the door knowing he had an ally.

At eight o'clock, Andrew let Mr. Jenkins in. Purposely he'd left the lamp burning in Harriet's room and the door cocked partially open, so that Mr. Jenkins could see inside.

"She's sound asleep. I think that soup your wife sent did the trick."

Mr. Jenkins nodded. "Always does."

They each took an end of the couch and lifted. It was heavier than Andrew had expected.

"What's this thing made of, lead?" Mr. Jenkins asked.

"Sturdy oak. Very hard wood. Very dense."

"Let's get on with it," Mr. Jenkins grunted.

They carried the couch down the narrow hall and out the front door. Shelton Street wasn't much wider itself. It wasn't wide enough to allow a wagon to pass, for if it had, Andrew would never have gone to so much effort. The block and a half to Mercer Street and then another block to the waiting wagon seemed like miles. Four times they had to stop for Mr. Jenkins to rest. With the driver's help, they lifted the couch onto the wagon bed.

Mr. Jenkins mopped his brow as he walked back to his house, and Andrew jumped onto the wagon with the driver.

The driver followed Andrew's instructions, including the suggestion they stop off for a whiskey at Grady's.

"I'm buying," Andrew said magnanimously.

The driver quickly accepted. By eleven o'clock the driver was staggeringly drunk and did not argue when Andrew told him he would make the delivery.

The London streets were silent as the wagon rolled over fresh snow toward the Thames, to the spot where Andrew had gone swimming on hot summer days with his sister. He knew right where that drop-off was, the one Amanda had found when she was only five. The river was frozen in parts, as the temperature dropped even lower as the night went on. The snowfall was heavier now, masking man and beast alike. Andrew pulled to a halt along the north bank.

He took the blanket he'd used to cover his legs and placed it on the ground. He pulled the couch onto the blanket, first one end, then jumped onto the wagon and finished shoving it off. He jumped down and grabbed the end of the blanket. Pulling the blanket over ice and snow on a downward slope wasn't as difficult as he'd thought. Once the momentum built, the couch started moving as if on its own. Andrew quickened his steps and then jumped aside as the couch went racing down the bank and into the icy Thames.

He watched only for a moment through the falling snow as the couch, weighted heavily as if made of cement, sank deeply into the drop-off.

"Good-bye, Mum. Finally your icy heart has found a proper home."

Andrew left. He still had much to do before he could leave London.

At dawn, just when the neighbors were starting to stir, when their eyes were not cleansed of sleep and their minds were not yet clear, Andrew pretended to be the dutiful son and took his "mother" to the hospital where she would receive proper attention.

Mrs. Jenkins swore to Mrs. Fieldstone that Harriet leaned quite heavily on her son as they walked down Shelton Street together. She knew it was Harriet because she wore that same red knit hat and her familiar wool coat. Mrs. Fieldstone commented on Andrew's ability to rally during times of crisis.

Andrew thanked God for the still-falling snow, charcoal skies, and little sunlight that day. For if it had been otherwise, everyone would have realized that he had stuffed his mother's clothing with the cotton from the couch and made this dummy he "walked" nearly a mile before depositing it in a rubbish heap.

On his way to work, he placed another cable to his sister, stating that their mother's health was deteriorating. Tomorrow he would cable her about Harriet's death and his forthcoming arrival in New York.

He would have no trouble dodging Lucy for another day or two. He would go about his business as usual, "visiting" his "mother" in the hospital. Then he would slip out of town at the same time he would tell the neighbors of Harriet's death. He would tell them he was too poor to conduct a wake and that he had arranged to have her buried in potter's field. They would understand that. He would tell them that Amanda had sent him the money to go to America. They would understand that too.

It was a perfect plan. It would never fail.

CHAPTER TWENTY-ONE

New York—February, 1896

Amanda tore the cable into tiny pieces, thinking if she obliterated the message she would also negate reality. It wasn't true. It couldn't be, she thought as she went to the window and looked out on the snow-frosted tree limbs that rattled against the panes. Just last week she'd talked to David about bringing her mother to America. He'd been against the idea at first until Amanda stated that Sylvia wanted Harriet to live with her.

"But now that can never happen," she said sadly to herself. Harriet would never know the man Amanda had married. Or see her in her fabulous new home, meet her friends. She'd dreamed of them working together on charity projects for Sylvia. Amanda had wanted to shower her mother with new clothes, take her to the theater, have lunch at Del's. Amanda had wanted to give her mother everything life had cheated her of. It was Amanda's turn to pay her mother back for her sacrifices.

Amanda's tears were hot and angry. *She* was the one being cheated this time. Life had cheated her and so had Harriet. "How dare she do this to me!" she sobbed.

David walked into the room and heard her outburst. Instantly, he was at her side. "What is it, dear? What's wrong?"

Amanda fell into his arms. "Oh, David. My mother . . . she's dead!" She let her tears flow as she found comfort in his arms.

He didn't know what to say. He'd never dealt well with death himself. When his parents died, it had been no more to him than a servant's passing. David had never been emotionally attached to people, nor they to him. His parents had looked upon him as an heir, not a child with a heart or soul. Simply, he was the one to carry on the family name. Hopefully, he would continue to make the Simon name worth something. Fame was more important to David than attachments.

His reactions, then, were mechanical, but Amanda was so grief-stricken she noticed nothing outside herself.

"I'm sorry, Amanda. Tell me what to do."

"Just hold me."

And he did.

A few hours later, Amanda had calmed. David felt helpless. All he could do was hold her hand and listen as she told him bits and pieces of her childhood. Some of the things she said made no sense and didn't jibe with her earlier stories about her life in Cornwall.

"Georgia and Mother were always close."

"I thought Georgia was the cook."

Amanda caught herself instantly. She hated this pretense she must always play. She realized now there would never ever be a time when she could relax, not be on her guard. The Lie must be sustained at all times—at all costs. "No, you misunderstood. Not Georgia the cook. Georgia Wingate, of the Sussex Wingates."

"I'm afraid I don't know that much about London society."

Amanda dabbed her eyes and sighed with relief. "I wonder where we'll put Andrew when he arrives," she said, almost herself.

"Andrew?"

She looked at David's confused face. "I . . . didn't mention that Andrew was on a ship headed here?"

David bristled. "No, you didn't."

"In the cable I received today. I must have forgotten . . . the shock of Mother's death . . ."

David didn't like this at all, but what could he do? He'd never seen Amanda like this. She didn't want to eat, she protested when he suggested an afternoon rest. She wouldn't be able to work for weeks. And he had those sketches he wanted to show the editor at *Collier's Weekly*. If he argued with her, she would only be further upset. For now, he would acquiesce. He would deal with the subject of Andrew later.

He put his arm around her shoulder. "Don't worry about anything right now. We'll put him in the spare room upstairs."

"I'd wanted to make that into a nursery."

"A nursery! Amanda, I think we're getting ahead of ourselves here. We won't need a nursery for a long time. Andrew will be here soon. Let's handle things one at a time."

"All right."

"Please try to rest. We have a dinner engagement with the Cannons and Elliots tonight."

"You'll have to send my excuses. I can't possibly go."

David knew this dinner was important. There would be close to fifty people at the table. Each one of them, through their patronage and gossip, would promote him. They loved Amanda and he knew it. He had to make certain her name and his appeared in the society columns in the morning.

David moved a bit closer and used his sincerest tones. "Where's that inner strength of yours? It'll only be for a few hours. And it might do you good to be with people. I don't want you to wall yourself away and dwell on the past. Your mother wouldn't want that, would she?"

Without his knowing, David had used key words.

"No, she wouldn't. She would say the same thing." She looked at him, her husband, thinking how kind he was to her. She wished her mother could have met him so she would know what a good choice she'd made.

Andrew looked at the Statue of Liberty, thinking what a ridiculous place to put a monument. Any fool could see it belonged in a park where people could visit it on weekends and holidays. He'd heard Central Park was very large. Americans. What did they know, anyway?

After the tedious wait while the immigrants from below decks were ferried out to Ellis Island, they were finally underway again. Andrew smoked a cigar as he paced along the railing waiting to dock. Somehow, during the entire trip, he'd feared that a cable would come through for his arrest. The body had been found, or someone had heard something. A child had seen him that night struggling with his mother. A British ship captain had the authority to arrest him and bring him back to London. Once he was safely on American soil, he'd relax.

It took hours to dock, forever for the porter to gather his luggage, and then there was the tiresome ride to Amanda's house. He was surprised there was no snow, but the driver explained it was the "January thaw . . . happens every third week of January," he'd said.

As he continued north on Fifth Avenue along Central Park, Andrew's jaw slowly dropped. He had intended not to be impressed by anything he saw, but he found he couldn't help it. No wonder Amanda loved America. Who wouldn't?

In New York the streets were filled with beautiful men and women dressed to the teeth. There were twice the carriages as in London; houses were twice the size and on bigger lots. There were more stores, more trees, more space, more everything.

Andrew saw his dream coming alive again . . . and growing.

The driver pulled to a halt.

Andrew looked up at the beautiful house with leaded glass windows. "Are you sure you have the right address?"

"Yes, sir." The driver jumped down and began unloading the luggage.

Andrew's smile was wide. If Amanda could do this well, so could he.

Amanda saw him from the window in her bedroom. She raced down the hall, down the stairs, and passing Casey, the maid, in the vestibule, she flung open the heavy front door.

"Andrew!" she cried jubilantly.

He ran up the stone steps and into her outstretched arms. He picked her up and whirled her around. He kissed her on the cheek.

"You look ten times—no, a hundred times—more beautiful," he said generously.

"I'm so very, very glad you're here . . . especially now," she said with that touch of sadness that grazed her days.

"I know," he said. "But we're together now. We should keep it that way."

"Oh, yes, Andrew."

David stood in the doorway, dressed in his paint-drizzled smock, which he wore over heavy tweed pants and a white shirt. He'd watched the reunion from his studio.

"Welcome, Andrew. I'm David, your brother-in-law." David shook Andrew's hand. "Come in out of the cold."

David ushered them in, noticing how Andrew left the payment of the driver up to him. In the salon, David propped his elbow on the mantle as he listened to Andrew's account of Harriet Granger's death.

"She was thinking of us both when she died, Amanda."

"Was there a large turnout for the funeral?" David asked.

Amanda stiffened. She hadn't had time to brief Andrew about her lie. In all the excitement, she hadn't thought to ask David for time alone with Andrew. Diversion was her best tack.

"David! What a callous thing to ask. Of course her friends were there."

"I'm sorry, Amanda. I don't know much about these things. I'm sure it was difficult for you, Andrew. Being the only family there at the time . . . making all the arrangements. I've never had to do that. My parents died when I was very young."

"I see," Andrew replied, wondering what kind of game Amanda was playing. But he did make certain his expression was solemn. "It wasn't an easy time, I can tell you that. I've never felt so devastated. I was always very important to her," he said directly to David. "I was to take care of her in her old age. She'd always said that, hadn't she, Amanda?"

"Yes, Andrew," she said, patting his hand.

"I thought I'd never get through those days, watching her there in that hospital. I'll miss her. But I survived that, and the trip over. I thought I'd never seen such terrible weather. I'm so glad I'm here, Amanda. I have wanted to come to America just as much as you. Maybe more."

David picked up his pipe and filled it. He wondered if Andrew ever spoke a sentence that wasn't prefaced with the word "I." David wasn't certain what it was, but there was something about Andrew that didn't ring true. He seemed sincere enough, but there was something else. Perhaps it was that peculiar glint in his eyes—a gleam that David recognized because he'd seen it too many times in his own eyes. He liked to think it was ambition. But in Andrew he could tell it was greed.

"Tell me, Andrew, what do you intend to do now that you are here?" David asked.

"Work, of course."

"Andrew was quite successful—" Amanda started.

"Business management. That's my interest. I can take a company that is in the red and show it how to turn it all around. I know the ways to make a failing business turn profits."

"You work miracles?" David laughed.

"I do," Andrew replied earnestly.

David lit his pipe, wondering if Andrew was always this pompous. "I'll see to the tea."

Andrew scowled.

Amanda turned to Andrew as David left the room. "Thank you for not giving me away. David doesn't know about my background."

"I know all about the story you and Mum concocted. Just not all the details."

"I'll tell you everything. If you intend to stay here, you'll have to play along. If David ever found out . . ."

"The party train would come to a halt."

"Precisely."

"Don't worry, Amanda. I didn't come here to disrupt your life. With Mum gone and all, there was nothing left for me in London."

"But what about Lucy?"

Andrew used his most crestfallen look. He even managed a misting of the eyes. "That was as great a blow as Mum's death. I found out she's been seeing someone else. I loved her too. Amanda, I don't know how to tell you this—she's . . . pregnant."

"Oh, Andrew. I'm sorry. This has been a terrible time for you. For us both. But we're together now and that's what matters. And it's going to be better. I promise."

Andrew's room was at the opposite end of the hall from the room Amanda shared with David. She and David rose early to work, and Andrew slept most mornings till nearly noon. Andrew's presence did not disturb their daily routine.

Amanda liked having Andrew to talk with at lunch when David normally left to meet with publishers. Most evenings, she and David had dinner or party engagements, and when they returned she found Andrew waiting up for her. He was always eager to hear about the evening. He grilled her on every detail from what was served for dinner to the waltzes that were played and who was there.

By the second week of his stay, Amanda was happy with their arrangement. David was not.

"He needs a job."

"He's still in mourning over Mother's death."

"All the more reason for him to find something to occupy his time. Look at yourself. You miss her, but your grief isn't pulling you down. All he does is sleep and eat.''

"You're right. Andrew was always very social. He liked parties and gay times as much as anyone. In fact, he hardly ever stayed home. He's grieving more than I'd thought.''

"You see? I'll talk to Quinton Parker. He's trying to get a new magazine going. If your brother is as good as he says he is, perhaps there's a place for him with Quinton.''

When Amanda told Andrew about the job, Andrew was angry.

"I'll find proper employment in my own good time.''

"I just wanted to help. It isn't good for you to dwell on the past.''

"Just leave me alone!" he stormed and retreated to his room.

Andrew flopped down on the massive burled oak bed. Christ! Why couldn't his sister mind her own business? He'd worked hard all his life. He was due a rest . . . a vacation. This was the kind of life he'd been destined for. He pulled a cord and his breakfast arrived. He rang a bell and his lunch was set before him on expensive china. He drank the best wines, read fine literature until the end of the day, and kept warm near one of ten—*ten*—fireplaces. Andrew was in heaven. How could there be more to life than this? He didn't want to work. He'd worked since he was ten. He'd like never to have to work again.

He got up and stoked the fire. He added more coals. This turn of events was not coming from Amanda, he reasoned. This was David's idea. If it was just manipulating Amanda, that would be easy. David, however, couldn't be fooled. That was obvious. He hadn't fooled David at all so far.

Andrew resigned himself to the fact that if he wanted to stay in David's house and receive David's beneficence, then he would have to follow David's rules.

Amanda rode with Andrew on Wednesday afternoon to Quinton Parker's office near Herald Square on Thirty-fourth Street off Sixth Avenue.

While she waited for Andrew to pay the driver, Amanda looked up at the giant clock, erected just last year, on top of the *New York Herald*'s two-story palazzo. She watched as the minute hand reached twelve and chimed the hour. Stuff and Guff, two bronze mannequins, struck at the big bell, with Minerva looking down on them from above.

Quinton Parker, a friendly-looking man in his late forties, greeted them. "Amanda! I had no idea you'd be here," he said, rolling down his white sleeves and shoving his arms into his jacket. "This is an honor."

"Don't be silly, Quinton. How's Sally?"

"Just fine. Sylvia's roped her into another project."

"Good for her. She needs something to occupy her time."

"What about me?" he teased.

"I know you too well. You're always here." She laughed. "Quinton, this is my brother, Andrew."

The men shook hands. "David tells me you might be the man I'm looking for. I could use some help getting this magazine off the ground."

"I'll do my best."

"Let me show you around first."

Quinton took them from the reception area where his office was located in a glassed-in area to the main editing room. Here, ten writers and editors worked on copy, stories, and layouts for the magazine. There were two secretaries who handled correspondence, he told them. The staff was shorthanded, but it was a fledgling magazine.

"What's the concept of the magazine?" Amanda asked.

"News. Any and all kinds. I want in-depth coverage of what's going on in the world—more than what one would get out of a newspaper with its limited time and space. I have what I think are the best writers in town. Unfortunately, this is their first byline, so they have no following—yet."

"No fiction?" Amanda asked.

"None. This isn't *Collier*'s."

"It sounds wonderful."

"My problem is that my reporting has mostly come from here in New York. I'd like to get something fresh from Europe or some kind of inside story about the Kaiser. But it takes money to send a guy to Munich."

"So you have to sell more advertising," Amanda said. "What sells advertising?"

Quinton laughed. "You!"

"I don't understand."

"As much as I don't want to admit it, New Yorkers are more fascinated by society, the Granger Woman and The Gibson Girl, than they are about a war in Africa, politics in Russia, or the economy of Italy. *I* want them to be world-aware, but they don't want to be.''

"So why not change the focus of the magazine?'' Amanda asked.

"Not yet. It could still make it, if I had the advertising.''

He showed them the printing presses, the cutters, the bundlers, and the dock where wagons picked up the magazines and then delivered them around town to newsstands. *Parker's Points* went as far as Philadelphia, Boston and Baltimore. Quinton hadn't been able thus far to produce any more than thirty thousand copies a month. He hoped, if he showed a profit by the end of the year, to buy an additional press.

Amanda and Andrew followed Quinton back to his office. There was an advertising layout for Lord & Taylor department store on his desk.

"Is that one of the ads?'' Amanda asked.

"Yes. I've taken it back three times but can't get their approval. Mr. Jameson down there is a pistol to deal with. He's never happy. Last month, we delayed the presses two days on account of him. But I need his money.''

"May I look at it?'' Amanda asked.

"Certainly,'' Quinton said as he went over to Andrew.

"Andrew, what do you think? Right now, you'd have to be a jack-of-all-trades. I can use any kind of input you've got.''

"My field is basically in the numbers business. If you aren't spending wisely, I can tell you where and what to do about it. I've never sold advertising before, but I think I could do it. I'm willing to try if you are. But . . . I don't come cheap.''

Quinton braced himself. "I can pay you twenty dollars a week.''

"Fifty,'' Andrew countered as Amanda gasped at his audacity.

"Thirty,'' Quinton replied sternly.

"I'll do it . . . for forty dollars. Take it or leave it.''

"I'll take it. But you'd better be worth it.''

"I am. When do I start?''

"First thing Monday morning,'' Quinton said and shook Andrew's hand.

Knowing he'd just received one of the highest starting salaries in publishing, Andrew turned to Amanda. "Are you ready to leave?''

Still stunned at the outcome of the bartering, Amanda replied, "What?"

"I'm ready to leave."

"Oh." She shook Quinton's hand as she came around the desk. "Give Sally my regards," she said.

"I will."

Andrew helped Amanda into the carriage. She straightened her wool plaid skirt and pulled a blanket up around her waist.

"I think we should celebrate," Andrew said. "What's the best place in town for a celebration?"

"Del's, of course."

"Delmonico's it is."

Amanda tried to listen to Andrew, enjoy her wine, and savor the braised beef, but she couldn't get her mind off that ad. There was something wrong with it, but even she was having a hard time figuring it out.

She had just finished her coffee and a sweet almond cookie, the kind Del's was famous for, when she exploded: "Too much copy."

"Beg pardon?" Andrew said.

"There's too much on the page."

"Amanda, dear sister, you've lost me."

"That ad of Quinton's. He's got too many words and not enough picture. The sketch of the woman's gown is lovely. Other than the name of the store and price, what else is necessary?"

Andrew shook his head. "All this time you've been thinking about that damn advertisement?"

"I'm sorry, Andrew. Of course I was listening to you. But I know I'm right about this. I used the same philosophy when I did posters for Sylvia's charities. I still do. And it gets results. When you go in there on Monday, you work on that ad. Then you take it to Lord & Taylor and just see what that Mr. Jameson says."

"I don't know, Amanda. Only the store name and the price? Nobody advertises like that."

"Well, they should."

"I think I'll leave that to Quinton."

"Andrew," she said firmly, "promise me you'll just try. On your first day, what could it hurt? Quinton could only blame it on lack of experience. However, if I'm right, you'll be a king."

Andrew didn't like taking advice from his sister. But what she said was true. On a first day one could make lots of mistakes and it wouldn't matter.

"He loved it?"

"Here's the check." Andrew handed Quinton a draft for three hundred dollars. "He wants to run a similar ad next month."

Quinton slapped his forehead in disbelief. "Tell me what you did."

"I have this philosophy about advertising, Quinton. Less is more." He pulled out ads from every magazine and paper in town. "Look at these magazines and newspapers. Every inch is filled. It's as if they thought they'd never get a chance to print anything again," he said, echoing his sister's words from the night before. He didn't tell Quinton that Amanda had stayed up past midnight clipping advertisements from *The Delineator* and *Harper's Bazaar* to prove her point.

"I also think, Quinton, that you should change the name of the magazine to *World Today*."

"Change the name? Never."

"What have you got to lose but your ego?"

Quinton carefully eyed this young man he'd only known for four days. "Ego, you say?"

"Ego. You and I both know you want your name on the cover. Why not really put your name on the cover? *World Today: Outlook by Quinton Parker*."

"Hmmm."

"The magazine is young enough that you can make these changes. You've only had two issues out, and so far you haven't burned any barns down from hot sales."

"I'll think about it."

Three weeks later, Amanda opened the March issue of *World Today*. Every advertisement in the issue had the kind of style she loved: clean, spare, and eye-catching. When not posing for David or attending one of his business lunches or dinners, she was helping Andrew work on the magazine.

She loved the work she did with Andrew. She'd never known anything as exciting, as creative. It was the first time she'd ever worked with her brother, and she liked it. He was receptive to all her ideas. He never rejected one as David often did when she was inspired by a particular pose or setting. David had become cautious with his success. He'd lost his sense of adventure. Now he was doing what he'd said he'd never do: copying Dana Gibson.

If Gibson's last sketch was of a girl in a swing, then so was David's. If Irene was posed on a golf course, then off Amanda would go and do the same. When it came time to pose her standing next to a carriage accepting a flower from a child, as Dana had Irene do, Amanda protested.

"I want to do something different, David!"

"No. I know what I'm doing."

"I don't think you do!" she said in front of the small crowd that was gathering.

David was well aware of their audience. To placate her he said: "What would you have me do, *dear*?"

Amanda looked around for a moment, stepped back and assessed the carriage and horses. Instantly knowing what she wanted, she lifted her skirts, grabbed a firm hold of the mane of one horse, and hoisted herself astride the horse.

Two women in the crowd gasped at the abundance of exposed, pantalooned leg. One elderly gentleman applauded and everyone else smiled approval.

"You see, David, they love it."

David harrumphed. "Will you sit sidesaddle, the way a *lady* would sit?"

"David, I *am* a *lady*. And *this* is how I sit."

Two young girls clapped.

"Oh, for God's sake," David growled, but quickly he sketched her, defiant smile, flashing eyes . . . and exposed legs. He'd never show it to a publisher, of course. No one would buy it. The Granger Woman was known to flaunt convention, but this could be taken as vulgar. He'd tear it up before they got home.

As soon as he finished, Amanda jumped down from the horse with no assistance and looked at the sketch.

"It's the best you've ever done. Give it to me."

"What?"

"I want it for myself," she said, sticking out her hand.

David handed it to her. "Now can we go home?"

"Yes," she replied, folding it in half and stuffing it inside her jacket. This was one sketch she would sell herself. And Quinton Parker would soon be making enough money to afford it.

David put his arm around her and kissed her cheek. "Tomorrow we're having lunch with a publisher from Boston. Don't forget.''

''I can't make it, David. I promised Andrew I'd help him with an ad.''

David withdrew his arm and sulked. ''God damn! I'm sick of Andrew this and Andrew that. Where do I fit in anymore? Will you tell me that?''

''I thought I was doing well, managing to help you both.''

''You need to rethink your loyalties. I've decided I want you to help *me* sell. Maybe you can talk these publishers into putting the Granger Woman in every issue.''

''David, of course I'll help you—you're my husband.''

''I'm surprised you remembered.''

Andrew tied his first white satin tie and slipped his arms into his first set of tails. He looked at himself in the mirror. His muscular legs and flanks moved against the light wool fabric. The coat fit his narrow waist perfectly, and his wide shoulders had never been displayed so well. He brushed his thick hair back with a sterling silver brush.

He'd never been to a debutante ball, but he'd listened to Amanda and read every society column and article he could lay his hands on. He'd been in America almost four months. Tonight was important to him. He'd proven himself at work by ingratiating himself with Quinton and using every single one of Amanda's ideas, suggestions and bits of genius she dropped on him like unopened rosebuds. He never once told Quinton about Amanda's role, and somehow he thought that Amanda wanted it that way. She was genuinely eager for him to succeed.

His only problem was David. As the weeks passed, David and Andrew had less and less to say to each other. David tolerated Andrew's presence, but that was all. Andrew didn't care. He'd stay and live off David as long as he could. He was saving his money; this was perhaps the only frugal time he'd ever known in his life. He knew he never could afford servants and a fine house like this. Not yet. He had a lot to gain from keeping the status quo.

The carriage David had ordered was more opulent than usual, with a gold velvet tufted interior, fine leather reins and bridle for the horses, and four shiny brass coach lamps. Amanda lifted her skirt as she entered.

"David, don't you think this is too extravagant?"

"No, I don't. We're becoming famous, Amanda. People expect us to arrive in style. It will look good in the columns in the morning."

Amanda wanted to retaliate, but she was tired of arguing. David's ideas about how to handle their business and hers was not meshing at all. One minute he wanted her advice and the next he would turn around and do exactly the opposite of her suggestion.

She knew David resented the time she spent with Andrew. But somewhere in all this she expected some understanding from her husband. He seemed to feel that she was his exclusive property. He didn't like any of her friends; more than once he'd cut short her time with Sylvia to the point where Sylvia rarely came around. Amanda sometimes felt she must lie to David to have time to herself. He was treating her as if she were a child. And she didn't like it, nor did she like his coldness to Andrew.

Her brother needed her right now until he was established. It was important that he meet the right people. Tonight would be a good beginning, but it was his first ball and she could tell he was nervous.

She watched David and Andrew as they tried to ignore each other. She wished she could make them like each other, but there was something between them that she didn't understand. She wanted them all to be a family. She could tell she was the only one who wanted it.

"How did your meeting with Quinton go today, Andrew?" she asked.

"Wonderful. He approved the ad layouts."

"Did you finally do these ads yourself?" David asked.

"David!"

Andrew was unperturbed. "I do all my own work."

"Not from what I can see. You two haven't fooled me in the least. Amanda gets out of bed in the middle of the night and works on those ads for you."

"Andrew has had some wonderful ideas—"

"He wouldn't know an original idea if he fell over it."

"I can do more than you . . . sketching pictures of your wife."

David nearly shot out of his seat with balled fists.

Amanda threw herself between them and held David back. "Stop it! Both of you. I won't have you ruining my evening!"

Andrew looked at David. God! How could he have been so stupid not to see it before? David was not only jealous of the time he spent with Amanda but of Amanda herself. David *had* to have Amanda. Without her, *he* was nothing. Amanda was David's link to fame, the only thing that gave David his drive.

What a pair they were, he thought. He, the brother, needing Amanda's fame and brain to get him what he wanted. And David, the husband, needing Amanda the woman to get the fame. Indirectly, then, Andrew needed David.

Andrew looked into his brother-in-law's dark, opaque eyes. David had never had to share his gold mine with anyone until now. Andrew could feel his hate burn through to his soul.

As the carriage turned onto a more smoothly paved street, David and Andrew sat across from each other, each assessing his opponent, analyzing the other's position. Each knowing he would win.

Christine Van Volkein stepped into a seven-hundred-dollar Worth crimson taffeta gown. She fastened a twelve-thousand-dollar diamond necklace around her ivory throat and clipped a pair of five-thousand-dollar matching earrings on her lobes. She stood back and assessed herself in the mirror.

It would do.

A little more than six months of marriage had shown Christine exactly how difficult it was to get the things she wanted. It probably wouldn't be so much work if she didn't want so much. But Christine wanted. How she wanted.

Manipulating Paul to buy the jewels, the gowns, the trips was the best part of marriage. Wielding her power over him had been a revelation. It had taken her over three years and a father's dying wish to get him to the altar. Thus, she'd prepared herself for long battles. She found that a trip to Tiffany's required only less than an hour of work. The only problem was that Paul didn't make the trip often enough to suit Christine.

Paul stood in the doorway looking at her. She could see his pleased expression in the mirror. She turned to him, knowing her smile was beautiful . . . and perfect.

"You like it?"

"I love it." He sipped his whiskey. "You'll be the most beautiful woman there."

Christine fought to keep her cheerful look. They both knew that Amanda Granger would be at the ball. The hostess had actually used Amanda's name in the paper to help publicize the event. Christine thought it vulgar, but the ploy had worked. Everyone in New York would be present. It nearly made Christine squirm in her hundred-dollar Parisian corselette to know that Amanda was this much of a celebrity, and that David was largely responsible for her fame.

Christine did not agree with Paul that David was an "amateur" painter. Christine had worked with Gibson. He was good, but he hadn't done anything wondrous for *her*. Christine's name was not bursting from everyone's lips. But Amanda's was. And, as Christine saw it, *she* was every bit as beautiful as Amanda. All she needed was someone like David. . . .

Paul put his arms around Christine's tiny waist. He lowered his head and kissed her on the nape of her neck.

Christine watched in the mirror as Paul's eyes closed and he lost himself in the moment. His breathing became more rapid. His lips parted and moved down her shoulder. Suddenly, he spun her around to face him. He dipped his hand inside her bodice as he kissed her hungrily.

"Let's not go, Christine. I can think of better things to do. . . ."

Christine let him linger a fraction of an instant longer before easing herself out of his grasp.

"No, Paul. We're expected."

"There has to be some time for just us. It seems we attend every party given in this city. I'd like to slow down." He put his arms around her again. "Let's go away. Just the two of us. Maybe some Caribbean island where we'll have the whole place to ourselves."

Christine laughed. "Paul! Don't be ridiculous. What would we do all day?"

"Plenty!"

She picked up her gloves and bag. She started for the door, but he was not following. She turned to look back at him. He looked so forlorn, she almost sympathized . . . almost.

"Paul, don't be like that. We have enough time together. Are you forgetting Wednesday night?"

"No," he said, remembering the pleasure . . . thinking of the seventeen thousand dollars in jewels it had cost him.

"There will be lots of Wednesday nights for us, Paul," she purred. "Lots."

White camellias, white lilies, and white jasmine perfumed the ballroom at the Waldorf as fifty debutantes danced their first waltz in the arms of a man other than their father or a relative. The thirty-three-piece orchestra occupied four risers amid nineteen potted palms, and waiters dressed in gold satin suits dispersed over a hundred cases of Piper Heidesik champagne to the five hundred and twenty-five guests.

Amanda took both the arm of her husband and that of her brother as she entered. It was as if New York society had never seen her before.

"She's a hundred times—no, a thousand times—more beautiful than his sketches," one matron declared.

"He must not be very good if he can't capture her any better than he has," another said.

But as they passed, Amanda noticed that the whispers were as much about Andrew as about her. Andrew was beaming.

They had just been ushered to their table when a harried-looking father was being dragged to Andrew's side by his debutante daughter.

"Amanda, David. I'd like to introduce my daughter, Sophie."

Amanda noticed that Sophie kept staring at Andrew out of the corner of her eye. "Sophie, this is my brother, Andrew Granger."

Andrew smiled and kissed the young girl's hand. He stifled the laugh that crept into his throat, for the young girl was so anxious to dance with him he thought she'd throw a tantrum if she didn't get her way.

"Would you care to dance with me?" he asked.

"Oh, yes!" Sophie nearly exploded. Then she led him to the dance floor.

Christine stood at the entrance to the ballroom, waiting to make her entrance. She'd purposely waited until ten o'clock, knowing then everyone would see her. She kicked the back of her gown to straighten the train and make certain the gown fell properly. She took Paul's arm. She led him directly to the hostess's table. After paying their respects, Christine knew precisely whom she wanted to see next.

By the time they reached David and Amanda's table, Christine had already heard the whispers about Andrew Granger. It didn't take her long to find him on the floor. He was without a doubt the most handsome man she'd ever seen. He was even better looking than Paul. She felt her breath catch in her throat as she watched him glide the strawberry blonde girl around the floor.

Christine thought again about the power she held over Paul. She wondered how many men she could capture with it.

"Christine," David began, "I thought Dana's sketch of you was one of his best yet."

Christine forgot all about Andrew. Her head spun around and she smiled widely at David. Absorbing compliments was Christine's favorite pastime. "Did you really?"

"Yes, I did. Other than two of Irene I've always liked, yours was by far the best."

Christine fluttered her fan. "You praise me too much."

"Never," David said, taking her arm and assisting her with a chair. "Perhaps you and Paul would join us for champagne. I'd like to talk to you about your work with Dana."

Amanda bit her lip to stifle her protest. She knew it wasn't Christine he was interested in but Dana. It was always the same wherever they went. Sometimes she thought David was obsessed with ambition. It wasn't healthy, the way he wanted to best Gibson. David didn't seem to care if his work was his personal best. He only cared that he get into the same publications as Gibson and beat his circulation and sales.

"David seems more concerned about his work than about his wife," Paul said, standing very close to Amanda. She could almost feel his heat through her clothes.

"He's quite dedicated."

"Quite." His tone was low and purposely sensual. "Let's dance."

Amanda nodded. On the dance floor, Paul took her into his arms and held her closer than was customary. His eyes never left her face.

"Why are you doing this, Paul?"

"Doing what?"

"Trying to make me think I'm the last woman on earth to you. You have a wife now. Isn't that enough?"

"Christine doesn't love me. She wants me for a lot of reasons, but that isn't one of them."

"You know what, Paul? I really don't care."

"I don't believe you. Until the day you die, Amanda, you'll care about everybody and everything. That's the kind of woman you are."

"Then you should know that I care about myself too. I'm not going to hide out in my house to avoid you, Paul, but I won't stand for this 'Pitiful Pearl' act you pull on me. I don't feel guilty over what happened. David and I have a wonderful life. I don't need anything from you."

"Okay, maybe it won't be me. But you need a whole lot more than David Simon will ever give you, Amanda. Look at him, for God's sake. The man's a robot. He's sitting with the second most beautiful woman in the room and he's talking business. If it were any other man, I'd already be defending Christine's honor."

Amanda was silent, wishing what he said wasn't true.

"I'll always love you, Amanda. But I promise not to push myself on you. If you ever do need a friend, though, I want you to know that you can count on me."

Amanda looked at him. No wonder all of New York loved him so. She could never again love him romantically as she once had. That Amanda had long since grown up. "Everyone needs a friend now and then."

Paul kissed her warmly on the cheek to seal the bond.

Christine tugged at her opera-length gloves, dabbed at her mouth, and pretended to listen to David. What a boor the man was! She didn't know how Amanda could stand it. Surreptitiously, Christine's eyes traveled to the dance floor where she saw her husband kissing The Granger Woman.

Christine felt her blood turn cold and the hair on her neck prickle. It wasn't the kiss, for Paul had kissed a thousand women since the day they'd married. It was the way he looked at Amanda. Paul had never looked at her like that. Christine had thought *she* had power over Paul, but now she witnessed a kind of power she knew nothing about. Scrutinizing them, she looked for other signs. Clearly, Amanda didn't feel the same about Paul.

"This is terrible," she muttered under her breath.

"Pardon?" David asked.

"Uh, it's terrible that you haven't been picked up by *Collier's*." Her smile was strained, but David continued droning on. Christine should have stopped Amanda a long time ago. Christine couldn't allow her to wrest Paul from her, not when she was only beginning to get what she wanted. She would think of some way to get back at Amanda. She listened to David and suddenly realized exactly the tack she would take.

"David, doesn't Amanda help you with your solicitations?"

"Sometimes. Not much, really."

"How strange. I should think she would be more actively involved. Why, if I were her, I would march right up to John Schultz—"

"You *know* John Schultz?"

"Of course."

"I've tried for months to see him. Do you think you could help me arrange something?"

"David," she purred, then sensuously ran her finger down his cheek. "What are friends for?"

It was the first time in his life that Andrew realized that to be successful he didn't have to do anything or say anything; he just had to *be*. None of these girls or their parents questioned him about his background, his family, or the circumstances of his arrival. They only knew two things about him. One, he had royal blood as did his sister; and two, he was a bachelor. A handsome bachelor with a famous sister who was married to one of New York's own, and who, from the first day of her arrival, had moved in all the best circles.

Amanda had done all his work for him. He'd never dreamed it would be this easy. For the first time, Andrew was confronted with *choice*. Not only could he have any of fifty debutantes but their older sisters too.

For weeks Andrew had wondered why Amanda hadn't introduced him to her society friends, and now he realized how effective her subtle strategy had been. She'd given him time to find a job, make a name for himself, and learn a little about the city. He'd absorbed enough about the society people through the papers and Amanda to know whom he should be impressed with and when to move on. There were no titles in America to ease the work of perception.

One particularly pretty girl, Meredith, with a slight frame and strawberry blonde hair, had somehow managed to have three dances with Andrew that night. It was flattering to know that somehow this girl had either bribed or blackmailed two other girls to exchange partners. Though she pretended to be demure, he caught her brilliant, fiery green eyes. He had a feeling that if he wasn't careful, he could find himself engaged before the night was over . . . willing or not.

"Papa said he wants to meet you," she said in a soft voice that could barely ruffle her fan feathers.

"Certainly. And Papa is . . ."

She raised a finely arched eyebrow. "I forgot. You wouldn't know Papa yet, would you?" She glanced around the room. She motioned with her head toward the second table to the left of the orchestra. "There's Papa. Herman Bishop."

"Of the railroad Bishops . . ." Andrew looked down at her. Her family had more money than God. He'd already done two ads for Bishop Railroads. They were bringing in a new express route from New York to Chicago and then an express to San Francisco. It was the most innovative idea in railroading in fifty years. Bishop had founded the New York-to-Cleveland express, which catered to the stock investors and brokers who needed to be at the Cleveland Stock Exchange every Monday morning. This gutsy, diminutive girl was his only daughter. Andrew couldn't believe his luck.

The dance ended and as everyone else applauded, Andrew held Meredith tightly and let his eyes drink in the possibilities.

"Shall we see Papa now?"

"By all means."

Herman Bishop was a rotund man, gray at the temples of his sandy hair, and smoked a gargantuan cigar. He blew out a cloud of smoke, gripped Andrew's hand like a vise, and, if possible, his smile was broader than his stomach.

"My boy! Pleased to know you. Know your brother-in-law, David. Fine fellow. He painted Meredith on her sixteenth. Sit down," Herman bellowed, for he didn't talk in normal speaking tones.

"I wanted to commend you, sir, on the fine operation you own. I've met John Childress in your advertising . . ."

Herman interrupted. "Know all about it. Good work there, Granger. Our sales went up ten percent."

"Ten percent?" Was he hearing right? His work—Amanda's ideas—were *that* good? It was incredible.

"I told Meredith to bring you over so I could offer my congratulations. She likes you, my boy. So do I." Herman Bishop puffed heavily on his cigar and exhaled a stream of Havana smoke.

Adulation had never been a part of Andrew's life. He knew now he could never live without it again.

CHAPTER TWENTY-TWO

Amanda's eyes snapped open. She jerked into a sitting position. "What is it?"

"You've overslept again, Amanda! All this time I thought you were dressing. How can you be so inconsiderate?"

"Inconsiderate?"

"Yes. We have a meeting with the editor of *City* magazine and you're still sleeping." David grabbed her lace robe from the divan and flung it at her. "Christ! I can't count on you for anything."

"I'm sorry, David." She stood woozily and tried to put on her robe, but she fumbled so much she gave up. As she walked to the bathroom, he was still berating her.

"I might as well call and cancel. We can never make it now."

"How much time do I have?"

"Twenty-five minutes."

She flung the door of the bathroom open. She was naked except for a towel she held in front of her. Her eyes were awake and flashing. "Then call for the carriage. I *will* be ready!" She slammed the door.

David went downstairs grumbling with every step he took. Amanda took less interest in his work as each day passed. Christine Van Volkien had been a hundred times more helpful and she'd only met with him once to arrange a meeting with Schultz. And the editor had bought. That sketch would be out at the end of the month. David felt as if things were really starting to break for him now. He needed Amanda with him at these meetings. The publishers wanted to meet The Granger Woman. They were as celebrity hungry as the public.

He didn't know what was wrong with Amanda lately, only that her interest in him and his work had definitely waned. For the past two weeks she hadn't wanted to go to parties or dinners. Their usual Thursday-night dinners for friends had come to an abrupt halt. Just yesterday, Sylvia had called to talk to David about it. Something was wrong, and David didn't like it when his business suffered.

Twenty-five minutes after she'd walked into the bathroom, Amanda walked down the stairs dressed in a stunning pale blue linen skirt and bolero jacket. She wore a yellow-and-blue hat with blue veiling streaming down the back. She pulled on blue gloves and smiled at her husband.

"Is the coach ready?"

Without complimenting her, he grabbed her elbow and ushered her quickly out of the house and into the carriage.

It was a beautiful spring day for lunch at Rector's near Herald Square. Amanda liked it, for it was very gay without being crass and it had the first revolving door installed in New York. Now it seemed that everyone opening a restaurant or saloon had a revolving door. There was a piano player, an accordion player, and a violinist who played ragtime music.

David had reserved a booth near the front so that they could talk over the music.

Max Solomon was a slight man, smaller in stature and bone structure than Amanda, but when he threw his weight around, the publishing world felt it. Amanda liked him instantly. Unlike the others, he didn't care about meeting a celebrity. He wanted to talk to *her*. Max was an unusual man.

"I hear talk that you could usurp Irene Langhorn. Do you think that's possible, Amanda?" Max asked pointedly.

"Anything's possible . . . given the right circumstances."

His tiny eyes peered at her over the top of his pince-nez glasses. "I've heard other talk about you, Amanda."

"Like what?" David demanded. Amanda noticed that he fumbled a great deal with his napkin. She wondered why he was so nervous. What was different about Max from any other publisher?

"I hear that Parker's ads look astonishingly like your charity posters. You have an unmistakable style, young lady."

"Is that something you heard? Or is that your observation?" she countered.

His thin lips parted in a genuine smile. It was his first of the afternoon. "Of course, you're right." He looked at David. "She's more than just your model, isn't she?"

David's laugh was strained. "She's my wife."

"Not your genius?"

"No! I pose all my sketches. It's my selection of background, my composition . . ."

Max placed a hand on his shoulder. "Don't take it personally, David. I'm trying to assess a situation here. I need to know my bargaining position."

"Amanda is a model . . . a very beautiful one. But it is my career that is on sale here."

"David, I think you're wrong." Max speared another piece of avocado and coolly let his words sink in.

David's mind was filled with defensive phrases, but wisely he remained silent. Amanda watched the wily publisher throw accusations and enticements into his cauldron. It was time for him to stop stirring things up and taste the brew.

"What I would like to propose, David . . . and Amanda . . . is a six-month exclusive on all sketches of The Granger Woman. You can't sell to any other publisher. In order to see Amanda, the public will have to buy *City*. According to my research, your last publication will be in July. From August to January of next year, I'll be your only publisher."

Amanda could see that David was instantly insulted. She knew he wanted to refuse the offer. Because David was an artist, he tended to sell himself too cheaply and too often. David would do anything to be as popular as Dana Gibson. Amanda realized that she was more in tune with Max's mind than David was. Max wouldn't have come to them with this offer if he didn't think that The Granger Woman could be a huge success. It was very possible they could beat out The Gibson Girl—if they negotiated the offer in their favor.

"How much?" Amanda demanded.

"Three thousand for six sketches."

"A thousand a sketch for six months. On the seventh month you'll run two sketches per month for fifteen hundred a sketch for another six-month period. David and I will have creative consultation rights."

Max's jaw literally dropped open. "Sorry, my offer or nothing."

Amanda daintly put her fork down and nodded to David. "Come, David."

David was still in shock over Amanda's counteroffer. Stiffly, he rose.

Suddenly Max appeared a bit jittery. "Now wait a minute. Maybe we can work something out."

David sank back in his seat. Amanda stood.

"Max, did your spies tell you that David recently sold to Schultz? His circulation goes all down the Eastern seaboard and west to Chicago and Kansas City. We're worth our price . . . and you know it."

Max dabbed at the perspiration on his upper lip. "Twelve hundred a sketch on the seventh month and thereafter."

"And we have creative consultation?"

"Yes."

"It's a deal," she said and stuck out her hand. "Have your attorney draw up the papers. You've just bought The Granger Woman."

Emasculation was an alien experience to David Simon. Suffering through it at his wife's hands was doubly humiliating. Somehow he'd make her pay for it. It didn't take a genius to know that Max Solomon would tell everyone in publishing that Amanda Granger had negotiated the biggest deal of David Simon's life. David had never had an agent in his life. He didn't trust them or like them, as a group. He'd be damned if his first agent was his wife and model.

But the deal was done, and there was nothing he could do about it now save to go on. He wished he could be magnanimous and thank her. If all went as well as Max expected it to, he could very well be sitting in Dana Gibson's shoes by the beginning of '97.

At seven o'clock, David left his studio and went down to dinner. There was only one place setting. He stormed into the kitchen.

"Charlotte, where's Mrs. Simon?"

"She wanted her supper in her room. I just sent it up," the cook said, surprised that her employer knew so little about his wife.

"That's twice already this week. Well," he said heading for the stairs, "I'll put a stop to this."

David took the steps two at a time and burst into the room. Amanda was nowhere in sight. "Amanda!" he called.

The bathroom door slowly creaked open. With sweat pouring from her pale face, Amanda leaned against the doorjamb.

"David, I'm very sick. Help me to the bed."

He rushed over and put his arm around her. She was trembling and cold.

"What do you think it is? You were fine at lunch today. Do you think it was something you ate?"

"I don't know. I haven't felt well for weeks. I thought it would go away."

"So that's why you kept cancelling invitations."

"It comes in waves. But this is the worst it's been. You'd better call the doctor."

And hour later, Dr. Trent closed his bag and joined David in the salon.

"You're going to be a father," he announced happily.

"What?" David was incredulous. "She has influenza, that's all."

"Mid-January, the way I figure it. She's only a month along. That's why she's so ill. But this won't last long. I left some medication to help her through the worst of it. Congratulations, David."

David walked the doctor to the door and watched as he rode away. This wasn't happening! Not now, not when he'd just started running in the big league. January—the month he'd chosen as a target date to finally beat Gibson. By January he *could* have had it all.

Whether he thought it demeaning or not, it was obvious Amanda was a good agent for him. He needed her now more than ever, though he would never admit it to her. But this baby was going to destroy it all—his dream, his life.

Amanda lifted a cup of strong tea and sipped as Sylvia studied her.

"David doesn't want this baby."

"What a horrible thing to say! What man wouldn't want a child?"

"I can see it in his eyes. He tells me he's happy about it, but I don't believe him. If I weren't so sick in the evenings when he wants to go to parties, perhaps he wouldn't be as upset.''

''Amanda, you're making too much of this. Parties aren't that important.''

''To David they are his lifeline to fame. You should see him, Sylvia. He nearly salivates when an invitation arrives.''

Sylvia wondered if she had misjudged David herself. He'd seemed genuinely in love with Amanda in the beginning. She'd never been sure of the union only because she'd known Amanda wasn't truly in love with David. Perhaps she should have given Amanda a stronger warning back then. However, it wasn't her place then or now to interfere.

''Give him some time to get used to the idea, Amanda. He'll come around,'' Sylvia said.

''I hope you're right.''

''Amanda! Would you please quit fidgeting!''

''I didn't move a muscle. How much longer will it be?''

''Christ! Sometimes you whine like a child. You know how important this sketch is. Max wants it by the end of the week. And you aren't helping matters any.''

''I'm just so tired, David.''

''Be quiet!'' he yelled and then buried his head in his sketch pad.

He was so intent these days, she thought, and always so angry with her.

June was unbearably hot. Even the oak trees seemed to melt in the heat. Pregnant or not, Amanda would have been uncomfortable anyway. The ''evening sickness'' had passed, though now she needed a nap in the afternoons. She hadn't gained much weight yet and was still able to wear most of her clothes. David insisted she cinch her waist ''so that no one would know.'' Amanda could count on one hand the people who knew about her pregnancy. David had wanted it that way.

She, of course, was joyful. She'd decided to combine the tiny sitting room and large walk-in linen closet next to their room to make the nursery. David hadn't liked that idea either. He wanted Andrew to leave, but Amanda wanted her brother with her. She liked the idea of a large family. Thus far, David had acquiesced to her wishes.

Amanda hired the painters, carpenters, and wallpaper hangers herself, since David wanted nothing to do with the nursery. It wasn't a large job, and thankfully the pounding and sawing were finished in three days. On the first day, David had stormed out of the house saying he couldn't work. Amanda didn't ask him where he'd been, for she was immersed in the decorating. She hired two seamstresses who swagged, draped, and tied the window, bassinet, and daybed in white eyelet. The chair rail was painted palest blue, with wallpaper of tiny rosebuds on a white background above.

Amanda smiled to herself as she thought about the room that was nearly finished.

"Amanda!" David tossed his pad down. "You're doing it again."

"Why don't we quit for the day? I have so much to do. . . ." she pleaded, thinking of the layette at Lord & Taylor's she wanted.

"Go on," he said as she pecked him on the cheek and rushed out of the room.

David waited until he heard her telephoning for a carriage. When she was gone, he picked up the telephone. "Plaza 7," he told the operator.

Christine had just finished her bath and was sitting on an apricot-colored chaise in her bedroom as she slathered rose water and glycerine lotion on her legs.

She picked up the receiver on the first ring.

"Christine?"

"David. What good timing you have. I just sent the maid on an errand. Paul's at lunch. What would you have done if he'd answered?"

"Hung up. As always."

"I hope that hasn't been too often."

"No. I need to see you."

"Of course you do."

"Today," he said eagerly.

"I can't. I'm having tea with Mother and some of her friends in an hour."

"Then tomorrow."

"Paul and I are meeting with our attorney. Something about the estate. Friday is good. At the usual place."

"Yes! That's perfect. Amanda will be at Sylvia's. At two?"

"That's fine," she replied nonchalantly and hung up.

Christine couldn't believe how simple it had been to seduce David Simon. She'd thought taking Amanda's husband from her would be her greatest challenge. Christine had also thought she'd be pleased with herself by succeeding, but she wasn't. David had been too easy. There was something wrong with that marriage. But all marriages were built on imperfection.

Christine picked up a crystal atomizer of French perfume. She lavished her entire body with it. Paul couldn't resist her when she wore it—David either. She wondered if it was simply that men were weaker than women realized or if there was something in their biological chemistry that made them easy prey for trappings like perfume, an overly exposed breast, a flash of leg beneath a gown. Didn't it bother men that they were so vulnerable, so pliable?

Christine was not a talented woman, nor was she smart. But somehow she'd been able to capture two of New York's most desirable men. She knew she was beautiful. Was that all it took?

Just as she had wanted jewels and a name from Paul, Christine wanted something from David. She wanted fame. David had the power to give it to her. Whether his good fortune was due to Amanda was a topic of debate for most of the city. Christine believed in David's talent. She would get him to sketch her again and again. If necessary, she'd sell the sketches herself. She had just as good connections in publishing as he did. Better.

Satisfaction glimmered in her eyes as she rose. It wouldn't be long, she thought. Soon she would be even more famous than The Granger Woman.

The Tenderloin was the area between the slums of Hell's Kitchen and the respectability of Fifth Avenue, from Twentieth Street through the Thirties. In the center was Herald Square.

Andrew had worked in Herald Square only three weeks when he'd learned the lay of the land. Under the El along the side streets of Sixth Avenue flourished the bawdiest revues, cafes, bordellos, and gambling halls. It was the underside of the New York his sister knew. It was the dark side of the Gay Nineties.

Six months after coming to New York, Andrew found himself in the same vise he'd known in London. He'd found a girl, Meredith Bishop, and that girl was very, very rich. He needed money to court her. The kind of money he needed would never come from Quinton Parker. He would have to go to the streets.

After the deb ball, Andrew had accidentally run into Meredith one day. She was shopping . . . alone. He invited her for a soda.

"Why haven't you called on me?" she asked, dipping her spoon into the tall glass.

"It's not that I haven't wanted to. I've been busy. My job, helping David with his work . . ."

"Oh." She smiled sweetly at him. But he could still see those determined eyes. "Have you been to Oscar Hammerstein's new theater?"

"The Olympia? No. Why?"

"There's a new play there I'm dying to see."

"You want to go there? Why? I mean, it's not in a very respectable area. The street isn't even paved yet."

"Andrew! Where's your sense of adventure?"

"My sense of . . ." He couldn't believe his ears. The Olympia was not just a theater but a block-long palace including a dance hall and concert hall. "What would your father think if I took you there?"

"He went last week . . . with mother. Now I want to go. So, will you take me or not?"

"Of course."

"Thursday night at seven," she said matter-of-factly and walked away.

Andrew still couldn't believe that one of the richest and prettiest girls in New York had blatantly courted *him*. He was flattered. And he was broke. He would need a theater suit, which, if he spent the last of Harriet's money, he could buy a proper one. But then, he needed money for a carriage, flowers—yes, he'd be expected to send flowers earlier in the day. Then there were the theater tickets themselves, a trifle. There would be dinner afterward and she would want to go to Del's . . . there would be all that champagne. Andrew quickly figured he would need two hundred dollars. There was only one place he could make that kind of money that fast—the streets.

By ten o'clock each night the working-class crowd of publishers, vendors, and secretaries gave way to the gaudy red satin and black lace of prostitutes. Rugged-faced men wearing bowlers and flashy suits spent money profusely. There were actors, singers, a few bohemian types; an alcoholic journalist and a bisexual artist. This was the world that Andrew knew best.

Andrew knew that Manny's Pub under the El was the favorite

gathering place for New York's night people, especially on a Monday night. He had four days till he saw Meredith on Thursday. He had to work fast, and that meant going after one of the princes of the underworld.

At the far end of Manny's, seated at a round table, was a tall, lean man with raven's-wing black hair and eyes that were blacker still. His cheeks were sunken hollows, and when he smiled his lips never parted, only cracked across his face like that of a jack-o'-lantern. His name was Vince Casal. He was the man Andrew had come to see.

On Vince's left sat a burly man in his middle thirties with an acne-scarred face. His eyes were like tiny raisins pressed into dimpled, pasty dough. Andrew noticed he kept refilling his whiskey glass before it was completely empty. Next to him was a blank-faced teenaged girl whose life in the streets had robbed her of the expected rose of youth. Her two girlfriends, one blonde, one dark-haired, whispered to each other. Andrew was quick to note the half-concealed caress of a thigh and the sensual gazes they gave each other. The second of Vince's thugs wore an exquisite dark suit with a red silk scarf in his pocket. His hair was meticulously combed, and had it not been for the bulge of a shoulder revolver, Andrew would have guessed him to be a banker.

They were an oddly assorted group, Andrew thought, pasted together by their curious needs and their struggle for survival on the night streets of New York.

Andrew boldly walked up to the table. "I hear you have the best game in town."

The expensively dressed thug stuck his face into Andrew's and snarled: "You heard wrong."

Andrew ignored him and never took his eyes from Vince. "Too bad." He reached into his pocket and pulled out a wad of bills. "I brought my friends."

Vince's eyelid twitched, but otherwise he remained a stone. "I can't help you out. But I've heard that on Tuesday nights a man with that kind of money can buy a good woman."

"Where?"

"Bessie's on Thirty-Third."

"What's the best time?"

"Eleven. Ask for Janey."

Andrew picked up his money and stuffed it back in his pocket.

He was not intimidated by Vince, for he'd known so many like
him and many who were much, much smarter. As he walked out
of Manny's he realized that Vince would be easier to deal with
than he'd thought.

Andrew walked inside the plain, three-story brick building.
From the outside it could have been anyone's house. But there
were too many bright lights, and the piano music was ironically
sad.

He was met by a bleached-blonde woman in her forties, who
had on too much lipstick and cheek rouge. She wore only a lace
corset, white stockings, and a sheer white peignoir. Nearly all of
her voluptuous bosom was exposed. She had long, lean legs and
small hips. There were many who would call her unattractive, for
her waist was not tiny and her hips were not large.

Andrew couldn't lift his eyes from her breasts. She smiled
widely. It was a warm, almost endearing, smile.

"Vince is upstairs," she said, not even asking his name.

She went first and at each step she turned to make certain he
could see all her bosom and all of her leg.

She stopped at the door before opening it. "After you finish, if
you have any money left—my name's Janey."

"I know," he said, filling his eyes one more time before she
left.

Andrew entered the room. There were six men at the table.
Vince was at the head of the table. There were two mousy looking
men, obviously accountants or moderately successful lawyers.
There was another, older man with balding red hair. He constantly rolled a pair of dice between his long, tapered fingers,
making an unnerving clicking sound. Andrew rightly guessed this
man was well acquainted with gambling. There was another man
of about thirty-five, with a thick black beard. One man was very
young, perhaps not even twenty, but he was expensively dressed.
Andrew guessed him to be a society type, getting his thrills from
the bad side of town. To a man like Vince, an unruly society boy
was the cream in his coffee.

Andrew dug into his pocket and pulled out his money. He sat
down.

"Glad you could make it," Vince said, shuffling and cutting
the cards. "You want a drink?"

"Yes." Andrew took a whiskey from a dark-haired girl. She

was the whore he'd seen the night before at Manny's. He glanced around and wondered where her girlfriend was. Andrew pretended to drink. He made a rule never to drink when working.

Vince started to deal.

"Before we start . . . may I see those cards?" Andrew asked politely.

"You questioning my integrity?" Vince laughed, but there was no humor in his eyes.

"Somebody might have slipped a marked deck in on you, Vince."

"Tell you what. To show my good manners, we'll start out with a brand-new deck. That oughta make everybody happy." He snapped his fingers and one of his thugs pulled out a new, sealed deck.

Vince took them out of the box. "You happy now?"

"Not quite. Let me see them."

Vince's eyes bore down on Andrew like branding irons. But he handed him the cards. Andrew rifled through them, then handed them back.

"They're okay," Andrew pronounced.

Everyone at the table breathed a sigh of relief. The game began. After seven rounds the two mousy types had folded. On the ninth round, the young society boy had lost to Andrew. Within the hour the other two men had bowed out, taking their winnings with them. Vince and Andrew remained.

"How about one last hand, Vince? High card wins all."

Vince had started with fifty dollars and now was up a hundred and fifty. Andrew still had his two hundred dollars. Vince's crooked smile cracked across his face.

"I'm in." He thrust two hundred dollars into the middle. Vince shuffled the deck, cut the cards, and reshuffled.

"You first," Andrew said.

Vince's smile was triumphant. He cut thin and turned up the ace of diamonds.

"That's pretty hard to beat," Andrew said as he placed his hand over the deck and cut. He drew the ace of spades. "I win."

Vince Casal's windpipe closed as he choked back his shock. He watched incredulously as Andrew scraped up four hundred dollars.

"Thanks for the game, Vince."

Andrew walked out of the room and shut the door behind him.

When he'd checked the cards at the beginning of the game he'd found they were indeed marked. It was a more sophisticated marking than he'd seen before. He'd allowed Vince to win the small hands, enabling him to make the big bet. He was positive Vince would call him for a rematch.

In the meantime, he thought he'd spend twenty dollars on Janey.

CHAPTER TWENTY-THREE

Amanda paced back and forth, listening to the maddening rustle of her taffeta gown. She'd sent the servants home, thinking David would have been back by now. It was past eight o'clock. If he didn't arrive soon it would be far too late to attend the Jones's party at all. She didn't really care about the party; in fact, she'd wanted to decline when the invitation arrived several weeks ago. David, however, had insisted. He'd said it was important for his career that they attend.

"To hell with his career!" she exclaimed and had started to undress when she heard the sound of a carriage outside the window. She looked out of her bedroom window.

"David!"

He raced into the house and up the stairs. He only glanced at her as he tore off his jacket. "Why aren't my tails lying out?"

"I didn't think you were coming."

"Nonsense. I told you this was an important night for me."

"Then where have you been?"

He stood, peeled off his trousers, and went to the closet. He took out his dress clothes and changed. He went to the bureau, picked up his brush, and smoothed his hair.

"I had a meeting with Max. I told you."

"That was at noon."

"He has some very specific ideas for the September issue. Ideas we didn't exactly agree on. It took more time than I thought."

"And do you both agree now?"

"Of course," he said smugly.

Amanda wondered just who had conformed to whose ideas.

In minutes, David was ready. Amanda gathered her gloves and evening bag and followed him downstairs.

As they sat in the carriage, she sniffed the air. There was a peculiar scent of jasmine that clashed drastically with her tea-rose cologne.

"David, what kind of cologne are you wearing now? That's not your bay rum."

David froze. He'd *told* Christine not to use so much perfume. Slathering herself in perfume the way she did, the fragrance seemed to imbed itself in David's skin whenever they made love. Usually, he had a chance to bathe it off. Tonight there hadn't been time. He had to think twice. He had to think fast. "You didn't like my gift?"

"What gift?"

"Don't tell me there wasn't a delivery from Lord & Taylor today?"

"There wasn't."

"After lunch, Max went out to buy a gift for his wife. I tagged along and well, I guess I'll have to spoil the surprise . . . I bought you a new French perfume. The girl at the counter told me it was all the rage in Paris. I guess she got carried away with that atomizer . . . spraying it in the air, on my wrists . . . just everywhere." He looked at her out of the corner of his eye. He wasn't sure if she believed him. "I *specifically* instructed them to deliver it so that you would have it for tonight."

"I never got it," Amanda replied.

Instinct told Amanda that David was seeing another woman, but other than the faint scent of perfume she had no proof. She'd never had reason to doubt him before, but his lie seemed too transparent to ignore. Alarm bells went off in her head. She wanted desperately to believe him, believe that their marriage was sound and that the new baby would make a difference.

David watched Amanda's face turn from suspicion to conviction. But there was still a chance to bring her back to him. He could not afford a schism between them. He smiled lovingly and took her hand in his.

"I know I've been neglecting you lately, Amanda, and I'm going to make it up to you. We should take a holiday next month. It'll be much too hot to be in the city. I'll tell you what. We'll go to Tuxedo Park. Griswold Lorillard invited me last year, but we weren't married yet, so I declined. What do you think?''

She looked at him. His eyes seemed filled with honesty. She couldn't tell anymore when he was lying or when he was telling the truth. Maybe his idea of a holiday was what their marriage needed. Perhaps with time alone they could become one again. And *if* there was another woman, perhaps David would forget her.

''It sounds wonderful,'' she said hopefully.

''I'll make the arrangements tomorrow.''

In Orange County, New York, amidst the Ramapo Mountains, Tuxedo Park had been conceived and built as a summer playground for the ultrarich. By 1896, when Amanda and David Simon alighted from the tufted velvet coach that had brought them to the mountain resort from the train station, Tuxedo Park was eighteen months old. Where once had been dense forest and impenetrable terrain, there now existed roads, sewer systems, a village, twenty-two cottages—each consisting of ten to fifteen rooms—and a clubhouse.

For their two-week stay, David and Amanda had been given exclusive use of a ''shingle-style'' house belonging to Griswold, who was in Europe for the summer. Amanda had four servants, a cook, and a gardener. A list of residents, their telephone numbers and planned dinners, parties, and activities was left on the desk in the main room. Court tennis, golf, and bridge tournaments were scheduled by hour of the day. At first glance Amanda could tell she would never lack for things to do.

Their first night was quiet and pleasant. It was cool in the mountains at night and David had made a fire. They snuggled on a sofa under a plaid woolen blanket.

''I think I'm going to like it here,'' Amanda said.

He rubbed her arm. ''It is wonderful, isn't it?''

She looked up and kissed him. ''Wonderful.''

Amanda slept late Monday morning. Two hours after lunch, she found it was a mistake she should never repeat.

David wore white slacks and a white linen shirt and had tied a white cardigan around his shoulders. With tennis racquet in hand, he came bounding up the hill to the cottage. He was not alone.

"Amanda!" he called to her as she sat on the porch reading a copy of *City* magazine. "Get dressed and come join us."

"I don't know how to play tennis, David. And aren't you forgetting . . ." She patted her stomach.

He stopped. "Oh, yes. So I have." He continued toward the front steps but at a slower pace.

The man behind him was quite tall, with broad shoulders and muscular legs. He was dripping with sweat. He had a thick crop of chestnut hair that gleamed in the sun, and from twenty paces his blue eyes sparkled at her. He was tanned, which made his even teeth seem twice as white beneath his dark mustache. She guessed him to be in his early thirties.

"Who's your friend?" Amanda asked.

David stood beside her and put his arm around her shoulder. Quickly, he leaned over and whispered, "Be nice to him. His family is probably the richest in New York."

The man stood on the first step, keeping his distance. He couldn't take his eyes off Amanda. He neither smiled nor spoke his approval. Amanda felt as if she could hear him reading her thoughts. Somehow, he'd found some inner link, some passage, to her innermost self. She was at once frightened and fascinated. She didn't know if she should fear him or accept him. But since he was important to David, she placed him in the category with all David's business associates.

"This is Matthew Wade," David said.

"How do you do?" Amanda said and extended her hand.

His smile was faint as he stepped up and took her hand.

There are times when one crosses boundaries of etiquette, when inaction becomes action. Matthew knew he lingered too long delving into Amanda's eyes, memorizing the touch of her hand. He should pull away instantly, recite the expected mundane cordialities that he used every day. But he couldn't. He'd never met anyone like her before. It was more than her beauty that intrigued him, or her Madonna-like deportment. It was the sadness in her blue eyes, nearly imperceptible it was, that intrigued him. He could tell that she thought she'd fooled him and everyone else. It was obvious her husband didn't see it. But Matthew saw it. He knew precisely where to look, for he'd seen that same melancholy in his own reflection.

Amanda glanced at David; there wasn't the first hint of jealousy in his eyes. Couldn't he see it—*feel* the vibrations between herself and Matthew? To Amanda it was as if she'd found an identical twin she'd never known about or some half of herself she'd lost in another life. Slowly, she retrieved her hand.

"Would you care for some tea, Matthew?"

"Yes." He sat in a white wicker chair on the opposite side of the porch.

Amanda tried to look at her husband when she spoke to him, but her head wouldn't turn. She could only look at Matthew. "How was the tennis match?"

"Matthew won," David said, pouring his own tea.

Amanda tried to concentrate on the tea, hoping she could break the spell. She floated lemon slices on top before offering it to Matthew.

"This is our first trip to Tuxedo Park," she said, looking him in the eye when he took the tea from her.

"Mine too. I've been in Europe for the past eighteen months, so I'm out of touch with what's been happening in the States."

"I see." Amanda was doubly flattered, for it was obvious he had no inkling of her fame as The Granger Woman. "Were you on holiday?"

"Hardly." He laughed softly. "It was rather boring. All business."

"Are the Wades opening branches of their bank in Europe now?" David asked.

As Matthew put his cup on the table, Amanda thought his face oddly stern. "I'm not involved in my father's business. Nor is he involved in mine."

"There's a difference?" David tried to be jovial, but obviously he'd hit some nerve.

"I abhor the banking business. I don't like anything about it. I've seen my father twist people's lives with the threat of a foreclosure, the denial of a business loan. He and I never seemed to get along. Clash of principles and goals."

"But the Wade banks are the most solid in the country. He's done a lot of good too," David said.

"I know that. And I don't have anything against success, either. Let's just say I have my own way of doing things." He rose quickly.

"I'm sorry if we've offended you," Amanda said.

"You haven't. It's been a long time since I've been around New Yorkers. I guess I'm not acclimated yet." He shook David's hand. "Good day." In three strides he was down the steps and had vanished behind the flowering wall of climbing red roses.

"What an odd man! His temperament was fine during our game . . . and what was that crack about New Yorkers supposed to mean?"

Amanda picked up the teacups and placed them on the wicker tray. "I have no idea. But I'll remember next time to choose my words more carefully."

Not realizing she was being facetious, David replied: "See that you do. He could be an ally for us."

Matthew strode angrily back to his cottage. He slammed the big walnut door behind him, went straight to the high-ceilinged, beamed living room, and flopped down on the leather sofa.

"Christ! You've made a fool out of yourself this time, old boy."

For eighteen months Matthew had cut himself off from the world of his father, where business and social standing fed each other. He wanted to make a mark in New York based on his own merits, not because he was James Wade's oldest son. It was difficult to do, and he was never certain if he was succeeding because of his father or on his own.

On his thirty-third birthday, Matthew had announced to his father that he was quitting the banking business and going abroad to find investors for his project.

James Wade had lifted his goateed chin arrogantly and, in tones that boomed like a cannon, said: "The hell you say!"

"You've known for years that my dream is to build a department store."

"I will *not* have the Wade name plastered on a common retail business like Macy's. Good God, Matthew! Have you no pride?"

Pride, Matthew thought. He had too *much* pride. He was too proud to live in his father's house, paying for his life-style with family money and then owing his father on his own life in return. Matthew had to follow his conscience.

Matthew sat up and ran his hand through his hair. Why had he been so rude to Amanda and David? He'd acted as if they were his enemies. They must think he was crazy.

"I *am* crazy!" he said, getting up and going to the terrace. He looked out at the mountains. "Crazy to think about another man's wife. . . ."

He lit a cigarette and flipped the match into a stone jardiniere. He would see her tomorrow, he knew. And the day after that. He'd never felt like this about any woman before. He was an intelligent man and had always been able to think things through logically. He was a realist. He didn't believe in love at first sight—or in fairy tales, time travel, or socialistic utopias. Matthew was a modern man; he believed in an explanation for everything. He was certain this was simply a passing infatuation.

Amanda dipped two toes into the freezing lake water and instantly recoiled. "The Thames in December isn't this cold!"

"Amanda!" David yelled from atop the embankment. "Are you going to swim or not?"

She lifted her face to him and shielded her eyes with her hand, but all she could see was the sun. "It's too cold! I think I'll take the canoe out."

"All right. We've got a foursome for golf. I'll be back around six."

"Good-bye." She waved.

Amanda walked over to the tiny birchwood canoe and tried to drag it from the shore into the water. It was heavier than she'd imagined, or this pregnancy had rendered her a weakling.

"Amanda!'

She turned again to the sun. "What is it, David?"

There was no response, but she could see him coming closer to her. "Did you forget something?" The sun shot between the tree limbs, nearly blinding her.

"You shouldn't lift that by yourself," he said.

She dropped her hand. It wasn't David. "Will you help me?"

"Yes," he said, standing next to her, looking into her eyes. The wind rustled Matthew's hair. He bent over and with one hand pulled the canoe to the water's edge. He extended his hand and beckoned to her. "Come."

She climbed into the canoe and sat on the seat in back. She picked up the paddle.

He pushed the canoe into the water and just as the tip left shore, he jumped into the canoe and snatched the paddle from her. "You didn't really want to be alone."

"I did, actually."

He watched as she opened her parasol to shield herself against the sun. "Do you want me to leave?"

"No," she found herself saying a bit too quickly. She felt uneasy in his presence. It reminded her of the days when she was a servant for the Kents. The Wade name was America's brand of royalty. They ruled over the Eastern seaboard with a strong and loud voice. Amanda had never been easily intimidated, but suddenly she felt herself shrinking from him. She didn't know much about him, except that he was easily angered. She wondered if it was safe for her to be out on this lake with him. What if he were a lunatic?

"You've never been out canoeing with anyone other than David, have you?"

"I've never been canoeing."

He watched as she struggled to avoid his face. He kept close to shore and pointed out the different kinds of flowers, the squirrels that scampered up the oak trees, and the place where he'd like to build a house. Slowly they circled the lake, he talking about nothing, she listening to his chatter. She felt comfortable with him, and she liked the soothing sound of his deep voice. But whenever she would look at him, she would see the intensity in his eyes, which caused a rush of excitement within her. It was an odd emotion—wanting to run away and at the same time wanting even more desperately to stay.

"You really love it here, don't you?" she asked.

"Yes. But I love the city too. I have a lot that I want to accomplish."

"But you don't like your father. . . ." She almost bit her lip. What possessed her to bring it up again, she didn't know. Curiosity?

"I apologize for yesterday. I'm normally quite controlled. It's just that I've worked very hard on my project—"

"Which is . . . ?" she quickly interrupted.

"A department store. On the south end of Central Park. I want something different even for New York. I want to handle only the finest merchandise from all over the world. Paris gowns, London men's suits, Irish sweaters and crystal, Chinese porcelain, and Russian diamonds. Everything the best, displayed elegantly. The entire first floor will be a mass of store windows. I went to Chicago to see Marshall Fields'. Well, my windows will be six feet higher. When people come to New York, my department store will be one of the sights they have to see."

''When do you break ground?''

''Next month. I bought the land two years ago. It took me five years to raise the money and arrange it. My father made certain every banker in New York thought I was certifiably nuts. I had to go to Europe to find investors. Now I'm ready.''

''What does your father think about it now that you have the money?''

''He doesn't know.''

''Why?''

''I came here straight from the ship. I needed some time to rest. To think. I'm not worried about my father. Nor am I afraid to face him. I know I can't be what he wants me to be, and I'll have to disappoint him. But I have to live my life for myself. Right now, I'm just trying to figure the easiest way to break it to him.''

''I should think he'd be proud to have a son like you.''

''He'd rather I be running his bank for him and going to his favorite charity balls.''

She smiled. ''If you'd been in New York, we might have met sooner. Perhaps at one of Caroline's parties,'' she said, trying to keep the conversation light. She ignored the compulsion she had to gaze deeply into his eyes and ask him profound questions about his feelings, his dreams. She wanted to know everything about him, but she had no right.

Matthew winced at the mention of the Astor name. He knew she'd been too good to be true. Amanda was one of those society matrons he hated . . . their lives were an endless party. He stuck the paddle in the water and pushed the canoe faster. But there was something about Amanda that told him the label didn't fit.

Amanda watched him as he seemed to paddle with a vengeance. ''Are you always so within yourself?''

He chuckled. ''Are you always this inquisitive?''

''How will I get to know you if I don't ask questions?''

He lifted the paddle and put it across his lap. ''And you want to know me, don't you?''

Their eyes met as an incredible stillness surrounded them. Amanda could hear the morning loons as they called to each other and the crickets chirp amongst the dense thickets on shore. But here in this canoe, she could swear she could almost hear their hearts beating. That same feeling of oneness she'd had yesterday when he came up her porch steps was here again now. Carefully, she stretched out her hand, wanting, needing to touch him. He grasped her hand in his and caressed it. She was tremendously frightened. She was, after all, another man's wife.

Amanda remembered her days on the ship with Paul. That was nothing to compare with the emotions she felt now. This was more than the sum total of her caring for David, her love for Andrew or her mother. This was beyond her realm of experience. And she didn't know what to do.

"I can't see you again," she said.

"Yes, you can. And you will."

"No. I'm married . . . and about to become a mother. I have a life. . . ."

"So do I. It won't be easy for us, Amanda."

Amanda tore her eyes from him. She was crying. "Take me back to shore. Now."

He said nothing. He turned the canoe around and headed back to the bank where they'd met. He jumped into the water and pulled the canoe to the beach. He helped her out. For a moment he stood with his hands on her waist, looking into her eyes. He wanted to kiss her, but he didn't.

"Good-bye, Amanda."

"Good-bye, Matthew," she said and started up the hill. When she reached the top, she turned around. The sun had moved to the west and again she found herself being blinded by its light. She knew he was there, but she couldn't see him. She put her hand over her eyes; still she saw nothing.

"Good-bye. . . ." She walked away.

For the rest of the day, Amanda could think of nothing but Matthew. She could still hear his voice, feel the coolness of his skin. She replayed the scene between them over and over. She became increasingly restless. She thought of going to his cottage, of telephoning him. She wanted to see him, but she knew she must not. When David returned from his golf game and informed her they were meeting two other couples at the clubhouse for dinner, she wanted only to get into bed and pull the sheets over her head—for about three weeks.

"I don't like that dress," he said casually as he tied his tie.

"What?"

"You look too . . . fat." He pulled a yellow cotton dress from the wardrobe. "Wear this."

"David! I hate that dress. Besides, I'm not fat, I'm pregnant."

"You don't have to go around broadcasting it."

"Why are you doing this? Don't you want this baby?"

"I don't remember being consulted about this."

"We're married. It comes as part of the territory."

David gulped a whiskey. "I don't want to talk about it. This isn't the time."

Amanda threw the yellow dress on the bed. "It's never the right time for you, David. We only talk about the things you are interested in, and only when you decide. You can't ignore this baby any longer, David. It is real."

"I'm more aware of that than you think."

Amanda glared at him, wondering how much of her anger was meant for David and how much for Matthew. At this point, she wanted nothing to do with *any* man.

"I'm wearing this dress," she said firmly, picking up a light mohair shawl.

David finished his whiskey, mumbled a satisfying round of obscenities to himself, and together they headed for the clubhouse.

Dinner was a casual affair, consisting of only five light courses and three wines. A string trio played faintly in the background. Amanda met the Henleys and the Petersons, both from New York City. They were well acquainted with Amanda's fame as The Granger Woman.

"That's a beautiful dress, Amanda," Elinor Henley complimented her.

Amanda purposely threw David a triumphant grin. "Thank you. I thought so too."

"You'd look marvelous in anything," Elinor replied. " I wish I knew how to put things together the way you do. You make it look so easy."

Janice Peterson concurred. "I have to rely on my dressmaker. And sometimes I think she takes advantage of me. Lately, she's made dresses that look like they were made from remnants."

"Maybe they were," Amanda said, remembering when her mother used to do exactly that to make larger profits. There wasn't anything wrong with it, if the seamstress was good. Obviously, Janice's woman was not.

David placed the wine order and then rejoined the two men as they discussed their golf game.

"Do you play golf, Amanda?" Sam Peterson asked.

"No. But I'd love to try."

"I thought perhaps you did, you being from London. It's quite popular there."

Amanda cringed. "I just never got around to it."

Elinor Henley had always considered herself an aware person. She went to the best parties, moved in the best crowds, and had been a guest of kings and queens. Elinor tried to be in the right places at the right times. It often took a great deal of effort, but always she'd found her reward. Elinor's passion in life was gossip.

She was not the kind to create false rumor where there was none, nor did she ever malign anyone. She rationalized that had she been born a man, she would have become an investigative journalist. She often felt like an archeologist uncovering an ancient tomb when she delved into the private parts of people's lives. She told herself she was helping them, for if she ever heard wild stories, she would replace the untruth with truth. Facts were important to her. She did not believe she was prying, though she'd been called meddlesome to her face. Elinor honestly liked people, and she likened herself to charity workers—she was a philanthropist.

"Did you have a nice canoe ride today, Amanda?" Elinor asked.

Amanda was surprised, though she shouldn't have been. "Yes, I did."

"And wasn't that Matthew Wade with you?"

David was instantly at attention. "Wade took you out on the lake?"

"Why, yes. We had a lovely ride," Amanda replied casually. "The water was smooth, no wind, and it didn't get hot until later in the afternoon."

Elinor played with the stem of her wineglass as she continued her investigation. "Did he say why he left so abruptly?"

"Left?" Amanda's surprise was scribbled across her face.

David's eyes narrowed. "We were to play tennis in the morning. I invited him for bridge later on Friday. How odd."

"It is, isn't it?" Elinor grinned.

"What did he say to you, Amanda?"

"Say?" She remembered the penetrating look in Matthew's eyes.

"He must have said something about leaving so abruptly."

"No. He was worried about his new store."

Janice Peterson broke out into laughter. So did Elinor.

"You mean he's actually going to do it this time?"

Amanda was confused. "He said he was breaking ground next month."

"Ha!" Sam Peterson said. "James will stop that."

"He seemed very determined to me," Amanda said defensively. "Matthew didn't impress me as a man who could be easily manipulated."

"Maybe so. But even Matthew can't fight James Wade. Sixty million dollars is a tough opponent."

David's jaw fell. "Jesus! Sixty million."

Elinor leaned forward. "Sam's being conservative." She looked pointedly at Amanda. "Even if Matthew could work his way around his father, I doubt the battle with Sydney would be worth it."

"Who's Sydney?" Amanda asked.

Elinor smiled caustically. "His wife."

CHAPTER TWENTY-FOUR

Morals were easier to deal with than emotions, Amanda decided two days after arriving home. Morally, she was able to banish the existence of Matthew Wade from her life. He was married and so was she. She was not an adulteress. Morals were cut-and-dried, black and white. Morals made life simple, clear, and defined.

Emotions, however, brought everything within the realm of possibilities. Emotionally, she was already attached to Matthew even when she didn't want to be. She was a disciplined person with a great deal of willpower. She did not telephone him; she sent no notes, no cards. She never saw him and even went out of her way to avoid that area of Central Park South where she knew he was breaking ground for his store. Amanda had successfully kept Matthew out of every part of her life—except her heart.

From the moment she awoke in the morning until her head hit the pillow at night, there was not a single hour of the day she didn't think about Matthew at least once or twice—a dozen times. After one week of inner battles, Amanda knew she had to do something to keep Matthew locked away. She met Sylvia for lunch in Washington Square.

"I want to co-chair the September Art Festival."

"You have so much spare time," Sylvia said facetiously.

"I pose for a few hours in the morning for David, and then he leaves until dinnertime. Which, of course, used to be his 'parade time.' "

"Pardon?"

"The time when he would show me off to publishers, investors. But now he's keeping me in the house. He's embarrassed by my pregnancy. It will ruin my 'image,' he thinks."

Sylvia wished she could take David aside and pound some sense into him, but she could only help by granting Amanda's request. "Are you sure you're up to this? We have only two months to get this fund-raiser off the ground."

"Positive. I feel wonderful."

"Very well. By the way, how is Andrew? I invited him for dinner while you were gone, but he already had an engagement."

"He's even busier than David. He's seeing Meredith Bishop now so he's never around for meals. I might as well be a hermit."

"It can't be all that bad."

"Well, I can't wait for this baby to come. At least then I'll have some company." Amanda looked down at her empty tea-cup. "I never knew I could be so lonely."

Andrew walked out of Bessie's with full pockets. He'd played Vince Casal for a sucker for over a month, but tonight's winnings were an exception. Andrew realized now that he'd been wasting time on Vince's two-bit games. He needed to move up to bigger stakes, but to find the kind of players he needed wouldn't be easy. He'd thought about discreetly going to Amanda's friends, the ones he knew liked to game once in a while, but there was too great a chance he'd blow everything he was trying to build in that world.

Up till now, he knew he was smart to keep his gambling confined to Vince's poker games at Bessie's. But the time had come for him to become a bookmaker again.

Summertime in New York was a bookmaker's heaven. Not only was there horse racing—both trotters and harness in New Jersey—but golf tournaments, court and lawn tennis tournaments, sailing regattas, swimming and diving meets, the still-unorganized baseball teams that played throughout the city, lacrosse, and cycling events.

Bookmakers in New York were not tolerated as they had been in London. In the past few years a reform movement had diminished the protective shield of Tammany Hall, and many bookmakers and gamblers had learned to be cautious. But none of this worried Andrew, for he looked upon it all as a challenge. He knew how to be discreet and when to advertise. He would have to choose his first "clients" very carefully and then rely on referrals from them to build his business.

Andrew went home that night from Bessie's determined to become his own businessman once again.

By Labor Day, Andrew's new venture was flourishing. Since "the house" always retained the best odds, his profits were good. But as he'd found before, Andrew needed more. If he made three hundred a week, he tried to double it the following week. He took on more clients. He found it necessary to rent an apartment in the slums where he could conduct business. He intended to move to Herald Square by October and then maybe on to Times Square. In a few years he knew that was where the action would be. Andrew prided himself on being visionary.

Andrew also realized that soon he was going to have to move out of his sister's house. She was becoming too inquisitive, and David was much too suspicious. Andrew wasn't all that worried about David, since he'd seen him meeting Paul Van Volkein's wife at an out-of-the-way hotel in Brooklyn just a week ago. Andrew could handle David. Amanda, on the other hand, was a necessary evil. He needed her to keep his relations with the Bishops on a good footing. Amanda was his emissary, his good-luck charm.

However, to move out of their house would cost money—lots of money—and he didn't have enough yet. But it wouldn't be long. For the first time since coming to America, Andrew could feel his dream becoming reality. Soon he would have everything he needed to propose to Meredith Bishop. Then he would never have to depend on Amanda for anything. He'd be so high up on the social ladder he'd have to look down to even see his sister. To Andrew, of all the dreams, the one he relished the most was that of besting Amanda.

Someday, after he'd taken from her everything she *owed* him, he would find a way to finally put her in her place. Then it would be her turn to know what it was like to live as he had.

Amanda picked up the morning edition of the *New York Herald*. Her eyes briefly scanned the society page and she was about to move on to the editorials when she spied a familiar name. She read the item three times before believing it. Instantly, she shoved her chair away from the breakfast table and hurried up the stairs. She went to Andrew's room, knocked on the door, and let herself in.

"Andrew! Wake up!" She nudged him, then shook his shoulder.

"What is it?" He tried to focus, but fell back on the pillow instead.

"Read this."

He glanced at the society page. "Oh, for God's sake, Amanda. Haven't you seen your name enough?" He pulled the blanket over his head.

"Andrew, this isn't about me. It concerns you."

"I'm in the paper?"

"No, but . . ." She pointed to the article.

It was the engagement announcement of Meredith Bishop. Andrew bolted upright. His eyes were saucers.

"It's a lie! I know how she feels about me."

"It says she's to be married in November. That's only a few weeks away," Amanda said. "You had no idea about this?"

"None. Why, just Saturday night she told me she loved me. I mean, bold as brass. I don't even know when this Rockwell character could have seen her. I thought I was the only one. . . ."

"I think you'd better talk to Meredith."

Andrew didn't go to Meredith. He made an appointment with Herman Bishop instead. As he waited in the reception area of the walnut-panelled office, staring at the gold velvet drapes and the pen-and-ink sketches of Bishop engines, rail yards and round-houses hanging on the wall, he knew he'd been right to come here. Andrew didn't have to convince Meredith to marry him; she was already hooked. He needed to win Herman Bishop, a task not unlike trying to fast-talk the devil.

The secretary ushered Andrew into an expansive office. Herman Bishop did not stand as Andrew entered, only motioned for him to be seated. "My boy," he said graciously. "How is your sister?"

"Just fine, Mr. Bishop. Thank you for asking."

Herman Bishop was never a man to mince words. He quickly lit a thick Havana cigar. "I suppose you're here about Meredith."

"Yes. I can tell you it was rather a shock, since she and I—"

"Andrew, Andrew. You didn't honestly think you had a chance with Meredith, did you?"

Andrew was surprised at his candor. "Yes, I did. I love your daughter, Mr. Bishop. She loves me. I can't believe she would agree to this engagement.''

"Well, she has." Herman Bishop leaned across his desk as he chewed on his cigar. "I can't allow her to marry you, my boy."

"Why not?"

"I know about your 'nighttime' activities."

Andrew gulped. This was worse than he thought. "I don't know what you heard, but I assure you it's all lies."

Herman held up his hands, fingers splayed. "Don't get defensive. It won't do you any good. My source is quite reliable. It's not that I personally have anything against gambling. Why, I gamble every day I walk in that door. What businessman doesn't? But I want something better for my daughter. Why, I wouldn't let her marry anyone like me—much less a bookmaker like you. Now, I understand about who you are, your background and your sister's, and that's all fine and good. But I wouldn't want Meredith to wake up some night and find her house filled with gangsters. You understand."

"Yes, I do."

"There's no hard feelings here, Andrew. This is a small town when you get down to it. We'll be seeing more of each other over the years. I assure you that I won't tell anyone about this or about your . . . uh . . . business venture. I would advise, however, that if you intend to court one of Meredith's friends, and you haven't altered your business goals, I will have to say something then."

Andrew cocked his head to the side. "You're telling me to clean up my act or else?"

Herman smiled magnanimously. "Precisely."

Andrew rose. "Good day, sir."

"Good day, my boy."

That night Andrew went to his Hell's Kitchen apartment to pay off his bets. He'd bought a second-hand table, two bentwood chairs, and a ten-year-old leather sofa whose coils needed retying. Aside from the bucket of beer he kept in the icebox, there was nothing else in the apartment.

Filled with anger and frustration over his encounter with Herman Bishop, Andrew had forgotten to go to the bank that day and withdraw money to pay off his bets. He'd been careless about many things as the day went on. He took bets he was certain to lose. He gave odds he shouldn't have.

By ten o'clock most of his customers had come for their payment. By eleven o'clock he was out of money. One particularly large winner had five hundred dollars coming to him. Andrew didn't have that much and so was obliged to make the man return in the morning when he could go to the bank.

The man was angry. Gamblers were not a trusting sort.

By eleven-fifteen, Andrew was ready to call it a night. There was a knock on the door.

"All bets are paid off for the night. No bets placed till tomorrow."

He went to the door and turned the key. The door sprang open.

It was Vince. He'd brought his friends.

Vince's three thugs circled the room and stood behind Andrew while Vince spoke.

"A friend of mine placed a bet for me. Then he comes back and tells me you can't pay."

"Oh, Louie? He placed the bet for you, huh? It's like I told him. I'll have the money in the morning. I just didn't get to the bank, is all."

"I hope that's all."

Andrew saw the burly man come around behind him and move a pace closer. He thought he could feel the man's breath on his neck.

"Looks like you got a good business goin' here, Granger."

"I do all right."

"Did I tell you I started a new business venture myself? It's called protection."

Vince signalled to his thugs. The man behind Andrew grabbed his arms and held them behind his back while the other two thugs slammed their fists into his ribs and stomach. Andrew couldn't breathe. His knees buckled under him. But the burly man held him up so he could take more punishment. They landed over a dozen blows before Vince stopped them. The burly man released Andrew. He slumped to the floor.

"It's like this, Granger. Every month, I take a little percentage of your business to protect you from ruffians such as these here. There's all kinds of things that can happen to a man in your position. This was just an example. You get my meanin'?"

"How much?"

"Five hundred a month. Paid on the first."

"Five hundred . . ." Andrew groaned.

"That's right. So tomorrow I want the five hundred you owe me for my bet and the five hundred for protection. Then we'll be even, Granger." He nodded to his men. "Boys . . ."

They filed out of the room. Vince was last to leave. He bent over and rifled through Andrew's pockets and took his last few dollars. Then he rammed his shiny black shoe into Andrew's ribs.

"You should never have taken me, Granger. You shoulda asked around. They would have told you . . . Vince ain't stupid."

He quietly shut the door.

David left at six in the morning. The new issue of *City* magazine was due out. He and Max intended to spend the day going over the layout for the Thanksgiving sketches.

Amanda was six months pregnant, and in the past week she seemed to have "blossomed." Nothing she owned fit properly anymore. She decided to spend the day at B. Altman's looking for maternity clothes.

She bathed and dressed and went to breakfast. She was surprised to see Andrew. He looked horrid.

"Shouldn't you be at work?"

"I don't feel well."

She put her hand on his forehead. "No fever . . ."

He grabbed her wrist and flung her hand away. "Oh, stop trying to be the mother. . . ."

"Sorry." She sat down, poured her coffee, and buttered a blueberry muffin. She pretended to read the paper.

Andrew watched her surreptitiously as he toyed with his eggs. He would have to be careful with Amanda. She was so pristine, so untouched by the real world, that he doubted seriously she would believe him if he told her of his bookmaking. She was always looking for the good in people. He knew for certain she'd never understand the concept of "protection money." He'd have to give her something that was plausible.

"I'm sorry, Amanda. I'm not sick, I'm in trouble. I need your help."

"What is it?"

"I need some money."

"How much?"

"Five hundred dollars."

"Why so much?"

"I borrowed from a friend I met in a pub near where I work. I had to do it, Amanda."

"It was for Meredith, wasn't it?"

"Yes," he said, wondering what she'd think if she knew he'd spent more than three thousand on Meredith over the summer. And for what? To have her father beat him down at the eleventh hour.

Amanda's heart went out to him. She thought him a romantic, falling in love the way he had with Meredith. He was courageous too, striving to best the odds against him. He wasn't wealthy, but for months, Meredith had been truly interested in Andrew. Amanda herself had begun to hope. She had to help him.

"I don't have that kind of money. Not without asking David. And I don't want him to know anything about this."

"Neither do I."

"I just don't know. . . ." Suddenly, the vision of herself sitting astride a horse in Central Park flashed across her mind. "Wait here a minute!"

She hurried up the stairs as fast as her pregnant body would carry her. In ten minutes she was back. She handed Andrew the sketch David had done over a year ago.

"David hated it. He said it was too vulgar."

"I think it's wonderful," he said earnestly. He still couldn't believe this was his sister. The girl in the sketch had so much spirit, so much will. In his mind, she and Amanda were nothing alike. But then, he hated his sister.

"Who will buy it?"

"Offer it to Quinton if he promises not to run it until January. David's contract with Max ends the first of the year."

Andrew took the sketch and rolled it up. He went to the vestibule and placed a call to Quinton. Amanda stepped over to the doorway so she could overhear the conversation.

"This drawing is highly unusual, Quinton. It's worth more than eight hundred."

Amanda was puzzled. Andrew had said he needed five hundred. Why was he asking for more. She strained her ears to hear.

"That's more like it, Quinton. And at a thousand you know you still got a bargain. By January, it'll be worth twice that. Think of the publicity angle to this. This will be the first sketch of The Granger Woman after the baby arrives." Andrew paused as he listened to Quinton. How clever he'd been to extract this price from Parker. Now he wouldn't have to dip into his savings at all to pay off Vince.

As Andrew replaced the receiver, Amanda quickly returned to her seat. Her brother was smiling when he entered the room. She was not.

"When do you meet Quinton?"

"At nine tonight . . . at the magazine. He has to work late."

"And when do you meet this man you owe?"

"An hour later at Manny's Pub."

Amanda stood. "I'm going with you," she said firmly.

"What? Are you crazy? It's too dangerous. It's a different world when the sun goes down."

"I'm well aware of the risks. And I'm also aware you lied to me. Just exactly how much money do you really owe, Andrew?"

"You eavesdropped!" he bellowed. "In my book that's worse than lying. The truth is that you don't trust me. What kind of family is this?"

"It's because we are family that I'm going to help you. How much do you really owe him? More than the thousand you'll get from Quinton?"

"No, just the thousand."

"Then it's settled. I want to make certain you pay this man off and that it's over and done with for good."

"All right. Have it your way."

"I intend to."

Amanda sat in the carriage waiting for Andrew to finish his "transaction." She watched as winos stumbled down the sidewalk or huddled in doorways. She saw women dressed in gaudy clothes and men in wild yellow-and-black checkered suits. She knew their kind, for they reminded her of Mercer Street in London. Andrew thought she knew nothing of these kinds of people, but she knew everything she needed to know. She knew their desperation, the loneliness and heartache they felt. They were no different from herself or anyone else. They were human.

The driver leaned down from above. He looked odd, upside down as he was, and she wondered how his worn top hat stayed on his head.

"I'm just goin' to check the harness. I didn't want you to worry that I was leavin', ma'am."

Amanda nodded as he jumped down from his perch. Even the driver didn't think they were safe here, she thought uncomfortably.

She wondered how it was that she'd almost forgotten this way of life, if anyone could, but that Andrew had not. There was something in his psyche that kept him tied to this world. It was as if he didn't want to leave it. Andrew had weaknesses, but she was convinced that if she helped him, he could overcome them.

They both had the protection of The Lie to sustain their positions, although she remembered too many nights she'd awakened in a cold sweat, afraid that David had discovered the truth. It was a precarious safety net she and Andrew relied on, but it was all they had.

She looked around the street and down the alley Andrew had taken. It was dark, but she could feel life in the shadows. There was something eerie about this night, this place. She hugged herself, trying to dispel the chills she felt. She wished he would hurry.

Once this was over, she would elicit a promise from Andrew never to involve himself with these men again. Next time she might not have the money to bail him out.

Soft whispers from the alley evolved into angry words and curses. Amanda leaned out of the carriage. She strained her eyes but couldn't see anything. Then she heard the sound of footsteps running. They came closer. She saw Andrew as he ran into the lamplight. There was a look of panic on his face.

Suddenly a shot rang out. The bullet ricocheted off the corner of the building. Andrew ducked. Then there was another shot.

The horses whinnied and snorted. The driver stood on the curb trying to calm them. But when the second shot hit the top of the coach itself, both horses panicked and jumped away from him, yanking the reins out of his hands.

A third shot narrowly missed Andrew's head.

"Open the door, Amanda!" he screamed as he raced toward her. He didn't see the horses as they reared back on hind legs and jabbed at the air with their forelegs. They whinnied and bolted.

Andrew's hand had just touched the door when the carriage shot off down the street.

Amanda screamed as she saw Andrew's frightened face suddenly vanish from her sight. The force of the runaway carriage slammed her against the back seat.

The horses ran faster, taking corners at breakneck speed. The carriage jostled back and forth over the cobblestone streets. They turned another corner and Amanda was thrown against the open door, nearly sending her into the street.

In the Tenderloin area of New York that year, many of the city streets were undergoing major reconstruction. Those that had been brick, cobblestone, and dirt were being paved. It was an arduous undertaking for the city but one that had been heralded by the mayor's office and the city council as a project long overdue.

That night, as Amanda's uncontrolled carriage sped down the streets, the frightened horses knew nothing of the street commissioner's construction project. There were huge open sewers among the bricks, ready to engulf the unaware. Narrow lanes of packed dirt and sand dropped off a full foot to unprepared ground. There were wooden barricades barring entrances to side streets and alleys. It was a dangerous maze.

Amanda screamed again and hugged her belly as the horses ran faster. She feared for Andrew, wondering if they'd killed him; she feared for herself, for surely she was about to be killed.

The thundering horses' hooves pulled the carriage around a perilously tight corner, where the horse on the left sank his foreleg into a pit of mud and soft tar. He broke his leg and fell to the ground. The momentum of the speeding carriage was broken by the grounded horse. The carriage rolled on top of him, killing him instantly, before it upturned on its left side.

Amanda was rammed against the side, hit her head on the burled wood door frame, and was rendered unconscious.

CHAPTER TWENTY-FIVE

David languorously ran his hand over the flat terrain of Christine's abdomen. "Promise me," he pleaded sensually, "that you'll never allow yourself to become pregnant."

She dangled her slender fingers over his head before allowing them to sink into his hair. "You aren't one of those men who find fertility erotic?"

"There is nothing erotic about a grotesquely deformed body."

Christine preened. "Amanda should have known better. Her first duty is pleasing you. I never want children."

David propped his head on his bent elbow and looked at Christine. She was coolly beautiful, and yet he knew the passion of which she was capable. "You and I think alike."

Christine dug her hand into his hair and pushed his head down to her breast. She didn't have much time, and talk was a waste of time. As he flicked his tongue against her skin she thought about her victory over Amanda. In the beginning it was enough to have stolen David. But now, as the months passed, Christine wanted more. She wished that Amanda could find out about this affair. But that was dangerous and could be too costly for Christine. She might lose Paul. And she never wanted to lose Paul.

She'd had a difficult time getting away the past two weeks. She could tell that Paul was finally suspecting something. Tonight, however, they were quite safe, since he had gone to Boston for a few days. This time had been heaven for her. She spent her afternoons at the jewelers and the best dress boutiques in town. She spent her nights with David. She didn't ask David what excuses *he'd* made. She knew he didn't have to work hard at it, for Amanda was stupid—she trusted David.

"More," she moaned.

Lust should be slowly savored, David believed. "In time . . ." he said, moving over her.

"We don't have . . . time," Christine breathed as she felt the pressure of their thighs coming into contact.

"It's only midnight. I'm not leaving until just before dawn."

"Oh," Christine groaned as his hand slid between her legs. She liked it when there was lots and lots of time.

Amanda's nightmare left her groggy, drained, and oddly wracked with pain. She had a difficult time opening her eyes. It was as if they were swollen shut. The sun was a peculiar shade of yellow, she thought as she felt its warmth on her face. She squinted at the light and blinked.

Slowly, the room came into focus. Gone were her velvet draperies, damask-papered walls, and huge bed. She saw a gold-tinted paper roll shade pulled down over the window. The ceiling was higher than she remembered. The bed was hard and cold. The air smelled of alcohol . . . and blood.

She tried to talk, but her mouth was terribly dry. She tried to move, but her muscles would not respond. Her arms and legs felt like lead. She prayed that she was dead. She could never live like this.

Tears filled her eyes and rolled down her cheeks. She whimpered.

"Amanda?" a voice came from the corner.

"David?"

"No, it's me, Amanda." Andrew came to her side. He held her hand and squeezed it.

She squeezed his back as the feeling returned to her arm. She wasn't paralyzed. She could see him more clearly now. His face was ashen, his clothes rumpled and dirty. His eyes were filled with fear.

"Thank God, you're all right," she said, remembering the gunshots. "I was so worried." She recalled the carriage overturning and then . . . nothing.

Suddenly she felt a sharp pain jab her stomach. She clutched her belly. And then she *knew*.

"Andrew! What's happened to my baby!"

He rubbed her arm more vigorously. "Amanda . . . it's all my fault. I should never have taken you down there."

"Andrew!" Every nerve in her body was immediately awake. Her brain was functioning at superspeed. Her hands ran across her flat abdomen. They knew there had been a mistake; a horrid, tragic mistake.

"No!" she screamed at the top of her lungs and bolted upright. "No!"

Two nurses scurried into the room, bringing medications and blankets and water.

Amanda searched Andrew's face with panic-stricken eyes. This was still her nightmare! He pressed his hands against her shoulders.

"Lie down, Amanda. Get some rest."

"No!" She fought him, fought the pills they tried to give her that would make her sleep again. What fools they were, she thought. Didn't they know she was already asleep? "You bring my baby back, Andrew," she hissed at him. "Now!"

He said nothing, only pressed harder against her shoulders. She was so weak and tired she couldn't fight him. "I can't get your baby, Amanda. It's dead. Do you understand?"

Her eyes were like saucers, filled with pain and fear. He'd never seen her like this. All white and limp and yet strong. He wished she would just go to sleep like the nurses told her. She had to accept the truth. She had no choice.

She flung her arm over her eyes. "Yes," she groaned with the voice of one who had lost all hope. "I understand."

Just then a doctor came into the room with an injection of a new medication. She jerked slightly when he sank the needle into her arm.

Andrew looked away. Within minutes Amanda's sobs stopped and she drifted off to sleep. He sighed heavily and followed the doctor out.

"When will she be able to go home?" Andrew asked.

The doctor removed his glasses and rubbed the bridge of his nose. It had been a long night while The Granger Woman aborted her child. "Not for a week. She's lost a lot of blood, and there's still a chance of infection. It'll depend on her spirits."

"She can't go home today?"

"Good God, man! Do you want to kill her?"

"No, of course not. I just didn't realize it was that serious. I want the best for her. She's my sister."

The doctor patted his shoulder. "I understand." He started to walk away, then turned back. "As soon as you locate her husband, I want to talk to him. Don't forget."

"I won't," Andrew replied as the doctor continued down the hall.

Andrew went to the nurses' station and for the sixteenth time telephoned David's house and woke the maid. This time, David was home.

While he waited for David to come to the telephone, Andrew tried to remember the story he would tell him. If David ever discovered the truth, there would be hell to pay for both himself and Amanda.

"Andrew! Where the hell are you? And where's Amanda?"

"I've been trying to call you since midnight. I have bad news."

David's sharp intake of breath told Andrew he was prepared.

"Amanda's at New York Hospital. We had an accident coming home from the theater. . . ."

"What theater . . . what kind of an accident?"

"We saw Oscar Wilde's play—"

"Jesus Christ! You took her down *there*? Are you out of your mind?"

"David, will you quit asking questions and listen? The horses bolted and the carriage overturned. David . . . she lost the baby."

David paused for a minute, letting the words sink in. What about her face?"

"What about it?"

"Goddamn it! Did she cut her face?"

"Her face is fine, David. She'll be posing again in no time. Your meal train has not left the track."

"Lucky for you, isn't it, Andrew? I'll be there straightaway."

When David entered the hospital room, Andrew rose from the wooden chair and greeted him coldly as he would any adversary.

It was no surprise to him that David didn't love Amanda. Andrew regretted his part in Amanda's accident. He felt badly about the baby, for it was an innocent. But this was the first time Andrew realized that David didn't want his baby. Andrew was learning a great many things about Amanda's husband. And all of it was ammunition Andrew could use against him.

David went directly to Amanda, not wanting to look at his brother-in-law. It was all he could do to control himself and not tear the man apart.

Amanda looked awful. She was so pale he could see the fine network of veins beneath her skin. Her sweat-soaked golden hair was matted to her head. He placed his hand gingerly on her stomach. It was true. He would no longer have to share Amanda with this baby. He wanted her head filled with thoughts of him, of their work together, their goals. Perhaps now she would see that being his wife, his protegée, was all she needed to be happy.

This miscarriage could be a blessing for them. He would have to convince her of that he knew, but he would do it.

Amanda opened her eyes as she felt the pressure of his hand on her stomach.

"David." She cried hot tears. "I'm so sorry. It was all my fault." She put her arms around his neck.

"No, Amanda. Don't talk like that. It was an accident. Andrew told me all about it. It wasn't your fault. It just happened. All I want is for you to get well and come back home. That's all."

"Oh, David, I don't deserve you."

"Why do you say that?" He smoothed her hair back from her forehead.

"Because you're so understanding."

"Don't look back, Amanda. I want us to put this behind us and go on. This was God's will. You have to believe that."

Amanda nodded.

Andrew stood in the corner wondering what possessed Amanda to accept David's platitudes. If he were her, he would have tossed David out on his ear. But then, Amanda had always been gullible. It was one of her qualities he cherished the most. Without it, he wouldn't be in America today.

"Rest, Amanda," David said. "I'll come back later and see you."

"David? Promise me we'll have another baby very soon."

"The doctor says you must rest for awhile, Amanda. We have all the time in the world for babies."

She started to cry again, feeling the emptiness inside her. "Promise me!" she demanded.

"I promise."

David kissed her forehead and quickly left the fetid room, knowing he'd made a promise he would never keep.

November could have been a grisly month, but it wasn't. The trees had kept their leaves longer that year, letting their gold, red, and orange colors decorate the city. It was warmer than previous autumns, so Amanda spent long hours on the terrace behind the house puttering in the garden, writing sad poems, and thinking about "what could have been." She refused to pose for David. He informed her he had hired Christine Van Volkein to sit. Amanda didn't care.

She didn't care what happened to Andrew or his gangster buddies. She was taking care of herself.

Sylvia stood on the back steps with a tray filled with teacups and a pot of tea. Quietly, she walked over to the wicker settee, placed the tray on the table, and waited.

Amanda placed a fistful of bittersweet in a basket and turned around. She was not at all surprised to see Sylvia.

"I had a feeling David would call you after awhile."

"David didn't send for me. I haven't seen you since the first week you were home from the hospital."

Amanda sat down and took the tea. It felt good running warmly down her throat. But it wouldn't fill her up. She was still empty inside. She started to cry.

Sylvia put her arms around Amanda and rocked her back and forth as if she were a child. "Let it go, dear. All of it. Cry as hard as you can. Cry like you'll never cry again."

Amanda clutched Sylvia's shoulders, knowing she was surely hurting her, her grip was so strong. But she couldn't help it. She felt as if she were dying. She cried as hard as she could.

Finally, Sylvia handed her a lace-edged handkerchief. "You needed me. You should have sent for me."

"I know." Amanda nodded. "I just didn't want to bother you."

"You know better than that."

Amanda looked her in the eye. "Yes, I do." She sighed. "You're about the only thing I'm sure of these days."

"That's understandable."

"I never realized how important the baby was to me until it was gone. I also never realized how *un*important it was to David."

"Sometimes tragedy opens your eyes to many things."

Amanda gasped. "You mean you saw it? Why didn't you say anything?"

"It was none of my business. It still isn't, unless you want to tell me about it."

"He won't allow me to talk about the baby at all. He won't consider having another one—ever. He said it could happen again. That the next time something might happen to me." She paused. "He wants me to go back to work."

"I think you should too."

"What?"

"It's not that I'm taking sides here. But it isn't good for you to spend your days dwelling on this. There is a time for grieving, Amanda, and you've done that. Now you should move on."

"But I don't feel like working."

"What do you feel like?"

"I don't know. I know I don't want to pose. I would like to see Max, though."

"That's a start. Why don't you arrange a lunch with him? Get out of here, Amanda. See your friends."

"Perhaps you're right."

Amanda met Max at the *City* magazine offices. He was frustrated, tired, and overworked.

"I can't believe it, Max. You've finally gotten what you wanted and now you don't want it?"

"I didn't say that. I love being the number-five magazine in the city in less than a year. However, I can't keep up with the demand. I had two editors quit and go over to Quinton Parker, of all people."

"He has a good magazine and you know it."

"Goddamn esoterics. They gave up a good salary here to write about some transcendentalist in the Himalayas. My adman moved to San Francisco last month. So here I am on the verge of making it big and I'm going to fold. I've got to find somebody fast."

He looked at her hard for a long time.

"I'm not an editor," she said.

"No, but you can do layouts. You can sell. You know good copy when you see it. Personally, I think you're a gold mine."

"I don't know, Max."

"I do. We'll keep the hours to a minimum for you in the

beginning. You tell me when you feel like taking on more. What do you say?"

"I say yes."

By Thanksgiving, Amanda was her old self again. She started going to parties and dinners with David as had been their custom before "the accident," and Andrew accompanied them.

Andrew found himself more in demand now, after Meredith had announced her engagement, than ever. It was as if an alarm had been sounded across New York City that Andrew Granger was available again. Though he hadn't found anyone in particular to court, he made use of the time to get to know not only the young girls but their parents. Andrew decided that the next time he spent any money on a courtship, he would make certain no father would put a halt to his progress. Andrew wanted only a sure bet.

David found his life to be intolerable. Something had changed in Amanda, but he didn't know what. She did not support him the way she once had. She still managed their business with Max better than he, but there was a new slant on everything these days. He felt as if she were cutting him out of her life, slice by slice. There was nothing he could point to as an example. It was simply a feeling he had.

"Do you have any new sketches of Christine ready? Max is ready to negotiate," she said one morning.

David poured a second cup of coffee. "They aren't quite right yet. Another week."

"We have deadlines, David."

"So what does that mean? You'll buy someone else's stuff? Gibson, maybe?"

"Maybe."

He glared at her while she buried her head in paperwork. "Don't forget our dinner with the Johnsons tonight. Wear that lavender gown."

Her head popped up. He *knew* she hated the lavender. "Fine."

"Emily Anderson wants you to attend her tea on Monday. I told her you'd be there."

"You know I'm meeting the Macy's people that day. Their account could be important to Max."

"I really don't care."

Amanda stood angrily. "I know you don't, David. Tell Emily

I'll be there." Amanda stalked away. She felt as if there wasn't enough of her to go around. And David was deliberately making things difficult for her. She knew he wanted her to quit *City* magazine. But she couldn't. This job had resurrected her from a depression she hoped never to know again.

David's possessiveness was not going to stop her. She couldn't live her life through him anymore. She had to have something all her own. She had to stay sane. If she were to remain in this house all day, wondering about *things*, she would go crazy.

"It's late," she said, going into the vestibule to get her coat from the closet.

David followed her. "See you tonight. Don't forget."

She pecked him on the cheek. "I won't," she said and left.

David waited until he heard the carriage round the corner. He went to the telephone and picked up the receiver. He gave the operator Christine's number.

"We have all day, if you can make it." He paused, chuckled, and did not hear Andrew as he quietly came down the carpeted stairs.

Andrew stood above the alcove where the telephone was located. Because he had a late breakfast meeting, he'd not left the house at his normal time. He knew David was unaware of his presence.

"Don't worry about it," David said. "Amanda hasn't the slightest idea. I'll see you in an hour."

Andrew walked up from behind David.

"Amanda may not know about you and Christine, but I do," Andrew sneered.

David spun around, his blazing eyes coming into contact with Andrew's defiant ones.

"You son of a bitch!" David hissed.

"I guess that makes you the brother-in-law of a son of a bitch." Andrew laughed.

"Don't think for one minute I don't have your number. If it weren't for me, your little setup wouldn't be quite so rosy now, would it? I don't think I'd stir up any trouble if I were you. You could find yourself with no roof over your head."

"Don't threaten me, David. Without Amanda you'd be nothing! And we both know it. The whole city knows it. The only one who doesn't is Amanda. But one of these days she's going to wake up and see what I see . . . a second-rate sketch artist who thinks he can make it in the big time."

David lunged for Andrew's throat, but Andrew drew back and delivered a solid punch. David fell back on the floor.

After driving three blocks from the house, Amanda realized she'd forgotten the B. Altman advertisement portfolio. She instructed the driver to turn around. She had just come in the door when she heard David and Andrew arguing. She saw Andrew hit David. She was about to run to her husband when Andrew's next words stopped her dead cold.

"You get the hell out of my house!" David had barked.

"Is that so you can move your mistress into my room? Or does Christine want it all? Does she want Amanda's place?"

Amanda's hand flew to her mouth, but she knew what Andrew said was the truth.

She had been home from the hospital three days when David stayed out all of one night. Still heavily medicated, she'd easily put it out of her head. But as the weeks passed, she realized that David was having an affair.

At first she blamed the accident. She was under strict orders from the doctor not to have intercourse. She assumed David was seeing prostitutes. Many men did. But he always smelled of the same perfume. It was the one he was supposed to have sent to her. She realized in a flash that it was the same one that Christine Van Volkein wore.

"David? Andrew?" She came forward.

Andrew froze. David pushed himself up and quickly rushed to save himself.

"Andrew is leaving, Amanda. I cannot tolerate accusations like he's been making. The situation here has not been good since the accident, and you know it. I've tried not to blame Andrew, but I do. If he hadn't taken you there that night, none of it would have happened. His anger toward me is quite apparent, as you have just seen."

"You're scum, David!" Andrew said and stalked away.

"No, Andrew, wait!" Amanda yelled.

Andrew turned to her. "He's right, Amanda. I *am* leaving. I can't stand him any more than he can stand me. I've got to leave."

Andrew raced to his room and took out his suitcases. He'd just cut his own throat, but right now he didn't care. He believed that in less than six months he would find the right girl and marry what he wanted. He didn't need any more of David's orders or snide remarks. David was right. They hated each other.

He crammed his clothing into the suitcases. At the bottom of the drawer he found the sapphire earrings he'd stolen from his mother. And the diary. He had half a mind to show it to Amanda. But this was his only insurance, and he might need it some day. He'd kept this diary for over two years. He would put it to better use than simply to spite David Simon.

Amanda stood dumbstruck in the hallway as Andrew breezed past her with loaded suitcases. She kept staring at David. She thought of her mother and all the things Harriet had told her about what to expect in America. She thought of the dream husband her mind had conjured over the years. He should have been a caring man, decent, loving, and faithful.

She looked at David. He was nothing like what he should be or what she wanted. David, she realized, wanted none of the goals she did. He was obsessed with fame, whereas she liked the work. He wanted friends only when they were useful to him; he didn't want her. He wanted Christine. Amanda was going to give him what he wanted.

"Tell her she doesn't have to settle for Andrew's room, David. Tell her she can have my place."

"Are you crazy? You mean you believe what he said? That's ridiculous. It's a lie."

"No, it isn't, David. Christine can be your new model. She can be your wife. She can be anything she wants to me. But she *can't* be The Granger Woman. I'll always be my own woman, David. I guess it's time I really tried it."

She pushed past him and went up the stairs.

He followed her. "Amanda, I think you've been under an emotional strain since you lost the baby. Don't you see? With Andrew gone, we can both relax now. Take that honeymoon we wanted."

She went to her dressing table, took out a key, and locked all her bureau drawers. She locked her closet. She deposited the key in her purse and pulled the strings tight.

"I'll send for my things. I have a meeting to attend."

He grabbed her arm. "You'll regret this, Amanda. You're nothing without me. I made you famous. I made you into what

you are today. There isn't a publisher in this town who'll talk to
you without me. I can make any woman I choose as famous as *I*
want her to be. You never understood that, Amanda. And that's
where you went wrong.''

''No, I didn't, David. I've closed my eyes to many things
about you because I believed in marriage. I didn't take my vows
as lightly as you did.''

She glared at him and looked down at his fingers as they
clamped around her arm.

''Now take your filthy hands off me.''

She jerked out of his grasp and hurried down the stairs. In
seconds she was out of the house and, she knew, out of his life.

David Simon had grown up in New York City. He had many
fans and many supporters. He told them his new protegée would
be the ''hottest'' star to ever grace the pages of New York
magazines. There was much fanfare when the January 1897 issue
of *Collier's* hit the stands with sketches of Christine Van Volkein.
But the sales did not increase.

David's ego was undaunted. It would take a few months for
Collier's readers to know to look for his sketches. He believed
he'd made a step forward, not backward. He was surviving the
scandal over his divorce, and he made certain that no one knew
about his affair. Amanda had cooperated in that area by keeping
the reins on her brother and by employing a divorce attorney well
noted for his discretion.

David believed in what he'd told Amanda. He believed in his
talent. He believed the day was still to come when he would best
Dana Gibson. He believed he did not need Amanda.

Book III

ADULTERY

CHAPTER TWENTY-SIX

In 1897, New York's Bohemia was centered in Chelsea. Literati and artists mingled with actors to compose one of the most colorful sections of the city. This was not the society world Amanda had moved in for nearly three years. It was a world of individualists and visionaries, of men and women who cohabited without marriage. It was a world where the mind and soul took precedence over the material. Women went to the theater to listen and learn, not to show off their jewels and outrageously expensive gowns. Men worked alongside women on major projects—books, plays, and massive sculptures. It was a world where Amanda experienced equality. It was a tiny world.

The world she had left behind did not take the news of Amanda's pending divorce lightly. Many sided with David, many sympathized with Amanda, but most adamantly agreed that divorce was immoral. What they desperately wanted, nearly craved, was information about Amanda's reasons for leaving David. Gossip flourished. There was speculation that Amanda had left David for a lover, that David was having an affair—some even rightly guessed it was Christine; others believed Amanda to be depressed after the miscarriage and thought she would return to David.

It was the choicest piece of gossip since Oscar Wilde's imprisonment in '85 for immorality. New York gave it proper billing.

Amanda's true friends rallied to her defense; the others she learned she could live without. Sylvia spoke for Amanda when she told *her* friends that Amanda had left "an intolerable situation." Amanda let people think what they wanted. She could never change their minds and it was a waste of time to try.

Amanda quickly learned that at this juncture in her life, she had to take each hour at a time. She couldn't think ahead to the afternoon or night, for it all seemed overwhelming to her. She had barely learned to cope with the loss of the baby when she was faced with David's infidelity. She wondered if shattered illusions could ever be restored.

Max turned out to be her best medicine. He never coddled her. He made demands on her, but never more than what he knew she could handle. He made certain that every night she went home with extra work. He never let her finish a project before the day was out. At six o'clock, when she left for home, he wanted her to be thinking about the next day, the next issue. He stimulated her brain, which in turn forced her spirits into second gear. By the end of six weeks, she awoke each morning looking forward to the new task Max would set before her that day.

Amanda loved the world of *City* magazine. The smell of printer's ink was like an opiate to her. She liked the noise of the whirring presses, the curses of the warehousemen and drivers, and, most of all, she loved the excitement that took place within her.

Her office was little more than a cubbyhole at the far left corner of the editorial room. There was a small typing pool of four secretaries; two artists who did cartoons, titles and borders; four editors; and a general manager. Max oversaw the entire staff.

City magazine could not afford to employ many reporters, so Max bought articles from free-lance writers. Amanda's first job was to read these articles, choose the ones she liked, and recommend them to Max for possible publication. Max met with her every Thursday to review the advertisements. Amanda's eye for placement, balance, and copy was fresh and new. And with each assignment, she became better.

As she worked with the artists she became fascinated with their views of what a city magazine should be.

"You can say more with one picture than with a thousand words," Cary said over a desk-bound lunch one day.

Amanda thoughtfully traced the rim of her coffee cup. "What kind of sketches are you talking about?"

"Not sketches at all. Pictures, Amanda. Photographs. Take a look around at what's going on in New York. There's renovation everywhere. The city is changing. How many thousands come here every month? Ten? Twenty? The neighborhoods alter every week. We should be chronicling everything on film."

"We just did a story on the annexations—"

"Who cares if Brooklyn is consolidated into the city? You see what I mean? That's not what is changing at all. Look at the faces of the city. They're the kind of faces we've hardly seen before. They can't speak the language, they're frightened, they're poor. They don't know what the future holds. But they're glad to be here."

Amanda thought of the first day she'd come to New York. She remembered the immigrant girl in the lifeboat. It was a picture that would forever remain in her brain. "I see what you mean, Cary."

"If Max would just give me the chance," Cary went on, "I could really do something with *City* magazine. But all he wants is to run those assinine sketches of David Simon's. . . ." His head snapped up, embarrassed. "Jesus. I'm sorry, Amanda."

"It's okay." She smiled out of the corner of her mouth. "Let me talk to Max."

"Max, it's a good idea."

"It stinks. And you know why? Because immigrants can't read English. What do they care what's in my magazine? But New Yorkers *do* read. And they spend hard-earned money on magazines. Forget it, Amanda."

"Max, I think you're wrong. New Yorkers need to know how the city is changing. It's relevant. It's now. And this idea of photographs—"

"Is too damned expensive. You know how much it would cost to renovate my presses? *The Delineator* started running photographs in their ads last year. It cost a fortune. They'll spend the next decade trying to pay them off. They have to ask twice for their ads what I do. It's a fad, Amanda. Face it."

"I understand about the cost factor, but I think you're wrong, Max. Photographs are going to be around forever."

"Maybe, but not in magazines. People still like the creativity of the artist. Not everybody can afford to buy an original sketch or painting. But they can buy it in *City* magazine and *Collier's* and all the rest."

Amanda smiled at him. "Is there anything I can say to convince you?"

"No."

Amanda turned and left, thinking that if she had her *own* magazine, she'd know precisely what to do.

Amanda didn't like defeat any more than the next person. However, one of the first things she'd learned while working for Max was that he had a mind set in concrete. Once he'd formed an opinion, even dynamite couldn't budge him. She would have to work around him and try to bring innovation in small parcels. If she couldn't have photographs, she would start with more relevant stories.

She ran two articles on the plight of women factory workers. Both received adverse letters from their readers. Amanda was undaunted. She coerced Max into allowing her to print an article on a free women's clinic that had recently opened in Greenwich Village. The article was severely lambasted by the public when a group of Episcopal ministers discovered that the clinic dispensed birth-control information to both married and unmarried women. The clinic solicited funds from progressive influential New York women and paid top price for a full-page ad in the next issue of *City*.

Again, Max and Amanda went head to head.

"When will you learn to play the game, Amanda? Bring me safe stories."

"Safe? What does that mean?"

"It means ones that will sell magazines to our market. Know your market, Amanda. It's the key to business."

"Max, the world is changing, and you aren't changing with it. Get your head out of the sand."

He threw up his hands. "Women! No wonder David couldn't get along with you!"

Amanda glared at him. "That's a rotten thing to say."

Max softened. "It was. I'm sorry. But damn it, Amanda, you cause me more headaches than the entire staff."

"Then why don't you get rid of me?"

"Because you're too damn good at what you do. But when you go on these offbeat crusades of yours, it's almost not worth it."

She put her arms around him and kissed his cheek. "Yes, it is, Max. It's worth it."

*   *   *

By the first of March, Amanda had two full issues of experience behind her. She felt more secure every day in her role at *City* magazine. She liked her apartment, her new neighborhood, her life. She did not see David for two months until he called and asked to see her at his attorney's office on the south end of Central Park. Amanda agreed.

Cecil Bateman looked exactly as Amanda imagined him. He was a tiny, turtlelike man, with a bald head, glasses, and lipless mouth. He bobbed his head up and down when he talked, seemingly taking shelter from the world's adversities in his humped shoulders. He didn't talk, he croaked.

"David tells me that you will not consider reconciliation?" It was a statement that he uttered like a question.

Amanda looked at David. He seemed defiant, sitting imperiously in his chair the way he was. She marveled that she seemed now to be seeing him so clearly. She watched as he calmly smoked a cigar. He never looked at her, asked her how she was. There was no trace of concern for her at all. She wondered if they had ever loved each other.

"It would be impossible," Amanda said. She wondered for an instant what their life would have come to had there been no Christine. How long would she have let him go on, dictating to her?

"You can't have the house, you know. I inherited it. And the furnishings, the paintings, all of it," David said.

"I don't want your family heirlooms, David. I just want a divorce."

His head swiveled to meet her gaze. He was incredulous, and it showed. He realized she didn't want him; worse, she'd finally realized she didn't need him.

"You don't want any of the property?" Cecil Bateman croaked again. He, too, couldn't believe what he was hearing.

"No. I only want David's assurances that he will do his best to keep the gossips quiet." She looked him squarely in the eye.

Because it benefitted his purposes as much as it did hers, and because what she asked required minimal time and no investment on his part, he agreed. "Done," he said.

She rose. "If there is nothing else"—she looked from one to the other—"then I'll be going."

David rose out of courtesy. For a split second he realized she was walking out of his life forever. Soon the papers would be signed, they would wait the required year, and then it would be official. She looked so sure of herself, standing in front of him. She was not afraid of the future—a life without him. He felt instantly shaken. He wondered if it was possible he might *need* her.

"Amanda, I was wondering if you'd join me for coffee . . . just for—"

"For what, David?" she interrupted. "To reminisce? I don't think so. I wish you luck, David. I hope your pictures of Christine will bring you the fame you want."

"Amanda . . ."

She walked out the door, though she knew he watched her from the doorway as she went down the hall. She hated him at that moment, hated him for killing her girlhood dreams, hated him for not ever really loving her, and she hated him for showing her that love was only an illusion.

Sydney Wade sat in her father-in-law's office seven stories above Central Park listening to the millionth argument between her husband and his father. Men. Whether they were twenty or two hundred they never grew up. They never learned anything past the bounds of their egos. Matthew would never give up his foolish ideas about a department store . . . even the sound of it made her teeth rattle. Nor would James Wade ever consider a compromise. He was determined to force Matthew into taking over Wade Banks. Sydney had been married to Matthew for over a decade and had learned that nobody ever forced Matthew to do anything. But like all men, Matthew could be handled . . . if done properly.

James Wade sat in a brown leather chair, supposedly designed to be three inches higher and wider than Kaiser Wilhelm's throne. James Wade liked to think he had a psychological edge on world leaders. Especially when their emissaries came to his office for money.

"You'll fall flat on your face in less than a year," James predicted.

"I have enough capital to see me through twenty-four months," Matthew replied.

"I hope you didn't ask any of *my* friends to back you."

"Believe it or not, some of them asked *me*."

"I don't believe it!"

"Are you calling me a liar?"

James glared at his son. "Then they're just as big fools as you."

Matthew stopped his pacing. "I can't figure out what burns you the most—the fact that the family name will be on a store-front or that I might make it."

"Your impertinence, Matthew, could see you riding out of town on a rail."

"Forget it, Father. That sort of thing went out of style twenty years ago. Nobody has that much power anymore."

"You *are* naive."

Matthew picked up his coat and hat. "Probably. But I'm not so naive as to think I can be bullied by you anymore. My store will be finished by June. You're welcome to come to the grand opening. Come Sydney, let's go home. I want to spend some time with Jacqueline."

Sydney tilted her heart-shaped face up, lifted her heavily lashed blue eyes at her husband, and smiled. "I think not. Dad and I have some things we need to discuss."

"What about Jacqueline? You haven't seen her in days."

"She'll survive. She has *you*, doesn't she?"

Matthew started to protest again, but it had been a long time since he'd been able to reason with Sydney. They'd come to an agreement long ago—she would go her way and he would go his. "As you wish."

Matthew left the room and went to the elevator. While he waited for it to arrive, he thought about Sydney. He remembered when they were very young and first married. He was making his first mark in the world, albeit as his father's protegé. In those days, Sydney was by his side, urging him on. She gave dinner parties for his best clients. She made certain his father was included in all their holiday gatherings. Sydney was the best adhesive his relationship with his father could ask for. They had both wanted Matthew's success then. But Matthew had changed. He was good at banking, but he didn't love it. For Matthew there had to be more passion in life, more excitement in his career. He wanted a challenge.

When he told Sydney about his idea to open a department store, it had been a severe jolt for her.

Sydney was from a background similar to his. Her grandfather had founded Hudson Railroad and after making twenty million dollars, he established one of New York's premier banks. He now ran the Brinkley Banks, and personally ranked with the top four banking families, which included the Morgans and the Wades. Sydney had always known wealth, just as Matthew had. She had gone with him to Europe, and although she did not follow him from city to city as he looked for investors, he had to thank her, for her presence showed his supporters a unified front. Sydney had kept herself, the nanny, and Sydney's then two-year-old daughter, Jacqueline, in London for nine months and later in Paris for nine months. She spent most of her time "renewing friendships," she'd said. Her father, Harlen Brinkley, had given her a list of dozens of people for her to speak with. At the time, Matthew had thought she was only being sociable. Once they were back in New York, Matthew had overheard Sydney and Harlen speak of these people as if they were accounts in a bank ledger. It was possible that Sydney's friends were nothing more than that to her. He and Sydney led such separate lives, he knew very little of what she did other than work at her father's bank every day.

Sydney seemed perfectly happy with their situation. Matthew was not.

Whenever Matthew raised the subject of the problems with their marriage and Sydney's inattention to Jacqueline, Sydney either changed the subject or brushed it off.

Matthew believed there should be a oneness in a marriage. Sydney believed only in separateness. Matthew gave up and concentrated on his store.

He spent nearly all his waking hours planning it, supervising the construction, and praying for its success. For besides his daughter, his store was all he had. He certainly had no marriage, and his father thought him a fool.

He breathed deeply and walked over to the window.

From seven stories up he could hardly tell if it was her or not. It was an extremely windy day and her hat blew off. He watched as she raced against the wind. Her coat flapped open and her scarf whipped in the wind. He watched as she finally reached for the hat, caught beneath a street bench.

The elevator door opened.

Matthew was glad the elevator whisked him to the ground floor. He dashed across the marble floor, past the bank tellers, and out the revolving brass and glass door. He shot his arm into the freezing air and waved to her.

"Amanda!" he yelled and rushed toward her.

She stopped when she heard her name being called. She would remember that voice anywhere. She turned. "Matthew."

For months, she'd thought she would be terrified if this moment came, but her life had altered drastically since that day on the lake in Tuxedo Park. The only problem was that Matthew's life was still the same. She knew the right thing was for her to leave—to be strong, as she had been when they'd first met. But as she looked at him and felt the warmth of his smile, saw the honesty in his eyes, she weakened. And though her conscious self continued to deny it, she decided she would allow Matthew into her life.

He didn't say anything at first, only looked at her, took her gloved hand, and held it for a minute. "Where have you been? I haven't seen you at any of the parties."

"Were you looking for me?"

"Well, uh, yes, I suppose I was."

"That's very flattering."

"You live around here, don't you?"

"I used to."

He paused and looked at her curiously. Then he remembered. "I'm sorry. I heard about your . . ."

"Divorce," she finished for him. "I'm getting used to the word. If I keep saying it over and over, it doesn't sound as nasty as it once did." She smiled. He seemed a bit nervous to her. "Really, it's all right."

"I don't believe in divorce," he said, thinking of his own life.

"Neither do I. But I believe in living."

He looked at her curiously. "Could I get you a cup of coffee? You look half frozen."

"I'd love it."

They slipped into a small restaurant, quiet and unpopulated this late in the afternoon. Waiters were sitting at a back booth comparing tips they'd received at lunch, guessing how much they could glean from the dinner crowd. Amanda ordered hot cocoa. She slipped off her coat. She saw Matthew's eyes travel to her abdomen.

"Was it a boy or a girl?"

Amanda's eyes fell and instantly stung. She struggled with

herself not to show her grief. She raised her head. "I lost the baby."

"Oh, my God." He didn't say anything else, only took her hand and squeezed it. He knew there were no words to express his sympathy. He thought of the first day he'd seen her. She'd looked like an angel then. Today she looked like a woman—a very, very beautiful woman.

The waiter brought the coffee and cocoa. Amanda scooped the whipped cream into her mouth. "That's your building across the street, isn't it?"

"Yes. It's coming along quite well. We'll be open the first of June if all goes according to schedule."

"I'd like to see it sometime."

"You would?"

"Of course. Besides the fact that it's your project, there could be a story in it for me."

"A story?"

She laughed. "I have a job now. I'm an editor at *City* magazine."

"I'm impressed. There aren't many women in your position who'd want to work."

"My position?"

"Amanda, you're famous, a society notable, you should have a good settlement from the divorce . . ."

"Stop right there, Matthew." She thrust her hands up. "I'm not getting anything from David. I can take care of myself, without his help."

"But he owes it to you. It's the law."

"If I let him do that, then he'd still have a hold on me. I won't give him any part of my life."

Matthew stared at her. She was the most perplexing woman he'd ever met. He couldn't decide if she came from heaven or from another planet. She didn't think like anyone he knew, male or female. He was beyond fascination; he was enthralled.

Amanda finished her cocoa. "Could I have another?"

"Of course." He signalled the waiter.

Amanda could not have cared less about the cocoa, but it gave her a chance to stay with Matthew a bit longer. She liked being with him. She felt that same excitement she'd experienced that day on the lake. But it was the simultaneous feeling of security that made her stay. She didn't know what it was about him, but she felt she could talk to him about anything. She should be wary of him, telling her feelings to him like she was. After all, he was almost a stranger. But no; she knew Matthew was special.

She stirred the cocoa slowly and glanced out the window. "I live on the other side of town. In Chelsea. I like it there. It's close to the magazine and I've made a few friends. Artists, mostly."

"I see," he said, realizing that she wanted him to know about her new life. He was flattered.

"It keeps me busy."

"That's important to you? Keeping busy?"

"Why, yes. Then I don't think about . . . things. . . ."

Matthew's eyes met hers. She was unaware that the wind had unravelled her hair, bringing long golden tendrils down from her upsweep. The afternoon sun filtered through the cafe window and wove through her hair. Her eyes sparkled at him, showing him a promise he'd never seen before. Matthew was a realist. He didn't believe in romance or its trappings. He told himself there was nothing special about this afternoon, the way her smile lifted her face or the way her voice seemed to sing in his brain.

Matthew was already married to probably the most beautiful woman in New York. Beauty could not have any affect on him. His reaction, then, he told himself, was due to a vulnerability within himself over the problems he was having with Sydney and his father. It was not Amanda. It was the timing.

He could nearly feel her reading his thoughts.

"Isn't that why you're building this giant building, Matthew? To keep busy?"

"No, it's a solid business decision. I'll make a lot of money someday."

"You already have a lot of money."

"There's a difference. This will be something I built myself. My way."

"It's your ego, then?"

"My ambition. My dream."

"Ah," she said. "I have a lot of that too."

"I wouldn't admit that if I were you, Amanda. That isn't a very feminine trait."

"But I'm not just another woman."

"I'm very aware of that, Amanda. Very aware." His tone was pointed and serious. He let his eyes rest intently upon her.

Amanda was responding to him more forcefully than she could have imagined. Often she moved boldly forward, using her heart, not her head, as her guide. This time was no exception. She wanted to know everything about Matthew, the good and the bad. And she was determined this would not be their last meeting.

"I'm fascinated by your project. But tell me, Matthew, why did you choose this location instead of building where the rest of the retail trade is? Say on Thirty-second or Thirty-fourth Street?"

"You think I'm crazy too?"

"No. I think you've got a good reason, and I'd like to hear it."

"I don't want to be near the competition, because I refuse to recognize any competition. Wade's will be superior to anything New York has ever seen. I'm building Wade's for *tomorrow*, for the next century, not for today. Look at what's happening in New York. Everything—retail, housing, art, theater—it's all moving north, toward the park. The best homes are built around the park. Now not everyone can afford to buy a home up here, but for a special outing, a stroll in the park—people will naturally gravitate toward Wade's."

"I agree!"

His eyes danced as he continued. Absentmindedly, he took her hand in his. "Wade's is going to be around a long time, Amanda. By 1910, I'd like to open a branch store in Philadelphia. I've projected that in less than twenty-five years, say by 1920, I should have half a dozen stores throughout the Eastern seaboard."

"That's incredible."

"And quite possible."

Suddenly he looked down and realized that she'd placed her hand over his. "I've never told anyone all of this."

"I'm glad you chose me."

"So am I."

Amanda was feeling a thousand emotions and all of them were underscored by the fact that right or wrong, Matthew was going to play a part in her life. But because she'd learned from David and Paul that romantic moments were faulty cornerstones in one's life, she struggled to keep her boldness in check. "I meant what I said about writing an article on your store for the magazine. Would you consent to an interview?"

"Isn't that what you're doing right now?" he teased.

"Yes." She laughed. "But could we continue this later?"

"Yes," he said, staring deeply into her eyes.

"Good. I'll talk to my editor tomorrow."

Sydney Wade rapped her perfectly buffed nails against the white silk damask-upholstered sofa. She wore a fabulously elegant black crepe gown, four strands of diamonds that reached deep inside her cleavage, and enormous square-cut diamond earrings. Her black hair was piled high on her head and wrapped with another chain of diamonds. She looked every inch the "princess of New York society" (in waiting to Caroline Astor) that the columns had dubbed her.

She looked at the solid gold clock atop the black marble mantle. "Where *is* he?" she muttered aloud.

She rose, went to the window, and looked out. "Damn it."

Sydney despised pacing; only animals and her husband did it. But tonight she was nervous and upset enough to embark on the habit. The meeting with James and Matthew had not gone well. It had taken her nearly three weeks to get them both to agree to meet, and rather than doing what she had suggested, they'd both thrown all her work aside and begun another round of bickering.

James needed to give Matthew a time schedule. He should ease his demands on his son, allow him to dabble in the store for two years. Then, when the store failed, he could take him back into the bank.

Matthew, rather than putting his shares of Wade Bank stock up for collateral to his European investors, could take out a loan from Wade Bank, repayable out of his inheritance, to pay for the failed store.

To Sydney's way of thinking, any fool could see that this was a more equitable solution to the problem than either of the men had embarked upon. James Wade needed Matthew's expertise at the bank. And Matthew had to get this department store experiment out of his system without jeopardizing his *real* future.

Sydney believed that Matthew was wasting his talent on this store. He was risking his father's wrath and a possible schism. Sydney also knew that in order for her to get what she wanted, she had to keep Matthew and James on speaking terms.

Banking was in Sydney's blood. She'd been born to it and at an early age had chosen banking as a career, even though most women were prepared solely for the career of marriage. But

Sydney's mother had died when she was three. Her only child-hood memories were of a male-dominated world, even at home.

Sydney's father, Harlen Brinkley, had taught her everything she knew. He was a demanding teacher, but Sydney was intelligent and wanted desperately to please him. But locked away in her memories was an incident that reminded her of the almost impossibility of ever pleasing Harlen Brinkley. . . ."

"Father, please help me with this arithmetic."

He took the piece of paper from her fifteen-year-old hands and scanned the twenty problems she was doing. "This is all wrong. Not one is correct. You must study harder."

"But this algebra is so hard for me."

"I understand . . . you're a woman."

"What's that got to do with it?"

"Men have mathematical brains. Women do not. But it's not your fault you weren't born a man."

Sydney did not miss the bitter tone to his words. "Then whose fault is it?"

"Your mother's."

"I see. . . . Father, would you love me more if I were a boy?"

Harlen's stern eyes glanced briefly at Sydney; then he looked back out the window as he spoke. It was a habit he seldom broke as Sydney grew. She felt as if he were ashamed of her and that he regretted not siring a son. "It isn't that I would love you more, it's just that things would be different."

"How?"

"If you were a man, you'd grow up and help me run the bank. We could work side by side. Father and son."

"Why not father and daughter?"

"Women have no place in banking."

"Why?"

"They don't have the brains."

"But I'm different. I'm a Brinkley."

"This is true."

"Let me try. I could start as a secretary."

"Yes. You could do that." He sighed heavily, and to her it was the loud sound of defeat. "But it's no use. You could never have any power."

"Power?"

"Money is power, Sydney. And only men have power. That's why the Brinkleys have always been in banking. We control businesses, politics, even people's lives. It's a tremendous responsibility."

"Father, I could learn everything you know. You could teach me. You'll be proud of me," she said. Then you will love me, she thought.

"I am proud of you, Sydney. And if you want to learn, I'll teach you. But you can't be something you aren't. You can't be a man. You can't have any power."

Sydney turned away from him and left the study. She closed the door. "Yes, I can Father. And I will. I'll have it all. You'll see."

Sydney learned as she matured that her father was correct when he'd said women had no power. However, it did not take her long to realize that she could rule *through* a man. She'd read history stories that talked about the "power behind the throne" and that oftentimes it was women who truly ruled, not their husbands or their fathers.

All through her teenage years, Sydney worked, listened, and learned. She did not go to college, for she couldn't stand the idea of being away from her father or the bank. She had all the education she needed at the bank. She intended one day to run it with her father, albeit she would remain in his shadow; still, it was enough for Sydney.

Sydney's father had always spoken of James Wade with respect. Though Harlen Brinkley did not force the issue of Matthew, he made his wishes clear.

"I see Matthew Wade graduated with honors this spring," he said one day, in his usual unemotional tones, as he sat at his office desk.

Sydney sat across from him taking dictation.

"He'll be a fine banker someday. Any girl with half a brain would do right to consider him as a husband."

"I don't want to get married—yet," she said, liking her world that included only herself and her father.

"You must marry, Sydney. It's the way things are. It would please me." He uttered the magical words.

Sydney believed, in her naivety, that despite Matthew's youthful reputation of rebellion (he'd refused to attend Harvard—his father's alma mater—and went to Princeton instead; gossip at the time said Matthew's actions were solely intended to defy his father), he could be manipulated. How wrong she'd been. For although she manipulated him into marriage, it was the last time she was to do so.

He'd been twenty-two, working for his father, full of energy, ideals, and dreams. He was New York's most eligible bachelor that year, and she was the most beautiful debutante. They saw each other at every party, dinner, and ball that season.

Sydney had never used feminine wiles as most girls her age had, because she had never been concerned with pleasing any man except her father. But she saw her father's wisdom: through Matthew she would gain the power she wanted.

Matthew was not in love with Sydney and she knew it. But at the age of twenty-two, he was not made of stone either. Sydney met Matthew for a Fourth-of-July picnic given by the Hendersons, friends of her father's, at their beach house on Fire Island. After a day of swimming, water games, and hunting for sea shells, the younger "couples" built a bonfire on the beach and sang songs while their parents played quiet games of bridge on the wide front porch of the Hendersons' clapboard house.

Sydney asked Matthew to walk along the beach with her. A hundred yards down the beach, she boldly turned to him and kissed him. The night was starry, sultry, and romantic. She pressed her breasts into his chest and put her arms around him. When he started to unbutton her white linen blouse, she didn't stop him. Nor did she object when he pulled her to the grassy dunes and lay on top of her.

For Sydney, sex would always be mingled with a sense of triumph: the following morning, she announced her engagement to her father. Matthew had never formally asked her, but she had guessed rightly that he was a responsible man. Four days later he produced the requisite engagement ring.

Sydney's marriage to Matthew was an intellectual decision. The ensuing ten years had produced a daughter and a mountain of tension between them. But she had pleased her father. Sydney was happy. . . .

Sydney went to the mirror now and smoothed her skirt and checked her bustle. The clock chimed eight. There was still no sign of her husband.

"Goddamn you, Matthew!"

There was the clippity-clop of horses' hooves outside. She raced to the window. Matthew hurriedly paid the driver and dashed up the steps. He waved away the butler as he raced into the house.

"Don't say it," he said rushing past her.

"You think they'll notice we're two hours late?"

"Since this is the first time in ten years that our tardiness will have been my fault, I'm not worried."

"You should be. The Wilsons will be there. He's one of your biggest backers."

Matthew walked down the hall to the nursery.

"She's asleep," Sydney said.

"Then I'll wake her. I haven't seen her since breakfast."

"For God's sake, Matthew. We're late!"

He spun around. "My daughter is more important than this dinner. Got that?"

Sydney backed down. She hated Matthew when he was like this.

He leaned over the bed and kissed his daughter on the cheek. Her eyes popped open.

"Daddy!" She threw her arms around his neck. "Did you think I was sleeping?"

"Of course not."

"Shhh!" she said, pressing a tiny finger to a perfect bow mouth. "Mrs. Collingswood thinks I'm sleeping. I fool her all the time." Jacqueline's long black curls bounced around her heart-shaped face.

Matthew smiled. There was no more perfectly formed child on the face of the earth, and her temperament was just as beautiful. "I love you, princess." He kissed her again.

"Come on, Matthew," Sydney urged.

"Good night, Jacqueline." Sydney pulled the covers up, bent down, and placed a light kiss on her forehead. Jacqueline's smile vanished along with her exhuberance. Sydney walked to the door.

Matthew took Jacqueline's hand. "See you in the morning."

"I'll wake you early and we can have honey and biscuits."

"Are you sure you'll remember?"

"Oh, yes! I'll remember. I love you, Daddy."

"Good night," he said and left.

Matthew went to his bedroom where Sydney was already waiting for him. Her arms were crossed over her chest. He ignored her as he quickly bathed and changed. Matthew had tried to understand Sydney's dislike for her daughter but couldn't. Jacqueline was the sweetest child God had made, but Sydney always acted as if there were something wrong with her.

Sydney's pregnancy had been difficult, and the birth long and painful. There had been complications and Sydney had nearly died. The result was that Sydney couldn't have any more children. He'd once asked her if she blamed Jacqueline.

"No," she'd said.

"Do you blame me?"

"No."

"Then why do you feel this way about us?"

"I don't want to talk about it, Matthew. Such things are not topics for discussion."

The matter was closed.

Not long after the encounter, Matthew overheard Sydney talking to the nanny.

"It's regrettable that Jacqueline was not a boy."

"Why?"

"Boys are perfect. Girls are not," Sydney had said and ended the conversation.

Matthew had questioned her about what she'd said, and Sydney denied it all. "You must have misunderstood, Matthew. That will teach you not to eavesdrop."

But as time passed, Sydney's attitude toward her daughter grew increasingly distant.

Matthew smoothed his dark hair and picked up his black silk top hat. He looked at his wife. "Why all the concern about this party?"

"It's important for your career. I want you to succeed, Matthew. I just have different ideas about how to go about it, is all."

"And this afternoon is your idea of how it should go?"

"If you would just listen to reason. . . ."

"My father and I will never agree. Sydney, take the pressure off yourself. Leave it alone. You're fighting a losing battle."

"I don't think so. Wars take years." She smiled charmingly.

He put his hand on the small of her back and pushed her gently toward the door. "Mark this day on your calendar, Sydney. The war ended in a stalemate."

"Don't be so sure," she said and closed the bedroom door.

Amanda let only three days pass before she saw Matthew

again. When she told Max she wanted to do a profile story on Matthew Wade, Max was in full agreement.

"Now that's the right angle. Why didn't you come up with this idea before? The new generation of New York wealth. I like it. I like it," he said, chomping on his cigar and waving her away.

Amanda telephoned Matthew at his temporary offices off Fifth Avenue. She purposely didn't call him at home. She didn't want to think about Matthew at home. It was there he kept his wife.

She met him at the job site. There were steel girders being welded at the very top floors. She could see men standing high above the city, face masks protecting them from flying sparks and pieces of steel. On the ground floor the marble and granite walls had gone up. The windows were boarded up, and so the structure looked like a blindfolded whale. Above the massive front doors was a huge German clock that was already in operation. As it chimed, Matthew walked over.

"It's still in its raw stages."

"It's magnificent." Amanda gazed up to the top. It seemed the epitome of progress to her. She wanted to see more. "Can we go inside?"

"Of course," he said eagerly.

He walked her around the concrete floors, pointed out the new Otis elevators that would take customers up and down. There would be two major dining rooms, a coffee shop, lounges on every other floor, walls of mirrors, enormous Venetian chandeliers, Italian marble display cases, and hundreds of employees. His enthusiasm was epidemic.

She stood in the center of the store and stared upward to open balconies that formed a rotunda all the way to the tenth floor.

"When it's finished the roof will open electrically. It's going to be finished in blue stained glass. I like the idea of refracted light spilling down into the interior."

Amanda's neck almost ached from looking straight up. "I like it too. Show me more."

He took her hand as they picked their way over boards, wire mesh, and nails. He led her to a makeshift desk made out of two sawhorses and a piece of wood. "Come into my office," he joked.

He took out four sets of blueprints and showed her the plans. "Each floor will be like a world of its own, each with a different theme. Sometimes we'll feature foreign countries and place their products on only one floor, sometimes on all floors. There will be holiday themes, of course. Special events. The possibilities are endless.''

Amanda watched him as he talked and she took a few notes, but not many. She knew she'd be able to remember everything he said. As he took her around the massive building describing the Art Nouveau ironwork he'd ordered from Paris and the special wall sconces from Florence, she felt IT again. This time, Amanda didn't have to wonder about the feeling. She knew she was falling in love.

Somewhere between Monday and Thursday she must have gone insane, she thought. For hadn't it only been then that she'd blamed David for showing her that love didn't exist?

From that very first time in the Ramapo Mountains she'd known there was something different about Matthew Wade. She'd pretended that she didn't dream about him at night. She had projected her romantic thoughts about Matthew onto David. Perhaps that was the reason she'd been blind to David's affair. When she lost the baby, she thought she'd never recover. But she had. Those first nights alone in her new apartment, she hadn't thought one time about David. But she had caught herself doodling Matthew's name on a piece of paper.

She had declined many invitations from friends over the months, telling herself she'd run into David, never admitting she feared seeing Matthew. She had known then, as she knew now, that once she allowed the dam of her emotions to break, she could never hold back. She knew then that although divorce was wrong, adultery was an even graver sin.

''Do you think you have enough?''

''Enough?''

''For your story.''

''Yes. I think so.'' She was still muddled in her thoughts.

''Will you be sending an artist to do sketches?''

''Yes. I think so. Maybe a before sketch, and then I could do a follow-up story in June when you open. It would be extra publicity.''

''I need all I can get.''

She walked toward the front. ''I'm very impressed with your store.''

''It's more than a store to me, Amanda.''

"It's your dream," she said, turning to him. "I remember."

Amanda saw Matthew again when the magazine sent Cary to do the sketches. She struggled to keep their conversations light. While Cary worked, Matthew took her to a small bistro nearby. She noticed that he didn't touch her, didn't linger over pauses in the conversation, and not once did he allow his eyes to delve into hers as he had done before.

Amanda was terribly depressed when they returned and found Cary had finished.

"Will this be in next month's issue?" Matthew inquired.

"Yes. The article is finished. I just needed the artwork."

"I'd like to see it," Matthew said quickly. "The article, not the artwork. Can you arrange that?"

"Well, yes. When?"

"Thursday evening would be good. After you finish work."

Cary stepped back and left them alone. He hailed a carriage.

Amanda was surprised. From his behavior that day, she didn't think Matthew would be interested in seeing her again. But then, she reasoned, perhaps it was only his concern for the content of her work. It *was* his store—his dream—she was writing about.

"I'll come to the magazine," he said. "I don't want to put you out."

She was right, she thought dejectedly. "I'll see you then, Matthew."

It had been a rotten morning, followed by a rotten afternoon. Max was feeling the pressure of the end-of-the-month deadlines. His top advertising salesman had quit to move to Florida, claiming his doctor had prescribed it for his respiration problems. Max had hired a new reporter who spent most of his time chasing women rather than news stories. Max had had four cups of coffee too many when Amanda walked into his office.

"I want to talk to you about the story on Wade's."

"What about it?" Max's head pounded.

"I think we should reconsider about sending a photographer. These sketches don't capture the real *feeling* of the place."

"No." Max thought his nerve endings would split through his skin at any second. Maybe he needed a drink—a lot of drinks. He shuffled through the stack of past-due bills on his desk.

"What if I paid for part of the cost? I can see other stories like this, Max. Why, look at what they're doing in midtown now. Look at the retail buildings. Did you know there's over a dozen new churches in construction this spring? Did you know building permits are up over one hundred percent?'' Amanda rattled on excitedly as she always did when her enthusiasm showed.

"No! No! A thousand times no!" Max pounded the desk. "Listen to me, young lady. I meant what I said the first time this conversation came up. We will not now, nor ever, do pictures. *City* magazine is quality. It's not a rag! Now you either learn to do it *my* way or no way at all.''

"I think you're wrong, Max. Dead wrong. I'll go on fighting for this as long as I'm here.''

"I won't change my position, Amanda.''

"Nor will I.'' Suddenly, she knew where the conversation was headed.

"Does this mean you're quitting me?''

"It seems inevitable.'' She held her breath.

Her words squelched the flames of Max's temper. "Don't be too hasty about this decision, Amanda.''

"I'm grateful to you, Max. I've learned a lot from you. But we're on opposite sides of the fence. I know you're shorthanded, and I won't leave you in the lurch. But as soon as you find a replacement, I'm going to have to leave.''

"And go where?''

"I don't know, Max. But I'll think of something.'' Amanda knew precisely what she wanted to do. She knew enough now to run her own magazine. For weeks she'd thought of nothing else. She wanted something progressive and interesting. She wanted to use photographs in all the ads, in features, everywhere she could. She wanted pertinent articles and she wanted to use slick, glossy paper like *Ladies' Home Journal* was using. Women paid a premium price for a favorite magazine. Amanda intended that her magazine would become every woman's choice.

Max smiled at her. He didn't want to see her go, but they weren't getting anywhere wasting their time and energy on arguments. He was holding Amanda back and she was stifling him. They were at an impasse. He wondered how it was that she saw things so clearly before he did.

"Yes, Amanda. You'll be just fine.''

Matthew stood outside the doors to *City* magazine waiting for

Amanda to emerge. He could have gone inside but didn't. He was too nervous.

Matthew didn't understand what was happening to him lately, only that everything in his life seemed to have been turned upside down since the first day he'd met Amanda Granger. He didn't know then she was famous, but he did now. He didn't know then what a determined, intelligent woman she was, but he did now. And now, he also knew that she commanded most of his waking thoughts and the entirety of his dreams.

He decided he was obsessed.

She wore a frown when she pushed through the glass door. But the moment she looked up and saw him, she smiled.

"Why didn't you come inside? I have all the material set up on the dummy. It's a good layout."

"I didn't come to see the article, Amanda."

"No?"

"I came to see you."

"Oh," she whispered, letting her eyes search his.

He took her arm and slipped it through his. "Where do you live?"

"It's not far. We can walk."

"Good," he said, pulling her a bit closer.

Amanda didn't notice the throngs of people on the streets now that the workday was over. She barely remembered what Matthew said as they stopped at the street vendors and purchased salad greens, a zucchini, tomatoes, bananas, grapes, and pears. He snatched up a fistful of jonquils and handed them to her. He overpaid the vendor. They stopped at a bakery and bought napoleons; he bought one bottle of Chianti and one of champagne at a store run by an Italian man who spoke no English and his tiny wife who spoke no Italian.

"They live on love," Matthew said as they exited and rounded the corner that led to Amanda's flat.

They mounted the steps to the brownstone. Matthew held their purchases while Amanda unlocked the door. He turned and saw a strange-looking man of about forty, gray corkscrews of hair flowing down his back, walking barefoot. The sun had gone down and so had the mercury.

"He'll catch his death of cold," Matthew said.

Amanda looked at Matthew and then at the man. "Hello, Philip!" She waved.

Philip nodded, never looked up, and continued on.

"He's eccentric," Amanda said.

"He's nuts."

Amanda occupied the first floor. There was a living room with a large fireplace, a second room equally as large, which should have been a dining room, but she used it as a workroom. There was a small galley-type kitchen and a large eating area stretched across the back of the house, with six windows that looked out onto a small terrace. The flower beds were well tended, with early hyacinths, daffodils and paper-whites jutting out of the ground.

She handed him the bottle of Chianti and two glasses. "I like puttering in the garden. I like to see things grow and change."

She started a pot boiling for fettucine. She washed the lettuce, sliced tomatoes, and chopped the zucchini while Matthew looked around at her collection of books and the rows of tiny clay pots filled with herbs she was "forcing" indoors.

"I like it here," he said, sitting in an overstuffed chair.

"It's not Fifth Avenue," she said, coming into the living room. "But it's mine."

He looked at her. "You don't want me here, do you?"

She shook her head. "No."

He took her hand. He kissed it. He let his lips linger over her soft skin. He pulled her down on his lap. He caressed her back.

"Yes. . . ." she breathed. "I do want you here."

Amanda lost herself in his embrace, in the sensation of his lips against hers. She tried to hold him closer, if it was possible. She kissed him over and over. She clutched him, clung to him.

She unbuttoned his jacket and then his shirt. She watched patiently as he slowly unbuttoned her lacy white blouse, peeled off her skirt, and then, with her clad only in her teddy, he lifted her and carried her to the bedroom and gently placed her on the bed. She wriggled out of her teddy as he kicked off his trousers.

She closed her eyes as he positioned himself over her. But as he entered her, she opened her eyes, wanting to see every inch of him. She looked into his eyes, kissed his lips, his cheeks and chin. Slowly she felt herself being spiraled to an ecstasy she hadn't known before.

He took his time, not hurrying either of them. She could tell he wanted the moment to last. Amanda thought she could feel her heart opening to him and accepting him. At that moment, Matthew took up residence in Amanda's soul. He would be with her forever, she knew. Until the day she died, she would never feel this way about another man. Matthew was hers for whatever small part of his life he could give her—a week, a day, an hour. But right now, she wanted any slices she could have. Her brain told her she was setting herself up for a life of misery and heartbreak. Her heart told her there were no options. Matthew was all she would ever know, all she would ever need.

Matthew was gentle and slow in his movements. He teased her nipples and massaged her breasts, thighs, and buttocks. Suddenly, she felt a pleasure so intense she couldn't keep her eyes open any longer. She thrust her head back and surrendered herself to Matthew.

Knowing she was spent, Matthew climaxed inside her. He was sweat-soaked when he lifted his head from her shoulder and looked into her eyes.

"I love you, Amanda."

"God help me, Matthew. I love you."

CHAPTER TWENTY-SEVEN

April found David Simon with no publisher, no income, and a dying love affair on his hands. A lesser man, he told himself, would be undone by his turn of bad luck. David reasoned that this was simply another challenge. He sought out publishers as far away as Minneapolis and San Francisco. He sold only two sketches of Christine. The demand was still for The Granger Woman.

David was undaunted by his problems. He believed in his talent, and he believed that he could make Christine famous. Because he was independently wealthy, he did not need income for sustenance, only for ego. To David they were one and the same.

Christine, however, had nothing in her life except the allure of fame. She didn't have any talent she could point to as an asset. She only had her beauty—an asset with a built-in depletion allowance. Christine wanted the excitement that fame would bring her. She wanted to be like Lillian Russell. She'd seen how crowds nearly mangled the beauty wherever she went. Christine wanted that kind of adoration. Christine was quickly realizing that David was not going to give her what she wanted.

"What about tonight?"

"Paul and I are going to the opera."

"Tomorrow, then?"

"I can't make it."

"When *can* you see me?"

"David, David," she cooed. "You're so impatient. I think we should be more discreet. Paul has heard too much gossip. I can tell you he suspects something."

"Me?"

"Of course *you*. Half this town suspects *you*. And I think it would be foolish to push our luck," she said, holding the ivory phone up a bit higher as she looked at the swell of her breasts in the reflection in her vanity mirror. She cocked her head to the side and studied her profile. No signs of her chin sagging yet. She'd heard that started around twenty-four, twenty-five.

"You sound as if Paul is more important to you than I am."

She had to be careful with David. She *did* still need him. "Not more important. But he is my husband, you know. David, please listen to me about this. Just think how special it will be after we've had a little absence from each other." She licked her lips sensuously and watched herself in the mirror. "I'll . . . make it very worthwhile, my pet."

"If that's the way it has to be . . ." David sighed dejectedly.

"Yes. It does." She placed the receiver in its cradle. She saw Paul standing in the doorway. She turned around slowly and slid the apricot silk strap of her dressing gown down her arm. She lifted her breast and cradled it in her hand.

"Take off your clothes, Paul. I've been waiting for you."

Sydney Wade wrapped a full-length sable coat around her perfect body, climbed out of the carriage, and stepped aside as Christine Van Volkein followed her.

"Wait for us," she told her driver.

They walked into Delmonico's and followed the maitre d' to their reserved table.

"I can't believe it's snowing in April!"

"I know what you mean," Christine said. "I'm sick of wearing winter fashions."

Sydney wondered if Christine had ever had a serious thought. The girl had a totally vacant brain. The waiter seated them and brought the menus.

"I'm dying for summer fruit," Christine said.

"Then order it. Del's has everything."

They placed their orders, and after the waiters finished their flurry of tasks, bringing water, butter, and rolls, Sydney took off her plum-colored kid gloves and laid them next to a new snake-skin purse.

"Tell me, Christine, why you had me cancel my meeting with James Wade in order to see you."

"You had to do that?"

"You said it was important."

"Well, it is important . . . to me."

"Christine, I hope this isn't another of your wild-goose chases you've brought me on."

"I'm having trouble getting rid of David Simon."

"Well, that shouldn't be too difficult. Just tell him you're tired of modeling and that you've decided you want to do some charity work."

"I don't think that would work," Christine said, looking around to see who else was in the room. She leaned forward a bit and lowered her voice. "You see, the situation is a bit more delicate than just my modeling for him."

It took Sydney only a moment to connect. "Good God! It isn't true, is it? Don't tell me you and David really are lovers?"

"Okay, I won't tell you."

"Christine, this *is* serious. Why, Paul has been asking all our friends—discreetly, of course—if any of them thought there was any truth to it. He just asked *me* two weeks ago at the Braxtons' party."

"And what did you say?"

"I flatly told him no. He knew I'd tell him the truth."

"You won't tell him now, will you?"

Sydney sighed. "No, I won't."

"Thanks. But you see the problem."

"Yes, *I* do. But do you? Really? You've got to end this."

"I know, but I don't want to. He's like an addiction to me, Sydney. Everytime I think about him I want to jump into bed with the nearest man."

"Christine! I'm shocked!"

"You are not, Sydney. You were no more a virgin than I was when you got married. Ten years ago we were only sixteen. You had to work damn hard to land Matthew Wade. You weren't so imperious then."

Sydney didn't like being reminded of her girlhood, when she'd been vulnerable and made mistakes. She was smarter now. And she certainly was never going to make a blunder like Christine was doing.

"Don't you realize what you could lose, Christine? You have to know that Matthew and I don't believe in divorce. He'd tell you the same thing. If Paul divorced you, you'd have a stigma you'd never get rid of. You'd be a social pariah in this town. You don't want that to happen, do you?''

"No, but there's my work with David.''

"Forget those damn sketches.''

"But I could be—''

"What? A new Gibson Girl or The Granger Woman?''

"Have you ever seen her?''

"I've known Irene for years.''

"Not her. Amanda. David's ex-wife.''

Sydney laughed. "Who hasn't seen David's sketches? But in person? No. By the time we got back from Europe, her marriage was on the rocks and she went into hiding. Besides, I've been too busy at the bank to worry over an artist's model.'' She paused. "What's the matter, Christine? Do you think she's more beautiful than you?''

"I think she's possibly more beautiful than even you, Sydney,'' Christine replied with a note of satisfaction.

Sydney looked upon her beauty as a dividend in her life. A bonus. It was not the key to her being or success that it was to most women. Beauty was a depreciating asset. Sydney only relied on appreciating assets—like wealth and power.

Sydney almost felt sorry for Christine. She only knew the power that beauty brought her through men. Thalia Whitley had done a splendid job rearing her daughter to be a perfect socialite. Unfortunately for Christine, the world was changing, and women like Christine could be left with nothing if they didn't play the game correctly. David Simon's about-to-be-divorced wife was a prime example. Who really cared if she was beautiful now? That's all she had too. Sydney had heard she'd been forced to live in some slum on the lower west side of the city. Sydney had known Christine since they were children. Sydney had been more fortunate than Christine, for her mother had died when she was three and she'd grown up in her father's world of business and commerce. She hadn't had to listen to female prattle every day. It was time Christine grew up.

"Christine, I don't care what you wanted from David. You must end this affair. If Paul divorces you, I don't know of anyone in this town who would help you.''

"Not even you, Sydney?''

"No, Christine. Not even me.''

*   *   *

After only four months away from the protective custody of David and Amanda's home and life, Andrew found that trying to make an honest dollar was ten times more difficult in New York than it was in London.

Andrew was not fool enough to engage any of Vince Casal's friends in a game of poker, but twice weekly he managed to hold small-pot games at his apartment in Hell's Kitchen. It gave him enough breathing room until he could think of something on a grander scale.

Andrew's job at Quinton Parker's had become easier, for he learned how to glean ideas from the best writers and salesmen. He listened over morning coffee while the salesmen talked about the difficulty they had in selling ad space. He asked questions, and when he heard suggestions and changes that could be made, he took them straight to Quinton, making certain he received all the credit.

Andrew utilized the fundamentals Amanda had taught him: clean copy, large visuals, and only the most pertinent information given. Though he did not make as large an impression on Quinton as he had when the ideas had all been Amanda's, he was holding his own, and his work was dependable. And above all, Andrew wanted Quinton to think he was dependable. This would give him power over Quinton, which he intended someday to use.

Still, his best source of new ideas was, as always, his sister, but that source appeared to be lost to him.

Andrew tried to see Amanda after she'd moved out of David's house, but it was not an easy task. Her first weeks away from David, she met him once for dinner, but their conversation was stilted and she seemed withdrawn.

By February, she had met him a few times after work at Rector's before going home to work on an assignment. She made no great overtures to indicate she needed his company.

Andrew was afraid that if he didn't keep in contact with his sister, he not only wouldn't get her advice on his ads, but he might lose all his connection to the world into which he craved entrée.

He shouldn't have worried.

He changed his mailing address to the magazine's post office box. There was a slight dwindling of invitations after the announcement of Amanda's divorce, but not much. There were still too many young debutantes who were enamored of his good looks and endearing charms.

Andrew had made his mark. He now found dinner invitations aplenty. He was gifted with theater tickets and opera and concert seats by fathers who liked him as well as their daughters did. Andrew's plan of wooing the families along with the girls had worked.

By the first of April, he had found the perfect girl.

Her name was Mary Alice Howell. She was a moderately pretty girl, with a moderately intriguing personality and a fabulously wealthy father. Jack Howell had recently decided that the publishing business was on the verge of a boom. Jack had bought two newspapers, one in San Francisco and one in Denver. He was a joint-venture partner in a book-publishing company in Hartford, Connecticut, but to date he had not taken the plunge in New York. He was fascinated by Andrew's involvement in publishing.

Jack Howell was sipping an after-dinner brandy as he read the evening papers in his library when Andrew arrived.

"Come in, Andrew," he said, motioning to a leather chair across from him. "Would you care for a brandy?"

"No, thank you, sir."

"How's everything down at Quinton's?"

"Just fine, sir. There's an article in the next issue that you might be interested in. It's about the new gasoline-powered automobiles."

"Automobiles? Do you think they'll ever replace the horse and carriage? I don't."

"Didn't they say that about the railroads?"

Jack howled. "So they did!"

Just then Mary Alice came down the red-carpeted white marble staircase. She wore a cream satin theater suit with brown velvet collar and cuffs. Her chestnut hair was piled on top of her head. Andrew noticed the fantastically beautiful ruby drop earrings she wore. They must have been ten carats each.

"You look lovely," he said breathlessly.

"Thank you," she said, pulling on her brown velvet gloves. "Father, you and Mother will meet us at the Waldorf after the theater, won't you."

Andrew smiled and gulped. He had only one hundred and fifty dollars in his pocket. He'd hoped to make it last a week or better, not just one night.

"That would be very nice."

Andrew shook Jack's hand. "Good! We'll count on seeing you then."

Andrew walked Mary Alice to the carriage, then followed her in. He noticed that when they drove off, Jack Howell was still standing at the window watching them. A protective father.

"You don't think I was too forward to invite you to this play, do you, Andrew? I mean, I didn't want the tickets to go to waste."

"No, that's fine," Andrew replied absentmindedly. He was still thinking about his lack of money. He had to find a way to get more of it—and fast.

"You look as if you're not happy about it at all," she said.

Instantly, Andrew remembered himself. He turned to her. In the moonlight she was quite pretty, with rosy cheeks and dark, round eyes. He touched her cheek with his hand and then traced the outline of her lips with his forefinger. "Mary Alice . . ."

He leaned over to kiss her. Quickly, she turned her head away.

"Andrew, don't!"

"What?"

"Don't kiss me. I don't want to be like all the other girls you've known."

"Don't worry, Mary Alice. You aren't."

She faced him. Her eyes were bright and stern. "*I* know I'm not. But *you* don't know me well enough to make that statement yet."

He chuckled to himself and leaned back in the seat. "You're probably right, Mary Alice. You aren't like anyone I've ever known." He wondered if it were possible that there could be two women like Amanda; and if there were, how had it been his misfortune to have them both in his life.

CHAPTER TWENTY-EIGHT

Amanda officially quit *City* magazine on April fifteenth. It was the first time Max had ever given a going-away party for an employee. Angela, one of the secretaries, baked a chocolate cake, Cary made an enormous card that everyone signed, and Max broke open a bottle of his best bourbon.

"Here's to the future, Amanda," Max toasted her. "I'd like to say you've been like a daughter to me, but I'd never want a child who caused me so much trouble."

Everyone howled as Amanda kissed Max's cheek. "I love you, Max." She blinked back her tears.

"So," Cary began, "what are you going to do now?"

Amanda kept her arm around Max's shoulder, looked at him, and announced: "I'm starting my own magazine."

Max's mouth dropped. "What?"

"Don't worry, Max. I won't be your competition. I'm going to start a woman's magazine and I'm going to call it *City Woman*."

"Clever," Max said appreciatively. "I wish you all the luck."

"I'm going to need it. I haven't raised the first dime for funding."

Max poured her three fingers of bourbon. "You'd better get to like this stuff if you're going to be a publisher."

"Amanda, will there be jobs for us if Max gets to be too much?" Cary asked.

She looked at Max and winked. "Absolutely!" Then she whispered to Max, "That ought to keep you on your toes."

Johnny, the errand boy, wound up the Victrola and put on a

ragtime record. Cary danced with Amanda and Max grabbed Angela as everyone else joined in. There was much clapping of hands and singing; it wasn't a solemn occasion, for both Amanda and Max knew that their association would never end.

Through the grimy window, Matthew watched the young man who whirled Amanda between desks and tables. She was happy there with her friends who loved her, wanted the best for her.

Matthew wanted the best for her, but he couldn't give it to her. He'd pretended for weeks that Sydney didn't exist in his life. They had never had a marriage. They were simply roommates—even less. Sydney had a life that seldom, if ever, intersected with his. She spent long hours at her father's bank and her evenings at society parties. Matthew only went to parties he couldn't avoid. Since Sydney usually was escorted by either her own father or his father, she was never the subject of discordant gossip. Sydney wielded enough weight among New Yorkers to keep rumors to a minimum. After ten years of their peculiar, particular marital arrangement, everyone accepted the Wades the way they were.

Amanda was putting a forkful of cake into her mouth when she happened to look out the window and see Matthew. She calmly put the cake down, made her farewells to everyone, and left.

Matthew waited for her at the corner under the street lamp. She rushed into his arms. He held her face in his hands and kissed her deeply.

"I didn't think I'd see you for days!"

"I *had* to see you," he breathed and kissed her again.

"Let's go home," she said.

"Yes. Home."

It was a lazy spring night, the kind New York poets wrote about. The breeze off the Atlantic washed the city in a salty, heavy glow that was neither fog nor mist. They walked slowly, savoring the moments of silence, of a quiet delighted giggle, of the sense of peace they felt at being together.

Matthew kept his arm around her waist and she put her head on his shoulder. Painters in lofts, chanteuses in cafes, and pedestrians on the streets knew they were lovers. Matthew and Amanda were recognizable faces not because of their fame or wealth or background but because they were part of the world of lovers who lived and flourished in Chelsea.

Amanda fixed them each a bowl of vegetable soup she'd made

the day before. There were muffins left over from breakfast. They ate in the bedroom where she could look at the mammoth bouquet he'd brought her three days ago.

He tossed his spoon into the bowl. "That was wonderful," he said as he picked the pins out of her coiffure. He watched the tumble of golden hair fall onto her shoulders. "I wish . . . I wish for a million things," he said sadly. "But tonight I wish I could take you to the finest restaurant in town. I wish we didn't have to slip around through shadows. It makes it seem . . ."

"Wrong?"

"No! Never wrong, Amanda. I've never been in love till now." He kissed her.

She huddled into the safety of his arms. "I don't want to think about anything but this minute. This is more than I dreamed for. *You* are more than I ever dreamed for."

"But I want so much for us."

"Shhh," she said, pressing her fingers to his lips. "Make love to me, Matthew. Show me you love me."

Matthew carefully eased himself out of bed without disturbing Amanda. He stepped into his trousers and put on his shirt. He looked at his pocket watch. It was nearly eleven. Sydney would be home in an hour, two at the latest. He picked up his jacket, shoes, and socks, deciding he would finish dressing in the living room so as not to wake Amanda. He tiptoed out and carefully shut the door.

He finished dressing, wrote Amanda a note, and started for the door.

"You think you can get away that easily?" Amanda stood naked against the doorjamb.

He smiled. "Get back in there."

"No!" she teased.

"What?"

"Make me."

"Amanda, I have to leave."

"I know," she said, walking toward him. She looked like a goddess gliding across the floor, unashamed of her nakedness. She seemed to revel in the gift of it that she gave him. She put her arms around his neck and leaned into him. "I love you, Matthew."

"I love you." He pulled her tightly to him.

"Surprise me again," she said. "The days are long without you."

"I know. I know."

He turned, and without looking back, he left.

As Amanda went back to the bedroom, she told herself that the pang in her heart was joy, not pain.

Sydney Wade's headache was the worst she'd ever had in her life. Sydney didn't believe in headaches. They were a fantasy dreamed up by women who didn't know how to control their husbands' sexual urges. Sydney had taken three headache powders and put cold compresses on her forehead, but nothing helped. She couldn't understand it. It wasn't the champagne, for Sydney never had more than one glass. She had to keep her wits about her.

It had to be the tension at the bank, she thought. Her father had been ill with influenza for almost a month, and much of the burden of running the bank had fallen on her shoulders. It was the day she'd dreamed of all her life. Clayton Saxon, the senior vice-president, had commented that she had as keen a mind as any banker in New York. Sydney was floating. And she didn't want it to stop.

Sydney's dilemma was to devise a plan that would keep her father in an advisory capacity and still allow her to make all the major decisions at the bank. It would take a great deal of thought. And that probably was causing the headache.

At midnight, Sydney went into her bathroom to run cold water on the washcloth for her head when she noticed that Matthew's light was on under his door. Perhaps he hadn't been able to sleep either.

She rapped lightly on the door and opened it, rather than waiting for a reply.

"Matthew, I . . ."

He spun around from the closet where he was standing still clad in his pants and shoes, but he had discarded his shirt.

She calmly placed the compress on her forehead. "Are we going out or coming in?"

"Coming in," he said flatly.

"Really?"

He looked at her. "Are you sick?"

"Just a headache."

"You never get headaches. Are you sure it isn't fever? Maybe you caught that thing from your father." He took off his trousers and hung them up.

"It's not influenza. Would you care if it was?"

"What's that supposed to mean?"

"Oh, nothing. I supposed you were still down at the site."

He sat in a chair and took off his socks. His smile was wide. "I wish you'd see it, Sydney. There's never been anything like it in the world. On the first floor I'm having an area sectioned off in glass blocks that will house fabulous jewels from all over the world. Even Tiffany's can't rival it. It'll be the best of everything. And I got a cable from Paris today. Those three designers you liked . . ."

"The apprentices at Balmain and Lanvin?"

"They took our offer. They'll be here in three weeks. You'll have the most beautiful gowns in New York."

Sydney dropped her arm to her side and placed her left hand on her hip. "It takes more than a designer to make a Parisian couture gown, Matthew. Any woman knows that."

"So do I. I've got four seamstresses and a fitter coming too."

"Good God!"

"What's the matter, Sydney?" he said with a self-satisfied grin on his face. "You think I just might make it, don't you?"

He stood and went to her. His eyes bore into her. "Give me some credit, will you? Just because I don't want to be a banker like you and my father doesn't mean I'm stupid. There's money to be made in every business. Now go back to bed. I'm tired."

Sydney didn't say anything. Sometimes, she thought as she retreated into her opulent bedroom, having the last word is a sign of weakness.

Amanda awoke to a pounding noise. Her neck was stiff, since she'd fallen asleep in the chair. Slowly, she opened her eyes and then realized that someone was at the door. She was still dressed in a skirt and blouse from the day before, and her lamp was lit. She stood and a stack of papers fell from her lap to the floor.

"I'm coming!" she said to the persistent knocking.

She unlocked the door. "Quinton! What are you doing here?" She rubbed her eyes.

"I'm sorry to come here unannounced, but it was very important. I didn't want to see you at my office."

His face was filled with concern. She stood aside and motioned for him to enter.

"I'll make some coffee."

Quinton sat at the kitchen table. "Amanda, I don't know how to tell you this."

She put the coffeepot on the stove and turned to him. "It's Andrew, isn't it?"

"How did you know?"

She remembered her brother's gangster friends the night the carriage overturned. She remembered a lot. "Tell me."

"I have reason to believe Andrew is skimming from me."

"Are you sure? Couldn't it be someone else?"

"I seriously doubt it. Three months ago I gave Andrew control over the books. He had a good background in accounting, and he wanted a raise and was willing to take on the job even though it would take some of his evening hours. Since I've done most of the bookkeeping for years, it wouldn't be easy to hide much from me. I guess he didn't think of that."

"You'll fire him, of course."

"Of course. But for your sake, I don't want anyone to know about it. If you talked to him . . . told him to give the money back, he could come in and resign. No one would be the wiser."

"How much did he take?"

"Four hundred dollars."

"That's a lot of money, but I'll make certain you get it back."

"I thought I'd deduct his next paycheck from the total. But even with his extra work it's only forty dollars."

"Quinton, you're being very kind," she said, knowing any other employer would have not only fired Andrew but pressed charges as well.

"You're my friend, Amanda."

"Thank you." Thoughtfully she said: "Andrew isn't bad, Quinton, I'm sure you can see that. It's just that he feels pressured to keep up with me, my friends. . . ."

"I heard he's seeing Mary Alice Howell. I can understand how he could be tempted. But you also have to know I can't take him back."

"I know, Quinton. You've been good to both of us. How can I repay you?"

Quinton laughed. "Call me if you decide you need to thrash him! I'd like to punch him out, if only because all this is upsetting you."

"Don't worry about me, Quinton."

"Well," he said, rising to leave. "If you do need me for anything, just call."

"It's a deal," she said and walked him to the door and let him out.

Amanda sank into the chair. Four hundred dollars was nearly all she had in the bank to live on. She didn't have any idea how to go about getting a loan to start up her magazine. She couldn't borrow from Sylvia, who lived off dividends from stocks. Amanda had thought of all her friends and didn't know any who would fund her magazine.

"First things first," she said and went to the telephone and placed a call to Andrew at his office.

They met at a tiny, hole-in-the-wall restaurant near Times Square. All the theater people were moving to the area, and many of the cafes and restaurants had become meeting places for celebrities and the journalists and columnists who kept the lights shining on their fame.

Andrew smiled charmingly to a pair of young actresses who passed by their table on their way to the restrooms.

Amanda stuck her fork in her salad and let it fall. She was too upset to eat. She looked at him. There wasn't a trace of guilt or worry on his face. How could he do it?

"I had an early-morning caller today."

"Oh," Andrew said, waving to an editor for the *New York Herald*. "Who was that?"

"Quinton Parker."

Andrew's head swiveled around. She had his attention. He placed his napkin in his lap. "What did he want?"

"You. Hanging by the throat from a gallows."

He forced a laugh. "What on earth does that mean?"

"He found you out, Andrew. He said you've been skimming money from him."

"It's a lie. Let him prove it."

"He *can* prove it, Andrew. So don't play the innocent here."

Andrew realized that his little sister wasn't so little anymore. She was growing up very quickly, and the tactics he'd used on her in the past weren't going to work anymore. She was not only older but wiser. She'd been out there working in the world for many months now. She'd survived David and the hypocrisy of half of New York society, and she'd come out of it stronger than ever. He'd underestimated her. And it made him very angry to know that once again she'd come up the winner. He used every bit of self-control he had to cover his real emotions. As always, his hatred for her wanted to surface, strike out at her, and beat her down. But Andrew kept his demons caged away and pulled out his most contrite tones and actions.

"Amanda, what am I going to do? Did he tell the police?"

"No. He told me. He's letting you off easy, Andrew, because you're my brother."

Andrew cringed. Of all the things in the world he didn't want to be was her brother. He didn't care if she *was* saving his skin again.

"Quinton told me that if you went in there today and handed in a letter of resignation and paid him back the four hundred dollars, he'd drop the matter quietly."

Four hundred? Andrew thought. He'd stolen over a thousand. Quinton was good, but he wasn't *that* good. He'd done a better job of covering his tracks than he'd thought. He looked at Amanda with penitent eyes.

"Where am I going to get four hundred dollars?"

"Quinton will keep your paycheck. I'll pay the other three hundred and sixty."

"You'd do that for me, Amanda?"

She sighed and looked at him. She thought of her mother and what she would want. She believed that Harriet would want her to help him. They were the only Grangers left. Faults and all, he was her brother and she loved him.

"I'll do it." She wagged her finger at him. "But it's the last time. And you're going to pay me back every penny."

"I will! You know I will."

"I know you will, because you're coming to work for me. And every week, I'm taking half your paycheck until you've paid me back."

"Work for you? I don't know . . ."

Confidently, she lifted her coffee cup. "You want to go to prison?"

"No." He sighed, wondering if working for his sister wasn't the same thing.

"It's settled, then. As of today you're the new managing editor for *City Woman*."

"Jesus."

"And Andrew—I know how to keep books too."

Bravado does not buy printing presses. Hope does not lease office space. And confidence does not hire employees. Only money could do all that, and Amanda didn't have any money.

Amanda decided to go where they did have money. She went to New York Life and Trust. She hadn't been in the loan officer's office for ten minutes before he flatly refused her. Lack of collateral, he told her. She went to Merchant's Bank. Then the New York National Bank. The story was similar at each place. No one wanted to talk to her.

She was extremely discouraged when she unlocked her door that evening. She went to the kitchen and as she took off her hat and was about to hang it on the wall peg, she looked out the French door to the garden and saw him.

She opened the door. "Matthew! What are you doing out there?"

"Waiting for you."

"How did you get in?"

"Through the back alley. I hopped the fence. It's not much protection, Amanda. Do you think it should be higher?"

"No!" She laughed and rushed out the door and put her arms around him. "Then I might not have seen you tonight. And I'm so glad you're here. It was a terrible day."

"Why is that?"

"I've been trying to get a loan for my magazine, and no one will even consider it."

He smiled. "What do you have for collateral?"

"God! If I hear that word one more time . . . !"

"I take it you don't have any."

"No, I don't have any."

He toyed with a lock of her hair. "And I suppose you went in person to see these bankers."

"Yes."

"And you talked to some vice-president or some assistant to the president or a loan officer."

"Yes . . ." She looked at him quizzically. "I'm doing it wrong."

"You're doing it wrong." He chuckled.

"This isn't something to be taken lightly, Matthew," she said firmly, trying to squirm out of his embrace. But he held her back.

"I'm not. In fact, I'm going to tell you just how to go about getting your loan."

"What?" Her spirits leapt.

"I could have gotten it for you all along, but you never asked."

"Well, I knew how you felt about your father. . . ."

"Oh, I'm not going to ask my father. Since you have no collateral, the only thing you do have is my word and my word with him couldn't get you five cents. No, I'm going to talk to Harlen Brinkley."

"Sydney's father?"

"Yes."

Bringing Sydney between them like this only pointed out to her what they were doing. Amanda usually was able to rationalize that they weren't hurting anyone, that Sydney didn't love Matthew, that he didn't love Sydney. All of which was true, but. . . .

Matthew knew instantly what she was thinking. "Don't, Amanda. We didn't plan to fall in love. The situation—"

"It's wrong, Matthew. You have a wife *and* a child. And I'm not officially divorced yet. I feel worse than guilty. Don't you understand? I've never done anything to hurt anyone, not intentionally, I mean. And now here I am, trying to make my own life, and I'm doing things that shouldn't even be options! Oh, Matthew. I can't live like this—it *is* wrong—for me."

"I know, Amanda."

She looked at him. Her heart was screaming for an answer, an end to the nightmare. "But I love you—too much, I guess."

"And I love you."

She slid her arms around his waist and put her head on his chest. "I want everything to be perfect for us. And it isn't."

"Life seldom is."

"But it could be more perfect than it is."

"I know it could." He lifted her face with his fingertips. "And I'm going to do something about it."

"You are?"

"I'm going to ask Sydney for a divorce."

"You'd do that?"

"I'm surprised you'd think I wouldn't. However, I think it

would be prudent of me to wait until *after* I've gotten your loan."

"Very prudent indeed."

Matthew was waiting for Harlen Brinkley when he entered his office. They shook hands.

"You're looking fit after you recent illness, Harlen," he said, though he thought otherwise. Harlen had been ill off and on for years but had always seemed to bounce back from bouts with bronchitis and pneumonia. Now, for the first time, Harlen looked every day of his sixty years. His face was pasty from being indoors and he'd lost a lot of weight, causing his skin to sag at the jowls. His hair was twice as gray as it had been three weeks ago. Matthew thought Sydney was right to worry about him.

"Goddamn doctors!" the stodgy old man said, bending down to a near crouch before he sat in his chair. "I think they keep a body sick on purpose, in order to make more money. If I had the time, I'd have the entire profession investigated."

Matthew laughed. "I see you haven't lost your sense of humor."

"Huh?"

"Harlen, I have a friend who is in need of a business loan. I was wondering if you might be able to help."

"What kind of business?"

"A publishing company. Magazines mostly, to start. Perhaps branch out into books later on."

"No newspapers?"

"No."

"Good. We've got enough yellow journalism as it is. I can't believe the crap they put in the paper these days."

"I agree. No, Harlen, this would be more upscale."

"What kind of magazines?"

"A women's magazine primarily. I understand from my friend that most of the magazines purchased are by women. *Ladies' Home Journal, The Delineator, Harper's Bazaar* are all making good profits. I was given this sheet of statistics to show you." Matthew handed Harlen a portfolio of information that Amanda had carefully compiled over the past few weeks.

Harlen studied it closely. "This looks good to me. How much money does he need?"

"Twenty-five thousand."

"That's a lot of money."

"It could be done for less, but I'm afraid the quality would suffer."

"What kind of collateral is he putting up?"

"That's where we have a bit of a problem. My friend is young and doesn't have anything but experience, ambition, and a willingness to work to offer as collateral."

The old man knit his hands together and peered at Matthew. "I don't think I—"

"Would you do it as a favor to me? If anything goes wrong, I'll back up the loan."

"Well, that's a bit different now, isn't it?"

"I'd like to think my word is worth something."

Harlen's withered face cracked into a smile. "Tell your friend he's got the loan. I'll have the papers ready for signing by the end of the week."

Matthew rose and shook his hand. "I can't thank you enough, Harlen."

"Don't mention it."

Matthew started out the door.

"By the way, Matthew. What's your friend's name? For the contracts . . ."

"Granger. A. Granger."

Amanda was so nervous she was fidgeting as she waited for Matthew to come back from the bank. She'd gone over to the empty warehouse on Twentieth Street to dream. It was perfect. The walls were sturdy, and it had adequate plumbing and had been wired electrically. She'd put the offices on the second floor and have the presses and loading docks on the ground floor. She'd have a special staircase installed leading up from the street to the second floor so that visitors would walk into a reception area and not into the deafening noises of the machinery.

The sun had gone down by the time Matthew knocked on the door. She yanked it open.

"Well?" Her face was filled with anticipation.

"He said yes."

"Oh, my God!" She leapt into his arms and nearly knocked him over. "I can't believe it."

"It's true," he said, shutting the door behind him. "There's a small matter that we need to be quite careful about."

"What's that?"

"I didn't tell him you were a woman."

"You told him I was a man?"

"He *assumed* you were a man."

"And so now we have to work around it." Amanda thought for a minute. "I know. We'll have my brother, Andrew, pick up the papers."

"You'd trust him with something this important? After what you told me he did to Quinton, are you sure you want to do this?"

"Yes, I am. You don't know Andrew—haven't even met him yet. He's not bad, really. He made a mistake with Quinton and I think he sees that now. Matthew"—she looked at him pleadingly—"he's my brother. He'll do it. I know he will."

"Well, if you're very sure . . . it just might work. The papers are being drawn up as A. Granger. I'll call ahead and tell Harlen you want them reviewed by your lawyer. Andrew will pick them up. Then you sign them as Amanda. Andrew will return the papers to a loan officer who will handle the transactions from there. Andrew will pick up the check and bring it to you. Then you deposit it in your bank."

Amanda shook her head. "All this scheming, just because I'm a woman."

Matthew smiled. "You wouldn't have any of these problems if you weren't so headstrong, so smart," he teased.

"It would have been better for me to stay married to David and play the dutiful wife?"

"Hey!" he said, coming to her. "Don't be mad at me. I'm glad you're the way you are. Otherwise you wouldn't have left David. I'm all for your magazine. I think it's great . . . and I think you'll make a success of it."

She looked at him. He was genuinely happy for her. She didn't see jealousy or any male sense of superiority. He was proud of her. And she loved him all the more for it. "It's important to me that you believe in me."

"I know. I'm just returning the favor," he said, thinking how enthused she was about his store.

Five days later, Andrew walked into the Brinkley Bank, signed for the contract papers as Andrew Granger, and told the loan officer's secretary he would return them in the morning.

The next day, Andrew returned to the loan officer's secretary with the papers. Before handing the packette to the girl he asked if she had the cashier's check. She pulled out an envelope from a drawer and handed it to him. He smiled the kind of smile that he knew would make her heart flutter. He purposely kept his eyes on her breasts to keep her off guard.

"Do you have to work on Saturdays?"

"Only mornings . . . till noon."

"That means if a certain someone were to come along about noon, you might be free to have lunch?"

She blushed. "I might."

He smiled again as he pocketed the check. He handed her the packette of papers.

"Good day," he said, winked at the girl, and left.

Amanda was waiting for him at her apartment. Not once during their plotting did Amanda think it was possible that Andrew might take the money and leave town. She never told him who had arranged the loan, for Andrew knew nothing about Matthew. In time, she supposed they wouldn't be able to hide their affair any longer. But in her mind, that day would never come, because she knew that Matthew would be divorced soon.

Andrew quickly alighted from the carriage, paid the driver, and sprinted up the steps to Amanda's brownstone. She opened the door and let him in.

"It went like clockwork," he said, proud of the escapade. "All it took was a little flirting and some charm—for which I am noted. . . ."

Amanda took the envelope. It was heavily sealed. And untampered with. She had been right to trust Andrew.

"So," he said cockily, "how much did you borrow?"

"Enough to ruffle every feather in New York publishing."

CHAPTER TWENTY-NINE

Amanda's back ached, there were calluses on her hands, and she hadn't washed her hair in three days. And she'd never felt better about herself. Two days ago, the sign painter had come and painted above the ground floor windows: GRANGER PUBLISHING COMPANY.

The presses were installed, as were the cutters and the binders. She hired seven drivers who were to work part-time only at the end of the month when the issue hit the stands. She intended to print only for New York her first six months; then, if she was successful, she would branch out to other markets. Boston, Philadelphia, Cleveland, and Washington were her goals in her first year. Max told her she'd bitten off more dream than she could chew.

The carpenters were putting the finishing touches on the outside staircase and her office was being painted. She'd found half a dozen used desks that were being delivered tomorrow. She would put the advertising salesmen together in one office for the time being, and they were to work on a large conference table.

Andrew hired three typists, a telephone operator, the typesetter, two men to run the presses and the warehousemen. Amanda hired the editors, and for the first time in publishing, she hired full-time photographers.

The editors were angry that the photographers were using the last remaining office for a darkroom, but it was the way Amanda wanted it. She didn't hire them to agree with her, she hired them to work. By Monday, they would be ready to work.

*　　*　　*

Sydney Wade sat at her desk in a blue-and-cream-appointed office adjacent to that of her father. It had become evident that his health was never going to improve. Harlen was now working only half days and took Fridays off completely. He turned over the majority of his business to Sydney. Harlen had finally become Sydney's "front man." And nothing had ever made her quite so happy.

In truth, most of the New York banking world marveled at Harlen: his ability to make decisions and not only to maintain his position as a leader in the banking community but to be forging ahead with industrious new acquisitions. There were many who spoke of Brinkley Banks with awe. All of this only served to inflame Sydney's desire to head Wade Banks.

She smiled to herself when she thought that none of the banking icons knew it was a woman running Brinkley Banks—not even James Wade.

As was her custom by now, each Monday morning Sydney reviewed her father's paperwork from the week before. She had just gone through a stack of contracts when she came to a name she recognized: Amanda Granger.

Quickly, she scanned the pages of the contract and realized that her father had approved a loan with no collateral. It was the first time she'd ever known of him doing such a thing.

Sydney left her office and went to the main floor, where the loan officer's secretary told her about the transaction. The girl told her emphatically that it was Andrew Granger she'd met.

Perplexed, there was nothing Sydney could do but wait until tomorrow and speak with her father about it then.

"Oh, that." He lit a cigar and coughed repeatedly. "It's a bit unconventional, but I'm not worried about it."

"There's no collateral."

"I have no doubts the loan will be paid. I have Matthew's assurance on that."

"Matthew? What's he got to do with it?"

"This Granger fellow is a friend of his."

She shoved the contracts in his face. "This Granger fellow is a woman. Amanda Granger to be exact."

Harlen put his cigar down. "The divorcée?"

"The Granger Woman." Sydney harrumphed.

"Why would Matthew deliberately deceive me?"

"He told you it was a man?"

"Not exactly."

Sydney's eyebrows rose. She didn't know which was worse—a doddering old man for a father or a husband who was the laughingstock of half the city. Lately her friends were calling his store Wade's Folly. She wondered how much longer she could stand it.

"I think Matthew and I should have a talk," she muttered.

The maid placed a veal cutlet in front of Sydney. She picked up her sterling silver fork and then halted in mid motion. She looked at her husband seated at the opposite end of the table. The candlelight from the eight-branched candelabra cast a soft glow on his face. He sipped his wine, glanced at her, smiled briefly, and went back to his meal.

She wondered if it was possible that he could be having an affair with this Granger woman. She'd never thought about Matthew in that sordid, truly banal context. She'd always believed him above that sort of thing. He was obsessed only with his daughter and his store. She wondered if he'd even have time for a woman. Of course, anyone could *make* time for the things that were important.

"I didn't know you were acquainted with Amanda Granger," she said flatly.

Matthew didn't miss a beat. He cut his veal. "Only in a business sense."

"How's that?"

"Surely you know, since you're asking me. I told Quinton Parker I would help a friend of his get a loan to start a magazine."

"And Amanda Granger was the friend?"

"Yes." He sipped his wine. He showed not a trace of the guilt she was looking for.

"I'm surprised Quinton would want to help someone become his competition."

"She's publishing a women's magazine," he said in a purposely derogatory tone.

"I see," Sydney said, catching his intonation. It instantly aroused her defense mechanisms. "Well, I hope she does very well with it. I'm a firm believer in women helping themselves. If you men would think more like women, this world would be a much better place."

He chewed his meat. "I know. You've said that before. And have I ever held you back?"

"No," she mumbled to herself. "Not that you could, anyway."

Matthew had desperately wanted to bring up the subject of divorce—tonight. But now he thought it wise not to.

He wanted a divorce from Sydney for the right reasons. He wasn't divorcing Sydney in order to marry Amanda, for his divorce was long overdue. He should have done it five years ago. But then, he reasoned, he wouldn't have his daughter. And there was nothing more precious to him than Jacqueline.

Matthew also could not risk letting Sydney know about Amanda. It would only make obtaining his freedom more difficult if Sydney knew she had an adversary. Sydney believed in territorial rights. To her mind, Matthew and Jacqueline were her property—rather like bank assets. She didn't love them, but she needed them to fulfill some emptiness within her. Matthew never fully understood it, but now after ten years of marriage, he knew that *he* was not the key to Sydney's happiness, though he'd tried for many years to be. But in Sydney's eyes, he'd always come up short. Sydney needed something he could never give her. He wondered if anyone could.

Matthew knew the right time to broach the subject of his divorce would come, and he hoped it would be soon.

Sydney watched him as he continued his meal. She should have known Matthew wouldn't be involved with another woman. He never had before. In fact, many would think Matthew was the perfect husband. As Sydney had matured, however, she'd found that no man was perfect—not even her father, and especially not Matthew. The less she had to do with either of them, the better. If she could have her way, she'd ask them all to leave her alone and let her run her banks. However, society saw things differently. She was forced by social dictum to keep both men in her life.

In the future, she must remember not to show her vulnerability to Matthew. She didn't want him to know that such things as his love affairs mattered to her. Sydney could not tolerate weakness—especially in herself.

"I need advertisers, Andrew."

"These guys have banged on every door in town."

Amanda pushed past him and picked up a stack of invoices on the file cabinet. "They'll have to do better. *You'll* have to do better."

"Me?"

"Yes. You work here too—in case you've forgotten."

"I have mountains of work."

"And most of it can be handled in one night if you'd stay long enough to get it done. I need you out on the streets, getting us some clients."

"What about my paperwork?"

"I'll do it."

Andrew grabbed his hat from the hat rack, snatched up a dummy copy of the magazine from Amanda's secretary's desk and left. He made certain he slammed the door.

Sally looked up at Amanda and grimaced. "A real professional."

Amanda shook her head and went to Andrew's office. She took the articles the editors had presented and the photographers' suggestions and went to her office. One hour later, Amanda had finished reading the material and had decided which stories she wanted and which could wait till later issues. She had Sally summon her two photographers.

Harry Sullivan was as Irish as the day was long. He had a thick shock of red hair, freckles, and brilliant blue eyes. He was almost pathetically thin, but she hardly ever noticed because she was always blinded by his smile.

Milton Wall had virtually no personality at all. She could hardly remember what he looked like from day to day, he was so bland looking, with brown hair, brown eyes, pale skin, and a medium frame. But when Milton placed his average-looking head behind a camera, he became a genius. It was as if he wanted to make the whole world beautiful. He saw things that only a Michelangelo could see. He worked magic with a camera.

They sat in her office on used, hard, hickory chairs. They showed Amanda the greatest respect, not because she was a woman but because she was going to make them famous.

"Gentlemen, as I told you when I hired you, I don't want conventionality. These photos you took for Pear's Soap might be fine for the *Journal* or *The Delineator*, but here, we have to do better. New York doesn't know it wants photographs in its magazines. We have to show them that they do. And here's how we're going to do it."

They both moved to the edge of their seats.

"I'm going to have the third-floor storage area here cleaned out. Then I want you to tell me what we need to set up a photographer's studio."

"You mean like an artist's studio?"

"Precisely," she said, thinking of David's studio with the

glass ceiling. "My idea is this. In the center section of each magazine, we'll show photographs of the latest New York fashions. No longer will women have to look at unexciting sketches. No wonder the masses of American women know very little about fashion. Except for the very wealthy, whose business it is to be fashion conscious, most women don't know where to start. It's your job to excite them. Show them photographs of real women wearing fabulous jewels, exquisite gowns, and furs. We'll have sections for everyday wear, party dresses, and accessories. *City Woman* won't be like any other fashion magazine in the country."

"I'm ready!" said Harry.

She looked over to Milton.

His smile was wan, but his eyes were filled with fire. "I know just where I want to start."

At the end of the month, Milton turned in photographs of an exquisitely beautiful young girl of about seventeen. She was dressed in a couture gown from B. Altman's and she held a nosegay of summer roses. Amanda looked closely at the young girl's face, the eyes that were sad and yet expectant.

She shivered as chills raced down her arms. It was the immigrant girl she'd seen three and a half years earlier on the boat at Ellis Island.

Amanda looked up at Milton. "I want this girl in every issue. Tell her she has a permanent job."

Love was a narcotic and Amanda was an addict, she decided. Though she kept every vessel of her brain filled with details about the magazine, she was amazed that there was so much room available for Matthew. In those first weeks as she began to create work patterns for herself, she noticed that she developed the habit of clock watching. It wasn't that she needed to know the time so much as it was an indicator of how many hours she must endure until she saw Matthew.

She could last two, even four days without seeing him. But on the fifth day, she became nervous, cranky, and preoccupied. She thought about him at least four times an hour. She didn't dwell on him, but the vision of his face flashed across her mind or the particular sound of his voice would invade her ears.

Because she kept her love affair confined to the borders of Chelsea and inside her own heart, she did not have to face recriminations from friends or society as a whole. Amanda fought pangs of guilt over the affair, but in her mind, Sydney Wade was a faceless person—a name that was never mentioned in their conversations, only implied. Amanda knew she was living a dangerous lie—one far more devastating than The Lie about her bloodlines, for this time she could lose her heart.

Amanda waded through an inch-thick layer of whipped cream before reaching the warm cappucino. She glanced out the window of the cafe. He was thirty minutes late. She pretended she didn't see the eyes of the waiter and the couple next to her. They knew who she was, and they knew that she had not intended to be alone tonight. The anxious look in her eyes gave her away.

Matthew had chosen this place, for he was an unknown here. This was not the world he frequented—his world was near Central Park. But as Amanda sat there, toying with her napkin and drinking her coffee, she realized that this was *her* world. It was the place where she was now familiar. She worked only six blocks from here. Her secretaries came and went in all these shops. And employees *talked*.

Once Amanda had been The Granger Woman. In the social circles of the Astors, Cuttings and Kanes, she was more than recognizable. The people here in the neighborhood had not known her then, and now they knew her as the owner of a fledgling magazine; nothing more. But tonight they knew her as a woman whose lover had not appeared.

In a week, a month, they would fit the pieces together. If she weren't careful, everyone in New York would know about herself and Matthew.

Amanda rose, paid her bill, and left. The summer night was hot and still. She felt desperately alone at that moment. She'd counted—too heavily—on seeing Matthew. She knew he would have been with her if he could. She also knew this was the price of loving a married man.

"You can't cut yourself off from the world," Sylvia said sternly as she loomed over Amanda's desk. "It's been six months since you left David. Everyone has had a chance to adjust. Even him. In the years to come you're going to need those people. Many of them love you, Amanda."

"And many don't."

"Don't argue. If you won't think of yourself, think of the magazine. You could benefit from their support. They could *make* this magazine for you."

"Are you saying that without them my ideas are nothing?"

Sylvia wagged her finger. "Don't twist my words. You know exactly what I'm saying."

Amanda rubbed her eyes. She was dead tired. "Yes, I do. I'm sorry."

"Caroline specifically asked me to talk to you."

Amanda's surprise showed on her face. "I can't believe it! I would have thought that having a divorcée among the guests would not be acceptable."

Sylvia smiled. "Caroline makes her own rules. If she is behind you, everyone will follow suit. This could be an important night for you, Amanda."

Amanda remembered the looks she'd received in the cafe two nights before. If bohemia was beginning to raise its eyebrows— for whatever reason—it was time she made the proper gestures. "You're right. I don't know why I bother to argue with you."

"I don't either. Have Andrew escort you. That will certainly squash any gossip."

Amanda was instantly at attention. "Is there gossip I'm unaware of?"

"Amanda, just the fact that you're on your own, living here in Chelsea, starting your own business, for God's sake . . . there's bound to be rumblings. So far, there's been nothing malicious."

Amanda let out a sigh of relief. Sylvia's keen eyes didn't miss it.

"Is there something going on I don't know?" Sylvia asked.

"No," Amanda lied. She looked at Sylvia. She hadn't fooled her a bit.

"I hope not—for your sake." Sylvia put on her gloves. "I'll see you Saturday night, then." She kissed Amanda's cheek and left.

Amanda leaned back in her chair, wishing she could tell Sylvia the truth. She needed to hear the sound of reason amidst this insane love affair.

CHAPTER THIRTY

Andrew had *not* received an invitation to Caroline Astor's party. The fact that Amanda had resurrected his intense jealousy of his sister. Andrew had not abandoned the Fifth Avenue crowd when he moved away, and Amanda had. He'd broken his neck trying to keep in touch with everyone, scraping together every nickel and dime he had to take Mary Alice to parties and dinners. It infuriated him beyond measure that when the party of the year was thrown, he had to rely on Amanda—again—to get what he wanted.

"Goddamn the bitch!" he swore as he tied his white silk tie.

He knew Mary Alice would be there, but he'd had to talk fast and fancy to explain away his predicament. Being the master of manipulation that he was, Andrew had distorted the truth in his favor.

"You know I want to be with you, Mary Alice," he'd told her. "But Amanda hasn't seen *anyone* since . . . well, since . . . you know."

She'd appreciated the delicate situation Andrew was in. "It must be hard for you, Andrew, dealing with this divorce."

"It is. It's the first in the family—that I know of. Going back eight generations, there has never been such a scandal. Of course, before that, I'm not certain. Mother never discussed it, if there was."

"How awful for Amanda," Mary Alice had said. "She must be heartbroken." Mary Alice leaned forward and whispered, "we've all heard about David and Christine Van Volkein. I'm

285

not prying and I don't want to know, but I'm on Amanda's side.''

Andrew took his cue from her. ''It's not my place to say, but I know Amanda did the right thing.''

Mary Alice smiled. ''Amanda is so lucky to have a brother like you—who watches out for her and her name.''

Caroline Astor's summer ball was held at the Waldorf Hotel. Because she was head of New York society, God smiled on Caroline and gifted her with a particularly cool evening so that none of her five hundred guests would be uncomfortable in the crowded ballroom. Only half an hour into the evening, one of the guests said that she'd overheard Caroline saying that what New York needed was a larger hotel, with more opulent accommodations, and that Caroline would call it the Astoria. The guest reported that everyone chuckled, but Caroline was serious.

Andrew begrudgingly escorted both his sister and Sylvia Hendrickson to the ball, complaining to himself about his stroke of bad luck. He'd wanted to be with the Howell family. It wasn't until they arrived, alighted from the cab, and were instantly photographed by half a dozen photographers that he realized his plight was not all that dire. There was a small crowd of onlookers ogling them, pointing to him. A young girl smiled at him. He liked the feeling of being a celebrity.

''What are they doing here?'' he asked Amanda, nodding to Milton and Harry.

''I hired them for the occasion.''

''What for?''

''It's a new idea I had for a column in the magazine. I thought I'd write a synopsis of this party, sort of like the newspapers do, but then run pictures of the guests besides.''

''Are you crazy? Who's going to want to look at pictures of us?''

Amanda smiled. ''A lot of people—I hope.''

Andrew shook his head. Amanda came up with the most outlandish ideas. He hoped they would get their first issue out without any more hassles than they'd already had. Coaxing advertisers to pay twice the going rate just to have photographs of their models in Amanda's magazine was tough. She didn't realize how hard it was to sell her ''ideas''—although he'd told her a million times. They had ten days left to deadline, and he knew they'd all be working around the clock just to get *City Woman* on the streets. At this point he was hoping their failure would only be minor.

Amanda went through the receiving line renewing old acquaintances. She remembered the parties she'd attended, the charity work she'd done for Sylvia, and she remembered how generously these people had opened their hearts and pocketbooks for her causes. She'd missed them more than she'd thought. And she realized that their approval meant a great deal to her. They were her friends and she'd underestimated them. She had done them a disservice.

She hugged Caroline especially tight. "Thank you for inviting me."

"You've stayed away too long, Amanda."

"I know that now. It won't happen again."

"I know it won't. I won't le. ."

Andrew excused himself as Amanda and Sylvia spoke with friends. Mary Alice had just arrived with her father and mother.

Amanda didn't see him, she felt him. It was as if all the sounds of human chatter and musical instruments faded away. She thought she could hear his breathing, his heartbeat. But then she realized it was *her* heart that banged so loudly. Slowly, she turned.

She saw him, dark hair gleaming in the chandelier light, eyes focused on her. He seemed to stand above the crowd, though he wasn't the tallest man in the room. Heads bobbed back and forth, cutting off her sight of him. He didn't smile, nor did he reveal his thoughts to anyone around him. Only Amanda knew what he was thinking, what he wanted.

She remained riveted to the spot, though her legs ached to run to him. She wanted to laugh and cry all at the same time. More than ever, she realized how desperately she was in love with him.

She wondered what it would be like to dance with him in front of everyone and not be the topic of scandalous gossip but simply accepted as any couple here. Instantly she cast the notion from her head. Such dreams were dangerous—for now. But someday, she knew, he would be hers.

Sydney Wade wore a startlingly brilliant blue Lanvin gown she'd bought last year in Europe. It was extremely low cut, which allowed ample room over her perfectly rounded breasts to display her six-stranded necklace of sapphires and diamonds. She wore her heirloom tiara in her hair and four diamond bracelets on her arms. As she surveyed the room, she was satisfied that she was the most exquisitely dressed at the ball.

Sydney stood with her husband at the far end of the ballroom as was her custom at parties. After the guests had paid their respects to the hostess, it was then Sydney's turn to hold court.

Using centuries-old pleasantries taught to her by her mother's friends, at her father's insistence, Sydney Wade kept the lesser beings of society at her side waiting for the crumbs she would toss, like an Olympian goddess. Sydney used these people, the ones she'd known all her life and the newcomers who by reason of birth or wealth were allowed to join their circle, for above all, Sydney knew their value.

One day she would inherit her father's bank, and in her heart she believed Matthew would come around to her way of thinking and take over Wade Bank. The thought of the kind of power she would have made Sydney giddy. She looked out at the sea of rich New Yorkers. She estimated there was more wealth in this room than in over four-fifths of the world. And someday she would have power over them all.

Preoccupied with her devotees, Sydney was unaware of Matthew's inattention. It wasn't until Dick Child repeated his question to Matthew twice that she realized something was wrong. Sydney prided herself on reading signals. She smiled and laughed as they conversed, but as Dick walked away and she struck up a conversation with the Dwyers, she kept a wary eye on Matthew.

She knew he thought he was being cautious, but Sydney was a master at detection. She followed his gaze and at first she saw nothing to be alarmed about. And then she saw her.

Sydney and Matthew had been in Europe during the time Amanda was finding fame as The Granger Woman. Sydney had seen David's sketches of her, had heard people talk about her. Since Sydney's return to New York she'd been overly involved with her father's business and had spent considerably less time attending functions that were not business related.

Though she was never completely out of touch with people like Sylvia Hendrickson and Caroline Astor, Sydney had found even she needed to make an extra effort these days to see them. Charity balls and parties did not fit easily into a hectic business schedule.

Because of Amanda's miscarriage, her divorce from David, her job with Max, and then the founding of her own company, she, too, had many reasons for abandoning the society circuit. Thus it was that not until the night of June 15, 1897, did Sydney Wade and Amanda Granger finally meet.

For the first time, Sydney knew what it was like to meet someone more beautiful than herself. Well, she thought, perhaps not more beautiful, but equally so, in a pale sort of way.

"Matthew, I'm terribly thirsty."

"I'll get some champagne," he said, spying a waiter passing near Amanda.

"I'll come with you."

"What?" Matthew was surprised, for Sydney never left her "place" in a ballroom until after she'd seen all her "subjects." He took her arm.

Amanda saw them coming toward her. She turned back to the conversation, hoping her hammering heart would quell itself.

Sydney took her champagne and walked directly up to Sylvia.

"Sylvia, I haven't seen you in ages. And it's entirely my fault." Sydney grazed her cheek with the expected kiss.

"And you've been missed. You look marvelous. How is your father, dear?"

"Holding up. I'm trying to help him all I can. It isn't easy."

Sylvia took Amanda's arm. "Of course you know Amanda. Amanda, this is Sydney Wade. Sydney, Amanda Granger."

Amanda forced back the lump in her throat. "We've never met formally, no. How do you do?"

"Quite well." Sydney glanced at her husband. "Matthew tells me he met you and David at Tuxedo Park." She cast her first line. "I couldn't make the trip."

Sylvia raised an eyebrow and said to Sydney, "I didn't know you weren't there." She eyed Amanda.

Matthew was quick to respond. "I was only there for two days; then I, too, had business I had to attend to."

"Seems you became fast friends," Sydney said. "You helped with Amanda's loan, didn't you, darling?"

Matthew didn't like the way the conversation was headed. He saw the probing look in Sydney's eyes. She suspected something, but he believed her to still be in the dark. "It was nothing at all," he said.

"Matthew was good enough to intercede for me. I owe him a great deal," Amanda put in.

"He tells me you're publishing a magazine. When do I get to see it?"

"In ten days," Amanda said proudly. She was glad the subject was business—it helped mask her emotions.

Sydney watched her, the beautiful girl who was having an affair with her husband. She knew they didn't think they'd given themselves away, but Sydney had caught them. It was the tiniest gleam in his eye as he glanced at her. It was the catch in Amanda's voice she was certain she had hidden. But even without these signs Sydney would have known, just as she was certain Sylvia now knew for the first time.

There was an energy between Matthew and Amanda that was unmistakable. It was not the kind of affair that lasts a few weeks and then dies a passionate death. Nor was Amanda a back-street mistress more dependent on a man for money than for love. This was the kind of romance Sydney had always feared, if she'd ever come close to fearing anything in her life. Sydney was shaken to the bottom of her feet, for Matthew was in love with Amanda and she with him.

"I'm very interested in this magazine of yours, Amanda," Sydney said, using every ounce of control to keep her voice calm, her thoughts clear. "Actually, that's not correct. It's not the magazine I'd enjoy hearing about—but you."

"Me? Why?" Amanda asked nervously. Did Sydney know? Had she given herself away?

"I've always been interested in women who take command of their lives. I think it's admirable. I'm glad Matthew arranged this loan for you. Had I known about your plight, I personally would have handled the transaction. I believe in women helping women."

Amanda was relieved. "Thank you. I'm glad to know I have everyone at Brinkley Bank on my side. If my first issues aren't successful, I may need your help after all."

"Now, now. Let's not talk like that," Sydney said condescendingly. "You're a fascinating woman, Amanda. Good luck to you."

"Thank you," Amanda said as Sydney took Matthew's arm and walked off.

Sylvia looked at Amanda. "I want to see you at my house tomorrow for brunch."

Amanda could almost feel her legs buckle. Sylvia knew. Amanda hadn't fooled anyone. She watched Sydney's retreating back. She wondered just how transparent she'd been. "I'll be there."

Matthew walked away from Amanda knowing he couldn't live this farce any longer. Because he'd been swamped with delays on the opening of his store, he'd been unable to see Amanda for more than a week. He hadn't even known she would be here tonight. He'd missed seeing her three nights ago and because there had always been someone in his office, because Sydney was always around at home when he was, he'd been unable to telephone Amanda.

It was a sick way to live and he wasn't going to do it anymore.

Matthew didn't know if *he* deserved any better, but Amanda did.

He'd promised Amanda he would ask Sydney for a divorce and he'd done nothing about it. When he wasn't working, he'd been with Amanda. He'd barely seen Sydney the past month. It wasn't going to be easy, but then, nothing in his life had ever been easy. Going up against Sydney was no worse than battling his father, except that now he had a lot to lose. He'd never thought twice about risking his family name on his retail store. But now he was risking a life without Amanda if he didn't handle Sydney carefully.

Depending on Sydney's attitude, she could make the divorce very ugly indeed. She could ruin Amanda's chances of success for the magazine. She could singlehandedly ostracize Amanda so that even if they were married, no one would ever accept them again. Such things didn't bother Matthew. He'd been the black sheep of the Wade family too long to begin worrying about what other people thought at this point. But she could demand custody of their daughter—out of spite, not maternal love. And this did bother Matthew—a great deal.

Andrew helped Mary Alice with her chair as they left her parents and went to the dance floor. He smiled and put his arms around her. Expertly, he waltzed her around the mirrored ballroom.

"I wish we were alone, Mary Alice. I'd kiss you . . . and hold you . . . so close. . . ."

"Andrew, don't. Please," she said, feeling the fever-hot blush in her cheeks.

"I'm glad you didn't come with someone else," he said facetiously.

"So am I. But Jack had to go to Baltimore on business."

"Jack?" Andrew panicked.

"Coster. I thought I told you."

"No, you didn't."

Embarrassed, she dropped her eyes.

This was worse than he'd thought. "I thought your father liked me."

"He does," she answered, perturbed at his statement. "*I* like you even more."

Andrew pressed his hand more intimately on her waist. "I know that. That's why I assumed that your father was forcing you to attend with someone else."

Mary Alice felt chills race up her back. She moved a bit closer to his chest. She clung a bit tighter to his shoulder. "He could never make me do something I didn't want to do."

"Are you trying to make me jealous with all this talk of Jack?"

His eyes met hers. Unused to using guile and flirtation, she said: "Yes, I was. You haven't telephoned me much these past weeks. We've only been out to dinner once and gone to two parties in the past month. I thought perhaps there was someone else. . . ." she probed.

"Mary Alice, I told you that I had to work."

"Nobody works twenty-four hours a day, Andrew."

"My sister does," he growled. "I'm glad things are out in the open, Mary Alice. I'm just going to have to put my foot down with Amanda. If I'd known that my work was jeopardizing my standing with you, I never would have allowed it. Don't you worry, this won't happen again."

"Promise?"

"Yes," he said, knowing that once again he was going to need some money—a lot of it and fast. Mary Alice wouldn't wait forever for a proposal and a solid wedding date. And it was obvious there were plenty of men ready to take his place.

Amanda watched them glide across the floor. They were the perfect couple, complementing each other's looks the way they did. She could hear the admiring whispers around her, paying homage to their princess, Sydney.

For the first time she saw herself as she was—a home wrecker.
Sydney was a victim in this mess she and Matthew referred to as
their love. And it was unfair and wrong. Suddenly, Amanda
wondered where she'd shelved her morals all these months.
She'd never met Sydney, and so she had pretended she didn't
exist. But coming face to face with real flesh and blood put the
situation into perspective.

Amanda rose from the table. "I think I need some fresh air,"
she said to Sylvia and the Cuttings. "Please excuse me."

On the terrace she inhaled the summer air, wishing it would
wash this sin from her. She didn't hear Sylvia walk up.

Sylvia placed her hand on Amanda's shoulder. "When are you
going to learn to talk to me?"

Amanda's eyes filled with tears. "Now." She sighed. "What
am I going to do?"

"I don't know. But I think you know what you *should* do. The
question is whether you can or not."

"Since the day I met him, he's been a part of me. Until
tonight I deluded myself into thinking we would always be
together—that things would get better."

"Oh, Amanda. I wish you'd said something. Sydney Wade
will never give Matthew up."

A tear slipped out of Amanda's eye. "She loves him that
much?"

"She wants that bank that much."

"What?" Amanda was confused.

"I'm not going to tell you what you did was right, but I also
don't want you going around blaming yourself for something that
isn't happening, either. I've known Sydney since the day she was
born. She's been spoiled and coddled by her father until I thought
no man would have her. She's been a handful for Matthew to
tame, I can tell you that. Any other man would have given up.
But he's allowed her to do what she wanted, and at the same time
he's never buckled under to her demands. For years, Sydney has
thought she was fooling the world, keeping in Harlen's shadow.
And possibly she was. But I know for a fact she wants only to
run that bank. I have never seen her reveal the first trace of
affection for Matthew or Jacqueline."

Amanda's tears dried in the light of Sylvia's words. "Poor
Matthew."

"True. He's probably as starved for love as you. But she'll never let him go, Amanda. Not in a million years."

"There's no hope?"

"None. The end is inevitable. I'm afraid that if you continue, you'll just be hurting yourself more. And you have to think of yourself. If I've figured out what is happening, it won't be long before Sydney does. She and her friends could ruin you and the magazine. Do you see what I'm saying?"

"Yes," Amanda said, feeling weak from depleted emotions. "I hope I can do it."

"It'll be the hardest thing you've ever done, but you'll do it. You have to."

Among the guests at the Astor summer ball were Paul and Christine Van Volkein and David Simon, who escorted Louise Thomas, his newest model. Christine had scanned the crowd, and other than Caroline Astor and Sydney Wade, she surmised she was the third best-dressed woman there. As she stood talking with the Brandons, she fingered her newest bauble from Paul, a fourteen-carat diamond pendant that she wore on a chain of rubies, which struck just at the crevice in her ample cleavage. Christine felt jewels should be sensual. She wore ruby earrings and a gold cuff of rubies and diamonds on her upper arm. She could tell by the comments that Monday morning half of New York would be rushing to their jewelers to have a copy of her cuff made. She pulled back the shoulders of her white silk dress, which wrapped around her like a sari. It was quite avant-garde to wear something with little waist definition. But tonight Christine had felt adventurous. She didn't want to look like the Gibson Girl or The Granger Woman anymore. She wanted to set her own trends. She took a fourth glass of champagne.

"I think you've had enough," Paul whispered.

"I can never get enough," she said, looking directly between his legs.

"Cut it out, Christine," he said, perturbed with her.

"You're no fun anymore, Paul," she said, kissing him.

Paul heard the sharp, stunned intake of breath from those around them. Christine was on the verge of making a spectacle of herself. "Perhaps we should go home," he said.

"What? And miss all the fun?" Her eyes fell on David as he danced past with Louise.

Paul grabbed her arm. "Don't even *think* it!"

Christine was still sober enough to keep her wits. "Paul, I was just thinking how pretty Louise looks. Don't you think so? In a conventional sort of way."

Paul had never really been sure about his wife's affair with David Simon. It was mostly conjecture. As far as the bedroom was concerned, he found it impossible to believe that any woman could want any more than Christine was getting from him. He sometimes thought he couldn't make it through the day, he was so exhausted from their lovemaking. He had finally tamed his wife.

"I don't care a whit about Louise Thomas."

She looked at him. He was more in her power than ever before. "Then dance with me, Paul. Hold me closely as you can."

Gladly Paul did as she asked.

It had been a long time since Christine had seen him, but she remembered thinking then as she did now that a more handsome man than Andrew Granger didn't exist. She watched as he whirled Mary Alice Howell across the dance floor at the Waldorf. She noticed the rapt expression on Mary Alice's face. And she also noticed the way Andrew looked at *her*. His eyes were like green emeralds—one of her favorite jewels. They were simultaneously icy and smoldering beneath thick, dark lashes.

She moved against Paul's body, feeling the pressure of his arm around her waist, her breasts crushed to his chest. She kept her eyes riveted on Andrew. When the dance ended, Christine was glad to see that Andrew had managed to be standing next to herself and Paul.

They applauded the musicians, who took a break.

Andrew turned to Paul. He offered his hand. "You don't remember me, but I'm Andrew Granger, Amanda's brother."

"Of course!" Paul smiled. "This is my wife, Christine."

"How do you do?" Andrew said.

Mary Alice knew the Van Volkeins well.

"It's a wonderful party," Andrew said.

"It's boring," Christine said bluntly as Paul's head snapped around. She frowned at him. "We're going home soon," she said, eyeing a waiter with a tray filled with champagne. "But not yet . . ." She walked off and followed the waiter.

Paul started after her when Mary Alice stopped him. "I'll go with her. Maybe she should go to the ladies' lounge for a bit."

"Would you mind, Mary Alice?" he asked gratefully.

"She's quite a girl," Andrew said of Mary Alice, but Paul mistook his meaning.

"Christine has been a bit restless lately. I've been trying to think of something that would amuse her, but she's rejected most of my ideas."

"Like what?"

"A trip to California. She's never been, and I thought she'd like to see some of the West. I bought her an automobile, but it frightened her to death. Even the jewels I buy her are losing her interest. God knows I've spent a king's ransom on them."

"Don't buy her anything anymore."

Paul laughed. "You don't know my wife!"

"No, I didn't mean it the way it sounded. Why not do something she's never tried before?"

"Like what?"

"Well, let's see." Andrew tapped his cheek with his finger, playing for the perfect cue. "Has she ever played poker?"

"Poker? Of course not."

"Don't you think that would be amusing for her?"

"Well, I don't know."

"It's a bit risqué. Make her put up her own money for the pot. Invite six of your choicest friends to your home. Make a night of it. I'd be glad to help."

Paul chuckled. "You know, she might like that. But it's too risky. She doesn't know the first thing about poker. I'd have to teach her."

"I'll tell you what. I'll help you teach her, then we'll set up a night and test her skills. If she had something to work toward, she'd concentrate on being the best she can be."

Paul considered the offer for a moment. "She just might like it at that. I'll talk to her about it and call you first of the week."

Andrew shook Paul's hand. "Glad I could help out."

David watched as Christine went to the ladies' lounge with Mary Alice Howell. He'd tried to see Christine for over two weeks, but she'd always been "busy." He didn't like being cast aside like a used pair of shoes. He would make Christine regret the dissolution of their affair.

He didn't understand Christine at all. One minute she couldn't get enough of him, and the next minute she acted as if she couldn't care less if he lived or died.

David had purposely brought Louise Thomas tonight to announce officially to New York that she was his newest protegée. *He* was discarding Christine Van Volkein in favor of a younger, more vital woman. David thought it appropriate that Amanda should also be present when he made his announcement. He wanted to show her and Christine that he didn't need them, that he'd never needed them. He wanted to show them that they were the losers for having brushed him aside.

Amanda saw him when he arrived with Louise. She hadn't spoken to him since the day at the attorney's office. For her, there was nothing to say. But here there would be no avoiding it. It was obvious to her what he was doing. Louise was being groomed as his newest ticket to fame. Amanda wondered if she should take Louise aside and warn her.

Amanda had seen him looking at her, during pauses in conversation, over the rim of his champagne glass. It was unnerving, and she knew she couldn't avoid him forever. She went to him.

"How are you, David?"

"I'm doing very well," he said, indicating Louise with a nod of his head.

"Max tells me you have a meeting with him on Monday."

"I thought you two were competitors."

"We'll always be friends. It was you and I who were competing. But now that I'm gone, perhaps you'll have a better chance to sell your sketches."

David bristled at her words. Though she was more beautiful than ever, he remembered all too easily how difficult she could be to handle. "My work has always found a ready market."

"You needn't be defensive."

"I was stating facts."

Amanda knew he would never change. He still considered her a necessary evil. Now that she could see him in a more objective light, it was obvious to her that he truly hated women, despite how much he professed to revere them. He would still like to control her—if she gave him the chance. But Amanda had come too far to let that happen.

"I wish you luck with your new model."

"I don't need luck. I have talent," he said pompously.

"We *all* need luck—or God—to see us through, David." She took a step back. "My friends are signalling to me. It was good talking to you."

David watched her walk away, shoulders held proudly, swanlike neck swaying just enough to make her movements fluid. God! How he hated her. He gripped his champagne glass so tightly he nearly broke the stem.

He noticed that as he'd spoken to Amanda, a small entourage had gathered around Louise and himself. Rather than admit the worshippers had come to see Amanda, he gathered their comments of admiration for himself.

Like an oracle he proclaimed: "Louise will be more famous than Amanda was as The Granger Woman."

"I didn't know Amanda was *not* famous anymore," Jessamine Winthrop said.

"Louise has great energy that shows through in the sketches," David said.

"Which magazines will she be featured in?" Sarah Jamison asked.

"I'm not ready to announce that quite yet," David hedged. How he hated them for always trying to pin him down. Didn't they understand the work involved in creating a legend? It was exhausting. If they had one iota of sense about art and its creation, they would cease such silly prattle.

David slipped Louise in and out of conversations and maneuvered her from one group to another clique. He made certain they all knew who she was. By midnight he was drained.

"But my dear," he said when she protested, "you need your rest. Beauty must be cared for."

He escorted her home and delivered her into the hands of her waiting elderly parents.

Rather than heading back uptown after leaving the Thomas residence, David instructed the driver to head for Herald Square.

The night was humid, and the streets were rancid with the stench of stale beer, animal waste, and degradation. David went to a tiny, rundown bar where derelicts and prostitutes ignored each other, each thinking the others were pathetic. In the back were four mahogany booths lined with stained red upholstery. There were red-checkered oilcloths on the tables that hadn't been wiped off in days.

In the last booth beneath the cracked Tiffany lamp with a

burned-out bulb sat a grotesque-looking man of thirty who looked fifty. His hair was white and unkempt. His face was pockmarked and he had one eye missing. He had few teeth.

He held the answer to David's problems.

David walked in unnoticed. The patrons were either too drunk or too used to seeing "society types" in their midst. He went straight to the last booth.

"Do you have any?"

"Of course. But the price has gone up."

"By how much?"

"A hundred dollars."

"That's crazy."

"Naw, it ain't. Supply and demand. You know that."

"Cocaine is that popular?"

"This week it is." As he grinned, saliva ran down his chin.

"I'll take it." David counted out two hundred dollars.

The grotesque man reached into a sack at his feet and pulled out a cold-cream jar filled with six ounces of white powder. David quickly placed it in his tuxedo pocket.

"Have a good time," the man said as David left.

CHAPTER THIRTY-ONE

Sydney Wade sat in a gilded fauteuil chair, scheming. She had been foolish not to have picked up on Matthew's affair with Amanda Granger before this. But she wasn't worried. She had been married to Matthew for ten years. One does not spend that kind of time with a man and not know his Achilles' heel.

"Jacqueline . . ." she mumbled to herself.

Sydney pulled her crocheted lace dressing gown around her and went to the nursery. She peeked in on the nanny, who was sound asleep in the adjacent bedroom. She pulled the door closed so as not to disturb her. It was hot and stuffy in Jacqueline's room.

Sydney tiptoed over to Jacqueline's enormous four-poster mahogany bed. It was ridiculous for a small child to have such opulent furniture, but Matthew indulged his child to a fault.

She bent down and could see that Jacqueline was sweating. The nanny had covered her with a heavy wool blanket and the window was shut.

"Stupid woman!" Sydney said to herself and pulled the blanket off her daughter and opened the window. "I must take better care of you now."

Just then she noticed a flood of light from the hallway. She heard footsteps. It was Matthew. He stood in the doorway wearing his pajamas but no robe.

"Is something wrong? I heard a noise."

Sydney shook her head. If Jacqueline so much as blinked in her sleep, Matthew was at her side. It was disgusting for a father to act like he did. Certainly *her* father had never pampered her like this.

Sydney did not realize she was jealous of her daughter's relationship with Matthew. She only knew that Matthew angered her with his behavior. She did not look upon it as strength of character.

"There's nothing wrong, Matthew. Go to bed."

He ignored her and went straight to Jacqueline. He touched her forehead. "She has a fever."

"She's just hot. It's summer. She's supposed to be sweating!" Sydney abruptly turned and left the room.

Matthew leaned over, kissed his sleeping daughter's cheek, and followed Sydney out.

Sydney went straight to her room and closed the door, hoping to keep Matthew out, but he was too quick for her and caught the door just as it was about to close.

"I'd like to talk to you, Sydney."

"Well, I don't want to talk to you," she said, knowing she needed more time to think.

"I think we should."

She sat in the chair and propped her feet on the ottoman. She couldn't force a smile. She thought of Amanda, of Jacqueline, of Matthew's store. "You've got everything you want, don't you, Matthew?"

"Hardly." He looked at her oddly.

"Yes, you do. You're successful, you have a beautiful wife, an adoring child, friends. But then, you *should* have it all." She kept incredibly calm. She was proud of herself.

"Why?"

"Because you're a man. Men have everything—and if they don't, it's because they are fools."

"Sydney, is there a point to any of this?"

"Of course, but you don't see it." Sydney wished she had the kind of temperament afforded to commonplace people. How she'd like to scream and yell at him, sitting there so smugly. She'd like to tell him how unfair the world had been to her. Blame him for the fact that he didn't love her—just like her father never loved her. She sometimes thought she hated Matthew, but she didn't. She was a woman, and her father had told her when she was a child that women were unable to hate. "Only men can hate," he'd said. It was another reason why she wished she'd been born a man. "What is it that you want to talk about, Matthew?"

"I want to talk about us."

"Us?"

"You and me—our marriage, or rather our living arrangement, since we don't really have a marriage."

"Of course we have a marriage, Matthew. We have one of the best marriages in New York. We're perfectly suited to each other."

"We aren't suited at all."

"That's your opinion. I'm quite satisfied with our life."

"Our life? We don't have a life. We don't do anything together—never have. We don't have the same goals, the same needs. Hell, I'm surprised we even live in the same house together."

"And what do you call Jacqueline?"

"A blessing."

"I suppose you fathered her all by yourself."

"Don't be ridiculous."

"Why not? You are."

"I'm trying to have an honest discussion with you, Sydney. You know as well as I do that this marriage is not working."

"I don't know anything of the sort."

Matthew knew Sydney was only playing with words right now. What bothered him the most was that she didn't seem shocked at all when he'd brought up their problems. An alert sounded in his head.

"Sydney, I don't want this kind of life anymore. We live in separate worlds. I want a divorce."

She sat calmly, keeping her hands folded neatly in her lap. She couldn't give in to her emotions, though she fantasized herself doing just that. How she'd like to ram her fist into his face. She knew very well that if it hadn't been for Amanda Granger, Matthew would never be asking for this divorce.

I must be careful, she thought. She didn't want a scene. She didn't want him to leave. She had to keep him here, for she honestly believed that though his passion for Amanda might not die, his intelligence, if not his daughter, would bring him back. Eventually he would grow tired of his store and return to his father's bank. Then, together, they would run the New York banking world. She would be more powerful than any man she knew—even her father. Then *she* would have it all.

"Do you have a mistress, Matthew?"

"No," he lied. "This is between you and me. Always was."

"Even if you did, it doesn't matter. A lot of men have

mistresses. Because if that's why you want this divorce, you have my permission to keep her."

"All I want is a divorce, Sydney."

"That's all, Matthew?"

"Yes," he said firmly.

"What about Jacqueline?" A tinge of victory stained Sydney's lips.

"She would live with me, of course."

"A child belongs with its mother."

Matthew was ready for her. He'd known she might take this tack. "You've never wanted anything to do with Jacqueline. You didn't want her when you found out you were pregnant; you've rebuffed her at every turn. You never spend any time with her—"

"What do we have a nanny for?" Sydney interrupted.

"A nanny is *not* a mother!" Matthew stormed, finally losing his patience.

"It's pointless to argue about this, Matthew. You *cannot* have Jacqueline."

"Why are you doing this? You don't want me or Jacqueline."

"You're wrong, Matthew. I *do* want you—be assured of that. And I'll never let you go—not without a fight."

Matthew's anger burned in his face. He stood over her and leaned down so he could see into her eyes. "Lady, you don't know what a fight is until you take me on. There are courts that decide these kinds of things. It may take months, but I'll find a way to get my freedom *and* keep my daughter."

Sydney gaped at him as he strode out of the room and slammed the door. She was shocked when she looked down and found that her hands were trembling.

Matthew went to his bedroom window and flung it open. He breathed in the summer air, trying to calm himself. Since the day he'd met Amanda, a year ago, he'd feared his life might come to this point. Matthew didn't know if he was a victim of fate or desire, but he'd found himself with a foot planted in two different, incomplete worlds, and the only thing he could be sure of was that he was miserable in both.

He could never go to Amanda and leave his daughter behind, and yet, as he looked at the stars, all he saw were promises of years ahead without Amanda—without love.

He needed them both. He had to have them both. But no amount of wishing would make this dream come true.

"You're wrong, Sydney. Nobody gets it all."

*   *   *

At nine o'clock the next morning, Matthew sat in a leather Chippendale wing chair across from his attorney, Joseph Ross.

Joseph listened earnestly to Matthew's story, turning his pencil upside down, sliding his fingers down it, then turning it over again and again. He would scribble a note, nod his head, then pinch the bridge of his nose with his finger and thumb.

Matthew had known Joseph a long time. He knew how his mind worked and he knew the signals Joseph was giving him with his gestures. Matthew's predicament was worse than he'd thought.

"It's going to be damn near impossible, Matthew."

"Jesus."

"Sydney has the upper hand here, just because she is a woman. She isn't a bad mother per se, just a disinterested one. She doesn't do anything any differently from half the society women I know. Jacqueline has not suffered at her hands. And it would be difficult for you to prove something like that in court."

"I know that Jacqueline would choose me if the court asked her."

Joseph leaned over his folded hands and looked at Matthew earnestly. "You've never seen a custody battle, Matthew. I have. I want you to be very, very sure you want to put your child through that. I've seen courtroom arguments so vicious, I thought we'd draw blood. I've seen children so torn apart they've had to be sedated. You've got the sweetest child I've ever seen. Something like this would tear her apart. My advice is, if you love your daughter, you'll think of something else."

"I want my daughter and I want a divorce."

"Well, there's nothing that I can tell you that would be an instant remedy. As your lawyer, I would say this: go home. Keep peace there and nurture Jacqueline's love all you can. Make certain she's on your side and that Sydney doesn't try to persuade her otherwise."

"I doubt Sydney would take the time."

"She's fighting for her marriage. She'll do anything she has to. Count on it."

"I guess you're right."

"And Matthew—no arguments. Until the time comes when we do think of something and can file those papers, I also want you to watch yourself."

"What do you mean?"

"I didn't ask if there's someone else, but if there is, be very careful. I'd even advise to break it off. Sydney could have you followed, and then she'd have ammunition to use in court. If you leave the house to live someplace else, she can declare abandonment. Then you'd never get Jacqueline. Keep peace in that house. Make Sydney think she's won—for now."

Matthew felt his heart sinking. "You're right. This does sound impossible."

"In order for you to get this divorce, you'll have to get Sydney's permission. She's going to have to want it as much as you do."

Matthew felt the last of his hope vanish. "She'll never do it."

Joseph looked at him. "I'm a believer in the right thing, Matthew. If this divorce is the right thing for you and Jacqueline—and for Sydney too—then, it'll happen. It just may not be as speedy as you'd like, and you may have some very painful times ahead of you—but it'll happen."

Matthew stood and shook Joseph's hand. "Thank you. I'll remember that."

Joseph watched as Matthew left the office. He shook his head. "There's not a chance in the world, my friend. Not one."

Matthew found it impossible to concentrate on his work. He went through the motions of making decisions, ordering materials, checking the incoming inventory. These were the most crucial days, just before opening, when everything had to be coordinated with the precision of a military general preparing for attack. Instead, his mind was on Amanda.

In an hour he'd see her. She was probably preparing his dinner now. He wondered if it had been a good day for her. Was she humming as she cooked? Would she have fresh flowers on the table? He could almost feel her arms around him now. He wondered how long he could wait until he told her.

Two days ago, he'd planned to come to her tonight with the news that he was divorcing Sydney. He'd wanted to take her out, perhaps to the theater, where he wouldn't have to fear his friends seeing them together. Instead, he had to be even more careful and secretive about his time with Amanda. How naive he'd been to think that because he wanted something he could have it.

To bolster himself, he reasoned that Amanda loved him and he loved her. In time, he would think of a way to coerce Sydney into a divorce. He would find a way to gain custody of Jacqueline. But for now, he was willing to take the risk of seeing Amanda whenever he could. He knew he could not live without her. He just hoped she would wait for him.

Amanda sautéed a handful of mushrooms in butter and then added chopped shallots. She diced a garlic clove and tossed it into the pan. She breaded the flounder filets. She looked at the pendulum clock on the wall. She was glad Matthew was late. For the first time, she almost wished he weren't coming.

Since the moment she met Sydney, Amanda had been wracked with guilt. From the day she'd realized she was in love with Matthew, she'd paraded through her days blindfolding herself to the truth. She'd allowed herself to succumb to love and all its feelings of giddiness and recklessness. She had selfishly never considered anyone but herself. Now that Amanda had met Sydney, she knew she was terribly wrong. Her guilt was even worse when she thought of Jacqueline. How pompous she'd been to think that *her* life, *her* love was more important than that of a child's. Both Sydney and Jacqueline had a claim on Matthew, a past and a present. All Amanda had was a stolen hour here and there, with nothing to call her own—least of all, a future.

The knock on the door broke Amanda's thoughts. She opened it. He wasn't smiling. He carried no flowers, no wine, but he scooped her into his arms and held her so tightly she thought he would crush her.

"God, how I love you, Amanda," he said. He buried his face in her shoulder. He inhaled her floral perfume. He kissed her cheeks, her nose and her eyes. It was if he'd been away at sea for years and this was his homecoming.

Amanda felt tears in her eyes, for suddenly she was afraid. Something was different about Matthew tonight. Although she tried to convince herself that she should not see him anymore, she wasn't as certain that she could go through with it. It had never occurred to her that he might have come to the same conclusion. Perhaps she'd hoped for a miracle.

"I made flounder. And a strawberry torte for dessert," she said with no mirth to her voice.

He pulled away. "My favorites. Are we celebrating?"

"I don't know. Are we?"

He loosened his tie and took off his jacket, carefully avoiding her eyes as she went to the kitchen. "I think everything is going according to schedule at the store. The mirrors arrived today. The painters have just about finished."

"Good," she said. She filled their plates and set them on the table. She sat down and placed a white napkin in her lap.

They ate almost in silence, though he held her hand throughout the meal. He mumbled compliments between bites. She could tell he knew there was something amiss. And she could see apprehension in his eyes. He kept the conversation on the store, the magazine, the weather.

Matthew's eyes almost hurt when he looked at her. He couldn't think of a way to tell about his scene with Sydney—or his attorney's advice.

She cleared the dishes. She watched as he stood, stretched, and then began pacing. It had never been like this between them . . . this tension. Already she felt devastatingly alone.

"Matthew, what is it?"

He looked at her, the soft light shining in her eyes. She loved him, and it made him feel whole. "I asked Sydney for a divorce and she refused. She said she'll keep Jacqueline from me."

"Oh, God," Amanda breathed, feeling as if the blood had just been siphoned from her body. She felt cold.

Matthew grabbed her hands. "It's only the first round. I talked to my lawyer. It won't be easy. We'll have to be even more careful about seeing each other. . . ."

"Why?"

"He told me that Sydney could hire a detective to follow me. It would make her position even stronger. But don't worry, I'll think of something—a way out for you and me and Jacqueline. I won't give up on us, not ever."

"Oh, Matthew," she said hopelessly. "Don't you see? What we're doing is wrong. I feel guilty, you feel guilty. And it's dangerous. Now you're asking me to further jeopardize your daughter's happiness. I've already done enough damage."

"What are you saying? That you won't wait for me?"

"I can't believe you would want a life for me that's lived in back streets and midnight rendezvous. What if she never gives you a divorce? All that aside, what if Jacqueline found out? She would hate you. It would destroy your relationship with her. I can't do that to you."

"Amanda, don't say this."

"I have to, Matthew. I know in your heart you feel the same way. How long would we last before we started hating each other for causing so much pain? We'd destroy each other." She grabbed him and clung to him. She sank her head into his shoulder and kissed his neck. "Matthew, I love you. But there's no hope for us."

He held her close, trying to somehow defy nature and press her inside him where he could carry her with him all his life. "I can't do this, Amanda. I have to see you." He knew she was right, but the reality of her words was too painful. He knew he couldn't risk losing his daughter either, and when the choice came, he knew he would protect Jacqueline, no matter how much he needed to see Amanda. He knew Amanda knew it too. He kissed her and as he closed his eyes, he felt his eyes sting with unshed tears.

Amanda wanted to back down, but she knew she had to be strong—for them both. "I'll always love you, Matthew. But until the day comes when I can have you freely—I can't see you anymore."

"Don't do this, Amanda."

"I have to."

He held her face in his hands and let his eyes delve into hers. "I promise you this. I'll find a way. I don't know how long it will take, but as God is my witness, I *will* come to you and we will be a family—you and I and Jacqueline."

He picked up his jacket and tie, kissed her passionately one last time, and left as quickly as he could. Strength could last only so long.

Amanda rushed to the window and banged on the glass. "Please look back," she mumbled, but he kept on walking. Before he reached the corner, she realized she couldn't see him anymore. There were too many tears in the way.

CHAPTER THIRTY-TWO

Andrew entered the plush vestibule of Paul Van Volkein's palatial home and waited while the butler announced him. He checked his tie in the Viennese gilt mirror, noticing the Vermeer hanging on the wall behind him. He couldn't help but be smug about this evening. For two weeks he'd heard nothing from Paul Van Volkein and then suddenly, today, Paul had telephoned saying he'd set up a poker game. Andrew had three hundred and fifty dollars in his pocket. He hoped it was enough. He heard Paul's voice behind him. He placed his most charming smile on his lips and turned to greet his host.

"Andrew. Welcome. We're all set up in the solarium," Paul said jovially as he put his hand on Andrew's shoulder.

Andrew was greeted by four other men, besides Christine. There were Jason McCauley, Bill Thatcher, Henry Hines, and Gerald Forestall. They shook hands and then all went straight-away to the poker table.

"Paul has been teaching me the basics this week. I hope you gentlemen won't mind a novice," Christine purred to the four wealthy men whom she'd known for many years.

Andrew sat across the table from Christine. She wore a black silk satin gown which showed her voluptuous bosom and high-lighted her newest ruby pendant. Andrew noticed that Paul seemed in a particularly good mood this evening.

Paul looked at Christine. "Where's your money, darling?"

She smiled coyly. "Right here," she replied and emptied a black purse full of bills onto the table.

Andrew sucked in his breath. He watched as everyone at the

table deposited huge stacks of bills. He would have to change his strategy. He'd planned to lose the first few pots until the stakes rose, but from all appearances, if he didn't win the first few, he'd be out of the game by the third hand. He smiled sheepishly.

Paul shuffled the cards and dealt. Andrew watched surreptitiously as Christine's face screwed up while she tried to judge the worth of her cards. Andrew had a pair of sevens, a jack, a ten, and a three of clubs.

"Ante is fifty," Paul announced.

Andrew gulped and put the money up as did everyone else.

Andrew watched the faces of everyone at the table as they betted, drew their new cards, and studied their hands. He noticed that Christine drew three, as did everyone except Paul. Andrew fanned out his cards. He'd drawn the third seven. He frowned so that everyone would notice.

Henry and Bill folded. Andrew caught Christine watching him. He knew he'd bluffed her.

"I'll bet another fifty," she said with a complacent grin.

Paul's face was granite. "I'm in."

Andrew tossed in his fifty. As did Gerald and Jason.

"Call."

Paul had a pair of queens; Gerald, a pair of aces. Jason had three twos. Christine smiled as she fanned her cards out. She had a nine, jack, queen, king, and ace.

"Where's the ten?" Paul asked her.

"Do I need it?"

"To win, you do."

"Oh," she said.

Andrew laid his cards out. "Looks as if I'm the winner this time."

Andrew scooped in the pot, feeling a bit more secure about the night. It was going to take some real skill to play with these people. They had pockets so deep they reached to China. This wasn't like playing in Hell's Kitchen where a one-hour game could wipe out all the players.

For the next two hours, cards were shuffled and dealt. Bets were made, and Andrew watched as his take increased to over two thousand dollars. At midnight, Henry went home. Bill was the biggest loser, but everyone joked about the fifty thousand he'd lost on board ship last spring when he'd sailed to Paris. Paul was about even. Christine had lost almost a thousand, but she'd learned to play the game rather well. Andrew liked that.

Christine watched him watching her. It was not simply complimentary to her that Andrew found her attractive, it was essential. Christine had decided that Andrew was to be her next lover.

She wondered if it would be any better to have sex with a man who had royal blood. Her friend Ancilla had married an English duke, and she'd said he was cold as a fish. But Christine could tell there was nothing cold about Andrew. She liked playing poker for high stakes. It was exciting to risk so much money on the turn of a card. She also liked having lovers, and it wasn't only the sexual excitement she craved but the thrill of the secrecy, the risk of losing Paul, her social standing.

Sydney had warned her about her affair with David, and Christine had heeded it. But what did Sydney know anyway? Sydney cared about nothing but her bank. Christine doubted Sydney had ever had the first sexual impulse.

Christine had found it incredibly difficult to concentrate on the game while sitting across the table from Andrew. Every time he picked up his cards, she watched his hands and wondered what it would be like to have those long-tapering fingers on her body, caressing her, massaging her. Whenever she looked into his eyes, she felt herself start to burn from the inside out.

After only a half hour, she'd felt a trickle of perspiration between her breasts. It was not a warm evening, only the lust she was feeling. She wished everyone would go home so that she could talk to him. She wondered how long it would take to get him into her bed. She'd heard that he was very serious about Mary Alice. Christine wasn't worried about Mary Alice so much as she was about the kind of man Andrew was.

What if he were one of those moral types—and would refuse her advances on principle? She took her eyes from her cards and glanced at him. He was studying her intently. No, she wouldn't have any problems with Andrew.

Play continued until nearly one-thirty. Everyone except Andrew and Christine was tired.

"Looks as if you did well for yourself, Andrew," Paul said.

"You didn't do too badly," Andrew replied.

"No, I didn't." Paul scraped nearly fifteen hundred dollars off the table. "You, my dear, need to learn a few more skills," he said to his wife.

Christine patted Paul's hand, but she looked at Andrew. "At least I didn't have to bet my jewels. But I agree, I need more lessons. How about tomorrow night, dear?'' she asked, turning back to Paul.

He shook his head. "You know I can't. I have to leave for Washington."

"Oh." She glanced at Andrew. "That's right. I forgot. But how will I learn if I don't play?"

Paul considered this a moment. He looked at Andrew. "I know this is asking a great deal, you being so busy with the magazine—not to mention Mary Alice." He chuckled. "But do you think you could teach Christine a bit more about the game?"

Andrew used his most sincere tones. "I am rather pressed this week." He looked at Christine's smoldering eyes. "I'll see what I can do."

Amanda waited impatiently as the first issues rolled off the presses. She had worked on the dummy so intently herself, she thought surely by now she could recite every line of copy. When one of the printers brought the copy to her and plopped it down in front of her, she was almost too frightened to pick it up.

The cover was magnificent, she thought. She ran her hand over the glossy paper and the picture of the young immigrant girl, Irene. There was a flag waving in the background as a salute to the nation's birthday, since this was the July issue.

Slowly, she opened the magazine and went through the pages one by one.

Andrew leaned up against the doorjamb and watched her. "It looks good."

Her smile had never been wider. Pride shown in her eyes, and at that moment he hated her more than he ever had, for she had accomplished her goal. She'd made her own dreams come true.

"It looks *great!*" she cried and jumped up from her chair. She went to him and hugged him. "We're going to make publishing history."

"You hope."

She was tired of his pessimism. When she'd told him advertisers would pay double for ads if he sold them correctly, Andrew had balked. He'd complained that the glossy paper was too expensive, the photographers were too critical, and the film cost too much. Andrew was forever finding fault.

"Don't, Andrew. Not today."

"In a week you may find yourself sitting here with all five

thousand copies and no buyers. I want to hear what you say then.''

''Well, it won't happen. If I don't think positive about all this, I'll never make it.''

''Fine. You think . . . I've got things to do.''

''Like what?''

''I have a life, Amanda. I have things to do besides work for this magazine. You should try it sometime.''

Amanda felt as if he'd shot her with an arrow. How could she tell him she had another life but chose not to indulge herself? How could she tell him that this magazine had been her lifeline to sanity these past weeks without Matthew? How could she tell him that his sister was an adulteress?

She watched him walk away. He would be seeing Mary Alice tonight. She knew he was getting closer to a marriage proposal. That was good. Andrew was entitled to some happiness.

She looked down at the magazine. These pieces of paper with their articles on the emergence of women, their fashion photographs, and their news of society darlings had become her life. She hugged the dream to her chest. It didn't hug her back.

''I don't have anyone to talk to but you.''

''I wish there was something I could say. Some salve I could use to make the pain go away so you would be healed,'' Sylvia said, fanning herself with a reed fan. It was nearly ninety degrees, and the sun had set over an hour earlier. She sipped a cool glass of lemonade.

''How do you stand it, Sylvia? Living alone?''

''I don't mind it at all. I miss Charles. I always will. And I do have my moments of feeling sorry for myself. But they don't come very often. I keep busy. I'm interested in people and they fill my life.''

Amanda realized that Sylvia was trying to say something. ''You think I've made work my life. Andrew said that.''

''Right now, it should be that way. You need to fill your head with work, busy activities. But the time will come when you can ease up on the controls a bit. Getting Matthew Wade out of your blood won't be easy.''

''I don't think I can . . . ever,'' Amanda said looking out to Washington Square where children were lighting Roman candles. They heard the *pop* and *bang* of firecrackers.

"Maybe you won't."

Amanda could feel tears well in her eyes. She thought she'd cried herself out. "I still love him, Sylvia."

"You'll always love him. But that doesn't mean that you can't make a life with someone else."

A sob nearly choked her. "I couldn't. Now now, not after knowing what it was like to be loved like that." She leaned over in the wicker rocker and studied Sylvia's wise eyes. "Could you ever love anyone else, Sylvia? Could anyone ever take Charles's place in your heart?"

"No," Sylvia said morosely. "No one could ever do that."

Amanda turned to watch the fireworks again. "I thought not."

Matthew shattered a magnum of Mumm's against the marble pillar of his new store. With a cheer from the crowd, the opening of Wade's was official. He cut a green satin ribbon with gold scissors and with a jubilant smile waved everyone in. Reporters and journalists shuffled through the crowd to get a moment with Matthew.

"Mr. Wade, our sources tell us that you more than doubled your original budget for the store. How do you justify such extravagance?" the pushiest reporter asked.

"This is New York. We are entitled to extravagance." He beamed.

"Is it true that Wade's bought over a million dollars' worth of jewels for the jewelry department?"

"It's true. As we near the Christmas season, we'll increase our inventory. We have a designer on staff who will custom make any piece our customers want."

Another reporter, more intent on taking notes about the opulent surroundings than he was on captioning statements, stopped and said to one of his colleagues, "Wade's can't fail; it's backed by the strongest bank in the country—Wade Bank."

Instantly, Matthew's anger flared. He thought that by now all of New York knew of his feud with his father. Succeed or fail, this was Matthew's dream. "Wade Bank has not underwritten one penny of this store," Matthew informed him emphatically. The young reporter was taken aback by Matthew's forcefulness, but he wrote the statement down in his notebook.

Matthew moved closer to him. "Neither I nor my store is affiliated with my father's bank. I assure you, he would want it that way." Matthew allowed a smile to cross his lips and when he did, the more seasoned reporters broke into laughter.

Embarrassed at his blunder, the young reporter blushed and went back to his description of the rotunda, the glass and marble display cases, and the pretty and efficient salesgirls, who were most willing to talk to him.

Matthew allowed photographs to be taken of the main floor, the dining rooms, and the offices on the top floor. He took the reporters on a tour, pointing out his innovations in retailing. There were appropriate "oohs" and "ahs," the wide eyes of surprise and pleasure. But Matthew knew that only the ringing cash registers would tell the true story.

The day was a long one, with a formal dinner for all the employees in the huge, walnut-paneled dining room where Matthew addressed them. It was a day of congratulations and expectations. And as he walked back to his office, closed the door, and stared out the window, he thought it the loneliest day in his life.

"She should have been here with me," he said to himself. "Amanda would have made it perfect."

He'd telephoned her those first days after their breakup, but she refused to talk to him, giving her messages to her secretary to relay to him. He told himself he understood, but he didn't. He was furious with her, himself, the world. Twice he'd started out for her office but then thought better of it. He couldn't put himself through the agony of another quarrel, especially when they both knew the outcome at the start.

"Damn it to hell!" Amanda was right, he thought.

He was trying to go on with his life, build his dream and plan for the future. But now still loving Amanda and not being able to see her was the hardest thing he'd ever done.

Central Park stretched out in front of him like a dark emerald, glistening in the moonlight. Soon the trees would be turning to autumn gold, and then the snow would come. Then it would be spring. He wondered if then he would find hope.

"I can't believe you would even set foot in this place," Christine said with a catty smirk on her face.

"Neither can I, but I'm doing a lot of things these days I never thought I would." Sydney instantly realized she'd revealed herself. She changed the subject. "Would you look around? There must be twenty people in line waiting for a table. He's actually done it. Matthew has made Wade's the only place to shop in New York."

"I heard he stole the chef from the Waldorf."

"He did. He's making it all work," Sydney said with a sigh.

Christine watched her over the top of her menu. Over the years she'd learned to read her friend. "You're disappointed. Is it your chance of getting him back to the bank that you're lamenting, or is it something else?"

Sydney put her menu down. She was nonplussed. "I'm not worried about Matthew. I can handle him. I have so far, haven't I?"

"I don't know. Have you?"

"I don't know what you're talking about."

" 'Fess up, Sydney. In the past weeks there's been a tension about both you and Matthew I've never seen before. Matthew isn't the kind of man who can be handled. I think he's shown you that and that's why you're afraid."

"Afraid? Me?"

"You haven't gotten him back to the bank, have you? I think you underestimate him. Look around, Sydney. The man is a genius. I think it's *you* who should come around to *his* way of thinking."

What? And give him a divorce? Sydney thought. "Since when did you grow a brain?"

"Did I touch a nerve?"

Sydney did not allow the first flicker of annoyance to cross her face. She remained cool and aloof. She wondered that if Christine could tell there was something more going on between herself and Matthew, how many other people were noticing it. Had Matthew said something to Paul? They had been boyhood friends. Paul would be the most likely of people for Matthew to confide in. No, she thought. Christine would have wanted to gloat had she any real knowledge of the situation. "I still say all of this is a passing fad. There are more important considerations in my life."

"Really? Like what?"

"The future of my family. That's something you've never given any thought to."

"That's not true. Paul was my future. I went after him and I got him," Christine said proudly.

Sydney raised a single eyebrow. "You weren't thinking about your marriage when you took up with David."

Christine smiled. "Ah, yes. David," she said slowly, thinking about their moments in bed. Quickly, she dispelled his image. "That's over."

Sydney waited while the waiter placed hot tea in front of them. She added sugar and cream. She studied Christine as she stirred her tea. She knew Christine was hiding something from her. Just as she was hiding the truth about Matthew's affair with Amanda Granger from Christine. "Who are you seeing now, Christine?"

"Does it show?"

"No. I was just guessing. I know you too well."

Christine's grin was a bit too wide and her eyes sparkled a bit too mischievously. "God, Sydney. He's unbelievable."

"You are such a little fool. Don't you have any brains at all?"

Christine put down her spoon. "Don't lecture me, Sydney. I need a friend, not a mother."

"Who is it?"

"Andrew Granger," Christine said proudly.

"Good God! Amanda's brother."

"None other. He's so exciting. You wouldn't *believe* some of the places we go. Bistros and honky-tonks—I even saw a gun-fight between two gangsters!"

"Christine! Are you out of your mind? Why would you take such chances? This is worse than anything you've done before."

Christine leaned over. Her eyes flared with exhilaration. "You don't know what it's like being married to Paul, who always does the right thing, says the right thing. He's so damn *boring*! Sometimes I think I'll go crazy. Andrew can't take me to Del's, and so we do outrageous things. I went to a burlesque show—I saw women strip down to almost nothing and dance. I'd heard about all these things, but never seen them. There's a world out there, Sydney—and I want to see more of it. I want to *do* things, experience things, before I'm too old."

"What is it with this preoccupation of yours? You aren't old. You don't look a day over twenty."

"But I am old. Thirty isn't that far away. I could die tomorrow, and what would I have to show for it? A stack of jewelry boxes, a closet full of clothes. I've got nothing, Sydney. . . ." Christine hissed.

Suddenly, they both realized what she'd said. Christine sat back in her chair, frightened of the emotions she'd revealed.

"Christine, it can't be all that bad."

"I'm not smart like you, Sydney. You have your work at the bank, Jacqueline—and you have Matthew."

"That's debatable. . . ." Sydney whispered to herself.

"What did you say?"

"Nothing." She fidgeted with her teacup. "Christine, be careful."

Christine patted Sydney's hand in a gesture of friendship. "I'll be fine."

It was late, and the light from Amanda's green-shaded desk lamp was not sufficient. She was tired, but this fashion article she'd been working on had to be ready by morning. A month ago she'd heard about a new designer working in a loft not far from Chelsea. Amanda had been told the woman's clothes were extremely avant-garde and that no one would buy them. Intrigued, Amanda had gone to investigate. What she'd found were undoubtedly the most beautiful evening clothes she'd ever seen.

The young designer, Katrine, used colorful beads, pearls, bugles, and rhinestones to decorate the bodices of her evening clothes. She chose the brightest-colored fabrics she could find, lamenting, as Amanda always did, that Americans were either color-blind or too frightened by the unusual to take the social risk of wearing something that was not white, cream, or black.

Amanda decided that day to feature Katrine's creations in this issue. Even if she couldn't convince New Yorkers to wear more adventurous colors, she knew Katrine would be swamped with orders to bead every bodice on the Eastern seaboard.

Amanda propped her chin on her hand as she scratched through another line and rewrote the last paragraph. She was so intent on her work she didn't hear Sylvia walk in.

"I know I'm disturbing you. That's why I came," Sylvia said, leaning over to kiss Amanda on the head. She sat in the chair across from her. "Have you had your dinner?"

"No."

"Good. Then we'll go together."

Amanda looked at her curiously. "What's wrong?"

Sylvia took off her gloves. "Why, nothing. Should something be the matter simply because I came to take you to dinner?"

Amanda put her pencil down. "Absolutely. You never come down here without making prior arrangements. And I've never seen you anywhere near here after the sun goes down."

"That's true. I've been meaning to speak to you about these late hours you keep. Where is Andrew? Who will walk you home? It's not safe on the streets at night."

"Sylvia . . . why are you here?"

"Amanda, you can't hole yourself up here day and night. It's not good. The world still exists, whether Matthew is in it or not."

"Oh, God." Amanda felt her stomach slide away at the mention of his name. She dropped her head into her hands. "I feel awful. I never knew I could be this lonely."

Sylvia got up and put her arms around Amanda's shoulders. "I know."

"I can't believe how perfectly I had fooled myself into believing we'd be married. I'd hoped so desperately. I believed we were special, that God would make some kind of allowances for us. But He didn't."

"No. I'm afraid you gave Him too difficult a task."

"I know that now."

"So," Sylvia said, "is this how you intend to waste the rest of your life? Staying at work all night . . ."

"I *can't* go home—I see Matthew in every room!"

"You have to face your demons, Amanda, but tonight, I'll go with you. Nobody ever said you had to face them alone."

Amanda looked at her—the woman who'd been mother, sister, and friend. God had given her Sylvia. In His wisdom, perhaps that was best. "No, I don't."

Amanda put her papers away. She turned out the light. As she walked out and shut the door, she thought how much she needed Sylvia's caring, her strength. When she looked back at the empty office, she thought the darkness had never seemed quite so vacant before—nor as frightening.

CHAPTER THIRTY-THREE

By November, five issues of *City Woman* had hit the stands. The critics had lambasted Amanda from the start. The magazine was too expensive, too avant-garde, and relied too heavily on pictorials instead of editorials. The editorials that did run were socialistic in nature, since they supported women's suffrage, better working conditions, and too many times debated controversial issues such as birth control and abortion. Every male byline in every paper in the city predicted that *City Woman* would not last out the year.

The publishing world despised her. But her readership increased. Amanda had already doubled the original print of five thousand copies. However, it was November when retailers would be spending the largest amount of their advertising budget. Every day, when Andrew and his sales force came back, the story was the same.

"They went with *Collier's*. *Harper's Bazaar* ran a special this month."

Because retailers wanted large ads and lots of them, Amanda's prices were much too high.

Andrew sat across the desk from her. "Face it. The articles last month about those striking women at the Virginia textile plant didn't help my salesmen when they went out to the retailers. Men run retail, Amanda. You can't get their dander up like you're doing."

"It was a well-written, incisive article. There should be more unions."

"Maybe so. But it's not your business. Your business is fashion—or so you said."

She pushed her chair back and rose. "I know."

"Well, I don't care what you put in the magazine. I just don't want to hear your complaints when I come back empty-handed."

"What about the ideas I had for the jewelry ads? Was anyone interested in those layouts?"

"A few. Harry Winston. And Wade's took out a full page."

Amanda's eyes opened wide. "Wade's?"

"Paid in full. I sent Sal over there to talk to the head of advertising. He was reluctant to do it, but word came from Matthew Wade himself to buy a full page. He wants photos of some specially made diamond necklaces. Wade exclusives."

Amanda suddenly felt weak. She sank into her chair. Matthew had saved her again. She had an impulse to telephone him and thank him, but she didn't. She knew if she heard his voice, even once, it would be a thousand times more difficult for her to get him out of her mind.

Amanda looked at Andrew. He was tired. They were all tired. She'd worked everyone harder than ever, trying to get the November and December issues ready. Work was a balm for her restless heart, but none of her staff knew that.

"It's getting tougher for me, Amanda."

"All right. You win. Tell them that for January we will double the fashion layout. We'll run a special issue on resort wear. We'll have the latest news about Saratoga, Jekyll Island, and Florida for our readers. How's that?"

"Better."

She leaned back in her chair and rubbed her eyes. She was getting weary of the fight just as everyone was. Perhaps she'd been too hard on Andrew, the staff . . . and herself. "How about coming over tonight for supper? I make wonderful pasta."

"I can't." He used his best brother smile.

"Seeing Mary Alice tonight?"

"Yes." He rose, not disclosing any more. He liked keeping Amanda out of his private life. She had too much of his life as it was. When he reached the door he turned back to her. "If everything goes well, you'll have a new sister-in-law soon."

"You're going to ask her tonight?"

"No. But I'm looking at rings tonight."

"Good luck," she said and went back to her work.

Andrew went to his office, called in his secretary, and gave her instructions. He wanted everyone on his sales staff to know of Amanda's new turn. Andrew made it a point to handle as much of his sales meetings out of the magazine offices as possible. He didn't want Amanda to know how little time he spent actually working. He relied on his salesmen to do the dirty work. Andrew always made certain, however, that Amanda knew that it had been *he* who had closed the accounts. His staff were underlings.

Andrew took his hat and coat from the rack and headed out the door for his most important meeting that week. He was seeing Christine.

Andrew had found that between his weekly poker games at Paul's house or one of his very, very wealthy friends' homes and the fistfuls of cash that Christine would give him, he wouldn't need his job at the magazine much longer.

How stupid he'd been to waste his time in Hell's Kitchen when the big pots had been sitting under his nose.

Christine liked that world, though. He took her to cafes where the patrons lived their lives in the shadows. He showed her one bawdy house after another. She liked the booze, the jazz music, and the gutter talk. Christine liked adventure, and Andrew made certain she believed she would find all the adventure she needed in him.

Andrew had to admit, however, that if it weren't for Amanda's Lie, he never would have bedded Christine in the first place. Many times when they had lain together, she would bring up the subject of his "royal blood."

"Do you think a king would be any better than you?"

"Not unless he was younger."

"Be serious. I mean it. I think royal blood does make a difference."

"How's that?"

She grabbed him. "You have a longer reign," she said and squeezed him—hard.

"I'll always be more than you can handle, Christine."

She moved over him. "We'll see about that."

Andrew smiled to himself as he walked toward the hotel where he was to meet Christine. He meant what he'd said when he told Amanda he would propose to Mary Alice. All he needed was the money to buy that ring.

* * *

"What is it?"

"Just something to make you feel good."

"I'm not sure," she said, rubbing the fine powder between her forefinger and thumb.

"Just sniff it."

Christine looked at Andrew while he pulled the rolled satin strap of her teddy down her arm. He cupped her breast and pinched her nipple.

"Do as I said," he commanded.

Christine obeyed.

"Now take some more. Do it again."

Christine sniffed the cocaine into her nostrils. He peeled off her teddy and then stripped off his shirt. As always when he looked at her perfect body, he became excited. Quickly, he stepped out of his trousers.

"I don't feel anything."

"You will," he said moving over her, teasing her nipples with his tongue. Slowly he caresed her rib cage, abdomen, and thighs. He breathed heavily into her ear. He sank his hand between her legs. Slowly, she began to twitch.

"Yes! Andrew, now."

"No."

"Please." She pitched back and forth on the bed as he teased her. Suddenly, the drug ignited every nerve ending in her body. She felt as if her skin was on fire. She wanted his hands everywhere, inside and out. None of it was enough.

"More!" she screamed.

"Patience," he said languidly, watching her twitch with excitement.

She pulled him over her. She shoved his head down to her breast.

"Damn it! Now, Andrew!"

"What'll you give me?

"Anything. Just please . . ."

"A thousand dollars."

"Yes. Yes."

"I want more, Christine. Two thousand dollars." He rubbed his penis between her legs, still not entering her.

"It's yours—just please . . ." She dug her nails into his buttocks and forced him inside her. He rammed her again and again. She felt she could go on forever. She raised her hips to him, craving more. She bit his shoulder.

He screamed when he climaxed. But she wouldn't allow him to move. She undulated beneath him.

"More, Andrew. It's not enough."

"I want more then too," he groaned.

"I'll make it three thousand. . . ." She smiled as she felt him grow hard inside her again.

"You can have anything you want, Christine," he moaned in her ear.

She threw her head back until her head was almost buried in the down pillow. Christine couldn't feel anything except one orgasm after another. She was drenched in sweat and her hair was mangled around her face. But she didn't care. With strength she didn't know she had, she rolled him over and sat on top of him. He shoved himself up into her until she yelped. She rolled over again and they fell to the floor. He loomed over her as he entered her again.

Christine was so high on the drug she didn't realilze she banged her head against the cold parquet floor with each of his thrusts. All she knew was that she could never, never let this end.

Exhausted and breathless, she said to him: "Promise me you'll bring the powder again next time."

"I promise."

CHAPTER THIRTY-FOUR

On Christmas Eve Amanda stood outside Wade's looking at the mannequins in the enormous window displays. There were red suede sleighs with silver runners, filled with brightly wrapped packages. Next to them stood groups of beautifully dressed mannequins carolling. In the next window was a Santa Claus surrounded by a sea of toys. Amanda hugged her bundles to her chest and walked away into the snowy night. She stood on the street corner beneath the lamplight wondering what would happen if she went in, knowing she didn't dare.

Streams of shoppers poured out the doors, loaded down with purchases. She still wanted something special for Sylvia. She'd found a rich mauve woolen scarf, but it seemed such a practical gift. It wasn't enough for the one woman who'd seen her through the worst six months of her life.

Amanda gathered her courage and entered the opulent, extravagant world of Wade's.

Enormous green trees rose from platforms placed above the counters. They were decorated with glass balls of frosted pink, green, and blue. Swags of gold satin encircled the trees and rippled at the base in a puddle of gold material. Amanda was dumbstruck. She hadn't seen the store since May, when she'd waded through sawdust, nails, and pieces of scrap lumber. Everything that had been said about Wade's was true. There was nothing like it on earth.

Amanda went from counter to counter searching for Sylvia's gift. She sniffed exotic perfumes, fingered delicate silk scarves, and marveled over Belgian linen handkerchiefs. But it was the

delicately hand-painted Limoges box that caught her eye. It was
edged in gold and had a tiny gold clasp. Smiling at the salesgirl,
she waited while her gift was wrapped in silver foil and tied with
an enormous green bow.

With only thirty minutes until closing time, Matthew had
locked his office and gone to the mezzanine railing to check the
number of customers that still remained. He'd thought that by
now people would be anxious to be home for dinner, prepare for
parties or midnight services. But Wade's was just as busy now,
at seven-thirty, as it had been at noon. No one seemed ready to
leave.

Working his way down, he checked each floor and found
people standing in line at every counter. Since Christmas repre-
sented more than fifty percent of his retail season, Matthew was
assured that Wade's would make a healthy profit its first year. He
was nearly giddy with his success.

He checked his watch. Sydney was to have met him over
twenty minutes ago. He'd wanted her there to help him present
his Christmas bonuses to his office staff. There had been plenty
of champagne, and he wanted Sydney to be involved with his
employees. To his surprise, she had agreed. He wondered now if
she had lied and had no intention of coming.

Matthew sighed. He didn't know why he expected anything
from her. Sydney hadn't been with him on opening day. Her
feelings about his store would never change.

On the second-floor mezzanine, Matthew signed his initials to
a register count for the linen department. It was only fifteen
minutes to closing. He leaned over the wrought-iron balcony and
watched the last of the hectic shopping come to a close.

And then he saw her.

She wore a dark maroon wool coat trimmed in black. There
was a small black lambs'-wool pillbox hat to match. Her cheeks
were still red from the cold. She smiled happily as the salesgirl
handed her a silver-wrapped box.

He wanted to shout to her, alert her to his presence, but he
didn't. He stood there bolted to the floor, knowing he had
nothing to say to her, nothing to give her.

"Thank you," Amanda said to the salesgirl and turned toward
the doors. Suddenly she stopped. She had the oddest sensation

that someone was watching her. She continued forward, knowing she must leave—now. She felt the hairs on the back of her neck prickle. She stopped, turned, and looked up into the rotunda.

She saw him leaning over the rail watching her.

"Matthew," she breathed. She felt cold chills cover her skin. He didn't move. It was if he was locked inside an invisible box. She knew she could not go to him. "I love you," she whispered to herself.

He saw her mouth the words and he knew what she'd said. He watched as she blew him a kiss and mouthed the words, "Merry Christmas."

"Merry Christmas, my beloved," he mumbled to himself.

Amanda turned away from him and continued through the doors.

At the moment Amanda was leaving, Sydney rode the elevator up to Matthew's office. She was glad all the hustle was over, though Matthew's late hours for the past month had given her precious moments of solitude.

She pulled her hands out of her white mink muff and unfastened her new silver fox coat. She didn't want to be here tonight, and it particularly disturbed her that she had to cancel a dinner with the Kanes for Matthew's employees. However, she felt she should indulge him, for after the first of the year, she intended to broach the subject of his coming back to the bank. If she could make him give up Amanda Granger, she could get him to do anything.

She exited the elevator and saw Matthew standing at the mezzanine railing. She walked over to him. "Merry Christmas," she said.

Still dazed at seeing Amanda for the first time in six months, Matthew was slow to react.

It was just enough of a nonreaction for Sydney's alarm system to go off. Surreptitiously, she scanned the crowd below them. She couldn't be sure, but it was her guess that the retreating blonde woman in the maroon coat was Amanda. She looked at Matthew. There was a misty gleam in his eye she hadn't seen for months.

Sydney felt oddly weak. She steadied herself and tried to organize her thoughts. Somewhere, she'd made a miscalculation. Was it possible his need for his daughter was not as great as she'd thought? Never having been in love herself, it was difficult for Sydney to calculate the extent of the hold Amanda had on Matthew. She knew secondhand of Christine's love affairs, her lust and need for men, but then Christine was weak. Matthew was not.

It was dealing with the unknowns of Matthew's feelings for Amanda that caused this increasing fear within her. It was a foreign feeling for Sydney and she didn't like it a bit.

As always, she knew if she relied on logic, she could easily rid herself of Amanda. Any fool knew that lovers could easily be duped, for love had the universal effect of rendering its victims mindless.

Sydney breathed easier. She would find a way to keep Matthew, her child, and Wade Bank.

"Are you all right, Matthew? You look as if you'd seen a ghost."

"Ghost? Yes. I think that's what it was. But it's Christmas. . . time for ghosts—of the past."

"As long as that's all it was."

"Yes. That's all it was."

Amanda watched as Sylvia unwrapped her gift. Her eyes lit up her face.

"It's beautiful. Thank you," Sylvia said.

"I'm glad you like it."

Sylvia tossed the silver paper to the side. "Did you see him when you went to the store?"

"How did you know I went to Wade's."

"I did *my* shopping at Wade's. They're the only ones in town using silver foil."

"Oh," Amanda said, looking into the fire. It was a viciously cold Christmas morning. The wind howled outside and the snow fell like a thick blanket, obscuring the view of Washington Square. "I saw him, but we didn't speak." Amanda rose and went to the fire. She rubbed her hands together. "I don't know why after all these months I felt compelled to go in. I wish I hadn't." Tears burned her eyes. She looked at Sylvia. "It's never going to get any better, is it?"

Sylvia's heart was breaking for her friend. "Time will help. You'll see, and you must keep busy." She checked the mantel clock. "You can start by helping me with dinner. I had no idea it was so late."

Amanda followed Sylvia to the dining room. She was glad Sylvia would not let her dwell on her problems. She *should* keep busy, and she had for a long time. Until last night, she'd actually found herself not thinking about Matthew for hours at a stretch. Six months ago, she wouldn't have thought that possible.

Amanda stirred the cranberries while Sylvia checked the turkey.

"Did I tell you that Julia has a beau? That's why she isn't here today."

"On Christmas it's nice to have somebody. . . ."

Sylvia wished there was something she could say to cheer Amanda. But she understood. "That's why we have each other."

Amanda looked up."Yes. We *do* have each other. And I'm grateful for that."

Just then the doorbell sounded. Sylvia untied her apron and went to the vestibule. She opened the door and greeted Irene and Dana Gibson. She was just about to close the door when she saw the Cummings' coach pull up. Fifteen minutes later, Amanda had just served sherry to everyone when the Kanes arrived. The quiet brownstone was suddenly transformed into a house filled with Christmas cheer.

Dana played the piano while everyone joined in to sing Christmas carols. When it came time for dinner Amanada helped serve. As she went from place to place she couldn't help but remember the Christmas dinners she'd served as a maid in Lord Kent's house in London. She no longer had the protection of a marriage to David to keep her from poverty, to sustain her social position. She only had her wits, The Lie, and the treasure of Sylvia's friendship to keep her from slipping through the cracks of New York society. If only she'd been truly born to royalty, she might have felt more secure. But she still felt as if at any moment some twist of fate would pull the mask from her face and reveal her to the world as she really was—a fraud.

The conversation was bright and energetic. Amanda thought it was all she could do to keep a smile on her face. She wanted to go home and pull the covers over her head and will away the holidays. But she didn't.

She sat at Sylvia's right, laughing at Everett Kane's bad jokes, sympathizing with Mildred Cummings about her problems with her household staff, and forcing Matthew's image from her mind. It was Christmas and she deserved some peace too.

After dinner, Amanda led the group in parlor games. Everett

Kane had just risen to take his turn when there was a knock at the door. Sylvia rose, but Amanda stopped her.

"I'll go."

The knock had become a continual pounding by the time Amanda opened the door. It was David. And he was drunk.

"Hello, Amanda . . ." he said, sliding against the doorjamb and then into the house.

"What are you doing here?" she demanded as she shut the door against the icy wind.

"I brought you a gift."

Amanda's eyes narrowed suspiciously. "What are you talking about?"

"We created a whirlwind in this town, didn't we, Amanda?" he said.

"Yes, we did."

He wanted to be firm with her. Make her regret what she had done. He pursed his lips, but they slid against each other, making him look like a buffoon. "I heard your magazine wasn't doing all that well. You should have stayed with me, Amanda."

"You heard wrong. I've doubled my circulation. I'm doing fine."

"It's nip and tuck all the way, isn't it?"

Amanda didn't know who was giving David the accurate rundown on her financial situation, but it was unnerving that he knew so much about her business. "Go home, David."

He straightened his shoulders, but in so doing he overcompensated for the movement and went tottering backward a step or two. He was angry at her for making him look foolish in front of the others. "You could stop all this nonsense. I might be willing to take you back."

"I'm not coming back, David. I don't need you." She was embarrassed for him and angry with him at the same time. He was trying to make her feel guilty for his career, for his lack of talent.

"Think you're too smart for me, don'tcha? Well, you're not. Because it's Christmas, I thought I'd be magnanimous. But I can see now you're the arrogant bitch you've always been."

"Leave, David." Amanda tried to grab his arm and urge him through the door.

"Don't touch me!" he hissed. "You think you're better than any of us. How long do you think they'll be your friends when

you treat people the way you do? Maybe you should just go back
to London. . . .''

Sylvia, still watching from the doorway, started toward them,
but Amanda signalled for her to remain where she was.

Amanda opened the door. She glared at him. ''Leave right this
minute, David, or I'll have you thrown out. It's your choice.''

David opened his mouth to hurl a harangue of insults at her,
but he thought better of it. He was not so drunk as not to realize
the scandal he would create. He wanted to see his name in the
press again, but only with triumphant horns blowing.

He walked past her out into the snow. He turned momentarily
and suddenly he looked quite sober to her.

''I hope you're happy, Amanda,'' he said with buried anger
and an unexpected touch of sadness to his voice.

''Are any of us really?'' she said and closed the door.

David placed his black silk top hat on his head and slowly
walked to his waiting carriage. He didn't know how to spend
Christmas now that he didn't have Amanda, nor was he welcome
in Paul's house. Nothing was as it had been. He needed a friend.
But he didn't have any. He shrugged his shoulders. It didn't
matter. Friends could be found in a cold-cream jar.

Andrew sat beneath a twenty-foot Christmas tree that held over
a thousand glass ornaments. Christmas was nearly over and he
hadn't had Mary Alice to himself all day. He'd gone to Christmas services with the Howell family, and dinner had been a
four-hour affair, with over ten courses. It had taken three maids
to clean all the wrapping paper and ribbons out of the main parlor
after fifteen nieces and nephews had done their damage to the
room. Now the children had all either gone home or were upstairs in the guest rooms fast asleep. Andrew had given Mary
Alice a box of chocolates, a mother-of-pearl set of combs for her
hair, and a pair of kid gloves. He knew she didn't suspect the
ring he still had in his coat pocket.

''This was the best Christmas I ever had,'' Mary Alice said,
looking up at the tree, then at Andrew.

''Not for me,'' he said, taking her hand.

''Why?'' she asked, suddenly worried.

''I never got to see you alone for two seconds. I've never had
a holiday with so many people around.''

''I guess we Howells can be a bit overwhelming.''

"Mary Alice, there's something I've been wanting to ask you."

"Yes, Andrew?"

Slowly he took out the ring box and handed it to her. It was unwrapped. "Would you marry me?" His smile was his most charming, his most endearing.

Mary Alice gasped. It was a beautiful ring. Set in platinum, the center diamond was easily two carats. It was surrounded by a ring of emerald-cut baguettes. "It's beautiful!" She smiled at him.

"Put it on," he urged.

She did as he asked. It glittered up at her in the soft lamplight. "Yes, Andrew." She sighed. "I'll be your wife."

He kissed her, happily. Then again, with more meaning, as he knew she would expect.

"Let's go tell your parents."

Mary Alice's smile vanished. "Must we?"

"Of course! Why wouldn't you want to tell them?" he asked, becoming concerned.

"Don't look so worried," she said, placing her hand on his cheek. "I just wanted to keep it a secret for a day . . . just for myself."

Andrew thought it a ridiculous thing to want. Women could be sentimental to a fault, he thought.

"I think I need to speak with your father, Mary Alice," he said firmly.

"I suppose you're right." She sighed.

They rose and went to the library. Andrew knocked on the door, then they entered.

Jack Howell was sitting in his favorite leather chair. Cigar smoke filled the air. He was reading a day-old newspaper.

"Father, Andrew has something he wants to discuss with you."

Jack Howell put the paper down, looked at his daughter, and then at Andrew. "So you finally asked her."

"Father, how did you know?"

Jack laughed. "We were all taking bets on you, son. Why do you think I had your mother get all those damned children out of here? Who could propose with all that ruckus?"

Andrew's confidence soared. He had Jack Howell in his back pocket. "Then I have your blessings, sir?"

"Of course." He stood and shook Andrew's hand, then kissed

his daughter's cheek. "Now, tell me," he said, sitting back down, "where's the house you intend to live in?"

"House, sir?"

"Where will you and Mary Alice live? She's used to the best. I know you can't afford anything this grand. For a wedding present I'll furnish the house for you. Anything and everything Mary Alice needs—linens, furniture, sterling, crystal. I just need to know where."

Andrew was stunned. He'd never thought ahead this far. A house? How could he afford a house? And yet Jack Howell would indeed fill it with a king's ransom of goods. They would never want for anything. "I haven't bought anything yet, sir. I wanted to speak to you about it first. Get your advice. I've never purchased real estate before."

"That's what I like about you, Andrew. You know when to ask for advice and aren't afraid to come forward to do it. I'll be very glad to help you out. Very glad. After all, we want the same thing."

"The same thing, sir?"

"For Mary Alice, of course. We want the best."

"Yes, the best for Mary Alice," Andrew said, squeezing Mary Alice's hand, smiling at Jack, and swallowing the hot lump in his throat.

Jack dismissed them, and as Mary Alice went to the kitchen to ask the cook for coffee for them, Andrew looked up again at the Christmas tree.

This was the worst predicament he'd ever gotten himself into. A house could cost a fortune. He knew he could coerce Jack into helping him arrange a mortgage. But he'd have to have a down payment or at least a considerable sum of money in the bank to show some solvency. It wouldn't be easy, but Andrew knew he could find the money.

This time, however, it would take more than a few thousand from Christine Van Volkein.

With the holidays behind him and two weeks of racking his brain, Andrew finally came up with a plan that would give him the money he needed to buy a house for Mary Alice. He would take out a loan from a bank, using Amanda's magazine as the collateral. To make the monthly payments on the loan, he would skim money from the magazine's accounts until he was married, ensconced in the house, and had Mary Alice's dowry put in his name. Then he would pay off the loan and no one, especially his sister, would be the wiser.

It took Andrew another three weeks to make up a false set of books that he could present to the banker for the loan. Andrew needed thirty thousand dollars. He could wheedle five thousand out of Christine, but he would need to borrow twenty-five thousand. Since the magazine was already leveraged for that much, he needed to show the magazine making nearly three times the profit it was.

Andrew selected a small bank with substantial capital, a bank that would consider doing business with Granger Publishing Company an asset. He wanted someone who was a bit starstruck with the Granger name, and one who would naturally assume, as he'd found once before, that A. Granger was a man.

Because he'd put a great deal of time and effort into his plans, Andrew was astonished at how easily he was granted the loan. The paperwork took less than three days. On the day before Valentine's Day, Andrew walked out of the New York Mercantile Bank with a cashier's check for twenty-five thousand dollars.

It was time for him and Mary Alice to go house hunting.

CHAPTER THIRTY-FIVE

Sydney Wade leaned forward while her maid plumped the pillow behind her head. She sipped her morning tea but ignored the freshly baked German pastries. The New Year had come and gone, followed by Valentine's Day, and with each passing week, Sydney thought she would find the proper moment to approach Matthew about going back to the bank, but she hadn't.

James queried her weekly about the matter.

"Give it up, Sydney. I have," he said. "I don't know what his Christmas figures showed, but the whole town is talking about the coup he's made."

Sydney chose to ignore Matthew's success. "Ridiculous. He's now into his slowest part of the retail year. His overhead is ghastly. It'll fail."

"I want him back as much as you do. But this time, I think Matthew has proved his point. And against some very strong odds."

"You sound as if you're proud of him."

James allowed a quirky smile to cross his face. "I suppose I am at that. He's my son, after all."

"Well, I haven't finished with all this yet!" Sydney exclaimed as she picked up her things and left. As she retreated through his reception area, she could almost hear his silent laughter.

Sydney put the tea aside. "Is Mr. Wade up, Violet?" she asked the maid.

"Yes ma'am. He's in the nursery."

"Oh, for God's sake! Won't he ever leave that child alone?"

Sydney did not see her maid's scowl as she scrambled off the bed.

She wrapped a burgundy velvet robe with black braid trim around herself, stepped into matching slippers, and went down the hall.

"I thought I'd find you in here," she said to Matthew.

He frowned. "A bit early for you to be up, isn't it?"

Jacqueline turned the page in her storybook. "Read this part, Daddy," she said, ignoring her mother completely.

Matthew started to read. Sydney grew impatient.

"Matthew, I'd like a word with you."

"Later," he said and continued reading. Jacqueline climbed onto his lap and stroked his hand as he read.

Sydney grew infuriated. "I'd like to see you now, Matthew! In the salon."

"I'll meet you there when I'm ready," he growled.

Sydney spun around and whisked down the stairs. Impatiently, she watched the clock. It was over thirty-five minutes before Matthew walked through the salon doors.

"You took your time," she said.

"It was important."

"A nursery rhyme? Important?" Sydney's father had never read to her. She didn't understand the reluctance to turn such duties over to the nanny.

"What do you want, Sydney?"

Sydney had created this moment. She wanted to use it wisely. There was only one way of dealing with Matthew. She came right to the point. "I want to talk to you about coming back to your rightful place."

"My what?"

"The bank."

"Oh, for Christ's sake!" Matthew started for the door. Sydney leapt to her feet and grabbed his arm.

"Hear me out, Matthew."

When he turned to her, Sydney thought she'd never seen eyes so white with anger or a voice so filled with venom. "Forget it, Sydney. You've already ransomed my daughter to keep me in this farce of a marriage. You can only use her once. Can't you get it through your head? I despise you, this place I live in, everything about my live except—*except* my daughter and my career. I'll be goddamned if I'll let you destroy them too."

Before she could utter a syllable, Matthew had stormed out of the house.

"I'm losing him," she mumbled, stunned with the realization. "I could have reasoned with him if it hadn't been for that Granger woman. This is all her fault. She's the reason he won't see it my way. How blind I've been! Well, not anymore. All I have to do is rid Matthew of Amanda and then everything will be perfect."

That afternoon, Christine flitted into Sydney's office in her usual blithe manner. Sydney was almost glad to see her. Christine was just the person to help her out of her problems with Matthew. Using Christine would be child's play. Sydney smiled at her. Christine was dressed to the teeth in a new designer gown. Sydney instantly recognized the workmanship.

"New ensemble, Christine?"

Christine preened. "Yes." She twirled around, needing to be admired. "Do you like it?"

"You bought it at Wade's."

"Yes, I did."

Sydney shook her head. "Since when have you left Marie at B. Altman's?"

Christine sat in a chair. "*Everyone* goes to Wade's now, Sydney. Face it, Matthew did what he said he was going to do. He's so successful, you'll never get him back to the bank."

Sydney revealed none of the tension that ate at the edges of her insides. "We'll see about that. Are you still seeing Andrew?"

"Of course. I'm meeting him after I leave here."

"I've often wondered how his sister is doing with her magazine."

"He says they are doing very well. The readership increases every month."

Sydney clucked her tongue and rolled her eyes theatrically. "I don't understand what the world is coming to."

"Why, what do you mean?"

Sydney lowered her voice to execute perfectly horrified intonations. "Where have you been, Christine? Everyone is talking about the bohemian life-style she is living. The idea—a woman living alone and running her own business." Sydney leaned closer. "I heard she has a lover."

Christine's face brightened. There was nothing she liked more than gossip—especially when she could compare her own scandalous life to that of others. "Really? Who?"

"I don't know that. Only that he's very wealthy. And very married."

"Andrew has never said anything."

"I doubt he would. He's no better than his sister. His engagement to Mary Alice Howell was just announced yesterday, and now you tell me you're seeing him today. I should have known they would be trouble from the very start—I still think it was vulgar for a woman to have her picture plastered across half the publishing world."

"I know," Christine said, with too much jealousy in her voice. "But you never said anything when David published my picture."

"That was different. I've always indulged you."

"Yes, you have at that." Christine smiled, thinking she held some mystic power over Sydney.

"Amanda never was 'our' sort, Christine. Her divorce was one of the most scandalous the city has ever seen. The rumors are still going around about that. Then she started this magazine. And the stories she publishes! Why, half of New York would like to see her run out of town. I even heard a minister stating that Amanda Granger was the kind of woman who was responsible for the demoralization of New York's young working girls."

"Oh, heavens, Sydney. You don't believe that, do you?"

"Who can tell? Just a few years ago, everyone wanted to be like The Granger Woman. Now that same woman is telling women where to go for birth control, to form unions. And she's living alone and has lovers!"

"I see what you mean," Christine said, succumbing to Sydney's theatrics. Suddenly it did seem as if there was something immoral about everything Amanda Granger did. To Christine's mind, her own antics paled by comparison.

Sydney looked at Christine intently. "You won't repeat any of this, will you, Christine?"

"Me? No! Of course not."

"Promise me," she begged earnestly.

"I promise."

"Good. I knew I could trust you."

On March twentieth, Matthew and Sydney Wade invited one

hundred and fifty of New York's most influential families to their daughter's fourth birthday party.

It was a gray day, with mist and fog encasing the city, making everything seem as if it were under a roof. Inside the Wade mansion, electric lights brightened the afternoon as uniformed maids passed silver trays of canapes and hired waiters poured from heavy bottles of French champagne. The children played indoor games and marvelled over the three-tiered birthday cake.

Jacqueline was dressed in an emerald green satin and white-lace dress her father had specially commissioned his design department to create.

Jacqueline delighted in seeing her friends, who all brought gifts for her. An hour and a half after the party began, Jacqueline played a strained and juvenile rendition of a Chopin piece on the piano in the music room, to the delight of her father. The moment she finished taking her bows, she raced to her father and threw her arms around his waist.

"Daddy, thank you for a lovely party."

He pulled her into his arms and kissed her cheeks.

Sydney was miffed at the lack of attention she received from Jacqueline, especially when many of the faces in the crowd looked questioningly over at her.

"Aren't you going to thank me too, dear?" Sydney urged.

Jacqueline's jubilance vanished. "Thank you very much, Mother," she said primly.

Sydney kissed her as was expected by the onlookers.

"Come, Jacqueline. Let's go cut your cake."

"All right," Jacqueline said, thinking she'd rather stay in her father's arms.

While Sydney was preoccupied with the ceremony of the birthday cake, Matthew stole a moment with his most special guest, Sylvia Hendrickson.

"Have you seen her lately?" he asked, keeping his smile in tact as friends stopped momentarily.

"Yes. How did you know I knew about the two of you?"

"You were never good at hiding things, Sylvia. Every time you look at me, I see your pity, your concern."

"It's that obvious?"

"Yes. Does anyone else know?"

"No. You can be assured of that."

"I want to see her. I want Amanda now more than ever."

"Then tell Amanda. Don't tell me."

"It isn't that simple. Sydney will never give me a divorce. And even if she did, she'd never let me have Jacqueline."

Sylvia looked across the room at her hostess. She was holding court, as Sydney always did at parties. Matthew was right. Sydney's edge was the child. It was a powerful hand she held. "I agree with you, Matthew. There doesn't seem to be any way out."

Matthew felt as if he would explode with tension and anger. "There has to be a way, Sylvia. I can't go on living like this much longer. Sydney doesn't love me, she never has. She cares even less for Jacqueline. She wants everyone to think she's the perfect mother and the perfect wife, but she's not."

"I wish I could help. . . ."

"You can't. And I'm sorry to burden you with this. It was wrong of me. It's just that talking to you makes me feel closer to Amanda. Tell her . . . I . . . love her."

"No, Matthew, I won't."

"Why not?"

"Because it would give her false hope. She's just learning to cope without you. It's not fair for you to run in and out of her life at your whim when you need emotional bolstering. Either leave her alone or fight with everything you've got to get her and keep her." Sylvia handed him her champagne flute. "Make a decision, Matthew. That's my advice."

Sylvia turned and went into the vestibule. She waited for a moment while the butler fetched her coat. The butler walked her to her waiting carriage.

Standing by the French doors, Sydney kept the conversation going around her, but her eyes were on the intense confrontation between Matthew and Sylvia. Sydney knew they were talking about Amanda. What she couldn't tell was whether Sylvia was leaving to deliver a message to Amanda or if she left due to a disagreement with Matthew. Matthew's expression was stoic, revealing nothing.

Sydney knew that if she watched Matthew closely for the next several days, she would find the answer to her question.

Amanda read about the Wade party in the columns the following morning. For two hours she waited until she knew Sylvia had risen. She made a second pot of coffee and continued going over the bills.

Amanda liked being in the office early when the presses were silent and she could concentrate. This was her world, she thought. Her apartment was the place where she slept, but this was truly the only home she'd known in America. She had never felt comfortable in David's house. None of it had ever been hers, nor did she feel he'd ever intended to share it with a woman.

And if she delved deeply enough into her heart, she would find that the reason she spent so little time at her own apartment was because it was the place she had shared with Matthew. Even though they hadn't been married, she'd *thought* of them as married. They were right for each other. They always would be.

She picked up the telephone and gave the operator Sylvia's number.

"You saw him yesterday, didn't you?" Amanda asked as Sylvia picked up the receiver.

"Good morning to you too, Amanda," Sylvia said lightly. "And yes, I did."

"Is he well? How did he look? Did he—?"

"Amanda, this conversation is taking you nowhere. I saw him. He's fine. Jacqueline is just as adorable as ever, very happy with her father. They seemed the perfect family."

"I see. . . ."

"Amanda . . . don't do this to yourself. He lives in another world, one that you have no part in."

Amanda felt as if she wanted to sink through the floor. "I'm always doing that, aren't I? Hoping . . ."

"Yes. And until the day he comes to you—which I see no evidence of—you have to go on with your own life."

"I know. But it's so hard."

Sylvia paused. "Why don't I come over today and we'll go out to lunch?"

"I can't. I have to much work to do. The bills are stacking up and I can't make any sense out of these ledgers."

"Let Andrew do it. He's supposed to take care of all that for you, isn't he?"

"Yes. But he's trying to find a house for Mary Alice. I never knew planning a wedding could take so much time and energy. She is forever telephoning him, needing his opinions. But I'm happy for him. He's finally found a girl he really loves."

"Good for him."

"I'm glad one of us has a chance at love."

"Amanda, please reconsider lunch."

"I will. And if not today, then tomorrow."

"Good. I'll talk to you then."

Amanda hung up the receiver. "God! I wish for once she wouldn't be so . . . *right*!" Amanda wanted the luxury of thinking about Matthew, pretending he was still part of her life, but Sylvia wouldn't let her.

Amanda was absentmindedly flipping through the bills thinking about Matthew when she abruptly stopped.

The bill from the paper supplier was one hundred and ten dollars higher than it was supposed to be. Amanda went through her files. She was certain that because they had increased their orders each month, they were entitled to a five-percent discount.

Andrew raced jauntily up the steps to the office. He'd had a memorable night at the opera with Mary Alice and some of their friends. They had all gone to Delmonico's for dinner, and Alexander Bissell had picked up the check. Mary Alice was going to meet him for lunch, and they were to look at a house just off Fifth Avenue and only two blocks from Central Park at two that afternoon. It was going to be a great day.

He twirled his bowler hat on his finger and flipped it onto his hat rack. He went next door to Amanda's office and stopped in the doorway. He noticed the ledger on her desk and the stack of bills she was double-checking.

"You're here early," he said merrily.

Amanda jumped with a start. "Oh, Andrew! I didn't hear you come in."

"What are you doing?" he asked with a smile.

"There seems to be a problem here. I distinctly remember the paper supplier telling me that we had a discount coming to us."

"Where's the bill?"

"Here." She handed it to him. "But they invoiced us for the full amount, and according to your ledger we paid the full amount."

"I remember this," he said. "They told me the new pricing would start next month."

"They did?" Well, I don't think that's any way to run a business, to promise us something and then renege. Perhaps we should change suppliers."

"Oh, I don't think we need to take drastic steps. After all, we're going to increase our order next month. Let me handle this. Perhaps I can get us an even better discount.''

"You think so?''

"Yes, I do.''

"All right. And would you double-check these bills? Some of this doesn't make sense to me.''

"How's that?''

"I don't know; I guess my head is rattled. The numbers don't match up.''

Andrew had to think quickly. "I know what's wrong! You don't have all the invoices here. Let me get them together for you. Then you can take them home tonight and work on them.''

"Tonight? I can't do it tonight. I've got two editorials to finish, and I have to go over the layout for the jewelry ads.''

Andrew held up his hand. "Amanda. Why do you take so much on yourself? This is what I'm here for, right?''

"I know. It's just you've been so busy with your wedding plans. . . .''

"Don't worry over these bills.'' He picked up the ledger and the invoices. "I'll get it all straightened out.'' Andrew wasn't worried. All he had to do was change a figure here, one there, and the books would look perfect, as they always did. Andrew was a master at embezzlement, though he would not call it that. He was simply getting an ''advance'' on his salary, he reasoned.

Amanda watched as he dashed out of her office, seemingly a bit too eager to start work. Andrew was not that industrious.

Suddenly, the memory of her confrontation with Quinton Parker flashed into her brain. She remembered the warning he gave her—not to trust Andrew. But she had countered then with the same feeling she had now. Andrew was her brother. If she couldn't trust her own family, whom could she trust?

Amanda came within an inch of picking up the telephone and calling her supplier to double-check. She had to stop and think about what it would mean to her relationship with her brother if she found him out. She wanted to believe that family was everything. It was incomprehensible to her that Andrew would steal from her. It was one thing for him to steal from Quinton, but to use her, her name, for his own selfish means—she couldn't believe Andrew would be that vile.

Trusting was probably the hardest thing for Amanda. She had never been able to trust herself with Matthew. She hadn't been able to keep her love alive long enough to trust that he would find a way. She couldn't trust fate or God to bring her the love she needed. She'd trusted God once with her child's fate and look what had happened. Trusting had always brought her pain. She knew she couldn't trust Matthew. But she knew she would have to, if only because she couldn't keep her love for him bottled in a tight can. What good was a love like that? Love needed to be used, nutured. She loved Andrew. She might not trust him, but she loved him. For that reason and that one alone, she hung up the phone and decided to let him prove himself to her . . . again.

Christine had gone to the gossips just as Sydney had known she would. When the May issue of *City Woman* hit the newsstands, New York critics were standing in line to take a shot at Amanda Granger. One journalist went so far as to suggest that the Granger Publishing Company be picketed.

Sydney noticed that the greatest outcry came from males, not females. And the story most lambasted was the one about a woman's right to choose a career rather than a family as her life's vocation.

It was too bad Sydney and Amanda were enemies, Sydney thought, for she agreed with Amanda's convictions.

However, the work Sydney had done thus far to discredit Amanda was not direct enough. She wanted more ammunition, and to get it, she had arranged this luncheon with David Simon.

He was wearing a brightly printed silk scarf around his neck, with his shirt unbuttoned at the neck, and a tweed jacket. Sydney had always thought his bohemian flare was too contrived. And she wondered if she'd chosen the wisest tack after all.

"David, how well you look," she said, motioning to him to seat himself.

They sat in the solarium, surrounded by blossoming begonias, daisies, and hothouse orchids. The maid brought tiny sandwiches and white wine.

"I was surprised at your invitation, Sydney."

"You shouldn't have been. I was under the impression you wanted to sell your art."

David was instantly flattered. "I do!"

She picked up a sterling fork. "David, I have given this matter considerable thought. I would like you to do a portrait of myself and my daughter."

"You what?" David was shocked. This was his first big offer in over a year. If Sydney Wade liked his work, she would tell her friends. This could be the beginning of a comeback for him. He would regain all the ground he'd lost since Amanda had left him, and then some. He'd be back on top.

"You still do portraits, don't you?"

"Of course. And I would love to sketch you and Jacqueline."

"I want to hang it in the salon," she said.

"Where everyone could see it," David said, his eyes growing wide with possibilities.

"Yes." She watched him as he ate and talked about what kind of poses they would use. He needed her right now in his life, and Sydney intended to take full advantage of the power she had over him.

"David, you can't know how much I sympathize with you over that nasty divorce of yours."

A bit surprised at the turn in the conversation, he said nothing.

Sydney sipped her wine. "All our friends still talk about how well you took it. I doubt I could use as much restraint as you've shown, knowing she's living down there in Chelsea . . . flaunting herself . . . her independence."

"It wasn't easy, Sydney," David replied, happy to have a sympathetic ear. "I'm sure you've heard the rumors that she's living with a man."

"Good God, no, David." Sydney offered the expected shock.

He nodded. "You have no idea the ridicule I've taken because of it."

Sydney watched him as he bent his head over his meal. No wonder Amanda had left him. He was weaker than any man she'd ever met. He nearly made her nauseous with his bleeding-heart pose. "How can you just sit there and take it, David?"

"Huh?"

"You're a man! Stand up for yourself. Fight back."

"How would I do that?"

"If I were you—as famous as you are—I'd go to the columns and tell my story. Denounce her in public."

David's eyebrows rose. "Well, I had promised her I would keep quiet about all this. She didn't force a financial settlement at the time."

"That was then. Her behavior is costing you clients, David. You can't overlook that."

"You're absolutely right," David said. It was time Amanda paid for the pain she'd caused him. "I'm glad you pointed all this out to me, Sydney. I hadn't realized that it was because of Amanda that my work has been suffering."

Sydney reached over and touched his hand. "We've been friends for a long time, David. I was unsure whether I should say anything or not—I didn't want to jeopardize our friendship. But I just couldn't let her go on abusing you the way she has."

David succumbed to Sydney's sincerity. "I had forgotten how important my friends were. Thank you for reminding me."

Sydney smiled in that cool, assured way that gave David confidence. "You can always count on me."

Amanda flipped the stack of newspapers over so she couldn't see the bylines or her name. In frustration she shoved them off the table, bolted to her feet, and screamed, "That son of a bitch!" The telephone jangled, but she ignored it. She flopped down into the overstuffed chair and drummed her fingers on the rolled arm.

There was something wrong with all this. Why was David coming out with accusations now? What did he care if she had a lover or believed in women's rights? David never did anything without a motive. He had to have something to gain. And then too, the whole thing didn't sound like him at all. For one thing, she reasoned, it was too clever. If he'd come to her office and created a scene, *that* would have been like David. If he'd purposely confronted her in a restaurant or at a party . . . *that* would be like David. He liked being on stage too much to pass up the opportunity.

Something was happening here, and she understood neither its reasoning nor its ultimate purpose.

Was it David's ego that simply wanted to see her magazine fail? Was that it? Or was this simply one of his drunken pranks?

"I don't care! I simply don't care!" she exclaimed to herself. "Let them all think whatever they want. Lies can't hurt me." She rose and gathered her things for work. She checked to make sure the windows were locked and turned off the lamp in the bedroom. She smoothed the bedcovers and as she did, a vision of Matthew's face flashed across her mind.

She wasn't frightened by David or newspaper columnists. From somewhere she had found the courage to get up every morning and face the day knowing she and Matthew would never be together. After knowing that kind of pain, everything else seemed insignificant.

Matthew angrily crammed the newspaper into his metal wastebasket. "Christ! What a vile little shit you are, David Simon!" he exclaimed as he read David's lies. Matthew went to the window.

The end of March had brought warmer winds than usual, and already the trees of Central Park were bursting into bud. Redbuds and a few dogwoods had blossomed, and everywhere there was the pastel green of early spring. It was a time for new life. And none felt it so poignantly as Matthew.

Jacqueline was the most wonderful child a parent could want. But each day as he got up to help the nanny bathe and dress his daughter, he was struck with how twisted his life had become. He had everything he'd always wanted, the success of a fabulous retail store, the growing respect of his father, and a beautiful daughter. He had everything but love. And even that was his for the taking if he would only have the courage to make the move.

But making that move involved the possibility that he would lose his daughter. Life was forcing him to make a choice, and it was one he wasn't sure if he should even be allowed to take. Wouldn't there be some retribution in the next life if he abandoned his daughter? And if he did not choose Amanda, perhaps God would punish him for that too.

" 'To thine ownself be true,' " Matthew mumbled to himself.

Not only were there no easy answers to his predicament— Matthew found no solutions at all. But he could no longer keep himself locked in a dreamworld where he and Amanda and Jacqueline were a family. He'd always been a man of action, a man who built dreams. Now life was putting him to the ultimate test. Matthew was well aware that reality negated the possibility of dreams.

Just then his telephone rang. It was his secretary. "Yes?"

"Mr. Wade, your wife is here."

"Send her in."

Matthew replaced the receiver and looked up to see his wife glide into the room swathed in a new black suede coat with ermine collar and cuffs. She'd bought it at Lord & Taylor, probably to make him angry. He didn't comment on the coat. The slight would make *her* angry.

"Hello, Sydney. What brings you down here today?"

Sydney was taken aback. "You mean you've forgotten again?"

"Forgotten?" He flipped through the pages in his appointment book. He had nothing written down all day.

She crossed her arms over her chest. "We're having lunch with your father."

"Ah," he said, knowing now why he hadn't made a note of it. "I can't make it."

Sydney's eyes narrowed. "Yes, you can. You've put this off for three weeks. He wants to see you. He's only asking for an hour of your time. There's nothing on your calendar, Matthew. I had your secretary look for me."

Matthew ground his jaws. "I must speak to her about that."

"Forget her. It's me you're angry with."

"How clever and discerning you are, Sydney."

Sydney realized she wasn't getting anywhere with this tack. She smiled at him, took a deep breath, and came at him from another angle. "I shouldn't have used your employee like that. I apologize." He was rigid and still staring blankly at her. "It won't happen again," she threw in, and he softened. "Matthew. I can't keep putting your father off like this. He only wants to talk to us about Jacqueline."

"What about Jacqueline?"

"I don't know. I assume perhaps a trust or something like that. James wants the best for her."

"Are you implying that I don't?"

"Good God, Matthew! What is the matter with you? Can't I say anything without you jumping down my throat?"

The muscles in Matthew's neck were taut, and already he felt his head pounding. It was true. Just Sydney's presence managed to set him off. He couldn't stand to be in the same room with her. When he saw her, he was reminded more intensely of Amanda. He wanted to explode and couldn't.

He let out a deep breath and flexed his hands, trying to gain control of himself. "All right. You win."

"Win? This isn't a war, Matthew. It's only lunch."

"Right. Only lunch," he said.

They met James Wade at a posh restaurant on the west side of the Park in the lower sixties. It was a new place for them all, and Matthew was surprised when Sydney knew the maitre d'. They were seated at the "best" table, which in Matthew's opinion was always the worst table, for he felt as if he were sitting on stage. Situated in the middle of the restaurant as they were, everyone would have to be deaf, blind, and dumb not to know of the Wades' presence.

The maitre d' flourished his arms about, signalling for their waiter, handing them menus, and incanting a dozen overly used compliments which he sprinkled over the heads of Sydney and James. When the man started to say something to Matthew, Matthew threw the maitre d' a cold look and he went scurrying away.

Sydney clucked her tongue. "Don't be so rude, Matthew."

"How do you know him? I've never seen him before."

"I don't doubt it. You never go *anywhere*. He was at the Hotel Albert, then briefly at the Waldorf."

"How do you have time for so many people's lives?"

"It's my business. Banking is people."

James interrupted. "That is precisely the reason why Sydney is good at what she does. In fact," he said, leaning back in his chair, smiling benevolently at his daughter-in-law, "she is one of the best bankers in New York."

Matthew looked at them, watching their mutual admiration feed and grow. Sydney received all the love and respect he'd wanted from his father for so many years. Curiously, now that he was at a point when he'd thought for so long that he would get what he needed so desperately, he didn't care. And it surprised him. He realized that he'd never had to prove anything to his father, but to *himself*. Now that Wade's was a success and its future looked bright, he wanted to break each month's records only to show himself that he could be better each time. It was competing with the goals he set for himself that mattered now.

He was glad for Sydney that his father liked her so well, admired her so much. It was no mean feat for a woman to garner that kind of admiration from James Wade. In her own way, Sydney was just as successful as Matthew was. He wondered if she felt as good about her accomplishments as he did about his.

Matthew looked at his father. "Sydney tells me you wanted to discuss Jacqueline."

James lit a cigar. "I do." He paused. "You know, I'd always counted on the first one being a boy, but, well, that isn't the case here. More time for that later, I suppose."

Matthew observed as his father, normally a man of little words, stumbled over this obviously emotional and difficult subject for him.

James tapped his cigar on the ashtray. "Working with Sydney and her father the way I have in the past few years has shown me that I need to make provisions for my granddaughter. Obviously, being a Wade, she'll always have money—provided she doesn't loose the whole kit and kaboodle in a card game." He laughed.

Sydney chuckled, but she could only think of Christine and the mess she was making of her life with no father to guide her. Christine would be the type to lose the family fortune in a poker game. Sydney shuddered. She prayed Jacqueline would inherit *her* brains and business sense and not Matthew's. Even though he was making a success of his store, Sydney still didn't trust it. He was too much the gambler for her.

"Jacqueline should have the best," James continued. "I want to see to it that she does, so I'm setting up an endowment for her. For a million dollars."

Matthew's eyebrows shot up and Sydney gasped aloud.

"I can see you both think it's generous enough."

Matthew was the first to regain his thoughts. "What's the catch?"

"Matthew!" Sydney said a bit too loudly and drew the attention of the chicly dressed matron and her daughter at the next table.

Matthew didn't miss a beat. He glared at his father. "I've known you too long, Father. You don't give anything that you don't get back. There's a million dollars sitting on the table right now, and you want something. What is it?"

"Matthew, you wound me."

"What's the price?" Matthew wouldn't relent. He brushed Sydney aside when she tugged on his arm.

James put the cigar down, his eyes deadly serious. "I want my granddaughter to inherit the Wade name and Wade fortunes. I want everything intact for her, just as it was handed to me by my father to run. You have repeatedly refused the family—"

"Never!" Matthew growled. "I've never rejected you. Just the job."

"It's one and the same."

"It's not. I'm a person, not an institution."

James's face was flushed, and the fact that Matthew remained calm but firm unnerved him. "Think of your daughter, Matthew."

Matthew leaned closer to his father. His eyes bore into those of the old man. "That's it, isn't it? Did you honestly think you could use my own daughter to blackmail me? Well, it won't work. By the time Jacqueline is of age, I'll be able to give her my own million-dollar trust. She'll inherit *my* Wade's. But I will never force her to make a choice between you and me. Who knows, Father? We might *both* lose."

Sydney couldn't contain herself any longer. "Matthew, think about what you're saying here. This is my daughter too. You can't make decisions that aren't yours alone to make. I won't allow this, Matthew."

"Allow? You won't . . . allow?" Matthew glared at her. For the first time in nearly a year the answer to his problems came to him in a flash of anger. "That's right, Sydney. You shouldn't allow any of this. If I were you, I wouldn't either."

She looked at him oddly, as if she were seeing a crazy man.

Matthew continued. "Father, you just said that Sydney was one of the most accomplished bankers you've ever seen. I would never do anything to stand in the way of my child or her future. I can't turn this endowment down since it isn't for me. What I am refusing is to be part of your scheme to get me back to the bank." He looked at Sydney. "I wonder just whose idea it was in the first place."

Sydney started to defend herself, but Matthew stopped her.

"Give the bank to Sydney. It's what she wants. It's the only thing she's ever wanted. Isn't that right, Sydney? There is nothing you desire, covet, love, more than the thought of running both your father's bank and the Wade Bank when James and Harlen die." He paused and could see that he'd struck home. "You want the million dollars for yourself. You want to play with it, invest it, but it isn't for Jacqueline that you need it. The one thing I won't stand for is for you to use *my* daughter as a pawn in your grab for power."

Sydney's eyes blazed as she glared at him, but she was at a loss for words.

He leaned so close to her, their noses nearly touched. "I'll give it all to you, Sydney. Everything your greedy heart desires—the bank, the future presidency, Jacqueline's trust. You can have it all. . . ."

Sydney's mind raced. She licked her parched lips. This was an offer that would never come to her again. The exchange would be expensive for them both. "And in return you would want—?"

"Custody of my daughter in the divorce."

Sydney was rigid, but not because she was in shock. She'd known for a long time the moment would come; she just hadn't expected it so soon. And she'd also known what her answer would be.

"It's a deal."

It was Matthew's turn to be shocked. But he made certain not to let it show. He turned to his father. "You are a witness to this."

James was stunned and couldn't speak. He only nodded his head.

Matthew rose. "I'll have my attorney contact yours in the morning."

"Very well," Sydney said, and she felt a cold rush when Matthew left the table with not another word.

When James finally managed to speak, he said: "You would trade your daughter so coldheartedly?"

"Don't preach to me, James. You were ready to blackmail your son to get what you want. We're exactly alike."

James realized she was right. They both knew how to deal at the highest levels and win. At that moment, James should have felt defeated because he'd lost out to Matthew again. But as he looked at Sydney, he finally saw that Matthew had no place at the bank; never did, never would.

"Don't worry, James. I know exactly what I'm doing. I haven't lost my husband or my daughter—yet."

Within an hour Sydney was back at her desk looking at the stacks of files from New York Mercantile Bank. Last week the smaller bank had requested the aid of Brinkley Bank in a series of bad loans one of their now ex-loan officers had made.

Sydney immediately picked up the file labeled Granger Publishing.

Sydney had never spoken more than obligatory salutations to Andrew Granger, and other than the fact that he was Christine's lover, she had never paid much attention to him or his business. However, after going over the loan that New York Mercantile had granted Granger Publishing, Sydney realized that it was time she did.

She perused the notes the loan officer from New York Mercantile had made about Granger Publishing. According to the accounts, Amanda's business was doing extremely well. Sydney's banker instincts went on alert. It was doing *too* well. Had Andrew come to her, she would have denied the loan. Which was probably why New York Mercantile was in trouble and Brinkley was not.

Sydney looked over Amanda's original loan papers. She went over the figures and compared them to figures she'd compiled on similar newly established publishing companies. She took some notes and wrote a list of telephone calls she would make in the morning concerning the publishing industry. She wanted to be very certain that if she made a move, it would be the right one.

Sydney was in a position where she could not afford a blunder. To her mind, she and Matthew were evenly matched this time. But this time, it was winner take all.

Matthew took long strides as he walked to his store. It was only forty degrees, and the gusts of wind stung his eyes, but he liked this kind of weather, for it seemed to stimulate both the senses and the mind.

In the past week since his luncheon with his father and Sydney, Matthew had been busy. He'd moved out of the house, met with his attorney, and filed for divorce. By the end of the month his new townhouse would be painted and ready for Jacqueline and the nanny to move in.

He knew that Sydney thought she'd come out a victor in the continual battle she waged with him. Matthew knew nothing could be further from the truth.

Sydney had deluded herself all her life into thinking that money was power. Sometimes her greed overshadowed her most life-affecting decisions, but even Matthew was surprised that she would give up her daughter for the bank. It shouldn't have, though. Sydney was just like his father, and there had never been a time that Matthew could remember when James was not preaching the credo of the almighty dollar. Matthew was glad Sydney had James to go to; they were two of a kind and deserved each other.

There was only one kind of power that Matthew believed in and that was the power of love. He knew from the moment he'd met Amanda that they were destined to be together. It was taking him longer to manipulate time and circumstances in his favor, but the result would still be the same. He and Amanda and Jacqueline would be a family.

He opened the glass door to his store and went in. It was hours before opening time. He took the elevator to his office and went straight to his desk. He picked up the telephone and placed his call with the operator. There was only one other person he knew of who would be at her desk this early—for he knew she was fighting the same demons as he.

It was picked up on the first ring.

"Amanda. I have to see you."

She had not spoken to him for almost a year. She had not seen him except for that brief moment on Christmas Eve, and suddenly she was afraid she wouldn't know how to act around him, what to say. Her hands trembled as she signed her name to purchasing orders, her voice cracked when she spoke to her employees that day. She couldn't think about work, she could only think about Matthew.

Noontime and her lunch with Max came and went. She tried twice to locate Andrew, but he was nowhere to be found. She assumed, as did the salesmen, that he was still out at Lord & Taylor's finalizing their ad.

She tried to bury herself in the stack of photographs Milton had given her, but her mind had gone haywire at seven that morning when Matthew had spoken her name.

"Why am I doing this to myself?" she demanded aloud and got up and walked around her desk. "He's married. He has a child. It's over." She checked the clock. Miraculously, it was nearly six. She looked out and saw that nearly everyone had left. With the most deliberate movements she'd used all day, she carefully put the photographs to one side, made notations for her secretary for the next morning, neatly arranged her desk, and then turned out the lamp.

She waited as the last of the editors left, and she locked the door behind her. As she slowly walked the six blocks to the cafe where Matthew had said he would meet her, she arranged her monologue in her head. She'd said all these things to him once before. Perhaps he just needed to hear them again. She could be strong again. Couldn't she?

She saw him through the half-curtained window, sitting at a table, impatiently playing with his teaspoon. He sipped his coffee, looked up, and saw her. His smile filled his face and instantly he was on his feet. He rushed outside and took her into his arms.

"Amanda. Amanda." He did not kiss her. He held her face in his hands and looked deeply into her eyes.

Amanda couldn't hold back any longer. She kissed him.

The flood of her emotions overwhelmed her. She felt as if she were tumbling over a waterfall, and she didn't want to stop. She held him tighter, trying to keep him as close as possible. In the back of her mind she knew this ecstasy could not last.

"I'll go to hell for this," she mumbled as he kissed her cheeks and eyes.

"That's a terrible thing to say."

"It's true."

"It's not. I love you."

"Oh, God, Matthew. Why are you doing this to me? Why are you torturing me?"

He pulled her closer. "This is nothing. Wait till I get you home."

"You don't understand what I'm trying to say."

"Yes, I do." He started walking toward her apartment. He kept his arm around her waist. She leaned into him.

She had tried to forget what it felt to be this close to him, to hear his voice igniting her mind and soul. But even her memories of him paled next to the reality of Matthew.

"I love you, Matthew."

"I know. And you needn't worry anymore."

They crossed the street, darted between young girls playing hopscotch, and then raced up the steps to Amanda's house. He unlocked the door for her and handed her back the key.

Once inside he took her in his arms and kissed her deeply again. He slipped her coat from her shoulders and rimmed her neck in tiny kisses.

"I've missed you more than you could know," she said.

"Oh, I have a pretty good idea. I wasn't exactly the happiest man myself. But all that is changed now."

Amanda stepped back from him. She was afraid to hope. "How?"

"I gave Sydney what she's always wanted. My inheritance—the bank."

"What?"

He took her hand and led her to the sofa. "I told you I would find a way to bring you, Jacqueline, and me together. The moment finally came when Sydney was ready to deal with me—on my terms."

"I can't believe this! You're sure she's really given in?"

"Let's say she had the collateral to make the bargain she's wanted all along. She finally decided to use it."

"Then Jacqueline is really yours. You'll raise her?"

"We'll raise her after we get married. If you still . . ."

Before he finished, Amanda threw her arms around his neck and kissed him, knocking him over on the sofa. "Of course," she said breathlessly.

Matthew held her, feeling the rapid pounding of her heart against his chest. He inhaled her perfume and stroked her hair. "It's going to take a year before the divorce is final. Can you wait that long?"

"Haven't I waited that long already?"

"I've already set the procedures in motion. I didn't want to come to you until I could offer you a life, Amanda. I wanted to give you more than just a promise." He reached into his pocket and pulled out a tiny box and handed it to her.

Amanda smiled as she opened it. She gasped when she saw the fabulous emerald-cut diamond surrounded by ruby baguettes. "It's . . . beautiful."

"Put it on," he said, helping her. "There. It's official. A year from today, we'll be married."

Amanda looked at the ring, then at Matthew. "I can't believe it. It seems too good to be true."

"Well, believe it. I never go back on my word."

Amanda's eyebrows knit together. "It's not your word I'm worried about."

"Sydney has what she wants, Amanda. And we have each other." He pulled her back to him and stroked her hair. "Everything is going to be wonderful from now on."

CHAPTER THIRTY-SIX

Andrew held his hands over Mary Alice's eyes as the carriage pulled to a halt.

"Don't you dare peek, Mary Alice," he said playfully as he took her hand and helped her down. She kept her eyes tightly shut.

"Now can I look?" she said, groping the air.

He steered her closer and stood her in the middle of the sidewalk so that the view was at its best light.

"Yes," he said proudly. "You can look now."

Mary Alice opened her eyes and gasped. "*This* is going to be out house?"

"Yes." He kissed her.

Together they gazed at the whitewashed Georgian facade townhouse. It was wider than most houses along Park Avenue. It had double doors beneath the portico, which was held up by two soaring marble pillars. The arched windows were sparkling in the morning sun. Just inside the black wrought-iron gate was a profusion of spring blooms that encircled the front steps and filled a three-foot-wide bed beneath the first-level windows.

Andrew reached in his pocket and took out the key. He handed it to Mary Alice. "It's yours."

She was giddy with delight. "I can't believe it! It's exactly the kind of house I would have picked."

"I know. I had inside help."

She stopped midway on the steps. "Father told you."

He nodded. "I wanted it to be perfect. He helped arrange the loan too. But I got the down payment on my own."

She kissed his cheek. "You're just as resourceful as I knew you'd be."

"That's the word for it, all right . . . resourceful." He paused, thinking of Christine. "Well, are you just going to stand there, or are we going in?"

Mary Alice excitedly unlocked the door and went in. The foyer floor was executed in pink-veined white marble, and the walls were painted a soft salmon with white trim. A soaring circular staircase twirled upward for four floors. On the left was a salon and an enormous dining room beyond. On the right was a library, and a small music room for Mary Alice. The kitchen was in the rear near the entrance to the herb garden.

"I thought you might want to have a landscape architect revamp the yard. There's much unused space behind the carriage house."

As they toured the enormous high-ceilinged master bedroom and bath on the second floor and the upper rooms, Mary Alice asked questions about the age of the house, the builder, the architect.

Finally, Andrew had to laugh. "Mary Alice, do you honestly think I would buy anything for you that wasn't the best?"

She put his arms around his neck. "No. You wouldn't."

He smiled most charmingly at her. "And now, young lady, comes the hard part."

"Hard part?"

"You have to decorate everything. And I think it would be wise if we started as soon as I sign the papers."

"You mean it isn't yours yet?"

"Ours."

"Sorry. Ours."

"The first of May. I wouldn't think of buying anything without your approval. I can't think you'd think I'd be that inconsiderate."

"Of course! How silly of me to think otherwise."

They walked to the end of the staircase and sat down. They looked at the wide expanses of area, looked at each other, and giggled.

"It's going to be great fun buying all the things for it, isn't it?" Andrew said. "I want good paintings for the walls. Something—"

"New. Light in color. Like the Impressionists are doing now in Europe. Perhaps we should go to Paris on a buying trip."

"Ah! Splendid idea," he agreed readily.

She turned to him. "I'm pretty set on what I want, Andrew. I think I should warn you now."

"How set?"

"I think we should have lots of French antiques. Quality pieces. Persian rugs. Silk drapes."

He watched as she stood and wandered into the salon. He followed her. He was awestruck as she bandied names about. His mind tried to tally the bill it would run, but he finally lost count. Thank God her father is paying that bill, he thought to himself.

"Sèvres china. Waterford crystal. Oh! And I have to have a chandelier from Florence. They're always in the best of taste. Viennese mirrors for the salon . . ." Suddenly she turned and clapped her hands together. "I can't wait to give my first dinner party."

"And who will we invite?" he said facetiously.

"The Astors, the Kanes, and, of course, the governor."

"The governor?"

"I'd like to talk to him about a few things."

"Really? Such as?"

"A referendum that would give women the vote."

Andrew tried not to let his face fall. For a moment he'd seen his future stretching out in front of him in a financially sound state of bliss, with nothing that would rock his boat. But then for a moment he'd forgotten the kind of woman he was marrying. His marriage to Mary Alice Howell would give him all the worldly comforts he could ever dream of and then some. But he was beginning to realize that with the life-style Mary Alice would demand came many treacherous pitfalls for someone like him. More than ever, Andrew realized he would have to take extreme care to keep his past—and his vices—in a tightly locked closet.

"I'll make you a bargain. You choose the guests and I'll choose the wine," he said.

"It's a deal."

Sydney looked at her calendar. April 10, 1898, would be a day she would never forget. Since the day Matthew had handed her his ultimatum, she'd decided what to do. It had taken her two weeks to gather all the information and have the paperwork ready. In precisely one hour, her bank auditors would call on Amanda Granger and demand an audit.

Sydney leaned back in her chair. She knew exactly what they would find. She was going through the motions now. Once it was discovered that Andrew Granger had taken out two loans against a company whose assets were less than twenty-five thousand dollars, she would have no trouble foreclosing on *both* loans.

The president of New York Mercantile Bank was elated that Sydney had agreed to do his dirty work for him. He'd gladly handed over his authority to her.

Sydney smiled, went to the window, and looked out toward the west, where Amanda lived. "Without that business, New York will finally see you for the whore you really are, Amanda. Adultery has its price."

Amanda looked at the pinch-faced man in his late forties. "I don't understand. I've made my payments. I sent copies of our books over to the bank in January just as Mr. Brinkley requested. What seems to be the problem?"

Stewart Anderson nodded to his partner Theodore Smythe, similarly dressed in a charcoal suit and bowler hat. "Miss Granger, the Brinkley Bank thinks there is some problem concerning the second loan that was taken out on Granger Publishing in February of this year. That transaction, as you know, came *after* your yearly audit."

Amanda shook her head. "There's been some mistake. I never took out another loan."

Stewart Anderson slapped his black leather briefcase on the desk and withdrew a copy of Andrew's loan papers. "No, that's correct. *You* didn't take out the loan with New York Mercantile. We have discovered that your brother, Andrew Granger, did. At the very least, Miss Granger, the bank feels there has been some misrepresentation here."

"Misrepresentation?" she mumbled as she took the papers and quickly looked them over. "This is incredible. . . ."

Theodore Smythe tried to eliminate the smug grin on his face, but he rather enjoyed watching people squirm a bit whenever he showed up on these audits. "You didn't know about the loan, Miss Granger?" He peered at her.

Amanda quickly gathered her wits. To admit anything to these men could result in criminal prosecution. "Oh, yes. *That* loan. For a minute, I didn't understand what you were referring to." She put the papers down confidently. "And," she said, motioning with her arm, "I'm sure you'll find our books accurate to the penny. Gentlemen . . ." she ushered them out and to Andrew's office.

Theodore sat in Andrew's desk chair as Stewart brought him the ledger books.

"If you need me for anything, I'll be right next door. I have a magazine to run." Amanda left them and went to her secretary.

"Yes, Miss Granger?"

"I want you to find Andrew for me. And don't even bother calling his accounts, because I'm sure he won't be there. Call the Howell residence first. If it takes all day—*find him.*"

"Yes, ma'am."

Amanda went to her office and closed the door. She picked up the loan papers. Her hands started to tremble as she thought of just how Andrew had arranged for the loan. He'd used the method Matthew and she had devised to hoodwink Harlen Brinkley on the original loan.

"This is enough to pay for a whole house!"

Amanda knew that twenty-five thousand dollars would buy a nice brownstone almost anywhere in the city. She suddenly realized that Andrew's expectations were even higher than she'd imagined. She wished now she had kept a closer eye on him, but she hadn't. She'd been too busy with the magazine, too busy with her thoughts about Matthew. And because of her negligence, she was now in a very precarious situation.

Worst of all, she'd trusted Andrew.

She'd paid no attention to the warning from Quinton Parker, to the rumblings from the salesmen about Andrew's lack of interest in the business. She's always covered up for him, even when they had lived with David. She thought she had been helping him. Instead, she had fostered this kind of behavior. She was just as much to blame as he.

She stuck her head out of the office doorway. "Did you find him yet?" she asked her secretary.

"The maid at the Howells' said they went shopping and then to a luncheon. I'm calling the restaurant now to leave a message."

"Good. I want to *talk* to him," she said angrily and shut the door.

Andrew and Mary Alice never showed up at the restaurant. Amanda talked to Mrs. Howell and left word for Andrew to telephone her at the office. Six o'clock came, and most of the employees left. Theodore Smythe and Stewart Anderson were still locked away in Andrew's office. They had not left all day. They never went to lunch or asked for coffee. They didn't speak to anyone, nor did they make any telephone calls. Amanda wondered if they were men or machines.

Fifteen minutes after six, both men emerged.

"We've completed our work, Miss Granger." Theodore Smythe carefully placed his bowler hat on his head. "The bank will be contacting you."

"About what? Isn't everything in order?"

"We found a few discrepancies in the books."

"Discrepancies?" She felt the floor sinking beneath her. She knew precisely what they were referring to. Andrew *had* been skimming the books. She'd been a fool to trust him.

"There is also the fact that you are heavily leveraged for the amount of income this company generates." Theodore Smythe smiled.

"*Heavily* leveraged," Stewart reiterated.

"Yes, well, I have to keep the presses running."

"Hmm. As I said, you'll be receiving a call from the bank. Good evening, Miss Granger."

They tromped out like retreating executioners.

Amanda flew to the telephone.

"I'm sorry to bother you again, Mrs. Howell, but has Andrew returned?"

"No. In fact, I'm glad you telephoned. He and Mary Alice decided to have dinner with friends, and then they are going to the theater tonight. Was it important?"

"Yes. But it can wait till morning. Thank you, Mrs. Howell."

Amanda did not replace the receiver but placed a second call.

"I have to see you," she said. "I'm in trouble."

Matthew arrived at Amanda's apartment in less than thirty minutes. Amanda was a bundle of nerves, pacing back and forth and wringing her hands as she explained everything to him. Matthew sat calmly in the upholstered chair, weighing matters. Amanda had a great deal to be concerned about, but Matthew was already seeing solutions where she was still dwelling on the problem.

"The simple truth is, Matthew, my brother is a thief!"

"Don't take it so personally."

"He's my brother!"

"He's not you!"

He went to her, put his arms around her, and tried to calm her.

"I'm sorry. I always seem tø be dragging you into my problems."

"It's allowed. I'm part of your life now. The good and the bad. But I think what we need to do is decide how we are going to handle everything."

She looked at him. "Did you tell Sydney about me?"

"No."

"She knows, though. I can feel it. I wonder how long she's known. It's obvious that this is all coming from her."

"I'm afraid you're right."

"It can't be the money. She doesn't need it. Would she press criminal charges, Matthew?"

"I've been wondering the same thing. I don't think so. I agree that she wants to see you destroyed. *But*, if she took this to court, there would be a lot of publicity. The press would find out about us, and it wouldn't look good for her image. If she has known about us for long, she'd made damn certain not to show it. That's *her* Achilles' heel. To a woman like Sydney, losing her husband to another woman would be a loss of power. No, I don't believe she would go to the law."

Amanda's face grew ashen. "I never would have thought anyone could hate me this much."

"Sydney probably doesn't even think of you as a person. Just as object in her way of getting what she wants. Believe me, I know."

"She's going to call the loans, isn't she?"

"Yes."

"Then I'll have to sell the magazine." She crumpled onto the chair.

"Hey! I thought you said I was part of your life."

"You are."

"I'll loan you the fifty thousand to pay both loans."

"I can't ask you to do that."

He tilted her chin up with his fingers. His face was stern when he spoke. "Damn it, Amanda. When are you going to realize we are a team? We may not be married yet, but we will be. If fate had been on our side, we would have met at a convenient time in our lives and had none of these problems. But we weren't so lucky. We're in this together. After we're married, you're still going to be running your magazine and I'm still going to run Wade's. What makes you think you're so special that you don't need any help once in a while?"

She looked at him, feeling all the joy and gratitude one gives a very special friend and thinking how lucky she was that he loved her too. "I can't do it all alone, can I?"

"Yes, given enough time, you'd find solutions on your own. But I'm glad you're forced into asking me."

"Why?"

"It shows you trust me."

She smiled. "I have had a bit of a problem with that in the past."

"A bit." He laughed and kissed her. "I can't help you with Andrew. That's a score you have to deal with on your own. But I'm behind you, whatever your decision is."

Amanda never had time to find Andrew that night or the next morning. Before the workday had begun she received a call from Harlen Brinkley's office summoning her to the bank for a ten o'clock meeting. Riding in the cab, Amanda thought about Andrew and Sydney. Both of them sought her downfall. And both of them had to be dealt with immediately.

Last night she had felt overwhelmed by all that was happening to her. But she remembered that it wasn't so many years ago when she'd had to deal with Lady Kent's dislike for her. Even though she'd been a child, she'd stood up for herself. In her naivety, she believed she could do anything, be anybody. Now she knew her vulnerabilities. She knew the risks she was taking, and she knew how much she could lose.

Sydney was only doing what any woman would do. She was trying to save her marriage. Amanda couldn't fault her for that. However, Sydney wanted her marriage for all the wrong reasons. She cared nothing for the man, for what Matthew wanted. Amanda wanted *only* the man, and she wanted him only because she loved him.

As she exited the carriage and went into the financial temple that was the Brinkley Bank, Amanda was confident again.

Harlen Brinkley, still pasty-faced, his old eyes tired from his bout with influenza, sat imperiously in his presidential chair. Sydney stood behind him, sun at her back, dressed in an excruci-

atingly expensive Parisian day suit. Sydney's smile was perfunctory as she motioned for Amanda to sit in the leather Chippendale
chair in front of Harlen's desk.

"Miss Granger. Finally we meet," Harlen cracked.

"I, for one, wish the circumstances would have been different," Amanda said politely. She calmly laid her hands in her lap
and sat easily in her chair. She looked directly at Harlen but
watched Sydney's face out of the corner of her eye.

Sydney crossed behind her father, went to the left of the desk,
and picked up a file. "My auditors gave us the report on your
company last night. I must say, we were greatly distressed by
what we found."

"Distressed?" Amanda stalled.

"Your books do not tally correctly, Miss Granger," Harlen
said.

"Those same auditors worked on my books at year's end. Did
they find any discrepancies in January?"

"No," Harlen said.

Sydney shifted her feet. Amanda noticed that her jaw tightened, but only by a nearly imperceptible fraction.

"Then these discrepancies you've found have been only since
the beginning of the year. Or more precisely, this past quarter. Is
that correct?"

"Yes," Sydney said firmly before her father had a chance to
respond.

"I presume you have a list to show me?" Amanda demanded.

"Yes." Sydney handed them to her.

Amanda glanced at it. It was just as she'd feared. Andrew *had*
been skimming from her, as he'd done with Quinton. The auditors had found over three thousand dollars that did not tally with
invoices and checks. Andrew's life-style was even more expensive than she'd imagined. She could live for nearly a year on that
kind of money.

Amanda smiled as she handed the copy back to them.

"Well, what do you have to say about all this?" Harlen
demanded.

"Nothing."

"What?" Sydney was taken aback.

"I hired a young and, I'm afraid, very inexperienced girl to
handle the books for me. Other than the fact that she'll be
reprimanded and I will have to hire a professional auditing firm

to do my books, I don't see that there's a problem. I think it was very nice of your bank to be so concerned with how I handle my business."

Harlen Brinkley was shocked at Amanda's lackadaisical attitude. "Is this how you run your business?"

"Not anymore. I just told you I would take care of my personnel problems."

Sydney quickly realized what Amanda's game was. She lifted her imperious chin. "The Brinkley Bank is founded on good business practices, Miss Granger. We cannot, in all fairness, give your mismanaged company the same privileges it grants others, who take such matters more seriously."

Amanda readied herself for the bombshell Sydney was about to deliver.

"We have also discovered that a second loan was taken out on your company. New York Mercantile Bank was the lender. The loan officer there tells me that the books he saw were quite different from what my auditors found yesterday."

"Did you see the copy of the books he is referring to, Mrs. Wade?" Amanda asked pointedly.

"No. But I trust his word."

"I wouldn't do that if I were you, Mrs. Wade. Don't trust anyone in business."

Sydney ground her jaws. This wasn't going well. Amanda's attitude was not what she had expected. Sydney had wanted her to grovel, to beg. Instead, Amanda acted as if she were at a Sunday luncheon. Sydney's instincts went on alert. She pressed harder.

"Miss Granger, I have known the owner of New York Mercantile Bank for years. He is an honest man. If he says they were different books, I believe him."

"That's your prerogative. What I'm trying to point out to you is that you have no physical evidence to prove his accusation."

Harlen Brinkley squirmed in his chair. He coughed. "What my daughter is saying, Miss Granger, is that you are overleveraged for the amount of income your magazine produces. My bank also feels that you are not using sound business judgement on a day-to-day basis."

Sydney interrupted him. She wanted to be the one to deliver the death knoll to Amanda Granger. "We're calling in both your loans."

"Both loans?"

"Yes." Sydney smiled.

"How long do I have to raise the money?"

"We want it by tomorrow." Sydney revelled in the moment.

Amanda was nonplussed. "That doesn't give me much time to sell the business."

"The bank will sell the company at auction," Sydney said.

"I see." Amanda rose. "And to whom would I give the check, if I had the money?"

Sydney wanted to smile victoriously, but instead she kept her lips firm, showing no emotion. "Either myself or my father."

Amanda turned to walk out the door. As she did so, she reached in her purse and pulled out a cashier's check for fifty thousand dollars.

Still with her back to them, she said, "Fifty thousand?"

"Yes," Harlen croaked.

Amanda turned around and walked back to Sydney. She stood very close. She wanted to look into Sydney's eyes as she handed her the money. She wanted to see if she had a heart, a soul. "You can have the money, Mrs. Wade. But that's all."

Sydney did not flinch. She took the check and continued looking into Amanda's blue eyes. She did not waver. She did not speak.

Amanda slowly turned and walked away, chilled to the bone as she realized what kind of woman Matthew had been married to all these years. And as she closed the door to the presidential office, she realized that she had saved her business and saved her brother from criminal charges, but she had not saved herself. Sydney Wade was not defeated. The war had just begun.

CHAPTER THIRTY-SEVEN

Christine Van Volkein blew on the dice as Andrew tossed them across the green felt crap table.

"A winner!" Andrew cried as Christine gulped another glass of champagne and dribbled a few drops down the front of her low-cut beaded gown.

She giggled, leaned her voluptuous breasts into him, and whispered: "I made a mess of myself. Why don't you lick it off?"

Andrew only smiled at her, took the dice again, and rolled them. Christine was so high on cocaine tonight it would be hours before she came down to earth. But he wasn't worried. Paul was in Baltimore on business, and they were spending the night at their favorite hotel. In fact, they'd spent so much time there, Andrew had moved out of his apartment in Hell's Kitchen where he'd lived since leaving David's house and into the Hampton House Hotel.

He spent his obligatory days with Mary Alice, took her to dinner, and always had her home by midnight. Then he would meet Christine and they would gamble, dance, drink, and make love till nearly dawn.

Andrew had not been to the magazine in five days. And he didn't care. Tomorrow he would be telling his sister that he was leaving for good. He had enough money from Christine and his winnings to keep him going until he and Mary Alice were wed in late June. Besides, he didn't have *time* to work. He couldn't believe how much effort it took to plan a big wedding. If he and Mary Alice were not discussing wedding details, they were shopping for the new house. There were luncheons and parties given for them nearly every other day. Andrew loved it. He hadn't had to pick up a check for weeks. Being the bridegroom had more advantages than he'd ever imagined.

"Andrew! You won again!" Christine squealed as she raked the money toward her.

Andrew picked up the dice. "Bet it all!"

Christine clapped her hands in glee. "How exciting! There must be over two thousand dollars there."

"Blow on the dice . . . for good luck." He waited as Christine did as she was asked.

Christine downed the last of her champagne. Her bloodshot eyes glanced around the table at the expectant faces.

Andrew rolled the dice. "Boxcars! Winner take all!" he shouted.

Christine dropped her glass on the table and started pulling the money toward her. "You're a king! I knew you'd win!"

"Come on," he said, picking up the last of the money and shoving it in his pockets. "Let's go celebrate."

They left the opulently appointed gambling room and exited through the rickety warehouse doors. Camouflage was the major calling card of the Spendel gambling operation, which had been in existence for only six months. But it was already the hottest place in town. Though it was located in Herald Square with all the rest of the bawdy places, its clientele was strictly uptown. Fortunately for Christine, the society friends she saw here were the kind that kept their mouths shut. Or so she hoped.

Once in the carriage, Christine couldn't keep her hands off Andrew. "Take me here, Andrew. Right now. I can't stand waiting any longer."

"You're going to have to." He pushed her away.

Angry at his rebuff, Christine tore at his clothes. "Don't ever do that to me again!" She grabbed him and then lowered her head.

"Christine, don't," he demanded. But within seconds he was in her power. He placed his hands on her head. "Yes, Christine. Do."

Paul Van Volkein arrived home a day earlier than planned. He had hoped to take his wife out to dinner and perhaps the ballet to celebrate closing a large real estate deal he'd been working on for over six months. However, when he arrived home at seven, the housekeeper informed him that Mrs. Van Volkein had gone to dinner with the Armstrongs.

Paul telephoned them and found that they had gone to Delmonico's. Too weary for socializing with friends, Paul took a hot bath, put on his velvet robe, and settled next to the fire with a novel. He would wait until Christine returned at nine.

Paul fell asleep and did not awaken until midnight. He found that his wife was not home.

By one in the morning, Paul was no longer worried but furious. He built a fire, drank a brandy, and paced. By two, Christine was still not home and the brandy bottle was half gone.

At four-fifteen he heard a carriage outside. He dashed to the window and saw Christine.

"Bitch." He poured another brandy, but not to give him courage; he knew what he was going to do. This was the first brandy of the night he savored.

Christine was still reeling from the cocaine when she opened the door to their bedroom. She sobered instantly when she saw her husband standing by the fire.

"Paul!"

"Where have you been?"

"I went to dinner with the Armstrongs."

"I know that. I mean afterward."

"I went for a drive."

"To where, Christine?" He walked forward.

"I . . . I was at Mother's."

"I don't think so. You would have been home earlier. Or stayed all night. Why didn't you stay all night, Christine? Afraid the hotel clerk would say something? Or the neighbors?"

Christine gathered her wits. Paul knew too much. She took off her gloves and hat. "I don't know what you're talking about."

He dropped his brandy on the floor and was instantly beside her. He grabbed her by the shoulders.

"Oh, yes, you do, bitch. I thought I had cured you of other men, or is Andrew Granger really all that good?"

"Andrew Granger?"

"You don't honestly think I'm that stupid, do you, Christine?"

"I . . . I—"

His grip grew stronger. "Maybe you're the one who is stupid," he said, pushing on her shoulders until her knees started to give beneath her. He pushed harder and harder until she was kneeling at his feet. She kept her eyes locked on him.

"What is the matter with you, Paul? You're acting crazy."

"I'm acting sane. A sane husband would have stopped you long ago. It's time we had this out." His eyes blazed with anger.

"Let me go, Paul."

"No. Get this straight, Christine. I don't love you. I've never loved you. And you don't love me."

"Paul, that's not true. . . ."

"Truth time, Christine. All you've ever cared about is wearing my name and jewels. You've never wanted *me*."

"What . . . what are you saying—that you want a divorce?"

His grin was malicious. She deserved this punishment. "Is that what you want, Christine?"

"No! Never!"

"I thought not. You worked too hard to get me. But you took me for a fool, and I'm nobody's fool—least of all yours."

Christine gulped. She felt as if the blood in her veins had turned to ice. She'd never seen Paul like this . . . so angry, so strong. It was exciting . . . he was exciting. "What do you want?" She licked her lips as she felt lust mounting within her.

"I want it all. And you're going to give it to me."

"Anything."

"I want a child. I need someone to love, someone who loves me back. Since you can't do that for me, a child will substitute nicely."

Christine nearly cringed at the thought. "I'll do it."

"I know you will. And I want you to break it off with Andrew and anyone else you're seeing."

"He's the only one."

"God help you, I believe that. I promise you this, Christine— from this day forward, I'll have you followed if you break your word to me. If I ever, *ever* find out that there is another man, you'll be out on your ear. No husband, no jewels, no clothes, and I'll make certain your reputation is sullied so that no man would ever want you again."

Christine couldn't help the smile that crept to her face. She'd always wondered what she would feel like if Paul became the master. She found she liked the harsh tones in his voice as he berated her, put her in her place. She wanted, *needed* to be told what to do and when to do it. She had needed a strong, dictatorial man. She'd never had a father. She'd never had a man to tell her "No." Now Paul was telling her just that.

She felt a wet stickiness between her legs.

"Take your hands off me, Paul. You're hurting me."

"I know," he said but did not move. "Promise me, Christine."

"I promise. So help me God," she said earnestly.

Paul removed his hands and put them on the side of her face. He leaned down to kiss her. "To seal the bargain," he said.

She kissed him with all the passion within her. "I can make you love me, Paul."

"Never," he said, thinking of Amanda, the one woman who would always hold his heart.

Christine unbuckled his belt, then unbuttoned his trousers. "I can make you want me."

Paul looked up the ceiling as he felt her hands caress his legs, then move up his thighs. "God," he said as she slowly rose, blazing a trail of hot kisses up his abdomen, to his chest, and then to his mouth. "I have always *wanted* you."

Amanda went to Andrew's apartment in Hell's Kitchen. Because they'd seen each other every day at the paper, she'd never asked him about the place where he lived. He'd never invited her for dinner. She rarely invited him to her apartment. When they did have a moment together, they usually shared a lunch at Rector's. She supposed their relationship was not much different from that between other brothers and sisters who, once they were grown, seemed to find their ways through life still connected but not familiar anymore.

So it was with her and Andrew. Until he met Mary Alice they had been much closer. But for over a year, she rightly assumed he was trying to woo his lady love and she was trying to build her magazine.

Now, everything had changed. Or at least Amanda's perspective on her brother had changed. She had to admit for the first time that Andrew probably did not love Mary Alice at all. He was using her just as he'd used Amanda. Andrew had stolen from Amanda; he would steal from Mary Alice. It wasn't just the money that bothered Amanda; in fact, that bothered her the least. It was his manipulation of her trust that hurt most deeply. And it was that pain that brought her here today.

She knocked on the door. There was no answer. It was very early and she knew he would still be asleep.

She knocked again and still there was no answer.

Just then, the door opposite her opened. A middle-aged woman with a tangle of long gray hair, wearing a soiled robe wrapped around her ample body, stepped out into the hallway.

"Who you lookin' for?"

"Andrew Granger."

The woman's eyes opened in surprise. "How would he know the likes of you?"

"I'm his sister."

"Bah! He wouldn't have no one fine as you fer a sister."

Amanda grew impatient. "I'm not going to argue the point. Do you know where he is?"

The woman smirked at her. "Some sister you are. Don't even know he moved out nearly a month ago. You from out of town?"

Amanda was rattled. He'd moved out and hadn't even told her. But then, she knew very little about her brother. "Yes. From California."

"That's a long way."

"Do you know where he went?"

"Nah! It's none of my business!" She retreated inside her apartment.

Amanda went downstairs and inquired of the apartment manager if Andrew had left a forwarding address.

"None given," the unshaven man said. "Said he was movin' uptown. I didn't believe him at the time. But now"—he eyed her up and down—"I'm not so sure."

Amanda left. She had no choice but to track Andrew down through the Howells. She would have to use extreme caution. She didn't want to upset Mary Alice. It was going to be a terrific blow to the young girl, but somehow Amanda believed Mary Alice would weather the crisis.

"He knows you're here tonight?"

"Yes. It was his idea."

"Christine, your husband is nuts."

"I came here to tell you that I can't see you anymore. It's over."

Andrew had many plans for his future. Losing Christine was not one of them. He tried to put his arms around her. She pushed him away.

"Christine, this is ridiculous. We'll just be more careful from now on, that's all."

"He's having me followed."

"Jesus!"

"I've got too much to lose, Andrew. Can't you see that?"

"You've always had a lot to lose."

"Not like this. This time it's different."

Andrew wasn't about to give up without a fight. He went to her. He let his handsome face hover over hers. His eyes smoldered with lust. "Tell me how you're going to make it through the hot, torrid summer without me." He picked up her hand and placed it on his chest. He ran it down his ribs, around to his back and to his buttocks. "Who is going to give you what I give you, Christine? I know just how you like it."

He kissed her, his tongue darting and probing her mouth forcefully. It was the kind of kiss that always melted her resolve. He felt her grasping his buttocks. She moaned.

"You need me, Christine." He pressed his hips into her. She moaned again.

Suddenly, she broke away. "I can't! I can't!"

"Yes, you can."

"No. I wouldn't know how to live without Paul's money. I have to have it. I have to have him. You don't know how he is now. So strong . . ." She started to cry.

"I'm stronger, Christine." Andrew was unrelenting.

"He doesn't love me, you know. He told me so."

"I love you, Christine."

"No, you don't. I should have known better than to get mixed up with Amanda's brother."

Andrew stopped. "Amanda? What's she got to do with anything?"

"Paul loves her. I've always known that. I guess that's one of your attractions for me, Andrew. I thought if I could get you, it would be getting back at Amanda. I've always hated her, you know. Her being The Granger Woman. David was spellbound by her. Just like Paul is. I wanted you so that it would make her angry."

"Really? I thought it was my—royal blood—you liked so much!" Andrew felt that ever-present rage unleashed inside him. He wanted to hurt Christine as she was hurting him. No man likes being emasculated. All his life women had been trying to push him down, keep him in the slums. Harriet had been the first—she had never believed in him. And then Amanda. Always

Amanda. She got everything she wanted and he got nothing. He deserved more out of life than any of them. He'd never met a woman he didn't hate.

As he stood there glaring at Christine, he realized how he could get back at her and his sister. God! He'd waited years to open his evil box. Now was the time.

"True. That was part of your allure."

"I thought so. Well, I've got a little piece of news for you." He walked closer, his eyes white hot with anger. He leaned very close to her. "There is no royal blood. You were never fornicating with a lord. It was all a lie." His grin was malevolent.

"What?"

"That was a little story Amanda and my mother cooked up to launch Amanda in American society. Before she came to New York, my little sister was a housemaid."

"I don't believe it."

"Ask her. Or better yet, ask Sylvia."

"Sylvia Hendrickson was in on it too?"

"Yes. Wouldn't your friends all like that little piece of gossip?"

Christine watched him, hate seething from his every pore. For a moment she feared for her life. "You disgust me!" she said and whirled away from him. She raced to the door and yanked it open. She never looked back as she swept down the hotel stairs and into her waiting carriage.

From the window, Andrew watched her leave. In a few days he would sign on his house. Tomorrow he would talk Mary Alice into eloping. They would still go through with the wedding and reception in June. But Andrew knew he needed to have her signature on a wedding certificate *before* Christine went to the gossips.

Andrew regretted his outburst. He shouldn't have given in to his anger, but a lifetime of hatred had come out at that moment. He knew it would destroy Amanda, but it could also hurt himself. It was a stupid mistake. But mistakes could be rectified.

If he moved quickly and carefully, his future could still be salvaged.

Matthew sat on the window seat holding his daughter. She wore a pink cotton dress and pink ribbons in her long curls.

"You look like an Easter present . . . ready to open," he said and tickled her ribs.

She squirmed around. "Quit, Daddy!" She laughed again.

"I missed you, Jacqueline."

"Not as much as I missed you. It was so lonely without you."

Just then the nanny came into the room. Sydney had dismissed Mrs. Collingswood, much to Jacqueline's dismay. Matthew thought she'd done it just to anger him. Mrs. Shane was in her fifties, thin and tall. She was immaculately uniformed, and though she did not hail from England as her parents had, her references were impeccable. Matthew was pleased with her, though he often wished she weren't quite so formal. However, she was one of the few applicants who did not snub their noses at a father who wanted to spend more time in the nursery than the mother did. He sensed that Mrs. Shane did not approve of Sydney's attitude toward Jacqueline any more than he did.

Mrs. Shane stood at the door smiling at him, with an armload of folded clothes.

"Are you packed yet?" Matthew asked.

"Nearly so. I arranged for a delivery man to take the heavier trunks and suitcases. Are you certain you won't be needing any of this furniture?"

"No. I have everything." He smiled and pulled Jacqueline closer to him.

"Everything, Daddy? Even toys?"

"New toys and all your old toys will be there."

"It's going to be wonderful, Daddy. But I don't care what it's like, just as long as you're there."

Sydney arrived at home after an exhausting day at the bank. She inquired of the butler about the mail and asked the cook about dinner. The downstairs maid took her hat, coat, and gloves.

"Were there any calls for me today, Edna?" Sydney asked as she flipped through the mail.

"None that I didn't refer to the bank." Edna's eyes travelled upward toward the staircase.

Sydney glanced at her and then back at the mail. "Did my new stationery arrive today? I asked the salesclerk to have it sent over."

The girl did not answer. She shifted back and forth on her feet. Edna's eyes were still focused on the staircase when Sydney looked at her again. The girl seemed unduly nervous.

"Is something the matter, Edna?"

"I don't know, ma'am."

"Out with it, Edna. I haven't got time for this."

"Yes, ma'am," the girl replied, still debating the placement of her obligations. "Mr. Wade came today."

"Matthew? Here?"

"He's here for Jacqueline. Mrs. Shane has been packing all day."

"It was today. . . ." Sydney said to herself, shoving the mail into Edna's hands. "I'd forgotten it was today."

Quickly, she picked up her skirts and mounted the stairs. In her desire to wrest Amanda from her magazine, she'd forgotten about her bargain with Matthew. She *had* told him he could fetch Jacqueline today. It was a day she never thought would come.

Sydney confidently walked into the nursery.

"Matthew." She nodded as if she were not surprised to see him. He would expect her to remember. "You didn't get my message?"

"Message?"

"Yes. About Doctor Peterson's advice."

"No, I didn't." Matthew stood, instantly suspicious.

Sydney smiled wanly at Mrs. Shane. "You needn't bother with those. Jacqueline will be staying here."

"What?"

In two strides Matthew was at Sydney's side. "Don't do this, Sydney. You break our bargain and there will be hell to pay."

"Goodness, Matthew! Your new life-style has done nothing for your patience. I didn't say I was breaking my word, now, did I? What I said was that Jacqueline must stay here for a few days until she's better."

"Better? What's the matter with her?"

"She's had a dreadful cold the past two days, and the doctor doesn't want her going out. Especially in the evenings. The trip might be too much for her."

"We're not going overland across the country. It's not even a mile away."

"I don't care. I won't let you risk a relapse. Maybe you don't take your responsibility as a parent as seriously as you should."

"I don't believe this," he said exasperatedly. "And I don't believe you." He turned to his daughter. "Jacqueline, are you sick?"

She didn't understand what was happening, but she answered

her father truthfully. "I did have the sniffles, Daddy. The doctor came. . . ."

"It doesn't sound too grave to me."

Sydney stood her ground. "Call the doctor, if you don't believe me. For an overprotective father, you certainly have changed."

"All right, all right. He'd say anything you told him to. You probably set this story up days ago. But just in case she is sick—"

"I'm only thinking of *our* daughter's health."

Matthew ground his jaws. Sydney knew just how to get to him, and he could tell she loved twisting the knife. She could play her games for now, but the end result was that he would have Jacqueline—very soon. He went to the chair and picked up his coat.

"Have it your way. I'll give Jacqueline a few days to 're-cover.' Then I'll bring my own doctor to look her over. I'll take her home with me then."

"Daddy . . ." There were tears in Jacqueline's eyes. "Don't make me stay."

"It'll only be for a day or two. I promise."

"Honest?"

"Yes. I'll be back for you. Count on it."

"I will," she said, holding tightly to Mrs. Shane's hand, her only ally in a world she couldn't control.

Matthew kissed his daughter and left.

Mrs. Shane turned to Sydney. "Would you like to read to Jacqueline?"

Sydney flashed her a disdainful look. "No," she said flatly and left the room.

"I thought not," Mrs. Shane said and hugged Jacqueline to her.

CHAPTER THIRTY-EIGHT

Amanda held Matthew's hand as they sat on the terrace. It was a beautiful April night. The tiny area was perfumed with the fragrance of hyacinths and lilac. All through dinner Amanda had been quiet, saying little of her day. Matthew, too, had been in a pensive mood.

She turned to him. "I know why *I'm* not good company tonight. What's your excuse?"

Without looking at her, he said: "I went to get Jacqueline today and Sydney refused to let her go. I'm going to have to use more forceful measures."

"Oh, Matthew. I'm sorry. You were so sure. . . ."

"One is never sure with Sydney. She's only stalling. She can't hold out forever."

"I wonder."

"What?"

"After my meeting with her yesterday, I think she's capable of anything. She's almost frightening, she's so coldhearted. But in a way I feel sorry for her."

Matthew's head swiveled around. "You feel sorry for her? Believe me, Sydney can take care of herself."

"She has nothing, Matthew. And she doesn't even know it. But someday she will, and the impact will be devastating."

"I doubt that day will ever come. She made up her mind a long time ago about what was important to her and what was not. She would never admit defeat. Right now, she is revelling in this fight."

"Do you think she'll really try to keep Jacqueline?"

"One never knows with Sydney. She's proving that she can be quite devious."

Amanda squeezed his hand. She didn't want to tell him that she thought his fears were justified. Sydney had never been just another woman. She was more than rich and powerful. She was intelligent and ambitious. She was used to getting what she wanted. And, Amanda sensed, she was a fighter. Just as she, Amanda, was.

Amanda didn't know how far Sydney would go, but she was counting on the fact that she was becoming desperate. Matthew was right; Sydney was only stalling for time. But why? What advantage would time give her? Amanda went over her business with a discerning eye. There was no way Sydney could take it from her now. Because Sydney's vulnerabilities lay in her business, she had assumed that for Amanda it was the same.

Unfortunately, now Sydney knew better.

Amanda wondered, as she watched the branches of the plum tree block out the moonlight, which one of them Sydney would attack next.

Mrs. Howell greeted Mary Alice with a kiss. She allowed Andrew to kiss her hand.

"How lovely you look this evening, Mrs. Howell," Andrew said, using his best charm.

"Why, thank you, Andrew. Would you care for some tea in the salon?"

"Thank you, Mother." Mary Alice removed her evening cape.

"Your sister telephoned here three times today, Andrew, looking for you."

Andrew had been avoiding Amanda's calls for days. Amanda had even tracked them down at Delmonico's at noon. He'd bribed the maitre d' to lie for him. It was ten dollars well spent.

"Oh, that." Andrew laughed lightly. "Just a minor crisis at the magazine. But we've taken care of it. I'll have to instruct Amanda not to bother you with these calls of hers."

"I don't mind, although the maid has mentioned that your sister seemed upset. Even said it was urgent."

Andrew smiled and took Mrs. Howell's arm as they walked into the salon. "Please don't worry your pretty head about such things. It's just business. Amanda sometimes gets rattled, with so much to do."

"I can understand," Mrs. Howell said, sitting on the settee. "A woman has no place in business."

"Mother!" Mary Alice exclaimed.

"You know very well how I feel about such things, Mary Alice."

Andrew laughed as he helped himself to some cognac. "Better not let my sister hear you say that."

Mary Alice scowled at her mother. Mrs. Howell rose. "I'll see to the tea."

Andrew watched her leave. "I hope Amanda hasn't caused any problems here."

"No. Don't worry about it."

He sat next to her and kissed her quickly and deeply. She didn't pull away but indulged him.

"I don't think I can wait till we're married, Mary Alice," he said, letting his eyes reveal more passion than usual. He kissed her neck and caressed her breast. "I need you—now."

"But we have to wait," she said breathlessly.

"No, we don't," he said.

"Andrew!" She pulled away. "I want to be a virgin on my wedding night."

"I'm not suggesting that you wouldn't be."

"What do you mean?"

"Let's elope."

"Andrew, that's impossible. All the plans have been made. There will be over five hundred at the reception. The columnists are already calling it the wedding of the year."

"I wouldn't deprive you of your wedding, Mary Alice. I like all the preparations, the parties. I want you to have everything."

"I honestly don't understand what you're talking about at all."

"We could elope. Get married by a justice of the peace. It would be legal. And then you'd still be a virgin on your wedding night. We wouldn't tell a soul. Only we would know."

"I can't do that, Andrew. We wouldn't be married in the eyes of God. The state is incidental to me. Man's laws change every day. You know that. It's God's laws I care about."

"Mary Alice, please. I want you so much."

"Then you'll just have to wait for me. It's almost May. It's only eight weeks till the wedding. Surely I'm worth waiting for."

Crestfallen, Andrew leaned his head over her hand so that she wouldn't see the panic in his eyes. He kissed her fingers one by one. "Will you at least think about it?"

"No. My mind is made up. That's just the way I am. Take it or leave it."

He looked at her. She was more self-assured than he would ever be. And why not, he thought. She was born to money and position. She had every reason to be confident. For the life of him he wished he'd picked a girl that was a bit less headstrong. Why couldn't Mary Alice have been more like her mother and less like her father?

"I'll take it," he said and kissed her lightly on the lips. He had no choice.

Sydney watched as the man approached her desk. By the common cut of his clothes and the everyday look of his face she knew who he was.

"Mrs. Sydney Wade?"

"Yes."

"Mrs. Matthew Wade?"

"Yes."

He opened his coat and pulled out a long white envelope. He handed the papers to her. Her fingers clasped around it tightly.

He tipped his hat. "Good day, madam."

She watched him leave, and as soon as the door shut, she dropped the papers as if they'd scalded her hand.

"God." She stared down at them. Her divorce papers. Matthew wanted her to sign them. If she didn't he would never turn over his inheritance to her. She wanted the position at Wade Bank—badly. But she also wanted to keep her marriage intact. There was no way of talking Matthew into leaving Amanda. She could only use Jacqueline to play for time. A week here or there really wasn't going to make much difference in the end, though.

Dejectedly, Sydney realized that she was running out of time and options.

Just then the telephone on her desk rang.

"Mrs. Van Volkein is here," her secretary said.

"Tell her . . ."

The door opened. Christine breezed into the office. "Put that thing down. I don't know why I bother with that woman out there anyway. When are you so busy you can't see me?"

"Christine, this is a place of business."

Christine leaned over and placed a perfunctory kiss on Sydney's reluctant cheek. "Be nice to me, Sydney."

"I can't."

"Why not?" Christine asked casually, slipping off her new spring coat and leather gloves.

"I'm not in the mood." Sydney rose and went to the window. "I guess you might as well know. In a few days it'll be all over town. I was just served divorce papers."

Christine looked up and blinked. "Why does this not surprise me?"

"Have you no sympathy?"

"For you? You never had any for me. Besides, you can take care of yourself."

Sydney crossed her arms angrily across her chest. "Did you come here to stick the knife in further, or was there some other pressing issue?"

"I came here to save your life."

Christine wallowed in the surprise on Sydney's face. She went to the fireplace, and looked up at the portrait David Simon had painted of Sydney and Jacqueline. "It turned out rather well. It's a touching gesture you should want the portrait of your daughter here at the office where you can see it more often."

"Will you quit blabbering about David's silly portrait and tell me what you meant by 'saving my life'?"

"I just want you to know that I'm your friend, Sydney. I took your advice and I broke it off with Andrew."

"Christine, please. I don't want to hear any more about your affairs."

"You should. This one is very interesting."

Sydney moved closer and sat on the sofa. She sensed that this time Christine was not playing games. Christine joined her.

"Tell me."

"Amanda Granger is not a 'lady' at all. In fact, she's miles away from any royal blood. She's not even as well born as you or I. The closest she ever came to having royal blood was being a housemaid to a lord in London."

"Christine, are you sure?"

"Andrew told me himself. He said that Amanda, his mother, and Sylvia Hendrickson concocted the whole thing to pass Amanda off on us. We've all been taken in by her. You, me, Caroline—"

"Matthew . . ." Sydney said, realizing the ramifications of what Christine had told her.

"Yes, Matthew," Christine said smugly. "Everyone knows about Matthew filing for divorce, Sydney. Joseph Ross's secretary has a loose lip. After I heard about it, I remember what you'd said about Amanda having an affair with a married man. I put two and two together and came up with Matthew and Amanda. I knew this information was too important to you to keep to myself. I'll tell you, Sydney, I was skeptical when Andrew told me this. When I think of all the time I'd spent envying her—her beauty, the fame David gave her. She never really had anything at all, did she?"

"No, and she still doesn't," Sydney said. It was all falling into place for her now. She knew what to do. With this information, Sydney could end this energy-consuming, time-wasting battle with Amanda Granger. For the first time in her life, Sydney felt close to another human being. Christine *was* a friend. And she had brought her a truly rare gift indeed—hope.

At precisely the same moment that Sydney and Christine sat beneath David Simon's portrait plotting Amanda's demise, the artist of that portrait was toasting his ex-wife.

He sat in his studio surrounded by hundreds of sketches of The Granger Woman. He splashed too much Mumm's champagne on the floor and not enough into his glass.

"Oops!" He laughed to himself. "Don't bother. The maid'll get it."

"I toast you, Amanda. My greatest creation."

He drank his wine and tried to focus on the portrait in progress. He picked up the charcoal again and sketched, but it wasn't coming out the way he wanted.

"No good. No good!" he stormed and slammed the charcoal on the floor. "Ah! I know." David went to the cupboard and opened the drawer. He pulled out the jar of cocaine. He filled both nostrils. He breathed deeply once, twice.

"That's better," he said and went back to his perch.

The sun was setting and the light was not as good as it had been earlier. He looked at the empty chair in front of him and then squinted.

"Amanda? Are you there, darling?"

Suddenly, she came into focus. She was angelic looking in a white lawn gown with pink embroidered flowers. She wore her

hair down, as she always had before they made love. She looked
at him with those hellishly cool blue eyes. The sun glinted off her
high cheekbones.

"You grow more beautiful every day," he told the apparition.
"I talked to Max. He's buying all my portraits of you. We'll be
very rich, darling, just as I said we would."

He scribbled on the sketch paper, pressing much too heavily
with his charcoal, but David's mind was so obliterated with drugs
and champagne that he could no longer see the grotesqueness his
art had become. Where once he'd been passingly talented, he'd
destroyed what skill he'd once had.

"My darling, when I'm finished, I'll take you to supper at
Del's. We'll see all your old friends, maybe even drive to
Washington Square and see Sylvia. You'd like that, wouldn't
you?"

David scribbled some more. He filled his glass. He looked up
again and the chair was empty.

"Oh, no! Amanda! Don't go! I have such plans . . . such
glorious plans!" He jumped up to follow the appartition, but he
stumbled on drunken legs and fell face first to the floor. He lifted
his head. Amanda was gone. He could only see the cold-cream
jar filled with cocaine. He reached for it.

Sylvia looked at the ring as Amanda held it to the light. "It's
magnificent, my dear. No one deserves happiness as much as you
two." She kissed Amanda and then Matthew.

"Thank you for having us to dinner," Matthew said.

"Nonsense. Every girl deserves an engagement party. Unfortunately, because of the circumstances, it'll be a private party."

Amanda smiled as Matthew hugged her to him. "You are the
people I care most about. This is all that's necessary for me."

"Very well, then," Sylvia said handing a bottle of champagne
to Matthew. "You do the honors."

Matthew opened the wine and poured three glasses.

Sylvia was the first to speak. "To love."

Sydney rode confidently in the carriage as it approached Washington Square. After a fitful night of planning, Sydney had
decided that the information Christine had given her must be used
judiciously. Were she to confront Matthew or Amanda, she
might not get the results she wanted.

Wisely, she realized that Sylvia could be greatly damaged, perhaps even more so than Amanda, should Sydney reveal the chicanery to their friends.

Sydney believed it was always best to use an intermediary whenever possible. Purposely, she wanted to surprise Sylvia with her visit. She wanted to play the role of the wronged wife. Sylvia would understand that, no matter how much she loved Amanda. She would use Sylvia to put pressure on Amanda and thus stop the divorce.

"When is the wedding?" Sylvia asked Amanda.

"As soon as Matthew's divorce is final next year. I want you to be my matron of honor."

"Gladly." Sylvia sipped her wine. "Have you told Andrew yet?"

Amanda looked anxiously at Matthew.

"Have I missed something?"

"A lot, I'm afraid," Amanda said. "There's a great deal I'd like to tell my brother, but I can't find him."

"Why not? Has he left the Hampton House?"

"Why would you think he'd be there?" Amanda asked.

Sylvia was confused. "You didn't know he moved there last month? I saw him the day he moved in. Stumbled across him, actually. I was having lunch with some friends. . . ."

"Amanda has been looking all over town for him," Matthew said. "It's very important she talk to him."

"Why?"

"He's been stealing from me, Sylvia. He even took out another loan on the business for twenty-five thousand dollars. If it weren't for Matthew loaning me the money, I would have lost everything."

"Who called in the loan?"

"Sydney," Matthew said between his teeth.

Just then the doorbell rang. Sylvia went to the door.

"Sydney!" Sylvia was flabbergasted to see her. "What . . . what are you doing here?"

"I know I should have called first. I'm sorry, Sylvia," Sidney said, using desperate tones. "But it's urgent we talk."

"I have guests, Sydney."

Just then Matthew appeared behind Sylvia. He seemed to loom

in the doorway, and the light behind his back made him larger than life.

"Come in, Sydney. Don't rush away on our account."

"Our?" Sydney said tentatively, placing one foot inside the doorway. Then she saw Amanda come and stand beside Matthew.

"Hello, Sydney," Amanda said evenly.

Seeing Amanda next to Matthew only gave Sydney renewed courage. "I'm glad we're all together. This eliminates legwork on my part."

Sydney strode imperiously past them, went to the salon, and chose the most imposing chair. She did not remove her cloak but sat regally as they seated themselves.

"What do you want, Sydney?" Matthew demanded.

"The truth. Once and for all, I want everything out in the open. And it should start with Amanda."

"Me?"

"Why don't you tell us all who you really are?" She paused to let the words sink in. She looked over to Sylvia. "But then, you already know who she is, don't you, Sylvia?"

Guilt cracked across Sylvia's face. Matthew didn't miss it. He looked over to Amanda. She hadn't even flinched.

"Why don't you say exactly what you mean, Sydney?" Amanda challenged.

"You aren't now, nor were you ever, born to royal blood. Except in your fantasies. Or Sylvia's fantasies. You aren't a lady—you're a former housemaid. You came over to America for the express purpose of finding a rich husband. When that marriage to David Simon didn't work out, you set out to find another husband. Only this time the one you chose is mine!"

Amanda thought the world had crashed around her. She saw the shocked look on Matthew's face, the panic in Sylvia's eyes. She knew this day would come eventually. No one could go forever without a lie like that coming back on them. For years she'd been afraid of this moment, of the unveiling. Here she stood naked before her greatest adversary, and she didn't have the shield of The Lie to protect her. For a moment she considered running out of the room. It would have been easy to let Sydney win, to not have to explain to Matthew, not to have to apologize to Sylvia for involving her.

But Amanda had never taken the easy way out for anything. She amassed every bit of strength she'd ever used or would use.

She rose to her feet to defend herself, but Matthew was too quick for her. He stood beside her and held her hand. Stunned, she realized she hadn't lost him at all.

"Sydney, I don't know what point you're trying to make with all of this, other than making yourself look foolish. Amanda never took your husband from you. I was never yours, and we both know it." He delved into her eyes. "And that's the part that's really killing you, isn't it?"

"Matthew! Why are you saying these things—in front of these people?"

"These 'people' love me, Sydney. They have all the right in the world to hear this. You came here to attack Amanda. That's the same as attacking me."

"Then save yourself, Matthew. Her reputation is ruined. No one will ever believe anything she says. You built your magazine on your reputation, Amanda. A reputation that is worthless."

Amanda spoke for herself. "I have always done as I said I would do. *That* is the reputation I have in this city, Sydney. It has nothing to do with where I came from or to whom I was born. That kind of thing is important to you. Not to me."

"Nor to me," Matthew said. "Please, Sydney. Go home. Stop fighting something that isn't yours to control."

Sydney's countenance had not altered in the least. The confident set to her head, the imperious lift of her chin were all there. She looked at Matthew and then at Amanda. They were like a stone fortress, strong and long-lasting. She couldn't fight them anymore. She wondered if she should even try.

She rose slowly. She did not tremble, she did not falter. She looked at them all, and at none of them. She walked to the door, turned back, and to Matthew she said: "I'll have my bank. Someday it will be the largest in the whole country."

"Yes," Matthew said. "You'll have your bank."

Sydney quietly closed the door.

Amanda fell into Matthew's arms, suddenly not feeling strong at all.

"Do you think it's over this time?"

"Yes, I do."

"And did you mean what you said?" She looked at him pleadingly.

"Surely you know me well enough by now—I love you, Amanda. I don't care what kind of blood you have, or who your

parents are, or how many lies you told to get me. Just so long as
you're telling the truth when you say you love me.''

"Oh, yes, Matthew. That's the greatest truth in my life. And
you know something else? For the first time, *I* believe all those
things I said to Sydney. I don't need The Lie to protect me. I'd
always thought if I had royal blood, it would make a difference.
But it doesn't, does it?"

He smiled broadly. "No."

Amanda and Matthew said their good-byes to Sylvia, climbed
into the carriage Matthew had hired, and headed uptown to
Hampton House Hotel.

"Are you sure you want to do this tonight?"

"Absolutely."

They arrived at eleven o'clock. "You stay here," Amanda
said to Matthew.

"Never! I'm coming with you."

"Matthew, I have to do this myself. He won't hurt me. He's
my brother."

"It's that kind of thinking that got you into this predicament to
begin with. And that's why I'm going with you."

She knew he meant well, and probably he was right. "Give
me twenty minutes. If I'm not back by then, come get me."

"Fifteen."

"All right. Fifteen."

Matthew kissed her quickly as she climbed out of the carriage
and went inside.

The hotel clerk told her that Andrew occupied room twenty-
one on the second floor. She took the elevator.

Andrew lay on his hotel bed, arms crossed beneath his head,
staring at the ceiling. Something was wrong, but he didn't know
what. He had no evidence that things had started to go awry for
him. Mary Alice was her normal, loving self. He checked the
newspaper columns each day to see if Christine had taken out her
vengeance on him. There was nothing. Still, he had the eerie
feeling that he was about to die.

Amanda knocked on the door. There was no answer. She
knocked again. Then she heard a rumbling from inside. The door
opened.

"Amanda? What are you doing here?"

"Did you think you could avoid me forever?"

"Don't be silly. I had no intention of—"

"Of course you did, Andrew," she said and pushed past him. She stood in the middle of the room. Her cheeks were flushed and her eyes curiously intense.

He shut the door.

"I'm here about the money, Andrew."

"What money?" He didn't like the tone in her voice. She'd already judged him guilty. He'd have a hard time talking her out of this one. But he'd do it. He always had.

"The money you stole from me. I'm talking about the money you skimmed off the books. You did to me just what you did to Quinton. Only worse. I know about the loan you took out against *my* business . . . without my knowledge. That's criminal, Andrew! But then, that's what you really are, isn't it?"

"Amanda! Where are you getting all this ridiculous information?"

"If you had answered my calls, Andrew, you would have known. In the past week I nearly lost Granger Publishing, thanks to you."

"Nearly?"

"The Brinkley Bank and your friends at New York Mercantile decided to foreclose on us. Shut us down."

He tried his winning smile. "But you said nearly. That means you saved the company. It wasn't all that disastrous then, was it?"

"Use your charm someplace else, Andrew. I have no loyalties to you after you tried to destroy me."

"You're being much too harsh, Amanda. I never wanted anything like that. I'm your brother, for Christ's sake."

"Exactly. And as my brother, you thought you had some special privileges in my life, in my business. You *used* me, Andrew. And there's nothing worse than that. I have a lot of enemies, Andrew. But none of them were as devious and cunning as you."

Andrew's rage boiled. Flashes of childhood memories peppered his brain. Suddenly, he was not an adult but a child again. He saw Amanda sitting on a new pony, being the delight of Lord Kent's eyes, while he wore thrice hand-me-downs from Church Street. He hated his sister—then and now.

"Don't preach to me, Amanda!" he yelled. "It was *time* I used you! All those years when you were living high at the

Kents, I hated you. *You* were the one with the new clothes and toys. *You* were the one who got the invitations to special outings and parties. Well, now I was just taking my turn, is all. You *owed* it to me, and you know it! You had everything—you still have everything.''

Andrew moved closer to her. She saw his fists ball and his eyes blaze, but she wasn't afraid. Her anger was just as great as his.

"You told Sydney Wade about The Lie."

"I told Christine Van Volkein—my mistress—Sydney's best friend. I didn't make her swear to secrecy. Why would you care what Sydney Wade thinks anyway?"

"Because I'm going to marry her husband once his divorce is final."

"Ha! That's a laugh. So you're not so righteous after all. Bet he turned tail and ran when he heard that piece of news."

"No, he didn't. He loves me, but you wouldn't understand that kind of thing, would you, Andrew?"

"I understand only one thing . . . survival."

"Good. Because you're going to have a life filled with just that."

Suddenly, Andrew wavered. "What are you talking about?"

"I want you to leave town, Andrew."

"Don't be ridiculous! Why would I do something like that?"

"Because if you don't, I'll have you thrown in jail for embezzlement."

"You wouldn't—"

"Try me." She glared at him intently.

For the first time in his life, Andrew feared his sister. He'd always been able to manipulate her, to coax circumstances and people into action that benefitted him and his motives. He'd always counted on his charm and wit to get him out of trouble.

"You won't do that. How would it look to the world if Amanda Granger's brother was a jailbird?" Andrew tried to think quickly. He was perched on the eve of getting everything he'd ever wanted. He'd be damned if he was going to let Amanda take it away from him.

"I don't give a damn about the world," Amanda said firmly.

"You should; they're your meat and potatoes." Andrew looked at her. His tack wasn't working. It should be. He thought of the fabulous house he was going to buy in a few short days. He thought of Mary Alice's enormous dowry. He thought of the treasures he'd planned to fill his house with, the European trip they'd planned. He had to stop Amanda. Now. It was obvious threats wouldn't faze her. He needed something more concrete to make her bend. He walked toward the bureau. He softened his voice and let pliant tones fill the room. "You'd better reexamine your position here, Amanda. If it is true that Matthew Wade is going to make you his wife, then you'll want to do everything you can to make certain that marriage takes place, won't you?"

"What are you talking about?" She was suspicious of the calm in his voice.

Andrew pulled out the top drawer. He withdrew a battered old diary. He caressed it, a gesture his sister would appreciate.

"What's that?" she asked.

"Your legacy." He handed her Harriet's book. "Read the page marked October 3, 1894."

Amanda opened it. Suddenly, she felt swept back in time, seeing her mother's crude handwriting. She was a girl again in a world she'd almost forgotten. Amanda read aloud.

" 'I love him. I always have. For over twenty years he's been my life, but I'm sure he doesn't know that. Just like he doesn't know so many things. He doesn't know that Amanda is his daughter, not Burt's. How I've wanted to tell him. But I daren't. It is my fate, my cruel fate, to love a man I can never have. I have to be content that were it another age, another country, Alvin would marry me. But not in this life—not in my life."

Tears filled Amanda's eyes. "Lord Kent is my father?"

"Yes," Andrew said smugly. "And you're his bastard. Now, little sister, what do you think your high society husband-to-be would think about that? He isn't gonna want a *bastard* for a wife!"

Amanda was too stunned by the shock to even hear what Andrew was saying.

Andrew went to the bureau and pulled out the earrings he'd been saving. "I suppose I should give you these. They were *hers*."

Amanda looked at them. She knew instantly that Lord Kent had given them to her mother. She could tell they were a gift of love, for he could have chosen something outrageously expensive and gaudy, as most wealthy men did for their mistresses. These earrings were not particularly costly but were in good taste. Amanda thought them romantic. "They're lovely."

She wondered if Lord Kent had ever known and not told Harriet. She thought of the particular way he would watch over her. How cautious he'd been when teaching her to ride that pony when she was only three. She remembered all the things he'd done for her; how Lady Kent had hated her, tried to get rid of her. She remembered how he'd defended her. "He knew," she said to herself. "He always knew."

Feeling more assured of his position with her, Andrew rocked back on his heels. "I thought you'd see things my way. You can't get rid of me, Amanda. You need me to help you through things. My ways may be a bit rough in your eyes, but—"

"What?" His words had started sinking into her brain. "I don't need you any more than I needed royal blood to give me confidence, or The Lie to protect me. I don't care if I'm a bastard or of legitimate birth. I've never needed anybody but myself. It took me a long time to learn that, but I know that now. I won't lose Matthew over this. In fact, he'll be happy for me that my father is living!" She clutched the diary to her breast as she hissed at him. "Consider this a gift from me, Andrew. I want you to get out of town. I don't care where you go, but if I ever hear of you, I'll destroy you. I'll make certain your reputation follows you. Never again will you be able to dupe another young girl like you did Mary Alice and God only knows how many before her."

"You can't do this—"

"I'm doing it," she said between clenched teeth. "Don't bother to pack. You leave here now, tonight. With only the clothes on your back and no money—*that* you owe to me."

"This is insane. I won't do it!"

"Then I'll call the police. Think about jail, Andrew. Think about that tiny little room, a bed with no sheets, living with men who smell like animals. Would you rather live like that?"

"I'd rather die than live the life you're condemning me to. You don't understand. I *have* to have money. I can't live without nice things, good meals."

"Fine. Then work for them the way everyone else does. *Earn* them, Andrew. I'm giving you a chance to make something of yourself."

"You're condemning me to hell."

"Only you would see it that way. Most people would think I'm being too lenient—again. I've overlooked your viciousness for the last time. Get out."

"Amanda . . ." he pleaded.

"Get out!" she screamed, still clutching the diary to her chest.

"Goddamn you, you bitch!" he screamed back and started for her throat. It wouldn't be the first time he'd killed. He was nearly ready to pounce on her when the door flew open.

Matthew loomed in the doorway, his voice deadly calm as he said: "You heard her. Now get out."

Andrew stared from one adversary to the other, then grabbed his jacket from the bed. In seconds he was in the elevator and gone from sight.

Tears streamed down Amanda's cheeks as she stared up at Matthew. "I lost my brother, but I found my father."

Matthew put his arms around her and rocked her gently back and forth as she cried.

EPILOGUE

Tuxedo Park, New York—January 1, 1900

Amanda leaned closer to the fire and warmed her face. She pulled the soft mohair blanket around her shoulders. She looked over at Matthew while he filled their glasses with champagne.

"Less than a minute," he said.

"And a new century will have begun. Doesn't it make you feel . . . I don't know . . . humble to think of all those years stretching out in front of us?"

He handed her the glass and joined her on the floor. He placed his hand over her rounded abdomen. "I can think of other things that are awe-inspiring," he said and kissed the top of her head.

"Oh, my gosh!" Amanda said, starting to get up. "I forgot to check on Jacqueline."

Matthew pulled her back to him. "I already did that. She's fine . . . sleeping soundly with her new doll and the stuffed puppy you made for her."

"She's so funny. She wouldn't even take her bath without that puppy."

He looked at his watch. "Ten . . . nine . . . ."

Just then the baby rolled over inside Amanda. "Did you feel that! This has got to be a boy. He's so active." She sighed. "I'm so happy, Matthew. Do you think it's possible anyone could be as happy as we are?"

"Nope. Eight . . . seven . . . six."

"I got a belated Christmas letter from Kent Manor today."

"What did it say?"

" 'My dearest daughter' . . . that's how he started it. Lord . . .

my father, I mean, wants us to come visit in the spring after the baby arrives. I'd really like to go.''

"I think that's a wonderful idea," Matthew said. "I'll need a vacation by then.''

"I should hope so. You haven't taken a day off since the opening. Not even for a honeymoon.''

"Until now. You have me for a whole week. Besides, I thought this was rather romantic . . . to come here, where we first met.''

Amanda laughed and stroked her belly. "I even look like I did when we first met.''

"I planned it that way." He laughed.

She looked at him. There was not a crook or cranny of her life that wasn't perfect at this moment. Although she knew it wouldn't always be like this, for life was not that kind to anyone, she also believed that they had won this moment in time, this slice of bliss. It was their trophy for believing in love, for never settling for second-best.

"I love you, Matthew.''

"Two . . . one. Happy New Year, Mrs. Wade.''

She kissed him passionately. "Happy New Year, my love.''